RISE OF THE WITCH

The Phoenix's Ashes, Book One
A Circus of Shifters Reverse Harem

By
Rebecca Ethington

Published by Imdalind Press

Production Management by Imdalind Press

ISBN (print) 978-1-949725-18-6

ISBN (e-book) 978-1-949725-15-5

Printed in USA

This Edition, September 2013

❀ Created with Vellum

CONTENTS

To My Kids

1

ELLIOT

I T WAS HOT.

We are talking planet plunging into the sun, surface of hell, grandma has back sweat, hot.

Yes, I know that is gross, but sweat was pooling on my upper lip and converging on the underwire in my bra in such a way that I was sure if it didn't stop it would consume me and I would drown in it.

Yes, I knew that wouldn't actually happen, but I was also fairly certain that people were not meant to live in this heat. I wasn't sure how anyone, including me, was meant to survive.

Which was saying something considering I burst into actual flames once a year.

"How you holding up?"

I looked up from the dusty trail I had been trudging along for the past few minutes to the owner of the smoky voice. Mr. Green Eyes, real name Brayden, had been something of a hovering puppy since the moment our tour guide had gathered the group at the trailhead.

Angel's Landing, Zion National Park.

It sounded calming. Everyone I had talked to said it was terrifying.

I was looking forward to both, but right now I wanted to feel like I wasn't burning up on the surface of the sun.

"Great," I said, forcing a smile that he instantly returned.

His wide grin sparkled in the sun, the light hitting against his teeth so perfectly that it almost seemed ridiculous. Especially when you added in the fact that he also had the perfectly shaggy blonde hair, and oversized muscles that most girls swooned over.

Hell, I was swooning over them, just a little bit. I probably would have been a little more interested in the advances he kept throwing my way if he wasn't quite so 'let me carry your fragile human body up this mountain using my big strong man-muscles.'

If there was one thing that was a turn-off for me, it was overly protective males. Yes, my five-foot-four frame may seem fragile and weak, but if I had to venture a guess I would say I could easily bench more weight than he could.

And that wasn't even counting the *other* stuff.

"Okay," he continued, his smile continuing to spread. "Let me know if you need any help with your pack or anything. I have been on this hike before, and I know the drop off ahead scares some people."

I blinked, carefully rearranging my shock into a smile as I looked at my "pack". It was a battered backpack I had found at a thrift shop earlier that day. It's sole purpose was to keep me hydrated, and due to my apparent death-by-sun status was almost empty. I think the thing weighed negative two pounds.

"Thanks," I cooed, trying not to sound too condescending as I fished out a granola bar. "I think I'll be okay. As long as I get a good picture at the top. I want to look like I am flying," or falling to my death, I added internally.

"I can help with that."

I could only smile.

As he spoke, the trees and rocks that had surrounded our path broke open, the trail continuing forward into what appeared to be nothing. Just a chain suspended over a narrow strip of rock that extended around a massive valley and sheer cliff face.

Angel's landing. It was beautiful. Even I couldn't help but be impressed.

"Perfect," I said under my breath, the single gasp swallowed by the wind.

"From this point on," our tour guide announced as he turned around to face the five of us, "you are welcome to explore. We ask that you remain near the chains that mark the trails. It can be deadly to exit the trails and unless you can fly it is not recommended."

Everyone else laughed with differing levels of discomfort, and Mr. Green Eyes turned to face me again, checking in.

Eyes forward, bud. I'm fine.

I shot him a smile, which seemed to suffice.

"Please enjoy yourself," the guide went on, "we will meet back here in approximately one hour to continue to our next destination."

Everyone nodded and broke off, one half of the married couple in front of me crumbling to tears at the terror of the sheer drop that was steps from us. A guy about my age was breaking off to explore, the fearless tourist not even bothering to grab the safety chain. I could tell by his high end pack and camera he was no stranger to adventure. Part of me wished I could have paired up with him; he had probably seen as much of the world as I had.

But nope, Brayden was turning toward me, concern clearly chiseled on his handsome face.

"You doing okay?"

Hover much?

"Yep," I said brightly, muscling past him with the full expectation that he would follow me. He did.

Right then, however, I didn't much care. Lost dog or not, he didn't detract from the beauty of this place.

The sheer cliff of stone was glistening red in the pending sunset, the jagged line of rock that shot up from the ground, reaching toward heaven like the wing of an angel.

The name suddenly made sense. But it felt like home more than any other place I had pulled this stunt.

I could already feel the song swell from deep inside my soul, the beauty calling to me, begging me to surround myself in it. To unfurl my wings and feel the heat of the breeze against face and feet.

The more the need to fly pulled, the faster my feet moved, my fingers only lightly touching the chain as I pulled myself toward the sandy stone ledge ahead. The jagged trail rose higher, pulling me closer to the clouds as a breeze circled over me. Warm wind tickled over my skin, igniting my soul's song until it was echoing through my mind.

"Soon," I whispered as I reached the top most point, the trail opening to a large flat overlook that was littered with hikers and tourists who had also made the journey. The majority of them were clustered near the center of the rock, as far away from the edge as they could get. No one paid me any mind as I walked past them, right to the chain that was meant to protect the fragile humans. Inhaling the hot evergreen air, I looked out at the canyon, at the specks of green trees far below, the ribbon of a blue river winding through them.

It was beautiful. But it was the clouds that were calling to me. It was the clouds that I wanted.

I lifted my face to the sun, breathing in the smell of dirt and damp that carried on the wind as the long strands of flaming red hair that had come loose from my braid slithered over my face.

"Soon," I said again as hesitant steps came up behind me. Brayden's ragged breathing was so loud that I was sure everyone within a five foot circle could hear him coming.

"It's beautiful, isn't it?" He asked, his voice so strained that for a moment I almost felt bad for him. "Have you ever seen anything like it?"

I wanted to tell him yes, tell him I had stood at the top of Mount Fuji, The Eiffel Tower and so many other places. I wanted to brag that I had felt the wind of the Andes, smelled the eucalyptus in Vietnam. Instead I nodded my head in agreement and shook my way out of the very empty water-pack and dropped it to the ground, sending a small plume of dust to tickle my ankles.

"Take my picture?" I asked as I turned to him, pulling the broken digital camera out of the front pocket of my cut-offs.

Brayden stood, heaving, his muscles constricting as he pulled his arms around himself, as if making himself smaller would somehow keep him atop the cliff. "How are you not scared?"

I shrugged, "Heights have never bothered me. Perks of being a corporate accountant, I guess."

He didn't seem convinced, which was fine. I had never

been a great liar. But, my stellar fibbing skills was not why I was here. I waved the camera at him a bit more.

"Or maybe I think I can fly."

With a curious twitch of his eyebrow he finally took the tiny beaten box I had found abandoned at a gas station on the way here. The chip in the corner was so large that I was surprised he didn't say anything.

"You don't need to be right against the barrier to get a good shot, you know." His voice was shaking so deep with nerves that I was a bit shocked he could form a sentence.

"Oh, I know." I twisted my face up as I watched him, suddenly feeling bad for the poor guy. As much as he talked, he couldn't handle the heights.

Ugh. This was going to mess him up.

I took one glance around but the fearless tourist had vanished, I was stuck with Mr. Scaredy-Pants. Now was not the time to second guess myself, I quickly kicked off the beaten sneakers, thankful to finally get out of them. They were a size too small, but all the thrift store had.

"There is something exhilarating about being right there, about facing death. Looking it right in the eye."

I said it darkly, and for a brief moment I could tell that he may have been concerned for my sanity. Then I took off my shirt and his look faded to shock.

"What are you doing?" He said, his eyes unabashedly staring at the bright red lace of my bra. The color perfectly matched my hair, and I kind of loved it. But I also knew it would look glorious on the way down.

"Taking a picture," I said, stripping off my cut-off shorts to reveal equally as lacey, equally as red panties.

"Umm... uh...." He obviously didn't know what to say, either that or his brain had shut off.

Fit, muscular girl in red lace underwear had a habit of doing that. No matter where in the world you were.

He wasn't the only one either. Men and women, they had all begun to turn toward me, the looks on their faces registering from embarrassment to confusion to a weird lust that always made my inner soul prickle.

"You're going to take the picture, right?" I snapped, quickly unwinding my braid and letting the long lengths of hair get pulled and tugged in the breeze that was starting to fill with the high operatic tones of my song, although I wasn't sure any of them could hear it.

"I... uh..." He couldn't seem to pull himself together, which was awesome because I was quickly running out of time.

More and more people were starting to take notice of me standing there in my underwear, and the tour guide was making his way over.

Great.

It's not like I was going to keep the picture anyway, even if there was one.

I shrugged my shoulders, gave Brayden one last look, and a chance to pick his jaw up off the floor, before vaulting over the chain and right to the edge of the cliff face.

The shock of everyone on the landing quickly turned to panic. Screams echoed around me as I bent down, setting my palms flat against the edge of the cliff face.

"Miss!" The tour guide's voice echoed over the screams as I quickly found my balance, my muscles rippling as I lifted my feet from the stone. Balancing on my hands, I pointed my toes and bent myself into a near perfect arch, butt against my head.

The shock faded, as I swayed in the air, my body flowing

elegantly in the wind as my bright hair rippled around my face.

Keeping my right hand firm against the ridge of stone, I lifted my left hand spreading it away from me like the wings that were inside of me, letting the wind tickle my fingers. Calling to me.

Sitting there motionlessly, my song lifted above the sound of the wind, and a hush fell over the screams for one single breath as everyone listened, as everyone felt the calm of my magic.

And then I sprang into the air.

I pushed my hands against the stone, vaulting myself into the air in an arch and a twist, moving and spinning like a diver from a board. Except there was no water, only air. Only the plunging abyss that my inner animal begged for.

The screams of panic from the people were swallowed by the wind as it ran over me, rippled through me. As I gave my soul what it wanted.

I danced through the air, spreading my arms from me as the ground grew closer... closer...

Warm air prickled against the gooseflesh of my skin as my body began to heat, as my inner fire threatened to break free.

"Not yet," I whispered, pressing against the heat as I attempted to keep her restrained. "Not yet."

I said it again, wanting to feel the air, feel the fall for one more moment, one more gasp.

"Now."

I couldn't hold it in anymore. With the snap of flame over my skin everything rippled and burned. And I changed.

Fire erupted around me moments before I hit the ground, my arms spreading wide as wings took their place and I arched up into the air, leaving a streak of flame behind me as the bird inside took my place.

My bright, beautiful song echoed through the canyon, the release of my soul playing in a masterpiece of sound.

I wasn't sure if anyone would hear, I wasn't sure if anyone would care.

I soared away under the trees, my powerful Phoenix refracting the light of the sun as the shifter I kept hidden inside of myself soar.

Letting myself be free.

2

ELLIOT

THE WARM BREEZE OF DAWN BLEW OVER ME, TUGGING AT MY hair and letting the ash that I lay in swirl over my bare skin. I knew I was exposed. I knew I needed to get out of there.

But, simply speaking, I didn't want to.

The heat felt good, and the soft touch of the ash my shifter left behind was a home I didn't get to experience very often. It was so peaceful, laying in the dim light of dawn as the sun tried to clear the massive mountains that surrounded this city. Everything felt right, right enough that I almost didn't care that I had chosen to return to my human form in the midst of a dark alley.

I was going to soak up every minute. So, instead of hustling my butt out of the alley and high tailing it into the hotel, I lay still tracing swirls and hearts over the layer of ash. The soft particles glistened in the early morning light, sparkling like glitter. Like fire.

"I'll see you soon," I promised the last remains of my phoenix as the hot breeze picked them up and whisked it all away.

Wind tugged at my hair, at the tiny shard of red lace bra

that hadn't been burned away, threatening to take me with it. I wanted to go. I wanted to soar on the back of the sun for a little bit longer.

Another hour.

There wasn't time. It wasn't fair, to only be able to fly, to let my phoenix soar, in these rare stolen moments that wasn't behind a cage. Hidden from the world.

Moments that were already freaking gone.

They will be back soon, Ellie, I promised myself.

I sighed with all the disgruntled frustration of the rebellious teenager I was and basked in the fact that in two weeks I would be eighteen. I may not know all of what that would mean, but I would sure as hell make sure it didn't mean hiding away.

I sat up with a smile, letting the last of the ash slide away.

Well, the last of what wasn't stuck to me. I looked a mess.

First order of business, a cold shower and lots of soap.

I scuffled to my feet and booked my naked ass to the stack of boxes by the dumpster where I had stowed a hotel pool robe before I left yesterday morning. I was sure the soft white cotton would be grungy and smell of rotten fish by now, but I didn't care. It was the key in the pocket I was after.

It was also what wasn't there.

Well, neither the robe nor the key were there.

"What the..." I snapped loudly, angling myself awkwardly behind the dumpster as I searched through the remains of boxes and trash cans and who knows what else in search of the robe, or at the very least the key.

Hell, I would even take a rot covered towel right about now--

"Looks like you are in need of some help."

Every single muscle in my body froze in place. The low,

mellow, male voice was very clearly trying to disguise a laugh, and it was no wonder. I was wrapped around the dumpster in such a way that my bare bottom was clearly visible, framed between wall and trash receptacle like a voyeur's day dream.

Perfect.

I could feel the blush heating my skin, coloring my cheeks. Both sets for all I knew.

"Hello?" He continued as if I wasn't wedged behind a dumpster. "Can I help you?"

Great, he wasn't even trying to disguise his laugh now.

"Ummm," I hesitated. "I'm fine. Just dropped something. I'll be fine. Please, go along your way…"

I twisted my arm behind me, waving him away as though he was nothing more than a fly. A pesky, irritating, in the wrong place at the wrong time fly.

He only chuckled more, the sound a deep mellow laugh that twisted deep in my stomach.

"Yes, it seems like you have everything under control."

I knew I had to move. I didn't have a choice, letting this guy talk to my ass was not going to work, but I was also far too stubborn to give in that easily. "I do, thank you."

My last ditch effort did not work, not even close. Mr. Intruder laughed harder, so I returned to my frantic search, the movement causing my tail end to wave back and forth.

"Why don't you come on out of there so I can help you."

I could tell he was trying to supersede the laugh with some kind of authoritative howl. It wasn't working.

"I'm really--"

"Or before I call the cops," he cut me off, causing me to swear quite loudly.

Fine.

I huffed, loud enough that he could hear, and slowly

backed out of the dumpster diving escapade, keeping myself close to the wall as I covered my breasts with my right arm.

I almost dropped it.

Mr. Intruder was not some punk hotel management with acne issues. Well, he might have been management. But, he was more likely hot as a sex god hotel management.

The suit he was wearing was not helping the heart palpitations I was feeling. The dark charcoal grey matched the black of his hair perfectly, and was cut so precisely that I could see every line of his trim muscles.

His green eyes were illuminated in the morning light, his dark hair pulled back into a curly man-bun. All he was missing to complete the look was the beard, but judging by the heavy five o'clock shadow he had going on I was sure it was a normal addition.

It took work to keep my jaw from dropping, but I managed it. Talking was another story, especially when he smiled at my obvious dumbfoundedness and revealed two dimples.

Damn it. Of course he had to have dimples. Let's crank the near perfection meter up to eleven, why don't we?

"Willa came out kay?" Yeah, that was English.

I sighed, took a step back, and tried to ignore the heart stopping smile he was giving me as I attempted to recenter myself.

"I'm really okay," I said, fully aware that at this point it was a lie. The odds were stacking up against me. "I am looking for my hotel key."

His eyebrow jerked up. "You threw it away?"

"NO!" I said a little too loudly, throwing my arms into the air and forgetting for a minute that I was covering myself. He smiled, I gasped, and the arm flew right back to cover myself.

"My friend... Dared me... it was a scavenger hunt..." Like I said, lying isn't my strong suit.

He looked me up and down, "A naked scavenger hunt? Did it also involve dumpster diving?"

"Yes?" Yeah, that sounded like a question. His smirk was making it hard for me to think, and I certainly wasn't going to fight him, or try to explain why I was covered in ash. "Listen, do you work here? I could really use a hand to get back inside. I need to get into my room..."

"Sorry, no," His smirk was growing, how was it possible that his smirk was growing? I swear the thing was covering his face.

"Well, thanks anyway," I said, ready to return to my dumpster dive, fully aware that it would mean turning around and sticking my hinny in the air. Again.

Could this guy leave already? I was starting to get irritated.

"But, I am a guest," he supplied, stopping my retreat.

My heart picked up into overdrive as he reached into his perfect suit and pulled out a key identical to the one they had given us at check in, complete with the pizza advertisement on the back.

Was he inviting me into his room? Umm no.

Right then, I think I would have been happier if he had been hotel staff, even with whatever repercussions would have come from that. There was something gleaming in those green eyes of his that was causing my phoenix to prickle under my skin.

"Down, girl," I hissed between clenched teeth, refusing to take my eyes off the man in front of me.

"Huh?" He asked, having heard me, I only shook my head.

"Great! So you can let me in," I said, quickly diverting

the subject, even though asking the question was putting everything in me right back on edge.

His heart-thundering smile was not helping that. Nor was the fact that he had the whitest straightest teeth I had ever seen.

"No can do, dumpster girl," he said giving me a nickname that instantly furrowed in my brow, something that only made him laugh further. "How do I know you are really a guest? I don't suppose you have any identification in your..." his eyes ran over my body, stopping briefly on the tiny shard of red lace underwear that clung to my hip, although how it was staying on I had no idea.

I shifted uncomfortably under his gaze, suddenly wishing I was an octopus and had any hope of covering more than the one strip of boob.

"My name isn't dumpster girl," I said, as if that somehow settled it. The twitch of his smirk made it clear that it did not.

"Well, if I knew your name I could call you that," he said with that same gravely voice, the sound spreading over me like a fire.

"You find me naked in an alley and expect me to give you my name..."

"And room number," he said with a wink. "Then I could call and check if you are staying here."

"Fat chance." I scoffed, he didn't.

He looked at me with eyes of liquid emerald, something there pulling at me familiarly, causing my chest to tighten.

Breathe, Ellie.

"Well, the cops would want the same thing..." He teased, twiddling the card between his fingers like he was about to throw the thing at me. "But then again, you are the one who is naked," he took a step closer, "and in an alley," another step.

He was so close I could see the subtle pin striping on his suit, his eyes so bright I swear they were absolutely glowing by now. I swallowed, my finger tips digging into the skin they were trying so hard to keep covered. I knew I should run, dodge around him and take my chances running pell-mell through the hotel lobby, but I was simply too stubborn. Besides, I might still have a chance for this guy to let me in.

Slim, but I think it was there.

"I'll start," He said, placing a hand against the wall and what I assumed was meant as a posturing move. "My name is Killian, what is yours?"

"Killian?" I asked, one eyebrow tweaking in curiosity. "That can't be your real name."

Yeah, that may have been a little harsh, but I couldn't stop the words from tumbling out. Who names their kid Killian?

Judging by the way his features darkened, it wasn't an unfamiliar question for him.

"Yes," he barked. I guess I had hit a pain point.

"Okay Killian," I said, taking a step toward him as I tried to posture him in return. Instead it sent my heart into overdrive and I took a step back. "What are *you* doing in the alley anyway?"

Any rebuttal he had planned slipped from his face and he flicked the card around his fingers, making it vanish from view as his eyebrows knit together.

"Let's say I was taking out the trash," the light teasing of his voice had become a rock hard caution that rippled up my spine in a million warning lights. Weird, desirable, warning lights.

Or at least that's what my human side was saying. My

phoenix side was pressing against my heart, everything heating and my skin pricked with sparks of electric fire. She wasn't wanting to escape, to attack, or to protect as she normally did, however.

No, she wanted him.

Hell, I wanted him. I wanted him bad.

Holy shit.

I swallowed, trying to force down the weird sensation that was starting to take over, but it clung on, burrowing deeper inside of me. With one dark syllable, his voice had somehow conjured a live wire inside of me, my phoenix screaming in a need I had never felt before. I shifted my weight, taking one large step back toward the dumpster, no matter how much I wanted to go the other way.

Want or not. I needed to keep my phoenix hidden. I needed to keep myself hidden, and the dumpster seemed like the best place to do that.

So much for my stubborn side, we were going into full on protect mode.

"I guess we both have secrets," I said, my voice strained as I forced a smile.

"I guess so," Killian said, that dark fluidity in his voice increasing as he leaned toward me until he was inches away, his breath rolling warm over my skin.

"What are you doing in the alley, dumpster girl?"

I couldn't breathe, oh lord, I couldn't even think beyond the heat that was covering me.

Breathe, Ellie, breathe.

I begged myself to break out from under him, to run, but at that point I would settle for one lone gasp of air.

I sucked it in as a loud snap echoed through the dark alley, a flood of light following behind the sound as the door directly behind Killian opened, the escape I had originally been hoping to make becoming available.

"Hey! What are you doing out here!" The man's voice was loud, and in charge.

I took the chance, and booked it.

Dodging under the arm of the green eyed sex god I bolted, buck-freakin'-naked toward the door, jumped around the burly kitchen worker and sprinted right into the brightly lit kitchen, my appearance causing one or two shouts before I was gone. Running around one corner, then another.

And another.

I was sure he was following me. Part of me wished he would. I didn't know what it was about him, but the fearful exhilaration, no, the absolute drowning need he was filling me with... Why was I running?

"Just keep going, you idiot," I scolded myself, darting into the pool area and right into the steam room. The tile of the large enclosed space slid underneath my bare feet, leaving ashy footprints behind.

The echoes of shouts and confusion bled through the crack in the glass pane door as I watched it close in its slow monotonous way. One painful inch at a time.

I backed into the room, as much as I wanted to pull it shut, I was trapped. If they saw me through the foggy glass it was all over. It probably wasn't a bad thing, I was a guest after all, but the repercussions...

Yeah, I didn't want to think about the amount of trouble I would be in.

The shouts grew louder, bouncing against the tile until the door closed with the softest of snaps. I flipped the switch the moment it sealed, filling the cloudy room with more steam.

The hiss of heat and damp consumed the room, fogging over the glass and stopping anyone from seeing inside. Stopping me from seeing out. If I was trapped before, I was even more trapped now.

A single note of phoenix song rang out before I sucked it in, restraining my soul inside as I grabbed one of the puffy white towels and held it over the steam. The already sticky towel grew damp as the normally boiling steam soaked it, steam and towel gliding over my skin, wiping the last of the ash away and sending it trailing down my body in rivers of glittering magic.

Beautiful lines of sparkling ebony.

Just like Killian.

Beautiful.

The thought was an unwanted twist in my gut and I flinched, towel falling to the ground as I turned to the door, sure he was there.

I swear I could feel him. Was that weird? Yeah, I am sure that *was* in fact, very weird.

"Pull it together," I scolded myself, fully aware that it was my habit of talking to myself and to my shifter had given me such a weird reputation.

I needed to get to my room and --

"I'm pretty sure you would need to pick the towel up before you pull it together."

Holy - - No. No-no-no. This could not be happening.

I whirled toward the smooth male voice, this time grabbing the towel and instantly moving to wrap it around me and shield myself from whoever was in the room with me. In the haste of my escape I had completely missed the broad shouldered man who sat towering in the corner. Sitting there, watching me. Watching me run my hands directly under boiling hot steam.

But there he was, sitting with a playful smile, charcoal eyes swallowing all the light in the room. He chuckled a bit at my reaction, his shaggy golden hair falling over his eyes as he threw an additional towel at me from where he had draped it over his shoulders. Of course, doing that revealed the perfectly formed mounds of muscle that covered his shoulders and chest, each line of his olive toned flesh dripping with sweat.

Was sweat sexy? It never had been before... but oh dear, I was starting to rethink that.

It's not like I hadn't seen muscles on a man before, in my line of work mostly naked muscular men was a staple. But him, there was something about him that had me struggling to find breath, and the increasing temperature of the room was certainly not helping.

"Thanks," I mumbled, using the towel he had thrown me to wipe down the sweat that was beading on my brow.

The towel was soft, wet and did not smell like the damp steam room. It smelled like smoke, mint and what I was sure was pine. The aroma assaulted my senses, shooting lines of electricity through my veins and I gasped.

That scent was doing a number on me.

I tried not to be noticed breathing in the heady aroma, but I was sure he caught me what with the way he was smiling, his dark eyes brushing over me with a touch so soft...

I swallowed, banning the lump in my throat away, right along with the twist of butterflies that was trying to take up residence.

"No worries. Feeling better?" He asked, a genuine concern painted on his face now.

I nodded, "Yeah, sorry I didn't see you there."

A smile twitched on the corner of his mouth as he sat

back against the wall, pressing his bare skin against the scalding tiles.

"I noticed, but it's really fine." He brushed some of his blonde hair out of his eyes, the concern glittering inside of their dark depths. "You seemed a bit spooked. Is everything okay?"

Yeah, just a phoenix shifter caught buck naked behind a dumpster, and now in a steam room.

I smiled.

"Yeah." Better to lie. "My friends challenged me to skinny dip and then took my clothes and ran."

Simple. To the point, and something every teenager in America does. At least that's what the movies say. Never mind that I was almost eighteen. And also not American.

His smile widened. "Figured it was something like that. You here on a school trip?"

"Something like that," I parroted back to him.

"I'm Jarron," he said, extending his hand as he leaned toward me, smile sparkling, his dark eyes looking into me so deeply that for a minute I swore he could see into me. I shuddered and held the towel closer, slowly extending my hand to his.

"El..." I began, only to have both words and breath sucked out of my chest the moment my hand touched his.

Warm. Soft. Electric.

Sparks of fire prickled up my spine at his touch, awakening that same desperate need I had felt only minutes before. It consumed me, my Phoenix heating me from the inside out, burning against my skin, desperate to reach him.

I wanted so badly to grab him, to pull him into me. To wrap my arms and legs around him and kiss him.

What was I doing? I had never been kissed before, and something told me that kissing a complete stranger, when we are both mostly naked in a steam room was not the way to go.

I pulled my hand away before either me or my Phoenix grabbed the poor man, or at least before he sensed the burning heat of my skin.

"Hi El," Jarron said slyly, his voice adding to the flood of warmth that was rushing through my veins. The soft look he was giving me was not helping, either.

His eyes were suddenly lighter, warmer, making me sure he hadn't felt the fire I hid inside.

And making it very clear I needed to get out of there.

Like, right the hell now.

"Goodbye Jarron," I said, holding the towels against me as I began to back step toward the doors. "Maybe I'll see you around."

I said it, I wanted it. But I also knew a lot more about my life than he did, and I knew that seeing him again, feeling that need again, would be far too dangerous for both of us.

"I have a feeling you can count on it," he said, his voice soft, and the electric butterflies went crazy again.

I gave him one sly smile and slid out of the room, into the thankfully empty pool area, where a row of fluffy white robes were waiting for me. It was as if they knew.

I honestly didn't know what was wrong with me. And I didn't know what in the world I was going to do with the way my heart was jumping around inside my chest.

One thing was clear, however. This time I was going right back to my room.

3

KILLIAN

As quickly as Killian had found her, she was gone.

He had been in awe of the girl from the moment he had turned the corner into the alley, his dragon perking up at the sight of her. He wanted her, but not her naked behind as she searched for something behind the dumpster, her.

Just her.

He needed her.

Not in his bed or in his court as was his normal fashion.

But with him. Protected. Wanted.

His.

She was his.

The thought tensed through his stomach, heating in his heart as his dragon fire began to burn, his shifter howling inside his mind in need of her. To feel her skin against his, to trace her lips with his tongue. To hold her. To protect her.

The new, frightening, emotions propelled him forward as he chased her, the dratted man that had opened the door and let her out of his grasp more than a few steps behind.

"Come back," Killian grumbled to himself as he turned a corner and faced yet another long, empty hallway.

How had he lost her? He was the fastest of his kind. He won every race, and defeated every enemy.

But this girl was gone. She had bested him.

It only made him long for her all the more.

"What in the world was that?" The hotel manager grumbled as he came up beside him, having also lost track of the streaming flame of her hair.

The balding man was panting, out of breath as he began to storm away, intent on catching her. A thunder of feet rattled behind him, at least ten of his staff ready to continue the chase.

"Freaking homeless people, they can't just come charging in here, bringing her filth..." Killian stopped the little man's tirade, and his retreat, before he could move more than a few steps away, his large hand wrapping around the man's wrinkled suit and pulling him back.

If this foolish little man thought he could insult the girl he had another thing coming. Killian's heart rumbled in his ears as he brought the man around to face him, holding him inches away as he let his nostrils flare.

"She is not filth," Killian growled, his voice rumbling alongside his dragon as the beast rose to defend the girl.

The manager was intent to rage at him, assuming he had been responsible for the girl's entry. He stopped short, however, any courage he had melting away at the sparks of fire in Killian's eyes. Killian didn't even try to restrain his dragon, he never did. A future king should never disguise his power. His father had made that much clear as he prepared him to take the throne. That was of course if the old man would die and let him take his place.

The thought mixed with the rage Killian felt, his need to defend the girl growing as he released the manager, leaving the man to stumble back, ready to posture Killian, although he was easily twice as large, both in bulk and in height.

His mistake. Killian's dragon snarled, his jaw squaring as his temper sparked.

"She is with me." Tweaking a smug grin, Killian produced the same room key he had shown to the girl in the alley, the ridiculous advertisement on the back making it clear where it came from. "Suite 405."

Making sure to emphasize the word *Suite*, Killian fixed him with a look that demanded respect. Even if the manager didn't know who he was, the room number alone should be enough to get the man to shut up. It was bad enough that Killian had been forced to stay in this tiny budget hotel down in the valley. He would much rather find a cave in the mountains, but considering what he was here for, the more they could blend in, the better.

No, the sooner he could get home and away from this stupid mission the better. It was dangerous enough to be here, he didn't need to be adding a girl to that.

Except that he could help it.

He wanted her. He had heard enough about this feeling to know exactly what it was, and that alone made everything he was here to do that much more dangerous.

It... couldn't be. She couldn't be.

"Mr. Cuelebre," the balding man gasped pulling Killian away from his thoughts as recognition set in.

Straightening his suit, the manager stepped away, trying to make himself look as put together as he could.

Not that it would help. The suit was a discount off the rack style, and could never compare to the perfectly tailored twill masterpiece Killian wore.

The suit had cost thousands, and been made by one of the finest tailors in Spain. It was one of Killian's treasures, and he was proud of it, if only because it was what his dragon desired.

The fact that it made him look amazing made it that much better. Of all the things to horde, at least his dragon had good taste.

"Yes," Killian affirmed, stepping closer as he took one last look around the corner, his heart thundering as it attempted to pull him toward her. "And I would expect my guests to be treated with as much respect as your staff have treated me and my..."

"Yes, yes, of course," the bumbling man cut in, bowing his head slightly. "Anything for our most esteemed guests."

At least the man had his priorities straight. The manager may not know exactly who, or what, Killian was, but even the mortal could sense the magic in him enough to yield.

"Then I trust you will leave me to my guest, and have your staff return to their work," Killian's voice was hard as he nudged his thumb behind him, pointing to the confused maids and kitchen staff that had joined the race.

"Yes, yes, yes," the manager blubbered, giving a backwards nod of dismissal to the others. "Anything you ask, sir."

This man was rubbing it on a little thick, and perhaps it was for good reason, it was clear by the state of the hotel that they didn't see many of Killian's stature here. The suite, if you could call it that, was well appointed, but the furniture was hard and the outcome of a bulk production company somewhere in the States.

Usually Killian relied on threats and charm to get his way, but this man crumpled like wet paper, ready to do anything for the dragon prince, even if he didn't know it.

"Wonderful," Killian crooned, stepping past the still

bumbling manager, toward where his heart was pulling him. "Then I will trust you will not get in my way."

The last words roared out of him, each consonant drenched in the deep rumble of his dragon, the creature speaking more to him than to the manager as it resumed its quest to retrieve its mate.

Mate.

The word jolted through Killian, stopping his heart with both fear and exhilaration.

Shifter mates were a powerful connection of soul and heart that many spent years searching for. Lifetimes protecting. Wolves mated once for life, the mates often dying within hours of each other. Pumas and many of the cats were the same. There was nothing stronger than a bond between shifters and their mates.

And in the case of a Dragon, nothing rarer.

Especially for the king.

It had been nearly three generations since one of the Dragon Kings, the Alphas of his kind had claimed a mate through a soul bond.

Soul mates were not meant for a king.

They were a sign of weakness. How could a king protect his kind if he was absorbed by a woman? Kings take what they wanted, claimed the woman or women they desired and kept his heart free to rule, and his bed free for pleasure. It was how his grandfather lived, how his father lived, and a life he had already begun to live.

But now, he raced through the halls toward her, every fiber of his soul stretching towards her in a need to claim what was his. To whisk her away and connect her dragon to his.

The thought made his bones ache for her, his dragon fire pulsing hot in his mouth.

He could nearly taste the steam.

Hot, moist, sweet like honey. Just like the aroma that had drifted from her. He couldn't seem to move his feet fast enough.

"Where are you going in such a hurry?"

The woman's voice was calm, sweet, and lined with enough ice that if it hadn't already doused the fire that was burning through Killian, the glare in her lavender eyes would have done it anyway.

"Dabria," Killian growled, slowing to a stop although he did not turn to face the dark figure.

The slender woman leaned casually against the beige striped wallpaper of the hotel as if she belonged there. Although, with her perfectly frayed black jeans, tall leather boots and shirt she could have easily been a smudge of ink against the white. Her long black hair lay in cords around her mahogany skin, making the bright purple of her eyes the only color in the smudge of black. They stood out like lights in the dark, digging right into Killian in an attempt to disable the muscular giant. Her seductive stare whispered over his skin, but for the first time he did not rise.

It was her eyes that had drawn his dragon to hers in the first place, the way they sparked in a danger that matched his own that had made his human form desire her.

Normally one glance of those lavender eyes and Killian would bend to her, take her. But right then he wanted nothing more than to push her out of the way and continue his pursuit.

It was a risk he could not take. Not right now. Not with this woman blocking his path.

Dabria was the reason he had been in the alley. He had been awaiting her arrival, and a message she had insisted on giving in person. Originally, he had refused her, but her demand had rubbed against him like sandpaper and he had obliged, knowing he needed to get rid of her, and that the manipulative woman wouldn't stop until she got what she wanted.

She was not part of his mission in this stinking mortal city, and if she discovered his reason for being here it could spell more than a little trouble for him.

More so if she even caught a whiff of what transpired only moments ago.

"I'm not used to having to hunt you down, handsome," she cooed, her voice a seductive lull as she pushed herself off the wall and stepped toward him, the tap of her heels against the worn carpet hitting against his heart like a nail in a coffin.

Killian's fists balled against his thighs in tight little rocks, pressing against his tense muscle in an effort to quiet the storm that was trying to take control.

Darting his eyes from Dabria, he took one last glance down the hall toward the invisible string that was still tugging at him. The strength of the girl's call was growing quieter by the minute.

He didn't have time for Dabria and her games.

"And I am not used to being summoned by haughty courtiers," Killian said with a snap, far too much of his frustrated rage seeping through his voice as his dragon growled, the air growing cold as it tried to suck her life from the air.

She didn't even flinch, she just smiled broader, used to his temper.

"Testy, testy," she teased, her hips swaying as she stepped toward him. "I've never seen you get so upset over a lost hooker before."

How dare she.

Killian's lip twitched, rage and bile rising in his throat as fire boiled in his heart. The bitter taste of ash filled his mouth, every part of him trying to control the anger at hearing the girl, his mate, being spoken about in such a way.

Mate. The word, the acceptance of it, calmed his heart, but not enough. The damage was already done.

"She is not a hooker," he barked, leaning toward Dabria as he let his eyes flash with flame, his massive frame threatening to swallow her, crush her into nothing but smoke and ash.

The devilish woman didn't even flinch.

"You tell yourself that, Killy," she crooned, stepping right up to him and placing her hands against his hips, the touch burning like ice, even through the heavy layers of fabric. "You know I can give you anything you need."

She whispered the words in his ear, lifting herself up on tiptoes to let her tongue dart out and taste his earlobe. Her hot tongue flicked at the long since closed piercing, the last remains of a defiant youth, well, if you didn't count the tattoos.

"I am everything you need," Dabria said, pressing the full length of her body against his, letting him feel every inch of her barely concealed curves.

Normally, her warm curves would result in him pressing her against the wall and take her mouth and body.

While he still wanted her against the wall, right then he would prefer to throw her away and watch her sliding down the bland striped surface in a ball of insolence and punishment.

How dare she touch him in such a way? His mate was waiting, his mate was ahead, and with every minute Killian wasted with Dabria, he was at risk of losing her. Who knew when their next chance encounter would be?

He couldn't risk losing her. But he also couldn't risk upsetting his father, and everything he knew of the dragon realm screamed at him to be careful.

His father should rejoice in a true mate for the future king, but Killian knew better than that.

He needed to be careful. Between the girl and his true purpose for being in the hotel, too much was at stake for the seductress to catch wind of something else going on, and share that news with the king.

She was the worst person to be here. Her dragon was powerful, and given the right opportunity could peer into his mind and pull his thoughts as easily as if she was reading a book.

He was sure she could do more, not that she had disclosed it in the hundred or so years he had known her, but he wasn't going to give her the opportunity to exercise any of her skills on him.

Dabria may lust after him, and he may have answered those calls on more than one occasion, but he wasn't a fool. He knew that it was the crown she wanted. Killian was only a vessel for her to get to her goal.

Killian's dragon howled in anger as he lifted the woman into his arms, pressing her against the wall as he had always done, using his wide hips to hold her in place as he gathered her tiny wrists in one large hand and held them overhead.

"Will you give me *anything* I need, Dabria?" He crooned his voice a low rumble and he leaned into her, running the rough scruff of his jaw against her. She shivered against the touch, moaning and melting into him.

Killian was good at this, at turning women to putty in his hands; both in the sheets and out. It was a benefit to both, a lustful tango of pleasure and desire.

Except this time Killian felt nothing, nothing but the

roaring anger of his dragon, the pulling pain of his heart taking him in another direction.

The lust was gone. The need had never arrived.

It was physically painful to be this close to another woman after he had felt so much with her...

The girl.

He didn't even know her name.

That fact alone only made his longing grow.

"Anything," Dabria breathed, her voice catching in her throat as he pressed against her, his dragon continuing to scream, demanding to rip her head off rather than continue the charade.

"Then I wish," Killian gasped, his voice husky as he pressed her hands harder against the wall, letting his breath roll over the hollow beneath her ear and sending a chill down her spine.

Dabria moaned, the escaped steam of his dragon awakening hers. The sound stabbed against Killian's heart, causing whatever thick band that was keeping his anger in check to snap.

He was done with her, and her games.

Killian pressed against her harder, her moan turning to a gasp as the air was forced from her lungs.

"Then I wish you to tell me whatever nonsense you *needed* to tell me, and leave my sight." Any forced seduction had left Killian's voice, leaving behind only the rage and frustration that was brewing inside.

He knew he should conceal it more, but the damage was already done and her violet eyes snapped to his, shifting to the blue ice of her dragon that she was known for.

"You will choose a mortal over me?" She seethed, affronted as she slipped out of his grasp. "You will choose the mortal whore."

The word was a hot knife through his soul, it sucked the air from his lungs and any logical thinking from his mind. There was only the dangerous growl of his dragon as it rattled in his chest, the sound vibrating walls and run down lighting fixtures.

"She must have the breasts of the gods," Dabria snarled, her lip curling as she leaned into him, daring him to counter.

Everything in Killian wanted to explode, to rip her limb from limb and cast her aside. But she had gone too far, she smelled too much. Forcing his temper, and his dragon, to back down he stepped toward the still fuming woman, wrapping his arm around her waist as he pulled her into him.

"Maybe she does," He crooned, keeping his voice soft as he looked into her eyes, the heat of his breath bringing a flush to her cheeks. "But sometimes I want to taste a mortal. I want to devour them. And right now I want to devour her. I can devour you anytime, my love."

Every word hurt.

He spoke them slowly, even though they sliced against his soul and sucked the air from the world until his bones ached. He had never felt physical pain like this. Not when his brother had stabbed him through the heart, not when he had breathed fire for the first time as child.

These words hurt in an indescribable way, but he couldn't pull away from them. He let them cut, let them stab like some kind of punishment for betraying the girl.

His mate.

There it was again, the same balm of calm that came with the acceptance of her.

"Then I will await that time," Dabria said, placing her hand against his cheek in a touch that was more like ice than the heat that it usually was. "And perhaps I will find my own mortal in that time."

Killian's lip twitched, crisis averted it seemed.

"I suggest you do," his words whispered over her lips, but before she had a chance to lean into them and make contact, Killian released her, letting her high-heeled boots hit the floor with a tap.

She did not stumble, however, she stood still and strong, her gaze still boring into his, although her frustration at the loss of a kiss, and more, was evident.

It took everything in him to restrain the rumble of his dragon that time.

"Now what did you wish to tell me, Dabria?"

"Just that we believe the Phoenix has been spotted."

If he had been holding something he might have dropped it.

No. It couldn't be.

His father had hunted that beast for as long as he could remember, his obsession with immortality ripping apart his kingdom, and his family. The phoenix was the reason he had come to this grungy city, and was staying in this low class hotel.

But not for the reason his father believed.

The back of Killian's jaw tightened, setting his jaw into a strong line that made Dabria's lip twitch.

"Where?"

"Southern Utah," Dabria said, now inspecting her perfectly manicured nails, as if what she was saying was as unimportant as whatever color she would get next. The fool. "A few hours ago, there was some chatter..." She waved her hand to the side. Flippant, unaware that what she was saying could easily end in her death. In the death of mortals, and wolves, and whatever else his father deemed as inferior. "Your daddy wants you to follow the scent. See what you can find."

If Dabria's seduction wasn't enough, there literally couldn't have been worse news.

"I'll find the beast," he barked, dismissing Dabria with his eyes as he turned from her, ready to high tail it back to the room, and into the air.

If only he could get there and back in time.

His mission had become much more complicated.

4
_____

ELLIOT

"You have got to be kidding me."

The newspaper slid in front of me before I even had a chance to take a sip of my coffee, the sharp voice of my best friend so familiar by now that I didn't even need to look up.

Not that I would have, the longer I could hold off the visual scolding the better.

"Good morning, Zoe," I said, keeping my eyes focused on the liquid black of my coffee, trusting in the aroma to wake me up before I had to get to morning training.

Living in a traveling circus meant a lot of things, but mostly it meant training. And training on no sleep was never a good idea.

I had finally made it back to my room about an hour ago, and even then the shower scalding I had subjected myself to wasn't enough to shake me out of the dream I am about eighty percent sure occurred.

Two hot guys... and whatever that feral *hunger* was. That couldn't have happened, and yes, I knew I was fooling myself.

I had washed off what was left of the ash my phoenix left

behind, and had just enough time to throw on tights, a leotard and my favorite hoodie, an oversized soft grey number emblazoned with bright pink lettering. Prague.

It had been almost a year since we performed in the ancient city, and I still missed it.

"Good morning, yourself," Zoe snapped, sliding into the booth across from of me.

Leaning over the scratched surface of the table, she came within inches of me and fixed me with an angry scowl before glaring into the hotel lobby, as if she was warding off any potential eavesdroppers.

Which she was. She was going full-blown protector on me.

"Look at it, Elliot."

I gave her a dark look over the use of my full name and slowly sipped at my coffee, letting the hot liquid burn my tongue a bit.

Zoe, however, didn't so much as flinch under my scowl, she held my gaze as the intensity in her grey eyes began to smolder, a tiny flare of red circling her pupil. She sat quite still in her cut off shirt, piles of brown curls pinned on top of her head. I was sure she didn't even try, and she still looked as though she had walked out of a magazine. The super scowl she had going was only adding to the look.

There was no way I was going to win this one.

Setting down my coffee, I groaned in that over exaggerated way she hated and picked up the newspaper. Leaning against the rough fabric of the tiny booth, I was ready to settle into the sob story about the girl who tragically fell to her death.

I could always count on Zoe to find my headlines.

As usual, she delivered.

Girl Falls to Death in Zion's National Park. Body Not Recovered.

It was a great headline, with a great picture of that beautiful canyon. I could feel my Phoenix prick up my gooseflesh just seeing it again.

Except, I could tell at once that I was in trouble. This newspaper was local.

"Crap," I hissed, scanning the story and turning to F8 as instructed in the hopes of finding as little information as possible about the girl, me, or what had happened.

Luckily, with the exception of one blurry picture from a spectator, they didn't seem to have any leads.

"Crap is right," Zoe snapped, snatching the paper from me and set it on the bench next to her, as if keeping it out of sight would help to keep it all a secret. One glance around the lobby revealed that to be impossible, there were at least five other copies filtered about through the others in our group. "That's a local paper, Ellie. I didn't even have to look that long this time. It was on my freaking door this morning. What were you thinking?"

I was thinking I was tired of being trapped in my skin. The response would have never made it all the way out, not with her. Not with anyone, really.

"I don't understand how that can be in a local paper."

My coffee was all but forgotten as I leaned toward her, our heads now millimeters apart as we hissed at each other. "I drove over three hundred miles away."

"Yes, and in Utah that is local, it seems. This isn't Europe."

I wanted to throw up. That one sip of coffee was suddenly not sitting very well.

"This is the United States, you can't drive four hours into another country and vanish into oblivion," Zoe sighed, finally leaning away from me and pulling my coffee toward her.

She immediately began to add copious amounts of creamer to it. Yuck.

"It was fine in California," I said, looking from the newspapers that were now everywhere in the lobby and twisted my hair around my fingers, the bright red more of a banner than usual.

Thank god dying your hair tomato red was kind of a 'thing' now. Didn't matter that mine was completely natural.

"Well, it's not fine in Utah," Zoe said, waving good morning to one of the other performers as they began to dish out some fruit at the buffet. "And even then, it hasn't been *fine* for a while."

"You know I can't keep her inside." I scarcely spoke loud enough for anyone, let alone Zoe, to hear.

Unlucky for me, Zoe had many of the same skills I had.

"And yet, I keep my dragon restrained…" she countered. I could tell she was trying to oppress me. It only bristled my defiant temper more.

"You can't for a minute think I believe that," I interrupted, narrowing my eyes at her as I stole my coffee back.

I remembered a second too late that Zoe had sweetened the concoction to death and I cringed the moment it hit my tongue.

"I have seen you during your act. It's pretty incredible how much more fire you are able to breathe. I mean… your baton doesn't have that big of a flame."

I was taunting her. I knew it, she knew it. And tease or not, she reacted with a snort, a tiny bit of smoke seeping from her nostrils as she leaned toward me again.

"Letting a little bit of fire out is different than releasing my dragon to soar over the Grand Canyon."

"It was Angel's Landing," I corrected her, her eyes flashing with flame.

"Does it really matter?" she retorted, stealing the coffee from me again. "You are still putting both of us in danger."

I froze. My phoenix's feathers were bristling, her frustration rising to meet my own. I narrowed my eyes at Zoe, fully aware that my own golden flames were looking out from behind my normally honey brown eyes, making them instead shine gold and threatening.

It was probably not the best idea to posture a Dragon, but I couldn't stop her either.

"It was one flight..."

"That you do every time we pitch the tents..."

"I never get to fly, Zoe!"

"Why are you in the circus, Elliot?" Zoe's soft voice cut through my rampage as she sat back in the booth, stretching the silence between us like a ribbon.

The chatter of the men at one of the tables beside us lifted above the stress-filled air, cutting through it as I pressed my arms against the hard ridge of the table. My skin was prickling with gooseflesh, the normally olive skin taking on a shimmering gold as my shifter moved closer and closer to the surface.

"Why, Ellie?"

I didn't have to answer, she knew the answer to that as well as I did.

"The dragon king wants to skin me alive and drink my blood or magic or something so that he can grant himself eternal life." As much as I tried to say that in a there's-no-way-this-is-a-big-deal way, it was a big deal.

A hugely, scary big deal.

I swallowed, the action impeded by a giant knot that had lodged in my throat.

I was five when my father had practically sold me to the owner, Suvi, an old Slavic witch that was older than Zoe. Unlike Zoe, however, she actually looked like she had seen a few hundred years. Zoe was a slender fire breathing goddess with hair the color of burnt wood and skin that glowed gold in the light.

Suvi was old, wrinkled and the perfect person to hide the first Phoenix shifter born in nearly three centuries. Her magic was strong enough that it only took one spell to mask my magic and my song from other shifters, and even most humans. As beautiful as the phoenix song was, I can pretty much guarantee that all those hikers witnessed was the wind and a bit of smoke. Suvi's magic concealed everything about my shifter. If anyone *had* seen anything they would probably think they had lost it.

Even to Zoe I was as human as little Xi who sat with her nose in the book in the corner, as she usually did. The only reason Zoe knew about me was because Suvi was hiding her too. Although Zoe had been a bit more closed lipped about her predicament than I had been.

I knew she was hiding from her dad.

"Your father wanted you to live," Zoe continued in a whisper, her words almost drowned by the quick Russian of the men behind us.

"I don't know what he wanted," I mumbled, folding my arms over my chest and slamming my back into the bench.

As angsty as I sounded, it was probably the only thing I really knew about my dad. I.e. nothing. I didn't know what he wanted, not really. Because I didn't know him.

Well, other than his name, Elliot. The name he had lovingly left with me. Other than that, it was bits and pieces.

I had been told my father was a Dragon shifter. I had been told he loved me. No one knew much about my mother, or how I had been born as a Phoenix and not a Dragon. But in reality it didn't matter. I was too young to remember either him or my mother. I don't even think I cried when Suvi told me of his death a few years after he had hawked me off.

I was a drifter. A loner.

Which from everything I had been able to learn about Phoenix shifters seemed about right.

"That was almost thirteen years ago, Zo, I am pretty sure they think I'm dead…"

"Phoenixes can't die," Zoe cut in, I restrained the need to stick my tongue out at her.

"Well, unless they are skinned and their song is stolen by evil dragon-shifter overlords." I spoke fast, angrily, and far too loud.

I immediately knew I had gone too far, I also immediately felt the guilt and worry that came with that. Not that I would let Zoe see either.

"Damn it Ellie," Zoe said, smacking her palm against the table and immediately going back into sentry mode, waving at the Chinese Pole team that were now looking at us with concern.

"You know it's true." I grumbled, spitefully chugging what was left of the coffee.

"Can you take me seriously for one freakin' minute?" She spat, the grey of her eyes shifting to red as her dragon threatened to take over. "You messed up. You got yourself on the front page with eyewitness accounts and some tough-guy named Brayden swearing he heard you sing as you fell."

Shit.

"And you did it here, of all places…"

"What's so special about this place?"

"What's so...?" Zoe stopped, her forehead wrinkling as she pinched the bridge of her nose as if I had given her an instant headache. Which I might have.

"We are surrounded by mountains. Some of the highest mountains on this continent."

I swallowed the last of the coffee, staring at her with a blank expression that aggravated her more.

"Dragons live in mountains," she retorted, leaning in close again. "I could smell them the second our truck rolled into this freakin' death trap. And you go throwing yourself off a cliff."

"Why didn't you tell me?" I could barely get the words out.

"Because I shouldn't have to." Zoe moaned, the red in her eyes beginning to fade. "You are almost eighteen, Ellie. You should know better."

Everything in me had turned to ice, which was saying something as I was pretty much made up of fire. But right then the heat was gone, drenched by an ice cold regret that as much as I wanted to hide away, I couldn't. I sighed, shoulders sagging as I ran my finger over the ridge of the now empty coffee mug.

"I know." It was all I could think to say. Sorry didn't seem to cut it.

"You have got to hide her away, Ellie..."

"You keep saying that. Suvi keeps saying that. But for how long? I can't stay trapped on the ground," I interrupted her, the words harsher than I had meant them. Not that it mattered, it wasn't my tone that had set her eyes blazing.

"You think I want to?" She hissed, causing the heads of several older women at a table nearby to turn. They looked away in haste with one smoldering look from Zoe; I didn't blame them. They didn't know her, and on first glance she could easily be terrifying, especially when her dragon was this close to the surface. "You think I like hiding? You think I like walking on two legs…" She faded off, waving and nodding to someone else before she twisted back to me, leaning over the table again. "I haven't shifted in over a decade years, Elliot."

Everything about her sagged and faded away, her own loss at what was as much a part of her as my shifter felt like a stab in the heart.

"I didn't know that," I said, my words sounding lame as the truth dug into me.

She had only been traveling with us for the last six years or so, I had assumed she had only been hiding that long.

I had obviously been a fool.

I had a problem keeping my phoenix in check, but most of that was because I was a baby. Well, a baby by the standard of shifters. I was only about eighteen years in to a three hundred year life cycle. Well, for dragons anyway. Phoenixes can't die. So I was almost eighteen years into eternity.

A baby. The thought made me want to roll my eyes.

Even with that, though, I couldn't imagine keeping my shifter locked inside for that long. I didn't think it was possible.

Looking at Zoe, I wasn't sure it was. I couldn't be sure that part of her wasn't dying.

"What I wouldn't give for just one more flight…" She sighed, her focus looking far past me at some memory that I was quite sure I could never understand. Maybe that's what I was looking for when I would throw myself off mountains, and towers, and anything else I could find.

"You have got to be more careful, Ellie." She finally said, her hand reaching forward to wrap around mine.

"I know, Zo..." I began, but she bowled me right over.

"The same people who are hunting you, are hunting me. And trust me when I say you do not want them to find you. I would kill myself before I let that bastard *king* take control of me again."

The tone of her voice shifted into a low hum of panic I wasn't sure I had ever heard from her before. All of my stubborn defiance went into high alert, heart pounding in confusion as her fear began to infect me.

The busy hotel lobby faded into nothing as our eyes locked in a battle of fire, the truth of what she was saying smacking against me like a battering ram.

That was the most she had said about her past, ever. I knew that I was hunted, I knew the basics of it, and as much as it scared me, nothing scared me as much as the danger that seeped from her voice.

She gripped my hands tighter, pulling any wandering focus back to her. "I would kill you before I let him get you. Don't give me a reason to do that."

I couldn't even bring myself to swallow.

5

ELLIOT

Circus Kaleydo was founded in 1983 in Turkey, and had traveled the world under the signature red and black tent every since.

Or, at least, that's what the website says.

The reality is that Kaleydo was founded sometime in the fifteenth century by Suvi's family, a clan of witches who travelled Europe under the guise of gypsies and later as circus folk in their attempt to blend in. After all, what better place to disguise yourself as a normal everyday human than in a freak show or as a palm reader.

They weren't the only 'gypsies' to do this, or at least that's what she says.

As time went on, the specialties changed and the traveling front became a full-fledged world-renown circus and less and less people hid underneath those red and black canvas tents.

Now we were more acrobats and contortionists than witches and vampires.

As far as I knew, Zoe and I were the only paranormal oddities here. Well, unless you count Suvi. But I wasn't about to go around asking everyone what animal lives in their subconscious or if they prefer to drink the blood of mortals.

I already had a reputation for being a little *weird*. Talking to yourself from a young age has a tendency to do that.

Sometimes I wondered how my father knew to bring me here. I mean, if he was truly hiding me, wouldn't he go somewhere that wasn't historically used as a paranormal creature hiding zone?

But then, what did I know?

I was raised here.

In a circus.

And yes, the circus was owned by a four hundred year old witch, but it was full of humans who knew nothing, and could know nothing, about me or anything about the world I came from. Which was probably fine because the only thing I knew about myself and my kind came from confusing websites created by fan girls obsessed with finding a hunky Dragon shifter to fill their bed. Websites and Zoe.

And Zoe wasn't talking.

Well, up until a minute ago.

Which is why I was giving her such intense side-eye that she looked ready to punch me.

"If you look at me one more time I am going to..."

"Kill me?" I cut in smoothly, my own stomach flipping as I said it.

"Shut up, Elliot," she hissed, her eyes sparking danger as she stared at me.

We walked toward where Suvi and her assistant Alan were gathering the performers for the morning grump, so called because Suvi was never happy in the mornings, and

Alan had a bulldog face that scared away most people shorter than him.

Considering he started as a flyer in the Chinese pole act tells you a bit. I think he topped out at five-foot-one. A whole three inches shorter than me.

You get the two of them together delivering the news of the day, before coffee had kicked in, and all you had was two sour-faced upper managers trying to sugar coat the performance stats and complaints from the hotel about how we are eating too much bacon.

Dust, chalk, and the sticky-sweet smell of rosin tickled my nose the moment we walked into the large white tent behind the main performance tent. Combine that with the smell of lighter fluid and smoke that always surrounded Zoe and her team of fire dancers and the tension that had wound up my spine at Zoe's declaration of prepared murder faded away.

Well, as much as it could knowing that my best friend was ready and willing to murder me.

Creepy.

I gave her another should-I-be-scared-to-go-to-sleep-tonight side glare, earning me yet another fiery scowl.

"Keep your eyes forward Ellie, you are starting to act neurotic." Zoe murmured out of the side of her mouth, raising a hand to a very groggy Ryn, her performance partner.

"You do realize that is easier said than done, don't you?" I hissed as the gangly Japanese teen began to make his way toward us. "You kind of knocked everything around me wide open."

Not to mention the fact that she had smoothly struck up a conversation with the stage manager, Becky, immediately after her grand proclamation.

I was left to sit there looking like I had eaten frogs. Something that didn't go unnoticed by Becky, who asked if it was 'that time of the month.'

I swear the woman had no tact, even if I did get a period I wasn't going to tell her. And I didn't. I more burst into flames every few weeks. But I still wasn't going to tell her that.

"I did not 'knock everything open'," Zoe said as she weaved through the meandering, half-awake company. "And even if I did, now is not the time to talk about it."

"You know something, Zoe," I stepped as close to her as I dared, fully aware that the look on my face and the near panicked levels I was reaching was starting to attract attention. "You know something about me, and about drag…"

"Shut up!" Zoe barked, loud enough that even Ryn, who had now reached us was looking a little concerned.

And he wasn't even getting the full brunt of her anger.

I had that luxury

I was stuck there, her eyes now glowing with a shade of red so deep I was sure anyone else would think they had become pools of blood.

I knew better.

My phoenix knew better. Although I could feel her prickle up in a need to protect, felt my heart warm and my skin began to chill as it did before a change. I forced my soul to stay inside. Instead, I swallowed and took one very meaningful step back.

"Woah," Ryn said in his deep Asian accent, "I don't think I have ever seen you guys fight. Is everything okay?"

His concern was clear, but I didn't move, and neither did Zoe. She let her eyes smolder for one minute more before she blinked and leaned into me. Slow, calculated, and with enough acid in her glare I was sure I could feel the skin on my face melt away. It took everything in me not to head for the hills.

I didn't want to be that close to her.

Hell, I didn't want to be in the same room with her. I may or may not have been second guessing my choice to be best friends with a dragon right then.

"I will talk to you later," she hissed, low enough that only a shifters ears could hear, and stepped away. "Everything's fine."

"Are you sure?" Ryn asked, casting me a look that made it clear that I was, in fact, melting.

Quickly arranging my fear-melted face back into place I waved him away, gave him a nod that he seemed to accept and sunk down onto one of the camp chairs that lined the massive practice gym.

Ryn gave me another look of concern before shifting his focus to Zoe, pulling the woman who was now refusing to look at me into a wrap around hug that instantly made me jealous.

And also instantly made me think of Jarron, and of that kind smile, and that wide chest that I was sure would feel wonderful to lean against.

I shook my head, trying to dislodge the image.

"What in the world is going on?" Ryn asked, low enough that I was sure he thought I couldn't hear.

"I'm wondering the same thing myself, Ryn," I mumbled to myself and sunk lower into the chair, ready to do anything to avoid being sucked into their conversation.

It was bad enough I could hear every word when he was trying so hard to be silent, add to that the special connection performing partners had for each other and I had accidentally been sucked into the seventh ring of hell.

Except now it was occupied by the still too fresh memories of two handsome men.

I had read enough Teen YA novels to know that when shifters found their mate it was this lifelong, protect to the death deal. I had never seen it. I had never felt it.

Well, until whatever had happened this morning with Killian and Jarron.

The squirrely warmth they had given me was still so fresh that sitting there listening to Zoe and Ryn was making that hunger surge again, the smug smile Killian had given me sending my heart into uneven palpitations. I guess it was burned into my memory. Ugh.

Mates.

It couldn't be true, could it? No, it couldn't because there were two and everything I had read had said one mate. One guy.

One Mate.

A line of fire pulled through my heart at the word, filling me with equal parts need and terror that was making my head spin.

I heard my phoenixes song a second before anyone else, a second before Xi looked up from her book to stare at me, and a second before the entire room froze.

Zoe and Ryn were locked in position, her smile wide as she placed her hand on his shoulder, laughing at some joke I had missed. Sasha and a few of the Russians were frozen in their balancing act, wide smiles in place as they goofed around before morning meeting.

For a second, I was sure I was being punked, and then I saw tiny Stacia, far above Sasha's outstretched arms, arms and legs perfectly stiff as she twisted and spun in the air. But she didn't twist. And she didn't spin. Her body was stuck as though someone had put a pin in her, tied her from a string and hung her from the ceiling.

No one moved, all sound was sucked from the room. All but the lone note of my Phoenix song, the sound stretching through the heavy air as I tried to jump up from my chair only to find that I could barely move.

The air was pressing against me.

I peeled myself away, slow, stagnant as if I was trying to force myself through the heaviest glue.

I was moving, yes, but everything was jelly, my mind going twice as fast as my body.

Even my heart was going double the speed in confusion as panic began to take hold. No one else moved, no one else seemed to have any idea that anything was going on, not even Suvi, the old witch having been my first guess as to whatever was behind this.

Her eyes were still fixed on Alan. She was as frozen as everyone else.

Was I causing this? It sure seemed possible, but I had never done anything like this before, the most I could do was burst into flames. I wasn't magical. Not like Suvi.

Not like the dragon king that hunted me.

"What the hell!" I bellowed in panic, the single sound echoing in a weird distanced reverberation. It came back to me end over end, my own voice distorted as though I was listening to it through some kind of heavy paste.

"Shit!" I yelled, and whatever spell had trapped us vanished. Leaving the Russians to finish their trick, Ryn to finish his joke, and my loud snap of a swear to echo so loud through the tent that everyone turned, leaving a hundred pairs of eyes fixed on me.

A few people laughed uncomfortably. The rest stared at me, sure gone off my rocker. Rightly so, I was sure I was looking at them in the same way, my mind still going into overdrive as to what the holy hell had just happened.

Slowly, those few laughs broke into loud chuckles, the sound of my embarrassment spreading over the tent in a wave. I fought the need to duck my head and pretend that I no longer existed, and instead met them all head on. Well, all accept Suvi, who was staring right at me with a look so severe that I did actually shrink into the tiny chair, the thing threatening to collapse around me.

"What in the world is going on?" Zoe demanded from behind me, any sign of her anger melted away into sheer concern.

Great, she thought I was losing it too.

She waited for me to answer, but the only thing I was able to do was release a few awkward duck sounds and gain more laughs from those around me.

"Settle down, settle down," Suvi howled in her scratchy voice as she looked right at me and Zoe, her eyes filled with so much rage that Zoe slowly sunk into the chair beside me, not letting her eyes deviate an inch from the old woman.

"What is going on?" Zoe whispered the moment Suvi had turned away from us, her eyes glinting with red as she shot me a powerful side eye. I could see the anger there, although I had a feeling it was not meant for me. There was too much concern in her voice, and the way she sat was almost... Protective? Weird.

Suvi and Alan's chatter about hotel policies we were breaking buzzed in the background as I turned to her. I was sure I heard the words 'swinging' and 'chandelier'.

I wish I had thought about that.

"I might as well ask you the same thing." I retorted, my heightened emotions from being trapped in glue knocking against me and making me volatile.

She gave me a look, a sigh, and then shifted her weight so my escape options were limited.

"Don't do that, Zo-"

"Later," she interrupted me as if that settled it, turning to watch Alan chatter on about some climbing gym that was giving us temporary memberships.

"Later what?" I did my best to keep my voice low, while also not looking away from Suvi, who was now looking at us so often I was sure she was hearing every word. "Later you will tell me everything, or later you will question me about my temporary Tourette's?"

"You're the one yelling--"

"Ladies," Suvi halted our conversation and once again pulled the focus of everyone else in the tent right to us.

"Please keep personal conversations until later," the rhythmic sound of accent was like home to me, but right then her frustration was a warning light.

Turns out, I could sink deeper into my chair.

"They are located on the other side of the complex," Alan said in his low drawl. "I am sure it would be a great opportunity to see what types of things Americans enjoy."

We had set up in a large parking lot of what we had been told was an old abandoned mall off the freeway. It was a much better setup than the weird field we had been given in Southern California. We had been on the site of an old amphitheater there, and the unkempt space would fill our tents with dust anytime a breeze picked up off the ocean.

The parking lot might be hot, but it was right by the hotel and gave us plenty of visibility. We had been sold out from the moment we started pitching the massive performance tent last month.

"Last order of business," Alan began, his accented voice stumbling as he bounced on his toes.

Everything about his demeanor had changed, it was almost like someone had flipped a switch and supercharged him. I wasn't the only one to notice, either. People exchanged glances, and a few that had been playing on their phones looked up eagerly.

All of that energizing buzz couldn't breach the weird sense of unease from the weird time freeze thing, and the way Suvi was looking at me wasn't helping.

Except she wasn't looking at me. She was looking right at Zoe, and Zoe was meeting the dead-eyed glare head on.

I swallowed.

"We have had such an interest in our production that we will be extending our stop here an additional two weeks," Alan continued joyfully, unaware of the daggers that were being thrown across the tent. Instead, he clapped his hands together joyfully as he bounced on his toes.

The reaction was immediate. Cheers, whoops, and instant conversations broke out through the tent, turning everything into an absolute tunnel of noise. The excitement was so thick that it was palpitating the air.

Extensions were great. More shows meant more money. And a higher ticket price meant more money. And all that money meant bonuses. So, more money.

I jumped a bit, my own excitement running amuck through my veins.

"This is bad."

Well, until Zoe said that.

"So, bad."

"Is that why Suvi looks ready to murder me?" I asked, chancing a glance at the old woman who was now making her way toward us, her tiny crumpled frame looking twice as large in the rage that was propelling her forward. Alan had let the meeting dissolve under the announcement and everyone had moved back into their own worlds, unaware of whatever showdown was about to occur.

I could take the guys this morning, sure. But Suvi? I was toast.

"She's not looking at you," Zoe mumbled as she reached us. "She's looking at me."

"Do you smell that?" Suvi asked, speaking to Zoe as if I wasn't there.

"It's stronger than last night, and a few minutes ago..." Zoe stopped mid sentence, giving me a look that made it clear I wasn't invited to that conversation.

Either that or she knew what had happened, and whatever smell they were obsessed with, came from me.

I had a sudden urge to smell my armpits. But there was nothing but the smell of my lavender shampoo and I was pretty sure the time freezes didn't smell like anything.

"My office. Now," Suvi snapped to Zoe, causing her to jump to attention, turning to look at me. "You, lock yourself in your room. I will be there soon."

"Huh?" I asked, shock still rippling over me as the two of them began to stride away.

Like hell if I was going to let them do this again, they couldn't lock me out of everything forever.

First, Zoe tells me she is going to kill me, and now I get stuck in a time sludge, thing... no.

My courage snapped into place as I jumped into action, catching up to Zoe and Suvi as they ducked under the heavy canvas to the outside.

"I'm not going to the hotel," I said, causing the two to turn as the canvas slid closed. "I'm coming with you. I need to know what's going on."

Suvi's eyes sparked curiously as the corner of her mouth ticked up, the twitch making the anger look that much more oppressive. Combine that with the full on fury that Zoe was projecting toward me and I almost lost my nerve.

"Nothing is going on that you need to worry about," Suvi began her voice harsh as she plunged into the same excuse they had given me for years. "Zoe and I are doing all that is needed to protect you, and we will continue to do so. Now, I need you to go to the hotel..."

"You can't protect me if you can't move," I interrupted, keeping my voice as strong as I could. "And if what happened a few minutes ago happens again then I am beyond toast."

The two of them exchanged a look that clearly said they knew exactly what I was talking about, and that it was anything but good.

The look punched a massive hole in my confidence but I wouldn't let it show. I needed to know what was going on, thirteen years of being in the dark was ending today.

"What are you saying, child?" Suvi asked, her eyes narrowing in a look so deep I was sure she was seeing past me and into my soul or some crap.

The glare sent ice down my spine and I shivered, although I refused to take a step back, no matter how much I wanted to. I met her eyes dead on, keeping my voice as stable as I possibly could.

"I am pretty sure I just froze time."

6

ELLIOT

Suvi's office was a relocatable outside of the main tent. There was a row of three of them that extended in front of the audience entrance, one for tickets, one for customer service and one where Suvi and Alan ran the whole show.

All three of them were hot, smelled of sweat and mold, and were full of strange outdated furniture. Alan's side of the relo was perfectly clean, arranged to his exact requirements and even had one of those old style drinking bird things.

Suvi's area was different, and if we hadn't stepped through the old metal door I wouldn't recognize it as a relo at all. Fabric of all colors were draped over the walls, tables, and windows, sending ribbons of jewel bright color into the heavily perfumed air. I had been in this room, or in ones nearly identical to it for the past ten years.

It was as home to me as the aerial silks and hoops I used in my act. In fact, I think much of these were old worn out silks that were no longer safe for flying.

"Sit," Suvi commanded me with one look, closing the door that separated her office from Alan's with a snap.

The tension in her voice whipped against my muscles and I dropped into one of the covered chairs as though someone had forced me there. Which she might have, I wouldn't put it past the old witch, what with the frightening intensity anything was possible.

Springs poking against my back as I sunk into the old wingback, my hands gripping the worn fabric of the armrests as if they were the only protection I had. I tried to get comfortable, but I knew it wasn't going to happen. There was too much panic in this room to even breathe adequately, and even then, every gasp of the dread filled air pressed against my chest in a paralyzing pressure.

I wasn't the only one who was drowning in the stress, Zoe was pacing the floor in agitation, continually peeking behind the heavy red silk that covered the window, as though she was waiting for something to burst through.

The action put me on guard and I stiffened, ready to attack whatever was moments away from busting in. Not that I could do much, I was sure even with the guy in the alley the most I could do was pin him to the ground and run.

The image blended with the memory and my stomach swooped, sending me back into the chair with an exasperated sigh.

Normally, I would kick my shoes off and throw my feet onto the coffee table, but I highly doubted such an act would fit this occasion, even if the surface wasn't covered with cards, bones, and candle wax.

"Zoella," Suvi's heavily accented voice snapped through the pungent air as she turned from the door, the old wood shimmering grey with some spell.

Magic. It had to be. I had never seen Suvi do anything like that before, and I couldn't stop staring. Dumb, I know. I burst into a phoenix at will, and a shimmering grey shield around a door was sending me into a tizzy.

"Do you still sense them?" Suvi asked softly, patting me on the shoulder as she passed and pulling my slack-jaw stupor from the door.

"No," Zoe said with a sigh, her lips pressed into a tight line as she once again looked out the window. "Whoever it was is long gone."

"Good." Suvi whispered, scuttling over to her desk, tapping once against the old cracked teapot there.

The porcelain immediately began to steam, big billows of violet clouds pouring from it's spout and filling the room with the scent of lilacs and mint. I had seen this trick hundreds of times before, but somehow seeing it alongside the shield made it that much more impressive.

"I will set more wards before the show tonight," Suvi said, her voice growing soft as she began to pour tea into three equally cracked mugs. "And I will need you to clear the perimeter."

Zoe stepped away from the window, casting me another one of those awkward glances from before and I shifted in my seat. My skin prickled, warmth spreading over me as my temper began to rise. It was clear she didn't want me here, that I was interrupting some secret club or something, and not, you know, being involved with something that I should have been involved with from the beginning.

I bit my lip in an effort to keep from exploding, although my phoenix was ready to do so at any moment.

"That will take me a good couple of hours..." Zoe began, giving me another look and I shifted in my chair.

"Then we should make this quick so you can begin," Suvi was calm, kind, but there was a tone of irritation and worry in her voice that snapped against my already taut temper.

"Make what quick?" I asked, unable to hide the irritated bite to my voice. "I would prefer if we take our time to go over everything. And I need to know everything. About me. About my dad. About whatever B.O. you are all smelling."

Suvi said nothing, she only fixed me with a wicked side-eye and popped a pipe into her mouth. The smoke that billowed from it stunk like old socks, maybe that's what they were talking about.

"It's not body odor," Zoe grumbled, crossing her arms over her chest as she leaned against the wall, the motion sending a few long sheets of fabric swaying. "You don't know enough to--"

"I don't know anything, Zoe!" I snapped, jumping in my seat. I would have jumped out of it too, if Suvi's focus hadn't shifted to me, her green eyes a haunting shade of disapproval that made me feel five years younger and not nearly as adult as I thought I was.

Exhaling with a shake, I attempted to center my frustration into something a little more adult and try again.

"Neither of you have told me anything." I looked from Zoe to Suvi, doing my best to stay as diplomatic as possible, even though my internal fire was still screaming. "Well, except that Zoe wants to kill me if there is a chance the dragon king would get me."

"Zoella," Suvi said, her grey curls swaying as she turned to face the now scowling dragon. "You should not say such things."

She took a step toward Zoe, puffing on her pipe as her dangerous looking green eyes dug into my friend. Her hunched frame barely came to Zoe's collarbone, but the tall Dragon backed down anyway.

Watching this showdown was making me strangely uncomfortable, not because I was watching Zoe cower before a four hundred year old witch, but because I think I may have been underestimating Suvi's power.

Or overestimating Zoe's.

"I'm only speaking of the truth," Zoe retorted, her dark eyes flitting to mine, glaring as though I had tattled on her. You would think I was the adult with the sass that was flowing off her.

"She is not ready for truth," Suvi said, setting the tray of tea, cups and biscuits. I would have been eager for the bready treats, but I couldn't given what she had said.

"Wait." So much for keeping my level head. "So I can know my best friend wants to kill me, but nothing else?"

Suvi sighed deeply from between pipe clenched teeth as she set the tray of tea down on the cluttered coffee table, sending a few of the bones rolling over the edge.

I grabbed them without thinking throwing them on the table where they fell on a tarot card, the two narrow bones landing end over end. Suvi's sigh deepened as she looked at them, her eyes growing dark.

"The crossed kingdom over death, the ruler of innocence" she said, with the pipe in her hands, eyes darting from the crossed bones to me. "The keeper of your fate seems to think that you are still not prepared for all that is coming."

"Good thing that keeper of my fate is not here," I grumbled letting the snark roll off my tongue like the bitter acid it was. "Otherwise, I would be concerned over the fact that I stopped time."

"Ah yes, I believe you may have accidentally been trapped in one of my wards. Tell me, child. Did you feel as though you were underwater and unable to move, or in a fog and unable to see?" Suvi's voice was kind as she picked up one of the ancient teacups, handing it to me without so much as a shake in her hands, her eyes not leaving mine.

I stared at her, fully aware of the delicious aroma that was drifting my way, although suddenly my stomach had tied itself up in knots.

When I had told them I stopped time before, Suvi had looked ready to scream, Zoe looked horrified as the two of them practically dragged me to the relo. Now I had gotten 'stuck in a ward', and she says it as though we are discussing puppies over tea.

The tea was there, but I didn't see a single puppy.

I'm calling bullshit.

I looked from Suvi to Zoe, the tall beauty chewing on her bottom lip as she stared at me, her agitation giving Suvi away.

She was very clearly hiding something, and the knowledge gnawed at me in an angry flame.

I took the cup grudgingly, refusing to look away from the old woman.

"It was both," I lied, watching Suvi for any reaction as I took a long sip of the tea, nearly draining the cup. "I could see, I could breathe and move, although very slowly. But everything was frozen. The air felt--"

"Heavy?" Zoe interrupted, her voice laced with all the dread I had expected.

See, bullshit.

"I'm sorry," I began, it was taking everything in me to keep both temper and shifter at bay. "But can you guys please tell me what is going on. Screw the bones. I am pretty sure we are past the whole 'protect a thirteen year old Elliot from herself' stage."

"I am not sure we are, child," Suvi said, rounding on me.

Her dark eyes were filled with the fear and a parental disappointment I had experienced before. "Any child that throws herself off a cliff is still in need of protection, and not ready to face the real world and the truths it holds."

My heart slowed with every syllable until I was sure it was nothing but a rock of stone in my chest. The teacup felt cold in my hands as my temper lifted, all of my rage directed right at Zoe.

"You told her?"

"I protected you," She clarified as if that made it all better. Spoiler alert: it didn't. And I was sure the glare I had fixed her with said as much.

"I don't need protecting!" I raged, standing so fast that I sent the forgotten teacup to the ground, the last of the deep purple tea spilling down my warm-ups and spreading over the plush rug in a violet stain.

Suvi looked at it sadly, sending more foul smoke into the air as she puffed on her pipe. I wasn't sure if she was mourning the loss of the ancient rug, or dissecting my future in the shards of porcelain, and I didn't care. I only had eyes for my meddling friend.

It felt like stretching to be calling her that, now.

"Yes, you do," Zoe began, but Suvi stopped her with a glare, sending the dragon into submission as she leaned against the wall of the relo.

"You will always need protecting child," Suvi's voice was calm, honest, and it did absolutely nothing to calm the rage that was brewing underneath my skin. "If not from those who would harm you, than perhaps from your own curious stupidity."

"Is that what we are calling my flights?" I said, emphasizing the word. I don't know why they were speaking about everything as if it was dirty and irritating.

"Revealing yourself to mortals, no matter how much you think you have disguised it is curious stupidity, and until you learn to conceal yourself, you are not ready to know the truth." The kindness in Suvi's voice had faded again, leaving me staring, my jaw hanging open in realization.

It wasn't my flying, or my attitude, or whatever time stopping I had been trapped in that was irritating-- it was just me. Everything about me.

"So what? I go fly once in a while, it's no big deal." I tried to make it sound like no big deal, even though by now I was well aware that it wasn't. Besides, my bi-monthly flying excursions weren't the problem here. "You two are apparently smelling demons or something and I can stop time..."

"It was a ward..." Suvi interrupted me, but that lie was the last thing I needed right now.

"Like hell it is!"

I roared, I screamed, and I knew for a fact that my eyes were the color of pure gold right then. I let it blaze, let the heat roll over my skin until I was sure if I focused I could throw fire.

The thought was terrifying.

First, time stops and I am sure as shit not buying Suvi's ward story. And now my hands feel like they are ready to explode.

I lifted the renegade appendages, staring at them with wide eyes as smoke rippled over my palms, the skin the color of lava.

No freaking way.

Panic increasing, I looked from my hands to the two woman in front of me, the look on their faces making it clear that they knew exactly what was going on.

And judging by the knowing look they exchanged, they weren't going to say a word to me.

"What is this? The old woman's club?" I asked, fully aware that my snark was growing out of control.

"Calm down, Ellie," Zoe pleaded, the fear in her voice melting to worry.

I opened my mouth to respond, ready to rage and demand answers. But the only thing that was ready to come out was the angry tears of rejection, of betrayal.

Instead, I balled my hands at my side and bolted out of Suvi's office and right into a very confused Alan.

"Is everything okay in there?" He asked, his voice lined with the usual irritation.

I didn't even bother to answer. I was pretty sure I couldn't answer without yelling, or crying, or both. Considering I wanted to do neither, I shook my head and charged past him, right out the door and into the biting desert sun that plagued this city.

"Wait," Zoe said, the door of the relo snapping loudly over the parking lot as she followed me out. "Don't leave like this..."

"Like what, Zoe?" I whirled on her, my long red hair flaring behind me as I turned, my temper exploding. "Like a woman who has been lied to for thirteen years. Like the freaking out-of-control wild animal I am. Like the liability you two see me as?"

I didn't even try to keep my voice down, I didn't really care who heard, maybe if they did Suvi would finally tell me something about who I was.

And why it was so freaking important for me to pretend that I didn't have a phoenix inside of me.

That I was nothing.

"Like you aren't my friend."

Her voice was calm, and strangely out of character for the fiery best friend I always knew her to be. It was almost enough to calm the hurt and anger that was rampaging through me.

Almost.

"You aren't treating me like your friend, Zoe," I said, low enough that the few performers heading toward the nearby businesses wouldn't hear. "You are treating me like I am some sort of problem. A canker in your life. And I am not sure why. I don't understand why you two can't tell me what's going on."

"Because you aren't acting responsible," she said, her own anger starting to ripple back into place.

"Why? Because I throw myself off cliffs? Because I want to feel like myself and not pretend there isn't something wrong? Because I'm not trying to hide like you are, scared of my own shadow, running away from some king like the coward you are?"

"That's low, Elliot." I could hear the hurt in her voice, but I plowed on, throwing myself into the friendship graveyard that I was building for myself.

"I would say the truth hurts, but I don't know what that feels like."

My voice was hard, every ounce of pain and frustration that had built up over the years flooding out in an attack that I could not control.

I didn't want to control.

I stood still, waiting for her response. Waiting for some apology, or promises of truth to come. I got neither.

"Go back to your hotel room, Ellie," Zoe said, her soft voice laced with hurt. "We will come get you when we know it's safe."

"Safe from what?" I asked, all the rage returning to her face as her jaw tightened.

"You know what," She snarled. "You may not know everything, but you know enough. Stop pretending we are doing this to hurt you."

"Aren't you?"

Zoe groaned, screwed her face up, and let out a frustrated growl that sounded a little too inhuman. I jerked at the sound, taking a step back as my rage ebbed, fear taking its place.

"I'm your friend, Ellie," Zoe said calmly, her tall frame towering over me as she stepped up to me, her hands sweltering through my hoodie as she placed them on my shoulders. I tried to shrug away from her touch, but she held me in place, her fiery eyes digging into mine. "I have been since before you knew yourself. You'll see that soon enough. Right now, however, you need to be safe. Go back to the hotel."

Zoe looked behind her as though someone had called her, her jaw tightening before she looked back to me, any sign of anger and frustration having evaporated.

"Go back to the hotel," she repeated, wrapping me in a hug I didn't return before she ran back into the relo, leaving me standing on the sweltering blacktop, drowning in my confusion.

I had no idea what had happened, and I was no closer to gaining any kind of information.

But I sure as hell wasn't going back to the hotel.

7

ELLIOT

"ONE HARNESS, ONE PAIR OF SHOES. THE AUTO BELAYS ARE ON the left, bouldering wall in the back, and your 'welcome class' will be in about twenty minutes by the yellow wall."

The perky girl behind the desk smiled brightly as she set what appeared to a tangle of straps on the bright blue counter. She pointed to each of the aforementioned locations in turn, smacking her gum as she spoke with an indiscernible accent, dropping her t's and l's in weird ways.

"Uhhh... thanks," I said, still not looking away from the tangle of the harnesses on the desk, fully aware that the girl was still staring at me. She had since the moment I had walked in.

Normally I would say it was the hair, but hers was equally as bright, she even had a nose ring to match.

I couldn't have any piercings. They caught on the silks. Part of me was jealous, but I wasn't about to tell her that.

"So, you're with that circus, huh?" She finally asked, breaking the silence as I began to gather the harness and shoes.

It was then I looked at her, and she smiled, revealing

perfectly straight, perfectly white teeth. The look was so unnatural it was a bit unnerving.

"Uh, yeah," I said, taking one quick glance to see if something about me had given me away. I still wore my Prague hoodie, although I had pulled a pair of warm ups over my tights and leo. "How did you know?"

She smiled brightly, smacking her gum. "The accent. I haven't never heard anything like it. Where are you from?"

I cringed at her choice of words, but managed to keep the smile in place. It wasn't the first time someone had said my accent was *interesting*. It's what happens when you grow up as a nomad, surrounded by a dozen different languages, and a dozen different accents.

I was a blend of all of them.

Hell, I spoke half of them.

"Europe," I answered with a smile, holding the harness against me as I whisked myself away before she could ask any more questions.

I was determined to figure this out and disappear into the air before Zoe found my note, and her and Suvi went on a rampage to find me.

Yes, I probably should have gone back to the hotel, especially considering I was no nearer to having any answers, and Suvi's response to that weird time freezing thing was anything but reassuring. I knew something was up. But I didn't know what or why, and all the worries in my head were multiplying in irritating ways. I couldn't take it anymore. I needed out of the trap they had wrapped around me, out of my head, and the rehearsal tent had too many snitches to even put it on the short list.

So it was this, or running, and running was too grounded for the amount of energy that was buzzing through me. This place was as to close to flying as I could get. I could already feel the electric buzz of my phoenix.

It was a sensation that only got worse when I walked into the large climbing area. High cathedral ceilings stretched twenty, maybe thirty feet in the air, the massive space lined with windows and climbing walls that were covered with multi colored knobs and fake rocks for people to hold onto. The artificial cliff faces surrounded the mats where dozens of people milled around, looking like little dolls amongst the majesty.

I couldn't resist it, I let out a sigh, any anxiety that had been tensed in my shoulders releasing into the air and blending with the sounds of chatter, weight room equipment and the booming bass of today's musical selection.

The space was huge. It was loud. And it called to me as much as my silks did.

I needed to get up there.

Sitting down on one of the long wooden benches that ran down the middle of the high walls, I pulled the harness around, ready to get started.

Ten minutes later I was still ready, but no closer to figuring this mess out.

Who had designed this? I had seen climbing harnesses before. I had worn climbing harnesses before when training a new move. But this was all canvas belting and buckles that didn't seem to go in any particular order. I contemplated charging my way back to the desk and asking for one that wasn't a nest of disappointment, but my stubbornness had gotten the better of me.

At least I had figured out the shoes. The shoes were easy. They reminded me of the tight fitting trapeze shoes I wore during parts of my act. Although the rubber made them significantly bulkier, they still clung to my feet like a second skin.

It was just this freakin' harness.

Losing patience, I growled at the straps as if that would set them straight and threw them to the padded floor, giving the awful thing a deep scowl.

"Crap," I said under my breath. So much for being quick and disappearing into the skies.

"It looks like you need some help."

I looked up at the voice and was met by a dazzling smile and the warmest brown eyes I had ever seen. I didn't even think eyes could reach that color, like warm honey and brown sugar.

I resisted the urge to lick my lips.

The lean muscle that was peering out from underneath his "Mountain High" tank top wasn't helping the sudden need for licking things. Like him. Or the jagged tattoo that covered the lean muscle on his left arm.

Down, Elliot. Yes, I was calling myself by my full name. That's how serious this was.

Instead, I settled for biting my lower lip and diverting my eyes, I was sure I was staring and the terribly sexy crooked smile he was giving me made it clear he noticed.

Ho-ly hell.

What was this, did all the hot guys in the world live in Utah?

All they had told us on the road was that there was a weird religion and something called a temple here. I originally wanted to jump off that, and I tried. But I hadn't been able to get the doors to huge granite building open before security was tapping me on the shoulder, asking me to leave.

The guy in front of me gave a slightly uncomfortable

chuckle and ran his hand through his shaggy chestnut hair before gesturing at the tangle of straps tangled around my feet.

"Would you like me to help you?" Mr. Tank Top rephrased the question, as if that would help to dislodge the lust bubble that was currently taking over all thought.

"Uhh, sure." I said, forcing my gaze away from the way his own harness was perfectly outlining his hips.

I swallowed.

"That would be great," I added hastily, hoping that he hadn't caught me ogling. "I've been climbing before. But this..."

I let my words trail off, gesturing to the canvas. He laughed, obviously having understood.

"Yeah," he said as he grabbed the tangle of straps from the floor. "These rental harness can be gnarly. I'm Drake by the way."

He cast me a smile as he began to untangle the mess, expecting me to respond.

"Ellie."

He smiled and held the harness out to me with an obvious grin of accomplishment, the crooked smile doing all sorts of flippy things to my stomach.

It was clear he thought he had achieved success, but it still looked like a mess of straps to me.

"Uhhh..."

Drake laughed, but it wasn't a sound of mocking, it was a genuine understanding that made me warm all over, the heat traveling through my veins in hot little sparks. Waking everything up.

My breath caught as the heat grew, as magic and fire pressed against my skin in a desperate need of escape.

A need to grip his shirt and rip it off him...

Oh my God. There was no way that thought had come from me, had it? Did I hit puberty overnight or some crap? I had no idea what was happening to me, and honestly I was getting a little scared. Or, at least I would be if I was able to think past the way he was smiling at me, his eyes melting into me.

"No worries," Drake said, unaware of the heart palpitations I was experiencing. "Stand up, let's get you ready to go."

I did as he asked, although that didn't get me any closer to understanding how this harness was supposed to work.

"So, are you from Prague?" He asked, leaning down to carefully arrange the straps in loops on the floor.

I looked at my hoodie, sure he was taking a guess in regards to my accent. Sure, it was as close to the truth as we were going to get. I was going to go with that. "Yeah."

"Awesome, I was there in August for a climbing competition. It's beautiful. What part of the city are you from?"

"Old Town," That one was easy, if I was going to pretend to be from anywhere, it was going to be there. The buildings, architecture, all of the high spires to fall from. I loved it.

"Nice," He said nodding his head. "I love it there, I'd love to go back."

"Me too," I said without thinking, the quick response earning me a sly smile before he went back to arranging the straps. There was a sadness that was hidden in that smile, twisting in my gut and pulling me closer to him.

I forced myself to step back.

"Well," he said, standing back up to face me, whatever sadness had hidden in his eyes from a second ago had gone. "You'll want to take off the hoodie. You can't climb in that."

Talk about cranking everything up to an eleven. I swallowed and stripped off the hoodie, remembering a minute too late exactly which leotard I was wearing.

It was black with wide straps and a cut out back that zigzagged over my muscles in gaps that stretched around my hips. The sheer material and tight fitting lycra didn't leave much to the imagination.

Circus people, dancers, anyone who performed really, wouldn't even give the warm ups a second glance. But this guy stared, smirked, and I swear his eyes melted into pools of honey. The color only increased the electric dance that was rushing in my stomach.

"You...you'll want to put your right leg through here," he said gesturing to the loop of red fabric he was holding out to me.

Not going to lie, it felt nice to take his breath away, and his tiny stutter was doing weird flippy things to my insides.

I stepped through the red loop, and then the other, our eyes meeting as he began to slide the harness up, his thumbs grazing over the soft fabric of my warm ups as he pulled the wide band over my hips. Neither of us said a word as he tightened the harness around my waist, shaking it a bit to make sure it was secure. Bringing me the tiniest bit closer.

Bringing his intense melting stare closer.

Bringing his lips closer.

I was pretty sure I had completely forgotten to breathe by this point. Drake was standing so close his fingers were millimeters away from my abdomen. I could feel the warmth through the sheer fabric of my leotard. I caught my breath, only to be assaulted with the sweet smell of his cologne as it mixed with the aroma of chalk that hung heavy in the air. His smell, his warmth, the brown sugar glow in his eyes, it all mixed together until I was having trouble controlling myself.

Or rather, I was having trouble controlling my Phoenix who was suddenly desperate to grab him, wrap around him, taste him...

I couldn't help it, I licked my bottom lip. The action bathed his face in that same crooked grin and he chuckled, looking down and breaking whatever spell had overtaken us.

"Th-that's it," he said, that adorable catch in his nerves making a return. "You are ready to climb. Who are you here with?"

Drake looked around the gym as if expecting some big tough guy to stake his claim on me, not like this guy couldn't take him. His muscle may be lean, but he certainly wasn't lacking.

"I'm on my own," I supplied, glad the twist of nerves and butterflies didn't make itself evident. "I was going to use the auto-belays."

I stuck my thumb behind me, toward where I hoped the "wall to the left" was, and smiled.

Drake dragged his hand through his hair and cast a very odd look toward the entrance of the gym before turning back to me, the smirk replaced by a weird gleam of concern that I didn't understand. It sent the formerly warm butterflies into a very twisty snake that might have been trying to stop my heart.

Looking toward the door in a panic, I half expected to see both Suvi and Zoe charging me down. But there was no one there, no one but the perky girl at the counter, who was now sitting on the counter playing on her phone.

"Would you like to climb me for a bit," He asked, the question catching me off guard and I jumped.

I couldn't help but laugh at that, and the sheepish look he gave me as he realized exactly what he had said, only made the laugh swell.

"I mean with me! Would you like to climb *with* me?" Drake laughed at himself as he gripped his neck, closing his eyes in embarrassment as a bright red flush began to stain his cheeks.

"Well, now that I have messed up any chances with you not thinking I'm totally into you..." He shrugged, flashing me with a full, heart-stopping, smile this time. The grin wrinkled the honey in his eyes, the color glinting in the sun that was streaming through the windows and turning them into pools of liquid gold. I was ninety percent sure that I was melting. Big puddles of goo, right there on the climbing gym floor.

Seriously. I was going to have to get my head checked. I never acted like this, and I sure as hell never needed to throw myself on guys as much as I have in the last twenty-four hours.

"You haven't messed anything up," I confessed, forcing my voice, and my smile to be as normal as possible. "And I can forget that you are totally into me, at least for now."

Or never. I was so logging that away.

"What do you say, Ellie?" The use of my name ignited the heat even further. I liked the way it sounded with that weird American accent of his. The low rumble of his voice rippled up my spine sending another round of pleasurable sparks across my skin. "Will you go climbing with me?"

More sparks ignited over my skin and I shivered, despite feeling so warm I was growing concerned that he could feel it.

"For a bit." I answered, using his phrasing from before, after all I wasn't sure when my boss was going to storm in.

"Good," Drake smiled and stepped toward the nearest wall, jerking his head for me to follow him. "I can belay you first, then teach you how. I don't know how long I have, I am supposed to be meeting someone."

The sparks vanished so fast I was sure someone had doused me in ice water. My heart tensed in a disappointment that I hadn't felt since I was thirteen and Suvi had given the lead in the new show to Xi instead of me. This was more than some juvenile disappointment though, it was a weird green envy that wrapped around my heart and sparked in what I could only explain as a murderous rage.

Flame wrapped around the skin of my arm, the scream of my Phoenix pounding in my head in a noise I had never heard before. The song I had always associated with my shifter was gone, instead I was consumed by a scream of anger. Need. Lust.

A million thoughts slammed into me, my mind flooded with ways to break up whatever date he was headed to, and whatever girl he was meeting.

Somewhere in the back of my mind I knew this was wrong, I wasn't some kind of home wrecker. And I certainly didn't need this man.

Except I did.

I really, really did.

Jerking, I forced my Phoenix to calm and any further ideas of meddling to leave.

So what if he had a girlfriend, I didn't need him. Hell, I didn't know him.

Although watching his back muscles flex and flow as he retrieved the ropes from the wall was doing weird things to me.

I stepped back, hoping to give my skin enough time to cool before Drake returned with the ropes.

"You're meeting someone?" I asked, hating that I was digging for information, while simultaneously not being able to control myself.

"Yeah, my brother is picking me up for some family thing," Drake answered as he turned back to me, his shy smile calming my heart even more than what he had said.

No girlfriend. Just brothers.

I could have sworn my phoenix was purring. Yet, another sound I hadn't heard before.

"But maybe," Drake said, taking one of the ropes and looping it through my harness in a knot. "I can see you again. Tomorrow, maybe for some coffee?"

My head jerked up from watching him weave the intricate knot, my heart absolutely thundering in my chest.

Yes! Yes, please!

He wasn't even looking at me, which was good, because I was sure that my jaw had disconnected and fallen to the floor, some weird choking sound emanating from my throat.

"Are you asking me on a date?" Thankfully I was able to pull myself together as he lifted his head. "Or do you just like coffee?"

I was trying my hardest to sound as nonchalant as possible and pretend that I hadn't been asked out on my first ever date by this man who had now fixed his melted honey eyes on me.

"Well, I don't know if you have heard, but I think I might be totally into you," he smirked, quickly securing the other end of the rope to his harness. "And I would like to see more of you."

"Is that so?" I looked down, "It's not like my top leaves much to imagination."

He blushed, "I mean, I would like to see you again."

"MmmHmmm," I was full on teasing him now. "I mean, I want to. But how can I know I can trust you?"

"Well, you are about to put your life in my hands," he teased, tugging on the rope that tethered us together and yanking me up an inch.

I laughed, I guess to him that was true. But he was no nearer taking my life in his hands than I was to actually being from Prague.

"Well, if you don't want to be alone with me, and don't mind hauty businessmen, you can always come with me and my brother to the circus tonight."

I froze. "The cir-circus?"

I guess it was my turn to stutter, but it wasn't for the heart stopping smile or the way his arm muscles had begun to bulge as he held the rope. There was only one circus in town from what I could tell, and I was currently on a renegade mission to escape the wrath of its owner.

"Tomorrow might be better. I have to work tonight." I barely got the words out, luckily he didn't seem to catch the whole deer in the headlights dead pan I had going on, he smiled, tugged on the rope again and leaned in until all I could smell was the heady aroma of him.

"Then it's a date."

The momentary panic was swept away into the chalk filled air as a joy swelled through me, spreading across my face in what I was sure was the biggest, goofiest, grin.

He didn't seem to care, the corner of his mouth twitched up in a smile that I was sure was going to be the end of me. It was some kind of woman lure, I could tell.

I quickly stepped away, needing to get away from him before I did, or said, something embarrassing. Like dance or squeal. Or kiss him.

All of which were a legitimate possibility.

"On belay?" I asked, turning back to him as I placed my hand against the hold.

"Belay on," he responded, his eyes shining as he gripped the rope and pulled, yanking me up an inch as he began to support my weight. "Climb on."

Giving him one last look, I turned away, ready to finally take to the air and conquer this wall. I was fully aware my time was at a null, and so I probably attacked it with a bit more vigor than he expected.

I was about half way up the wall when I realized exactly what he had said, and exactly what that meant.

He had invited me to the circus. My circus. The circus that had been sold out for weeks.

Meaning he not only had tickets, but he was going to be there. I don't know why it didn't sink in before, but now it was hitting me like a ton of bricks.

Holy hell.

Luckily I wore enough face paint that I was sure he wasn't going to recognize me. Knowing he was going to be there, however, did weird things to my insides.

And sent my phoenix singing.

One long clear note broke free, rippling through the empty air and bouncing off the false rock faces as it grew and blended with the low thrum of the music.

I cringed, freezing against the wall as I pulled every ounce of strength up to restrain my soul and keep my shifter locked inside. It was really hard to keep myself hidden when controlling the magic inside of me was a full on power struggle. Luckily, this time I won, the song fading away to a shadow of bells. I was pretty sure no one could hear it over the heavy bass of the music, but I had to be sure.

Continuing to climb up the wall, I pinched my fingers

around a bright yellow hold and lifted myself up, ever so casually looking around me to see if anyone had heard the still lingering note.

Everyone seemed blissfully unaware. Everyone except Drake, who stood frozen about fifteen feet below me. The rope was slack, his focus no longer on me, but instead on the door where two men were entering the large hall.

I guess it wasn't my song that had pulled his focus.

"Drake," I called down to him, not that I was scared of falling, but unless he gave me some slack I was technically stuck up here.

Drake nodded to the men who began to make their way over, their broad shoulders and bulk covered in far too much fabric to be ready to go climbing. I was pretty sure one of them was wearing a suit.

Family thing, huh? What was this, a mob hit?

Judging by the tension that had taken over Drake, I was starting to question. I could feel the anxiety all the way up here. It was like acid against my soul. I was pretty sure I wanted to be anywhere but stuck on the wall, this was not a reunion that needed crashing.

"Drake!" I said, my voice louder now, pulling his focus with a jump. "You can let me down now."

He nodded once, and the slack increased, giving me enough that I could let go of the wall and slide through the air back to the ground.

I don't think I had ever been so glad to be on the ground, although I was quite ready to get out of this cloud of drama I had landed in.

"You're early," Drake said behind me, the same tension smacking in his voice.

Any trace of the awkward teasing was gone, leaving behind a subtle panic that strained my muscles. My hands tightened into little balls as I fought a sudden, frenzied, need to whirl around and smack whoever was here.

Down girl. Last thing I needed was to pick a fight with two mob hit-men. I needed to untie this knot and get out of dodge.

That was if the freaking knot would even give!

"I figured it was better not to wait," one of the men responded in a bark, his voice swirling awkwardly against the protective roar that was growing in my chest. "I don't need you running again, Drake. Your pansy ass got here, and I was going to take what's mine before you bolted again."

That's it. Mob or not, I was going in.

I whirled around, ready to rampage. Kick, punch, pull hair, whatever it takes! I didn't get that far.

In fact, I didn't get anywhere past a one syllable shout and a furious finger point before I froze in place; my jaw, really and truly, hung open so far that the three sets of familiar eyes looked at me with varying degrees of concern and humor, the faces of the two newcomers spreading into a wide smile.

"Why hello, Dumpster Girl."

What. In. The. Hell.

8

ELLIOT

"Dumpster Girl? This is the girl from the steam room that I told you about."

Jarron, at least I think his name was Jarron, turned toward the man in the suit. Killian's five o'clock shadow and curly man bun were looking even more breathtaking in the bright sun of the climbing gym. Especially now that he wasn't cornering my naked behind in an alley and I could see the tail of what appeared to be a tattoo peeking around the collar of his perfectly pressed white shirt.

Killian smiled brightly at Jarron, his voice taking on that same darkness that rippled up my spine with all sorts of unnatural need.

"Naw, this is my Dumpster Girl," he smiled, those darn dimples popping up again. "I'm pretty sure I'll never forget her."

I tried to take a quick step back, forgetting too late that I was still tethered to Drake, and therefore still caught in this uncomfortable reunion.

"Do you two know each other?" Drake asked, looking between me and the two mob bosses with a disappointment that was sending shockwaves through my nervous system.

"No!" I shrieked, holding my hands out as the other two nodded an enthusiastic yes, Killian looking me up and down so slowly I was sure he was envisioning our accidental alley rendezvous.

This was so not okay.

"Knock it off," I barked at him, letting my voice ring out as he threw his palms up in defeat and took a micro step back. It was so small I wasn't sure it counted.

Drake continued to look between me and the two suited men, the lines in his forehead furrowing deeper and deeper.

"It sure seems like you know each other," Drake said, this time directing his question at me and not at the mob bosses. Although with the way my stomach was dancing in twitterpated excitement I was having a harder time seeing them as such.

I mean, Jarron's dark eyes were so deep... so kind.

Shaking my head, I pulled myself out of that rabbit hole. Drake had asked me on a date. My first date. No way was I messing that up.

"I don't *know* them," I began, the overemphasis not enough to clean up the mess I had walked in on. "I just ran into them this morning. I got into a little bit of trouble at my hotel..."

"Locked outside on a dare..." Killian interrupted with a wide smile as Jarron grinned sheepishly and said, "Skinny dipping accident."

The two looked at each other and laughed, poor Drake looked like he had been sucker punched. I needed to find a way to fix this, and fast.

"Listen," I said, my fingers furiously twisting and tugging at the knot and the harness that had trapped me in the middle of this mess. "I am pretty sure I am intruding on something, and as much fun as this is..." I continued, finally getting the harness off my hips and wiggling my way out of it. "I would really like to go."

I practically fell over the harness as I tried to step out of it, Drake catching me before I tumbled head first into the padded floor. Not that it would have caused any damage, but I was pretty sure I had had enough of creating the world's most embarrassing day. I didn't need to add anything more to it.

"Thanks," I said hastily, pulling myself away from Drake, even though the soft touch of his hand on my elbow was twisting pleasurably through me. "Will I still see you tomorrow?"

I waited for an answer, but instead of an eager, flirting, response his brow wrinkled in frustration, his brown sugar eyes darkening with veins of crimson.

The color caught me off guard, and I blinked, but before I could get a good look it had vanished, the deep scarlet color swallowed by the spark of the sun.

"That depends," Drake finally responded, "It seems my brothers may already have dibs on you."

Walking away gracefully wasn't going to happen. I was ninety percent sure my feet had turned to lead.

"Brothers?" Amazingly, I was able to get the full word out. My shock slapped harder against my spine as I registered what else he had said, causing my voice to come back loud and clear. "Dibs!?"

No way was I leaving that there.

"You don't get to call dibs on me!" I shrieked, whirling around on the three of them as I frantically tried to find some familial connection.

Besides being about the same height and covered in

rippling muscles of varying bulk, there was nothing. And, I wasn't even sure the muscle counted. That's just too much time in a gym. I had those.

Looking at them, I could tell they were as different as oil and water. If I had to guess by the way they were welcoming each other before I stepped in - they mixed just as well.

If Killian wasn't a mob boss, he was a club bouncer. With bulk, style, and the perfect combination of long wavy hair, beard, and tattoos to be branded as dangerous, he was the mirror image of the guys I had dreamed would sweep me off my feet and steal me away from the circus. No wonder looking at him was still sending waves of comfortable need through me, little butterflies dancing around my heart, begging me to take a step closer.

A polar opposite of his brother, Jarron looked like he had been pulled out of a magazine. His wavy blonde hair framed his strong jaw and high cheekbones so perfectly that I couldn't look away. So I didn't, I stared at him, my chest growing warm as his shimmering charcoal eyes smoldered into me, pulling me further into the pleasurable warmth.

I gasped; pushing the pull I felt for him aside and turned to Drake, who couldn't have been more different than both of them. He had the same bulk, although his muscle was leaner, and spread over his arms and back in ribbons. He was dark, rugged, and didn't seem as stereotypical hotty like his brothers, but that didn't make me want to jump into his arms any less.

Damn it.

"Dibs might be the wrong word," Drake finally said, dragging his hand through his hair, a sheepish grin spreading over his face.

"You think?" I don't think my voice had hit that octave

ever. "Besides, they didn't ask me out on a date, you did. So, you technically have 'dibs.'"

I groaned at my use of the word, everything about it igniting my temper into a white-hot heat. Something I didn't need given how hysterical I was sounding.

Could you blame me? It wasn't every day you found yourself face to face with three veritable sex gods, two of which had seen you in varying degrees of accidental nudity hours before.

A warm blush creeped over me at the memory, those swirling butterflies kicking into overdrive.

"Hey now," Jarron said, his voice calm as he stepped toward me, his hand outstretched the same way it had been in the steam room. "I would have asked you out, beautiful, if you had given me a chance. I know you would have said yes, too."

"Slow down, Jarron, she was with me first," Killian interrupted, that dark timber of his voice ripping through me as it had that morning. Oh lord, the warmth that was filling me with. "Besides, I am pretty sure we connected."

Killian stepped closer, his eyes boring into me as my soul pressed against my chest, pulling me towards him like he was the match I needed to ignite the spark. It took everything in me to stay still. I did, however, forget to breathe, which caused me to gasp as he leaned in, the smell of campfire rolling comfortably off him.

"See, there it is." He said, smiling at my inhale as his dimples indented his scruff. He reached out to me, tracing his finger over the crook of my bare arm and sending a visible shiver over me.

Gasping at the contact, I clenched my hands against my thighs in an attempt not to grab him, to touch him, to ignite more of the burning fire his touch had left behind.

Fight it Ellie, I chastised myself and stepped back, right into Drake's hard chest.

"I know you feel it too, Dumpster Girl," Killian's eyes burrowed into me, devouring me as he whispered in a calm reassurance that was swallowed by the growl that I could have sworn was emanating from Drake, the resonating sound rumbling against my spine.

"Ellie," Drake corrected sharply, his palms cupping my bare shoulders as he held me against him, almost as if he was protecting me from them. I wanted to tell him I didn't need protecting, but I didn't want him to move away either. "Her name is Ellie."

I knew my skin was hot, my phoenix had practically ignited in the desire that was overtaking me, but somehow Drake was hotter. The rough palms of his climbing hands ran over my shoulders like burning stones, prompting me to melt into him.

To let his arms wrap around me. To let him keep me safe, and warm. I leaned into the touch, pressing my back into him as the strange heat that was seeping from his hands wrapped around me.

And I thought I was a radiator. I turned to him in confusion, only to find myself millimeters away from the melting warmth of his eyes. From his soft lips...

The need to kiss him was so strong that I forced myself to pull away.

Unfortunately, I may have used a bit too much of that force and instead I stumbled, right into Jarron's waiting arms. I collapsed against him, his long arm wrapping around me as he held me against him, his fingers tracing the seam of my leotard. His lip twitched as he stared at me with those deep charcoal eyes...

Fuck. I wasn't breathing again.

"Wow," Jarron said, his arms tightening around me, his hand weaving over my back to push a strand of my long red hair out of my eyes. "I knew I felt something, I just didn't expect it to be this. I didn't expect it to be you."

To be me what? Confusion tried to swim past the mind numbing lust that followed these men around like a lost dog. My jaw flopped around like a fish out of water, attempting to force words or air or anything out.

Drake beat me to it.

"Wait," Drake said in a clipped tone, the panic behind the single word pulling everyone's focus.

He wasn't speaking to me, however, he was clearly looking between his two brothers in curious frustration. The odd look of betrayal had gone, instead it had been replaced with something else, something I really didn't understand.

"You feel the connection too?" Drake said to Jarron as he held me against him, as though he was scared someone would pull me away.

"I felt it when her fingers touched mine this morning," Jarron said, his voice so soft in my ear that I twisted in his arms as if in response, my breath catching in my chest as he smiled down at me, something overtaking the darkness in his eyes. Something golden.

It was beautiful.

"It's even stronger now," Jarron said, the low groan of his voice making my head fuzzy, something that wasn't helped by the way his fingertip began to drag over my jaw, tracing my skin and causing my breath to catch.

A tiny voice in the back of my mind hissed, prompting me to get out of this mess and leave before something happened. I heard the warning, I felt the nerves, but I couldn't respond to it, I had the clear distinction that this was where I wanted to be. Held tightly in Jarron's arms.

"I felt it when she looked at me," Killian said, the deep rough sound of his voice pulling me from whatever spell Jarron had trapped me in.

I looked toward the sound only to find myself ripped from Jarron's arms and pulled right into Killian's.

I let out a tiny squeak at the quick movement, but I didn't protest. As comfortable as I was with Jarron, it felt the same with Killian, if not a little dangerous. A little more possessive.

His large hands fanned over the exposed skin of my back as he pressed me against him, the touch sucking the breath from my chest as I was plunged into his heat, into the liquid green of his eyes.

Into a world that I never thought existed. I couldn't help it, I melted into him.

"Hello there, Dumpster Girl," He whispered, the corner of his mouth twitching in a smile and sparking his dimple.

Damn dimple.

"Hi," I wasn't even sure the word made it out all the way.

"I feel it too," Drake said, his voice awed now.

I wanted to turn toward him, to ask him what was going on. But I couldn't pull myself away from Killian's heat, from the way his finger was pressing against my neck.

"You are so warm," Killian said, leaning closer as his eyes began to search mine, mine doing the same as I tried to figure out what this spell I had been trapped in was. "Your power is so strong. I've never felt anything like it. What are you, Ellie-girl?"

The question pulled through the fog of passion like a whip. It smacked against the haze and the need I had for all of them faded away, all of the rough emotions dissipating and twisting into a panic.

"Wh---what do you mean?" My voice shook as the panic

grew, the warning I had so easily dismissed before smacking against my skull in a bright red warning light.

I had been so caught up in that, whatever *that* was, that I hadn't listened. I hadn't seen what was happening.

I had been caught. I was sure of it.

I tried to step away from him, but Killian held me against him, my stomach twisting as he lowered his head,

"I have been waiting my entire life for my shifter to bond to another, and now it has." The dark moss in his eyes were glowing, shining with an exhilaration that I didn't feel. "What are you?"

"I don't understand," I forced all the panic into my voice, the clipped words snapping out of me as I roughly pushed him away, sending him stumbling back a few feet.

I didn't even have time to dwell on the fact that I had enough strength to push that wall of muscle away before he had bounced back, the three brothers now closing in around me.

"You can't have bonded with her Kills," Jarron said, his voice hushed as he leaned over me, his hand running down my arm. The touch that had previously brought me pleasure was now only a panic inducing weight against my flesh and I flinched. "My shifter has claimed her, and I can feel hers answer..." he hesitated, and stepped closer, his eyes digging into me hungrily. The look sparked the same need, the same all-encompassing desire that ripped through me. My phoenix pressed against my skin, sending gooseflesh over my arms in a need for him.

Screw that I didn't need anyone. Or anything. Well, except to get out of there. "But you're right. I can't tell what her dragon is. Something strong. I knew I would bond to something strong."

He smiled, the look kind and understanding. I wanted to

drift into it. I wanted to trust him. But I couldn't. I really, really couldn't.

I stepped away, trying to weasel my way through the cage that they had built around me.

"Will you guys knock it off," Drake snapped, folding his arms around me and for one brief second I thought it was all a joke, I was sure that I was safe, and that Drake would make it all better. "There is no way we have all bonded to her."

That was it. Panic gone, my fight or flight reflex went into full on assault mode. Unluckily for them, both reactions fired at once.

"What in the hell?" I practically screamed, tearing away from Drake as the faces of the people who had been openly gawking at us until a minute ago slipped into concern, a particularly angry looking woman stepping forward, her high bun tipping over.

"What are you doing over there?" She asked, lifting her voice to us as she waved down a few of the wandering staff members. "Leave that girl alone!"

Her voice picked up as Killian grabbed my arm in an effort to stop my escape, his fingers hot little points on my forearm. I whirled around to face him, fully aware that my eyes had shifted to the golden gleam of my phoenix.

I didn't try to hide her flames as I faced him head on, the woman continuing to yell as she began to approach us, two employees on her heels.

"Let me go, Killian," I growled, ripping my arm away. His face was aghast in shock or fear, I wasn't quite sure. I hoped it was fear. "Leave me alone!"

I screamed the last words, letting them fuel my escape as I turned, ready to bolt away from the three men, to tear out of the building and take off into the sky if I needed to.

As long as I got out of there. I didn't care how I did it, or what the repercussions were.

"Ellie!" A deep grumble sounded behind me, making me sure that one, if not all, of the brothers were following me.

I chanced a look behind as I continued to charge towards the doors and caught Drake's sad, confused stare. Jarron and Killian were engaged in a furious debate with the group of people that had surrounded them. Drake's eyes had reduced to the color of caramel, the color crashing against my heart and pleading with me to run back to him, to fix everything and pretend that this joke had never happened.

To go back to just being asked on a date.

That wasn't possible anymore.

I pulled myself away, my soul screaming in agony as I bolted out into the setting sun, the large red and black striped tent giving me the only promise of safety I knew.

I didn't think I could get there fast enough.

9

DRAKE

HER LONG RED HAIR STREAMED BEHIND HER AS SHE RAN, THE color reflecting the sun in a flame that pierced Drake right to his soul. The color, the way the light reflected around her like magic.

Her dragon must be glorious. He couldn't wait to see it.

Of course, Drake had no way of knowing what element would rule her dragon, or even if the feeling that was wrapping around his soul was real.

She had escaped to the parking lot before he or his brothers had a chance to move, their way blocked by three mortals who looked ready to rip their heads from their hides for the supposed assault.

Normally, Drake would charge past the mortals and continue on his way, leaving them strewn about like broken matchsticks. If he had learned anything over the past ten years of his banishment, it was the overall inconsiderate bull headedness that mortals possessed. Most would scream and grumble and think you an "ass" before going about their day, happy they had won some unseen war. Charging through a crowd was as much an everyday occurrence as the sun rising and setting. And Drake made it a point to witness each and every one of those.

Charging through these three to reach his destination should be nothing, but with Killian here, those cards were off the table. He didn't trust his irritating brother enough to chase the girl down and leave him alone with fragile mortals. No matter how much his heart and soul longed for Ellie.

Drake hadn't seen his oldest brother in nearly ten years, and the last time he did the self-proclaimed heir to the throne was ripping heads from their father's mortal slaves, using them as emotional weapons in a war Drake did not win.

No way was he going to trust him with these three. Hell, he didn't trust the brute at all.

The fact that Drake had agreed to meet with Killian was a miracle enough. Add to that, the three of them bonding to Ellie and his hackles were up, everything ready to jump into action. He would protect Ellie from Killian if he had to, even if it meant the end of his own life.

"Move, vermin," Killian growled, the tone awakening every reflex that Drake had spent ten years restraining as his dragon continued to arouse from its long induced slumber.

The creature had been subdued upon his banishment, knowing that if he was to shift just once his father would not only track him down, but destroy him. One touch of Ellie's fingers against his, however, and all the work and training he had gone through to keep the creature at bay had been for nothing.

His dragon was as alive and alert as ever, fire burning through his belly as a need he had never experienced began to grip him.

He couldn't lose that.

The heated need in Drake's chest was replaced by frustration as Killian pushed through the mortals, knocking down every mortal in his path to the door.

"Apologies," Drake mumbled to the three who were looking after Killian, lines of horror covering their faces. "We need to..."

Both words and pursuit was frozen as the woman grabbed his forearm, her nails digging into his flesh as she began to sputter in anger, that ridiculous bun bobbing atop her head.

"I will call the cops," she barked, "you don't treat women that way. That woman was scared – hey!"

The lady called out as she pushed past Drake, shoving the wiry man aside and charging right for Jarron, who had begun to make his way toward the door, and after Killian.

On any other occasion, Drake would have been happy to see the two go, but not now, not when they were both making a beeline for the girl that his shifter had bonded to.

That their shifters had bonded to.

The thought was a rock in his chest, a million questions nagging at him and pricking up something possessive. The emotion made him feel dirty, he could not own this woman. He could not take her, not in that way. He tried to push them away, but his dragon would have none of that, the treacherous thing rising louder.

Ellie was to be his mate, that much was clear, he would have to figure out the rest later.

His dragon purred at the imagery of her, at the thought of her belonging to him, of being with him, of him holding her against his... The pleasure shifted into a low roar as he approached one of the other accusers, a staff member who was now on a cell phone.

The feral sound emanated from his chest so deeply that it pulled the worker's attention, the teens eyes sparking fear as he caught sight of Drake, his jaw squared, his eyes hard and full of threat.

He may not be aware of what was happening between his brothers and Ellie, but he knew enough to keep the mortals out of it. Calling the cops would only lead to danger. For the mortal peacekeepers, for the girl, and even for him.

If the clan of Dragons caught the three of them together it would only end in disaster.

He needed to end this game, but after ten years of restraining his dragon, he wasn't sure if he could. It would be a miracle if his dragon answered to the call and the deep magic still worked, but he had to try. He didn't see another option save attacking, or running, and he wasn't sure if either of those were possible.

Letting the fire burn in his belly, he stepped up to the staff member, pressing himself closer until he was inches away, invading both space and air with the burning furnace of his heat. The boy flinched, not wanting to disregard his manhood and bolt from the towering dragon, although it was clear he wanted to. The air was drenched with his fear, his hand shaking as he spoke to the 911 operator.

Clearly, Drake's dragon was peeking out. Perfect. Now, if only the power will work.

"Please, give me the phone."

Drake let his fire swelter as he spoke, the words smooth and calm as the kid looked at him in confusion. His eyes were cloudy, but not enough that it had worked. Cursing silently, Drake tried again, letting his fire burn deeper as his dragon perked up, tasting his rage for the first time.

"Give me the phone."

The dark brown eyes of the teen went white as he calmly handed the phone to Drake, his tattoos flexing over strained muscles as he seized the device.

"Go back to work." Drake commanded as he spoke into the mouthpiece, his focus still on the kid, even though he spoke to both him and whoever was on the other line. "Nothing happened here."

Unease swam through Drake as the teen walked away, the call disconnecting with a tiny click before the screen returned to the tile blocks of a menu. Drake crushed the phone in his palm, the sound of cracking glass loud in the cavernous space.

"There is nothing here," Drake said a little louder, dropping the remains of the cell to the ground. Several of the people around him blinked at his voice, walking away as their minds buzzed and their memory shifted into the fog.

Their reaction added to his guilt. Drake hadn't used the gift in over ten years, and before that much of his skill was forced into being by his father.

It was not something he was proud of, nor was it something that he wished to use. It was not a gift, it was a curse, and one that he still harbored regret for.

Not only for its use, but for his refusal to use it when it was his and so many other lives on the line.

Three words and he could have changed everything, instead he bore the branding of loss, the attempted coup a black mark on his soul. Instinctively, he looked at the winding scars that spread over his left arm, the long spirals cut so deep into the weak arm that it was amazing the tattoos covered them at all. Or that he had regained as much strength as he had, it could nearly hold his weight on good days.

He wondered if Ellie had seen. The thought was both a twist of worry and rush of need in his soul and he exhaled, his heart pulling him toward her. Needing to reach her, with or without his brothers.

"You have my word on the girl's safety," Jarron promised as Drake approached, the woman with a ridiculous bun and a severe expression still blocking his way. "I can promise no harm will come to her."

His voice was as golden and smooth as it always had been, the tone enough to melt any woman. Well, any woman who wasn't already on an irate tirade. This woman would clearly not be drawn in by his charms.

"You don't get to charge away, I will protect that girl," the woman continued, she and Jarron moving into a battle of wills that Drake was keenly aware the woman could not win. He was actually surprised he hadn't bolted past her already.

"Nothing happened here," Drake said in the woman's ear as he reached her, his stomach twisting uncomfortably as he stepped past the now dumbfounded woman, and his awe stricken brother.

Drake chose to ignore the open mouthed stare that Jarron was giving him, his brother's shock quickly turning to amusement. Both looks twisted Drake's nerves, bringing up a million angry irritations of years past.

If Jarron knew what was good for him he would drop it. Drake's dragon had been restrained for far too long, and its sudden awakening was stressing the already tense command he had of the inner beast.

Something that Jarron knew far too well. He had been the one to search him out years before. Drake was confused that the fight hadn't left a scar on his brother's pretty little face. Although, knowing Jarron's vanity, he probably paid some mortal to fix the mark.

"Leave it," Drake grumbled in warning as his brother caught up to him, the colorful woman at the desk ducking down a bit, as if the two men were going to vault over the desk and ravage her.

Foolish mortals.

Jarron, however, never knew what was good for him and walked as easily into the briar pit as he would into a brothel.

Both things that Drake had seen far too much of from the man.

"Still silver tongued, I see," He said energetically as they walked out the door, Drake's heart calming at the sight of Killian standing in the middle of the parking lot. His wide chest heaved as he searched the lot, peering through the glistening windows of each vehicle.

At least Killian hadn't found her.

"I told you to leave it," Drake hissed, refusing to look at Jarron as he bounced beside him, clapping his hands once in wicked excitement.

"But did you *tell* me," Jarron interjected, the choice of emphasis sitting heavy on Drake's chest.

Drake shot his foolhardy brother a warning look, letting the glare of his dragon set in the deep red veining that matched the monster he kept hidden inside of him. The look had no effect on the man, and Jarron only laughed loudly, the sound gaining the attention of Killian who turned, a look of murder clear in his eyes.

In one snarl of the older brother's lips all joy was sucked from the air, and in Drake's case all air from his lungs. He had seen that look, and he had every reason to fear it.

"Oh shit," Jarron murmured, all humor draining from

him as Killian began to speed towards them. as Drake's insides began twisting.

"You promised on your life that I would be safe, Jarron," Drake spat his insides twisting.

It was the only reason that Drake had agreed to this meeting. He would have lived a long and happy life never having to see Killian again, especially after what the older brother had done to him.

But, they had a similar goal now.

Knocking their father from the throne.

Drake had been passing Jarron information for years as they began to hunt the one thing that could overthrow their father. It had been dangerous work.

If they were caught, they would be killed.

If Jarron and Killian had been seen with Drake, they would be killed. Any dragon associating with the traitor would be. It was one of the reasons Drake had been hesitant to work with Jarron in the first place. But when Killian had wanted to see him face to face when the information Drake had collected about the child was given, it felt like too much of a trap.

Safe was the word that Jarron had thrown around; Drake was suddenly second guessing his hasty decision to trust him.

Asphalt cracked with each step of Killian's pristine loafers, the long curls of his hair beginning to break loose as the heir postured his baby brother. To any fledgling dragon it would appear that he was nearing a shift, but Drake knew better. Killian was nearly three hundred, and was accomplished in both restraint and control of his beast. Even more so than the last time Drake had seen him, it seemed.

Killian's dragon was right on the surface, his eyes jet

black as the monster took control. As his skin began to smoke.

"Damn it, Killian!" Jarron roared, rushing his brother in a rage, intent on stopping him any way possible.

Good. Someone had to stop Killian and it sure as hell wouldn't be Drake. He couldn't follow even if he wanted to. He was having enough trouble restraining his own shifter. He could feel him, pressing against his heart, growling in his soul, ready to rise, ready to fight. Which was ridiculous, his dragon was as broken and useless as he was.

What in the world was the point of using glamour on those mortals if they were going to turn into dragons anyway?

Drake stood still, trying to drown out the sounds of his brothers bickering as he closed his eyes, letting the hot summer wind blow through him, the hidden aroma of cottonwood trees carried on the back.

The smell was so faint that no mortal could sense it. The soft earthy scent drifted from the mountains, whispering through what rivers remained in the valley as it journeyed to the open air past the hills.

Beautiful. Calming. Enough to restrain his dragon.

"Don't command me Jarron," Killian roared, the anger in his voice snapping like a whip, although not as aggressively as it had a moment before.

"Then do not act like you need commanding." Jarron howled in a low roar as his temper brushed the surface. His face inches from Killian's.

Drake had seen these two fight often enough in his youth that he could very nearly see the strings of gold in Jarron's eyes, his dragon brimming over in an arrogant battle he could not win.

But he always tried.

Jarron very rarely knew when to stop.

"Your dragon is too near the surface, Killian," Jarron advised, the roar of his voice drifting to a calming lull. "You must calm if you wish to continue this venture."

Jarron was trying, Drake would give him that, but Killian would have none of it.

"I will not calm, brother," Killian snapped, the hatred in his eyes growing as they shifted from Jarron to Drake, the youngest fixed with a look that he had seen far too many times. The hatred was clear, it was the thirst for blood that many people missed. "And I will not continue any venture with a blood traitor!"

The animosity in Killian's words rattled Drake's bones, the memories bubbling up and shattering what little calm he had forced his dragon to find. They were the same words his father had thrown around so carelessly, and Killian knew that. He let the words slice and bruise.

Drake's dragon snarled, the sound rumbling in his chest so loud that the others both heard it, their eyes widening. Jarron in worry, Killian in victory.

"You have brought this outcast to me only so he could steal the woman my dragon has claimed," Killian continued, his voice dragging dangerously through his brutal tirade, pushing and prodding. "He has bonded with my mate."

His mate. My mate. This time, not only Drake's dragon snarled with territorial need, his own heart ached, his heart pulsing and throbbing for the girl whose fire had so easily kindled his own.

The fire he thought was dead.

He wanted to scream, wanted to rage, but neither of those things would get him closer to finding Ellie. Neither of those things would keep him, or her, safe.

"I did nothing of the sort," Drake spat, taking a step

toward his brother even though he knew better. Getting closer to the beast only drew him closer to death. "You say these things as though any of us can control them!"

"Will you two calm down?" Jarron yelled, stepping between them with his arms stretched wide, his skin gleaming gold as he prepared to stop the eruption, his own was inches below the surface. "Or are you forgetting that my shifter has fused to her as well. All three of us, fused to the same dragon."

Fused. The word seemed wrong, but in so many ways it was exactly right. He had seen as much in the gym. Seen the way they held her, the way Jarron looked into her eyes. The thought that the others had claimed his mate was made of fury, the reality rumbling angrily. There wasn't just anger there, however, there was something deeper, something that didn't make any sense. More than a need to claim her, Drake felt a deep desire to save her.

Was that part of being a mate? Drake could not be sure.

What he did know, however, was that three Dragons should not be able to *fuse* to a single female.

"It shouldn't be possible," Drake said, more to himself than to the others.

"It isn't," Killian spat, answering the query with a grunt as he once again began to posture the youngest of them. "She is mine alone. And I don't share."

Drake knew better than to battle his brother, but that was becoming harder the more he tried to lay some prehistoric claim to the girl.

Ellie deserved better.

"Even beyond that," Jarron said, his palm flat against Killian's chest in an attempt to stop any supposed advance. "It shouldn't be possible because we are sons of the King, and kings do not have mates. Kings haven't been granted a bond like this in centuries."

That was it. Of all the lies and barbaric claims that had been going on, this one rubbed Drake raw.

"You know as well as I do that that isn't true," Drake said. He would not stand there and let them be so disrespectful. "The rightful heir was granted a mate. A mate that our father—"

"The *rightful heir* is no longer with us." Killian's voice was a roar, his eyes hard as they dug into Drake, his snarl only igniting the battle further. "You will do well to respect the one that has taken that place."

Even Jarron knew better than to step in between this one, which was good. He wouldn't want to lose an arm. The thought was a slap and Drake almost lost his gall. Almost.

"You mean yourself, Killian? I will respect the ones that earn it."

"You are still the same pathetic excuse for a dragon, Drake. Tell me, has your flight returned. How about your fire?"

"Will you two knock it off!" Jarron roared, his hands rough as he muscled in front of Drake, separating the two before they did something stupid.

It wasn't enough.

"I was wrong to trust you." Drake snarled, pushing past Jarron in a mad attempt to reach Killian.

No matter how foolish the action was, Drake could no longer stop himself, every emotion and past frustration was now bubbling to the top ready to explode.

He could feel it brewing, all it would take was one more word from Killian.

He wanted it.

He wanted the fight.

Instead he got a fist to the jaw.

"Stop!" Jarron bellowed, his fist intersecting with Drake, and then twisting to batter Killian, although the latter was quick and observant enough to stop the fist before it made contact.

Darn it all, Drake had been too long out of practice. That was going to leave a bruise.

He would have to thank Jarron later for the not so subtle reminder of what he was up against. If he had gone through with that fight he was likely to have lost something more precious than a wing.

"We have both been working to find that wretched child for the last three years. We are so close to finding it and ending our father's reign. And you two... You two are going to ruin it all over a girl," Jarron's voice was a hiss of a warning, and it was clear he had meant it to be assertive, but his face betrayed him, the tiny flinch of pain around his eyes giving him away. Drake saw it immediately.

"You feel the same things we do..." He said, rubbing his palm over his still tingling jaw. Damn, he forgot how hard Jarron hits.

"I do. We all do," Jarron said, his focus drifting from his brothers to stare longingly at the mountains. It seemed like the logical place for a dragon to hide, and the mountains here were crawling with many of their kind. But Drake's heart pulled elsewhere, tugging him in the opposite direction as though the girl was feet away, hiding in one of the parked cars.

No wonder Killian had been scouring them.

"But I cannot tell you why. Or what it all means. I want her too. Right now I would give anything to hold her in my arms..."

Killian growled, the sound loud as he once again turned

toward Drake, as though he himself had started all of this. You would think that sense would have been knocked into him with a punch like that, but no, Drake met the glare head on, not so much stubborn as defiant to a fault.

"Drake," Jarron snapped, his voice a bark as his pulled the two from the silent dagger throwing competition. "You informed me that you have found something about the child?"

"Yes," He snarled, pulling away from his brother's glare, trying to ignore the way everything was boiling inside of him, ready to escape. He could almost taste the smoke and ash of his dragon, something that hadn't happened in nearly a decade.

"I was able to locate the monks that you found mentioned in the letter," Drake continued, biting the words through the angry tension in his jaw. "They were near Nepal, luckily there is good climbing there or I think I would have drawn too much attention. They gave me the name of a witch who has helped our kind in the past. She is the last of the long line of Romanian royalty. She runs the circus that is in town, and I have bought us all tickets."

He reached into his pockets and produced the three narrow strips of cardstock, the paper striped in red and black and emblazoned with the circus logo like the tent over a hundred yards behind them.

Honestly, Drake hadn't expected Killian to show, and had offered the ticket to Ellie on a whim, unable to ignore his need to be beside her.

Now, he was glad she had refused. If only because then they could get in, get the information they needed, get out, and then search Ellie out.

All of that, however, relied on a circus that his brothers seemed to be less than amused about.

Up until now Drake had been proud of the work he had done, it had taken months to plan the trip and get away without anyone following his tracks. It had taken work, and that wasn't even counting the days he had spent with the monks, convincing them of his trustworthiness. Promising over and over that he would not harm the child.

It had all been for naught, and all of that work felt as insignificant as a dog with a bone given his brothers' reactions.

Jarron cast a wary glance toward the gaudy monstrosity, obviously doubting the intel. Killian, however, never looked away, his eyes flashing with the dark flame of his dragon as he glared into his baby brother's eyes.

Drake didn't even flinch.

"You are sure of this?" Killian snarled, one of his eyebrows arching and pulling his jaw into a tight line.

"The child is either there, or the old witch will know where she went," Drake said, his heart pulling

"Perfect," Killian turned toward the tents for the first time, his eyes squinting against the sun as he glowered at the towering canvas, the stripes looking ominous in the setting sun. "We can find the child and dispose of it, and then we can find our Ellie. Who knows, maybe the old bat will have some idea as to what has happened to us."

"I wouldn't get your hopes up." Drake grumbled, earning a glare from the other two.

"Let's go hunt a phoenix." Jarron said, changing the subject and slapping his hands together like an eager child waiting for the buffet to open.

Drake didn't know why, but the sound of the clap was like a knife straight into his heart, the pulling pain making him regret ever having accepting Jarron's offer in the first place.

That phoenix nearly led to his death twenty years ago, and would lead to many millions more if it was found, and his father received the eternal life he wanted.

Which is why they needed to kill it first, before their father discovered it, something that was becoming more and more likely.

Even Drake knew that the crazy old man was right on their heels.

10

ELLIOT

I RAN OUT OF THE BUILDING AND INTO THE PARKING LOT SO fast that I steamrolled an older gentleman with a scarred face, a woman laden with gear and a child who I was pretty sure was celebrating their twelfth birthday.

Well, at least that's what the lady screamed at me as I sprinted away. Her rant was full of far more profanity that I would ever use around a child. I probably would have turned around and said so, if I wasn't so focused at making my escape into the tents that were magically a million miles away.

I could not get there fast enough, and I didn't care who I had to take down to disappear behind the red and black stripes. I would get there before the heat that was taking over me exploded, and my shifter took control.

I needed to get away from the brothers, if they even were brothers, before that happened.

Of course, that was a lot harder than it should be. Every footfall rippled through me like a string that was tethering me in the opposite direction. Pulling and tugging in an electric buzz that was begging me to run back and right into their arms. It didn't even matter which one, I wanted them all. That devastating need mixed with the growing panic in a way that was burning not only in my skin, but in the warm wet tears that were threatening to boil over.

The fear and desire fought against each other, creating some kind of emotional cocktail that was making me want to punch myself.

I would deserve it too.

How could I have been so stupid?

I should have listened to Zoe and Suvi and stayed in my freakin' hotel room. Stayed away from men and shifters and a combination of the two that would surely end in my death, or capture, or satanic ritual skinning.

Whatever.

First, I am trapped in some kind of time sludge and now I am being hunted by three sex gods who claim to be shifters. Yeah, I was toast.

"Chill out, Ellie," I scolded myself.

I was really letting my emotions get out of control. It was obviously nothing. Yes, I was totally attracted to three really hot guys, and honestly I would be concerned if I wasn't. I mean, they were crafted by gods or something.

But that was it. If it wasn't for their excessively poorly timed joke I would probably still be drooling over them. Because that's all it was - a joke.

It had to be.

They couldn't be shifters. Let alone dragons.

A joke.

I wasn't about to let it derail me.

Releasing what I hoped would be a calming breath, I darted between two parked cars and across the steady flow of incoming traffic that was beginning to surround the performance tent.

We must be closer to show time than I thought, people had begun arriving and I could smell the lingering aroma of paraffin oil and smoke that usually accompanied the show that Zoe and her troupe did outside of the gates before the house opened.

The smell was a comforting haze that took a bit of the edge off, although not enough for me to either slow down, or calm down enough that I wasn't a walking furnace.

Heat radiated from me as I ducked through the heavy canvas of the practice tent and into the mostly empty rehearsal space. Those who were still lingering and warming up were already in full costume and makeup.

"Shit," I said, not even bothering to keep my voice down. Stacia, one of the contortionists, turned at my outburst and shook her head. Judging by the level of frustration there, she had been hoping that I wouldn't show up.

I'm surprised she wasn't already in my costume, ready to go.

"Shit is right," A voice snapped behind me, causing me to jump.

I turned around to face a very angry, very frustrated Alan who was looking a bit more frazzled and harassed than usual.

A little wave of guilt assaulted my frayed emotions and I stepped back, willing to give him some room before he exploded.

Or I did.

Both were possible.

"You're late, Elliot." Ugh, I hated when anyone used my full name, but hearing it from him made me especially grumpy. I was scarcely able to restrain my scowl. "Please tell me you are warm or I am going to cut your act."

"I'm warm," I promised him with a gasp, fully aware that

the shake in my voice was from the emotional gymnastics I was accomplishing and not from the fact that I had run over a mile without breaking a sweat.

Even without sweat I knew I was good to go. Or at least, I was in theory, every part of me was shaking, and the idea of hiding away was really appealing to me right now.

Which was so unlike me, that I was once again faced with the reality of needing a good solid punch.

"Fine," Alan said with a snap, "check your rig and get in first makeup. You have forty minutes until curtain and we won't wait for you."

He gave me a sharp look that clearly told me he wanted to do more, like dock my pay and cut me from the show.

Both of which he had done before.

I wasn't about to push my luck. Casting Stacia a smug look, I bolted over the soft floor of the tent and towards the backstage and catwalks.

The theatre was the dark shadowy maze it always was. I had grown up here, these shadows were home. But tonight they all seemed a little too long, all little too dark. My frayed nerves were putting ghosts, monsters, and shifters in the dark crevices where they didn't belong.

My skin pricked up in lines of goose bumps as my phoenix settled against my heart, every part of me ready for an attack.

"Calm down," I whispered to my phoenix as much as myself and walked into the dusty blue light.

The aroma of chalk and sawdust lingered over me as my edge of panic began to sway, replaced instead by the electric buzz that always accompanied performing.

A hum of voices swelled in time with the music, and the last of my nerves evaporated thanks in part to the hundred or so who showed up early. There were always earlies, eager to soak up the energy of the circus and see what secrets they could discover. Unluckily for them, our show only began with a single bed on the main performance space, and even then it was more of a surreal framework that kind of looked like a bed depending on where you were sitting. From backstage it looked more like a collapsed jungle gym with a patchwork bubble in the middle. Pretty much everything else was moved in later, or stored up on the catwalk in the rigging. That's where I would start my act, falling from the ceiling, about sixty feet in the air. Right now though, it was knots and holes that I was checking my fabric for.

The long white silk was about forty yards long, the center knotted around the aerial-8 carabineer that I would connect to the rigging after the opening act. It was important that both the knots were tied properly and the fabric was free from snags and holes. One hole could end in a ripped silk and a deadly drop. Hence the importance of no piercings. That and I had seen a silk grab far too many pretty little piercings and rip them clean out.

No, thank you. Just because I could handle the pain did not mean I was interested in feeling it.

Cringing at the bloody memories, I quickly checked both the knots and the silk and stowed the long lengths away before darting back out to the practice tent, where Stacia was now gossiping with Jin, a trampoline performer, and walked into the dressing room.

The full length red flame unitard was one, very quick costume change, the hair and makeup however was a different story. I was well aware that the thirty minutes I had left was cutting it close.

I was going to have to cut some corners.

I hadn't even finished my foundation when the door to the girls dressing room burst open and a cloud of smoke filtered in, followed by Zoe, who was clad in full costume, full makeup and what was clearly a fresh burn on her midriff. Although thanks to her shifter blood, it was nearly healed already. I was sure the bare skin that wasn't covered by her leather halter top and floor length skirt would be flawless by the time she opened the second act.

"She lives!" Zoe said hesitantly, her dark eyes sparking in two little pools of worry among the wide sweep of black charcoal that covered her face like a mask.

As perky as she sounded, I could tell she was testing the waters. We hadn't exactly left things in the best place, and if it wasn't for the incident at the climbing gym I would probably still be fuming. Hell, I still was, just for a different reason. Zoe didn't know that, however. I wasn't foolish enough to believe that even with all her trepidation that there wasn't some kind of dragon fueled danger lurking there.

"I live," I said forcing out a half-hearted reply, waving my hands with an exaggerated flare before going back to my makeup.

"Not changed out for a fairy prince or something?" Zoe teased as she began to change out her skirt for a tiny pair of leather shorts, and resecuring her turban so as not to burn any hair during her act.

Not that her hair would burn. But it's what the mortal, non-shifters, had to do, so its what Zoe got to do, too.

Tucking the brown curls away, I was hit with a memory of similar wavy brown hair, tucked into a similar bun. That's all it took to send the emotions I had been trying to ignore into overdrive. Warmth flared in my chest like some kind of hormone firework, everything growing warm and needy in places that shouldn't feel warm and needy. I was clearly failing at banishing the sudden rush of emotion. The blush that was taking over my cheeks was making it impossible to get my makeup to cover evenly.

Damn it all. I was seriously starting to wish I had never gone down to that silly cliff. Just stayed in my hotel room and watched cartoons, slept in.

I wasn't able to restrain the groan in time.

"My joke wasn't that bad," Zoe said, misunderstanding my frustration.

I swallowed, not quite sure what to say. After what happened in Suvi's office I didn't trust her enough to tell her what happened, and why I was really groaning. I didn't have any guarantee she wasn't going to freak out, or lie to my face. Both possibilities made my insides writhe, so instead I sat still, refusing to be the one to break the silence that was stretching through the air with enough tension to drown a goldfish. Stubborn to the end, I shifted my weight and tried to focus on my makeup instead of the uncomfortable minefield.

Yes, I was being childish, and no, I didn't care.

"Would you like some help with your hair?" Zoe finally said, her question choppy as she stabbed at the silence with a blunted knife.

I wanted to say no. Correction; loud stubborn part of me wanted to say no. But I knew I couldn't. I didn't have the time to do everything, and Zoe was right there...

"Sure." Yeah, I sounded way surlier than I meant to.

Zoe smiled sadly, closed her locker and grabbed my hair kit out of mine as she came up behind me, comb and brush at the ready.

"Thank you," I whispered, grabbing the large red glitter pen I used in my makeup as Zoe began to pull my hair back in preparation for the long braids that made up the base of my updo.

"Of course." Zoe teased, her eyes glinting mischievously as she leaned down, staring straight forward and looking at me through the mirror. "Doing hair, covering for you with Suvi when you didn't go back to the hotel room. It's what friends are for."

I bit back the fire that was boiling my blood and stared intently at myself in the mirror, refusing to look at her. I couldn't guarantee any sort of control if I did, and I wasn't going to risk it.

"I told you I wasn't going back to the hotel." The snap came out anyway.

"I know, and I think we kind of deserved that."

The makeup pen froze against my cheek, leaving a large blotch of red glitter behind. I hadn't expected that response. My eyes darted to her, but she wasn't looking at me, her focus was on the long thick strands of my hair as she twisted the wavy strands end over end.

"Yeah, I know. I can't believe I said it either," she whispered, answering my stare with one glance before returning to my hair. "Sometimes we want to hide impending death from my cute little best friend."

This time her referring to herself as my friend didn't bug me, it felt normal. Well, as normal as a casual conversation could when following the words "impending death."

Any of my previous warmth had faded into a crippling cold, the kind of dread inducing shiver that built a little house in your bones and lived there. I don't know how a dragon could fill me with ice as much as Zoe did.

But she did.

"Is death coming?" Even asking the question made everything squirm.

"Not from me," Zoe said, giving me a sly smile that I was sure she thought would only feed into the joke. I may have believed her too if she hadn't threatened to kill me only a few hours before. "Suvi, however..."

She let her voice trail off, rolling her eyes in that signature way that always preceded a joke. It calmed down my emotional gymnastics a bit, but not enough that I trusted in the safety of my soul.

"How mad was she?" I pinched my face together, as she smiled, the glint of mischief in her eyes only promising more trouble.

"She was pissed," Zoe said with a smile as she went back to braiding, her eyes leaving mine and giving me room to breathe, even if not much else. "There may have been some ranting involved, and I was..."

Zoe hesitated, shaking her head, as she secured the first braid with a tiny red elastic.

"Overjoyed at my independence?" I already knew that wasn't going to fly.

Zoe let out one loud scoff that scarcely qualified as a laugh, "Actually, yeah. Standing up to me takes guts."

She beamed and this time I actually did laugh, although it was more like a nervous choking noise.

"Well, Suvi doesn't seem to have the same problem." I said, "You were running away from her like she was going to sell you to some supernatural zoo."

"Maybe she was."

"Suuure."

"I'll tell you a secret," she paused, leaning down and flashing me a grin through the mirror. "Suvi is terrifying, and I wouldn't go against her in a fight, but she isn't that scary. In truth, she turns into a potato at night. Old and wrinkly, and a hundred eyes looking in every direction."

She twisted her eyes around, waggling her tongue as she made a noise between a dying cat and a witches cackle.

The look was so weird that I couldn't help but laugh, the deep sound breaking through the pressure that was smothering the room.

I loved Zoe. She was my best friend, but I was also fully aware that we handled our shifters very differently. She played by the rules, and after breakfast this morning I may have gotten my first hint as to why.

That realization was a slap after my candid camera experience this afternoon. I may be starting to see the wisdom in her ways, didn't mean I was going admit it.

Yet.

And I still wasn't ready to tell her about my interlude with three sexy brothers. I needed to trust she wouldn't blow me off, and she hadn't quite proved that yet.

I sighed and leaned forward, stubbornly finishing the last twirl of glitter as Zoe continued to braid my hair.

"I'm not doing very good at this pretending to be normal thing," I mumbled, grabbing the dark charcoal colored powder that I used to add a bit of depth to the glittering flames I had drawn and went to work, chancing a glance at the clock. Ten minutes to curtain.

"It's not so much pretending to be normal, as it is restraining your shifter." The tone in her voice made it clear that she wasn't a fan of it either, which wasn't making me want to jump on the ignore your very needy and loud shifter band wagon.

"Well, that sounds miserable." I let that sarcastic sass fly and Zoe closed her eyes in that 'lord, give me patience' way I had always associated with old ladies.

Which I guess Zoe was.

"I know it sucks, Ellie," Zoe sighed, her voice soft as she quickly secured the second braid and began to twist the two together. "But you have got to start listening to us. I know where you are at, and I am here to…"

"To what?" So much for not diving back into our fight, the reaction jumped out of me whether I wanted it to or not.

I dropped the brow brush as I finished the last dark line and fixed her with a glare through the mirror that was dangerous enough, even without the wicked golden gleam in my eyes.

"To help? To keep everything from me? To command me to follow blindly?"

Even as I went on my tirade, Zoe didn't look away, and her shifter didn't rise to meet my own. She kept the dragon perfectly restrained. Which only pissed me off more.

Could she not be perfect.

Just one freakin' time?

"I need you guys to start telling me what's going on," I whispered, my voice a harsh hiss as goose bumps rippled over my arms, the tale-tale sign of a phoenix escape plan.

I knew I was riding in on dangerous territory, and I tried to calm myself, hissing instead of yelling. As if that would work. "You can't leave me in the dark anymore. And you can't tell me to go wait in hotel rooms for hours, waiting to be murdered, or scolded or both."

Zoe jabbed the last bobby pin in my hair with a little bit too much force, and took a glance at the door to make sure we were alone.

I, however, looked at the clock. Five minutes to go.

She sighed and sat down in the booth beside mine, pausing to tuck another strand of hair that had come loose from her turban back into place.

"I know. We never meant to, you know. But when you were still so little we didn't have another choice, and teaching you to use your shifter meant that Suvi couldn't shield it. We needed to hide you more than we needed to train you."

I couldn't move. If she had turned me to ice before it was nothing to now. After this morning I thought I had lost any chance of getting information out of her. But right now? She chose to open up right now when we had, I checked the clock, four minutes before the overture began and I needed to be bounding onto stage like the fire sprite I was.

We were out of time, I needed to run, but I couldn't move. I sat still, staring at her as my jaw began to unhinge herself.

"I didn't think it was a mistake, but it was..." She stopped mid sentence, her nose wrinkling as if she was smelling something sour.

"Do you smell that?"

Any calm that had been in her voice before had vanished, leaving behind a heavy bark of what I could only describe as fear.

"What is with you and smelling things?" I tried to push a laugh into the joke, but it couldn't shake free. Her panic was infesting me and I shifted away from her, watching in confusion as she ducked to the floor, grabbing at the leotard, tights and warm ups that I had hurriedly shrugged out of thirty minutes earlier. Her eyes were wide as she sat back down in her chair, her hands full of my clothes, her nose buried in them.

The image would have been comical if her eyes weren't dangerous, if her skin didn't seem to be smoking. I had never seen her dragon so close to the surface before. Every part of her iris had faded to a red so deep that it almost looked as if they were on fire. Maybe they were.

The image was terrifying and I scooted away, glancing toward the exit in a need to make a sudden escape. Even if

Zoe would let me, her eyes were making it very clear I was going nowhere until she got an answer.

"Do you smell that?" She repeated shaking my clothes towards me.

That was of course if I had an answer to give her.

"Smell what?" I shrieked, her panic infecting my confusion as I pulled away from her, genuinely scared now. "What are you talking about?"

"When were you around a dragon?" Her voice was a low hiss, the words cutting painfully into me. "Who found you?"

"F-found?" I stammered, the way my heart was thundering making it very clear I knew who had found me and exactly what Zoe was talking about, as much as I was pretending I didn't. "Dragon?"

"Who have you been around, Elliot?" I don't think I had seen her so scared, I don't think my name had ever sounded so bathed in dread.

But maybe that was just me. I mean, it was all a joke. It had to be.

Although the more I said it, and the more Zoe's panic began to boil, I knew the lie I had been telling myself wasn't going to hold.

"There were these guys," I began, Zoe's eyes popping so much I was half expecting them to explode out of her head. "They were bro..."

"Hey!" Becky the stage managers voice ripped through the tension causing both of us to jump. "What the heck is wrong with you two? Get on stage now!"

Becky charged toward us in a rage, ready to herd us out and to our first positions.

"Stay in the catwalk after your acts." She demanded as we began to race towards the backstage, making it clear I had no other option, even if I was going to question her.

"Either I or Suvi will come and get you the minute we can."

"Get moving!" Becky roared, making it clear we weren't moving fast enough. Which we weren't, I could already hear the opening swells of music.

"I need you to promise me you'll stay put," Zoe begged as we began to run, Ryn opening the large canvas flap that separated the changing area from the backstage and handing her a baton as the music hit its high note. Xi's voice rang out in a single note as we joined the cast and burst onto the stage, the circus exploding around the tiny girl as the show began.

"I promise." I said, although I wasn't sure she heard me over the roar of the audience, over the explosion of flame as her and Ryn began to dance around each other.

Vaulting into a tumbling pass, I landed right alongside the two contortionists atop the metal bed frame. I tried to sneak a glance to Zoe as I moved into a handstand, but she was lost amongst smoke and flame now, swallowed by the entire cast in a mess of bodies and noise as the show began.

"Look who decided to show up," Stacia jeered as we all balanced together, bending our backs into a low wave, our feet pointed toward the center. Every move was perfectly in sync with one another, perfectly executed. "I'm surprised you made it."

The tone of her voice made it clear she was pissed, she had been vying for my part for years, and she assumed that any misstep got her closer to her dream.

Unluckily for her, I couldn't focus on her pettiness right now. I was too lost in the dread of a few minutes ago, the emotion was like a dead weight against my chest.

It was hard to breathe, let alone keep my hands and back moving in time without feeling like I was going to explode.

Dragons. They were dragons.

You know, like the ones who hunted me and wanted to skin me alive. The panic of before was clearly not that far off, and it really wasn't helping. The tension built through my shoulders and knotted through my stomach, making it hard to keep my balance. It was hard to tell when I was balancing on one hand like this, but I was pretty sure I was shaking.

If there was such a thing as a do-over for the last twenty four hours I would like to sign up for that right now, please.

I was pulled from my near panic attack as the hoop that would start the show by pulling the little girl into a fantasy land lowered beside me. I lifted my body into the Lyra, grabbing the girl, Xi, by the hand as the rest of the cast melted into the backstage, leaving her and I alone. She gripped my wrist as she spun, sending to two of us into a rotation as the hoop began to raise, Xi coming right with me.

Her legs kicked, false panic lining her face, as she performed seamlessly, my own movement of greed matching her own. The audience gasped as I dropped her hand, letting her drop about fifteen feet onto the soft crash pad of the bed.

The bed deflated, nearly swallowing her as I began to dance alone on the hoop, my hands continuing to call to her, to reach to her.

Strapping my left leg over the hard metal loop of the Lyra, I raised my hand, shifting my weight into a long gazelle pose as the apparatus continued to spin. Higher, higher. I was about thirty feet up when gasps rang out as I dropped my hand, hoop and body falling a bit as I settled into a single knee hang, stretching the opposite leg over my head.

It was a beautiful pose and one that I loved if only for the awe involved. I pulled the leg more, shifting it past my head and into my opposite arm as the spin of the Lyra began to slow. Shifting my hands back to the hoop, I dropped my legs into a dancers pose, hanging by my elbow as everything turned to dread.

Not because I was going to fall. Not because I was now a good forty feet in the air.

But because, there, sitting on the front row, were three faces that I recognized at once, all three of them trained on me with differing levels of awe and recognition.

The dragons were here, and they knew exactly who I was.

11

ELLIOT

Music thundered through the tent in heavy thumps of tribal music that shook the rafters and rippled over the canvas in waves. The heavy material shivered over my head in a twisted dance, the thick stripe of black only a dozen feet above where I lay on the narrow catwalk, stretching my hips, legs and back in a effort to stay warm.

Zoe had told me to stay in the catwalk, and after seeing the three men sitting on the front row, I wasn't going to break that promise.

I had gone down long enough to retrieve my silks before making the long trek back up the ladder to the top, foregoing my usual mid-show stretch.

Although I had half expected either of the two women to show up before my act, neither had. I wasn't one hundred percent sold on that being a good thing.

I needed to tell them the men were here. That was if Zoe hadn't already smelled them, but who knew how far her super smell extended.

My heart beat so loud I could hear it over the drums; my nerves were so twisted that I was sure if you peered inside my soul I would be nothing but a tight little pretzel. Neither of those things bode well for a good show, especially one that began with me twisting through the air from the ceiling.

There was no other way to put it, I was scared, and not because I had seen three super hot dragons in the front row.

But because no matter how hard I tried to restrain it, my phoenix desperately wanted them, like jump out of the sky and land on top of them want them.

I was pretty sure that at this point I should be afraid for my sanity.

I was lusting after three men who were possibly sent to capture and kill me.

That was normal.

I didn't even try to restrain the eye-roll.

The only thing I could do to combat such ridiculous emotions was ignore them, which left me with fear. Fear and tension plagued me as I lay still, silk locked into the rigging, tied around both my left leg and waist in preparation for my descent.

Both heart and drums reached a crescendo and I pinched my eyes shut, running through my act one last time as I always did, knowing that the Russian Swings act was coming to a close.

Left leg around, flamenco grip, twist out, Rebecca Split, Camel twist, creature to a flip...

"You ready, Ellie?"

I nodded once, not opening my eyes as Spencer, the riggings master, began to lift the silk into place and do his final checks on the carabineer and locks.

Twist to a secretary sit, eggbeater to an s-wrap, windmill drop to a leg hang...

"Yeah," I finally answered as the music began to change, the long violin of the transition music beginning to sing out.

"Set to prep," Spencer said in full voice, nodding once to his assistant as I shifted to the small outcropping on the catwalk, weaving the silk around my waist one more time before holding it in front of me, ready for the opening drop.

"Prep." I responded, holding the long length of silk in one hand, and the tight pole above my head with the other. Setting my legs in a Peter Pan stance, I exhaled as the rigging lifted and my feet left the metal grate of the floor.

The silk tightened around me, settling me into the secure wrap that I would begin my act in. Flexing my feet, I did my final check, verifying that everything was in place and ready. As many times as I had done this exact piece, as often as I had free fallen from the ceiling, I would still check. You get one thing wrong, go left instead of right on a turn and everything would end in one over-dramatic splat on center stage.

"Dropping plank," Spencer announced before pulling the pins and letting the small section of catwalk swing down. "Position one."

I nodded in understanding, shifting my weight until my hands were behind and above me, leaving me looking like one of those ladies they carve onto the front of a pirate ship. As though I was sailing through the air, the rigging began to shift out until I was aligned with the center of the stage, Spencer, the catwalk, and his assistant about twenty feet to the left now.

I was on my own, ready to fly, all that was missing was my cue.

Xi was far below me, dancing through fog as the last of the Russian swings act left, leaving the little girl alone as the tribal beat took its last thump and the violin took over.

"To point A," Spencer said, his voice a whisper now as the two men took control, their cues as memorized as I was. Spencer had controlled my rigging for as long as I had been allowed on stage, I had the utmost trust in him.

So when the music hit its low rolling note of my arrival and I released my hands, I knew he was doing the same to the silk, both me and my apparatus falling toward the ground. I swung forward, purposefully slowing the drop by locking my knee over the tight pole of fabric before releasing it as I flung myself in reverse, grabbing the tail over my shoulder as I swung back again and began to spin through the air.

The usual gasps broke over the slow violin as the drop ended, my silk now having descended over twenty feet from the catwalk, leaving me a good twenty feet above the ground. My fragile frame swung through the air, suspended in the long angelic clouds of white. Billowing sheets of silk mirrored the fog that Xi danced through as she watched me prance above her, making the entire stage look like the girl had been transported to heaven.

The music, the clouds, the way the silk felt against my hands as I gripped them, everything was perfect. My heart had been thundering a minute ago, my nerves tangled as I thought of those three men in the front row. Now I wasn't even sure if I remembered their names, let alone what they looked like. There was only this.

And this was magical.

Twinkling lights surrounded me in rows of magical stars, the glittering lights shining through the fog as it reached up to swirl against my toes. Everything feeling like it did last night, when I soared through the canyon, when I danced through the clouds.

My phoenix rejoiced at the sensation, but instead of

song, it was only the calm sigh of contentment. It was only joy.

Pulling the silk toward my head, I arched my back until my feet stretched to rest against my shoulders, twisting myself into the perfect cyclical backbend. Releasing the hold, I swung up, arching myself forward to wrap my arms around the silk in a double hold and extended my arms into a move called a crucifix, although the way I was suspended by just the wrapped fabric over my arms I looked more like an angel. Freeing my feet from their crochet, I pranced through the air, the audience gasping and applauding before I spun into an invert, my legs stretched over my head in a split. Locking my knee around the silk I pulled myself up weaving the silk over my waist as I turned and spun into a Rebecca Split. My legs stretched wide and I pushed into a bow and arrow, my body and silk stretching to look like the weapon before I released cupid's bow.

The music peaked as I fell into a twist, the silk lowering as I moved myself into a butterfly, the silk wrapped over torso and legs, legs stretched toward the ceiling as my hands stretched down, toward Xi.

It was the perfect move for a solid base.

Xi stretched up to me as I stretched down to her, her face full of longing as she silently told the story of wanting to dance among the clouds to greet me.

She jumped high, her legs spread into a split as she missed my hands, her fingertips swiping against my own. The rigging continued to lower and with one more over dramatized leap our hands wrapped around each others wrists, the strong hold one that both Spencer and the musicians were waiting for.

The rigging lifted, she began to spin, suspended from my hand as she moved into a split, then a hang, and finally, with well-practiced timing jumped from one hand to the other, both of our hands wrapped tightly around each others wrists as she began to flex and contort through the air.

The audience gasped, they applauded, and as she touched down I quickly spun out of the hold, blood rushing to my head as I stepped beside her, the two of us engaged in a silent conversation.

Her character wanted to touch the stars, but I could not take her among them. As the emotion flooded out of her, I grabbed the silk, the two of us dancing through the long lengths of fabric like they were trees, jumping back and forth as the music changed, as her happiness grew.

But I, as a star, could not stay, and so I grabbed the edge of the fabric, letting the long widths trail behind me like a kite as I ran toward the audience, right to the three men.

My heart dropped to the pit of my stomach, slamming against my nerves and turning any joy I had felt to dread.

While their eyes were wide in shock, my stomach was twisted in knots as I leapt over their heads, white wings sailing behind me. The rigging lifted again as I jumped, sending me in a wide circle over the audience. Using the silk as the wings I could not reveal, I twisted, contorting my body into beautiful shapes.

Or at least that was what I was supposed to be doing.

I was having trouble hearing the music over the beating of my heart and I kept losing track of what I was supposed to be doing, which only made everything that much more frightening.

I couldn't remember how many times I had circled the audience, I couldn't remember which move I was supposed to be doing. One tiny tug of the fabric however, pulled me right back into place.

Spencer was lifting the rigging for the last drop, the action slowing the circles and pulling me back to the center. I couldn't let myself get lost in this crap. I needed to focus.

Pulling myself out of the panicked stupor, I began to prep for the final drop, carefully counting each move and each wrap as I stretched and contorted myself.

I knew the emotion had shifted to fear on my face, and in some ways it fit, so I didn't worry. Although, the look that Xi gave me as she stood now a good twenty feet below me clearly said she knew something was wrong.

The silk steadied as I hovered in place, heart pounding as I prepared for the final drop.

The music swelled, Xi shook her head in a frantic no, and I released the fabric and shifted myself forward into the drop. Then like the idiot I was, turned and looked right at them.

The three men looked at me in amazement, their faces full of awe and passion, and above all worry. I hadn't expected it, but it didn't matter, because the moment I looked at them I had something much more to worry about.

The air had turned to glue again, and time had stopped. Well, time had stopped for everyone but me.

I still twirled through the silks, the actions slow as I plunged through the sticky air, everything pressing and tugging against me. Forget barely being able to move, I could barely breathe. The dense air was a heavy pressure against my chest, the panic I had tried to ignore up until this point swallowing me whole. The frozen world turned to a blur as I looked from face to face in search of help, of someone who could stop it. But the only ones who knew that something was wrong were the three men, their faces lined with the horror that now crippled me.

It only took a moment, but as the world shifted from the

sludge, and time picked back up I already knew it was too late.

I had lost count of my rotations and although I bent my leg, wrapping it around the silk to stop the drop as I always did... there was nothing there to stop me.

I had begun to free fall.

Desperately arching through the air, I reached up to the silk but it was too far away, and the ground was growing far too close.

My phoenix screamed, the sound rattling in my head as she begged for escape, begged to save me and to soar through the air.

"No," I cried, as much to my shifter as to myself, the pain of what I had to do stabbing in my chest.

I needed to die, well as much as this audience was concerned. I could not die, but all they would see was the impact of my body against the hard stage, and the end of any life here.

There was no other choice.

They were too close. I didn't know if Suvi's shield would work.

Screams of fear drowned the tent, the music having stopped as the musicians stood in panic. I took one last gulp of air and closed my eyes, waiting for the hard impact of my flesh against the center of the wooden stage.

It never came.

Screams turned to cheers as strong arms caught me, warm hands pressing against me as I was held against a heaving chest, the muscles tense as they pressed against me.

My eyes popped open, expecting Zoe or Suvi, or even Ryn to have attempted to catch me. But there were only the deep charcoal eyes of Jarron, his face masked in anger as he gripped me against him.

"I got you," he whispered, his voice hardly audible over the cheers, before they too were smothered as the silks fell over us.

White fabric billowed around us, Spencer having dropped the rigging after me in the usual safety protocol for situations like this, but right then it only made me feel more trapped. Pressed against someone that I wanted to be a million miles away from.

Or at least an inch or two.

I swallowed, resisting the urge to wrap my fingers around his collar, or burrow myself in his neck. Both of which seemed like the perfect antidote for the panic that had now reached a heart-attack inducing high.

"What are you doing?" I demanded, pushing against him as I wiggled out of his arms, only to be swallowed by the silk, unable to get very far away.

"Protecting you," he whispered, his voice smoldering with playful concern. The sound was like a balm, and as much as I wanted to fight against it, I could tell he was genuine. "I will always protect you, darling. I have bonded to you, my place is beside you."

Jarron's whisper paralyzed the lingering panic, and as he reached toward me I found myself leaning into him, wanting him. Desiring him. Even if the limited space had made it possible to avoid his touch, I am not sure if I would have been able to force myself away. His fingertips grazed against my jawline, sending pleasurable shivers over my body as my phoenix lifted in response. My song swelled through me, the dark charcoal of his eyes shining in glittering gold as mine did.

"What are you, Ellie?" The tip of his fingers moved down my neck, tracing a warm line over the skin as it fanned out, his palm setting every nerve ending on fire. "What are you doing to me?"

I inhaled sharply at the pressure, unable to look away, unable to move. I opened my mouth to respond, to tell him what I was and what I needed, before I could get even one syllable out the music began to thump around me and the silk began to lift as Xi stuck her head between the swathes of white.

"Suvi says to go up. Both of you," I don't think I had ever heard the little girl sound so serious. She cast Jarron a curious look before she vanished behind the slowly ascending fabric, leaving me staring at the blonde Adonis who still held me in place under his warm touch.

The contact made everything swim in a comfortably fuzzy haze, although not comfortable enough to drown what I had been instructed to do.

"Well, crap," I said, watching the silk unravel from the floor. We had seconds before we would be revealed from our temporary hideout. I had to figure out what to do with the magazine model that was now holding my hand.

Minutes before I would have gladly flown away from him, now I couldn't tear myself away. I didn't want to.

There was a very large part of me that was rejoicing at that.

"Please tell me you aren't afraid of heights," I said over the music as the show continued around us.

"Our kind aren't afraid of heights," he said with a teasing grin, his perfectly arched eyebrow quirking up.

My stomach dropped at the reminder, but I ignored it, grabbing the edge of one of the tails of the fabric and wrapping it behind me, concealing us from the audience as much as I could.

"Well, this is different, trust me," I sasses as I held his

hand out, grabbing the other tail and quickly wrapping it around his wrist in a lock. "This is secure, but don't let go, otherwise you are going to break your wrist."

His confidence wavered a bit at that, but I paid it no mind, the rigging and the silk was still ascending, and now that he was wrapped into it, it was taking him right along with it. Jarron's eyes grew wide as his hand raised above his head, pulling him up as I wrapped my own wrist. Grabbing his free wrist, I kicked off, sending both of us spinning around each other as the silk lifted from the ground, me prancing through the air as the crowd clapped, him hanging from his arm like a deadweight.

He was going to hurt himself hanging like that, but I couldn't fix it now, we just needed to disappear into the sky.

Luckily, the tumblers had already taken the stage and much of the audience's focus had left, everything that had happened having been whisked away into the magic of the circus.

Well, everyone but Jarron's brothers. They had been sitting in awe on the front row, now all three seats were empty, one of the folding chairs collapsed to the ground.

"Where did they go?" I asked, suddenly panicked, expecting the other two to fall from the ceilings like bats.

No, not bats. Dragons.

"Checking the perimeter," Jarron said, the spin tightening as he wrapped his arm around my waist, pulling me against him. "They will protect you too."

My soul caught fire at the feeling of his body pressed so tightly to mine. My stomach twisted in pleasurable warmth, my skin rippling in fire as my phoenix swelled inside of me. Looking from the empty chairs to Jarron, I almost lost control. He was so close that I could see the golden strings of color inside of his charcoal eyes, I could see the flecks of wet that danced on the tips of his eyelashes, I could smell the heady aroma of smoke and pine, I could taste his warm breath on my lips.

Inhaling with a snap, I tried to pull away, knowing I was too close. Knowing that I wanted those lips to press against mine. The better part of me knew that I shouldn't kiss him, not yet. The much louder part of me didn't give a damn.

It was that part I was listening to as the two of us moved closer, as my free hand lifted to wind around his neck.

"I would not seal your fate just yet, young prince," Suvi said from behind me, her old wizened voice pulling us from the spell we had been caught in.

We both jerked, twisting in each others arms as we remained suspended in the air, our arms strung above our heads.

The old woman stood on the catwalk, her palm extended toward the rigging as she brought us in, her finger tips glittering in the faintest purple. Spencer and his assistant were nowhere to be seen, although judging by the milky gleam in her eyes they were inevitably close by, caught under her spell.

That was one trick I had seen her perform. I doubt they would remember anything about today come morning.

Jarron held me closer, his eyes narrowing at the old witch.

"I knew her protector would arrive soon, but I never thought it would be you."

"Protector?" I asked, looking from Suvi to Jarron, who didn't look as confused as I was.

"Who are you?" He asked, his hand fanning over my back at the supposed danger.

"I am Suvi," She said, the glowing in her finger tips vanishing as our feet touched down on the catwalk, although her palm remained up. Her eyes were kind as she looked only at the golden haired dragon who held me. "I am from the old order and traveled with your kind many hundreds of years ago. I have been this child's protector since her birth, and was until your soul pulled her away yesterday morning."

"What?" I questioned as the music swelled from far below us.

Just this morning she was telling me that I am too young to know anything about myself and now she is talking about souls and protectors like I was trapped in a medieval fantasy. Forget the love-sick butterflies I had been swarmed with, I was now wide awake with a swarm of angry, confused bee's rattling around inside my head.

"Yes, child," Suvi said, as she finally turned to me, her eyes kinder than I had seen them in years. "This one I have been waiting for. He is your key."

I opened my mouth to respond, trying to weave through the dozens of questions that were infiltrating my mind. Instead, they all got caught in my throat at the same time, making some kind of choking sound that might have had me question my sanity.

"Are you okay, darling?" Jarron asked, his finger tracing my jaw and making it even harder for anything coherent to escape my lips.

Besides my tongue, when I lick him.

Oh my.

Perhaps it was better if I kept my mouth shut and opted for a solemn nod. Thank god it pacified him.

"It's not just me," Jarron whispered, as I sunk into him, the sound of his heart like a torrent in his chest. "It is my brothers too."

This is new. But only in that I felt drawn to them in the

same wildly inappropriate and uncontrollable way. Beyond that, and mixed with this whole protector nonsense, I was pretty sure I had been hit by a metal bazooka.

Judging by the way Suvi's jaw dropped she had been hit with the same thing.

I hadn't expected that.

"All of them?" Suvi asked, the alarm in her voice sending my focus between them like a poorly timed ping pong match. "Are they here?"

"Unfortunately," Jarron nodded, his hand running possessively over my arm as his body plastered to mine so tightly that I could feel his worry in every twitch of his muscles. The sensation pulled a blush to my cheeks.

"Well then, we might have a problem," Suvi said with a light heartened laugh, "Because I can't see your father letting any of you live if your souls have all bonded to hers. This has become much more dangerous."

12

JARRON

She was so warm that pressing her skin against his was igniting a million strings of energy that Jarron had never felt before.

He had been with many other women, loved dozens of shifters in his centuries of existence, but this girl was different. She awakened something inside of him that filled every gap and loss inside of him. His dragon so close to the surface that his skin glittered, something that thankfully wasn't as apparent in the dim backstage of the circus.

The muscles in Jarron's arms were tight cords as he reached for Ellie as she descended the high latter that led from the catwalk. Her motions were easy, calm, it was clear she had done this a million times before, but it didn't matter. Jarron still reached for her, he still wrapped his arms around her, bringing her into him the second she touched the ground. He needed to know she was safe, And to be honest, part of him was still desperate to know she was real.

That she hadn't died in the fall.

He was still amazed he had caught her.

The three brothers had jumped into action the moment her hand had slipped from the long strip of fabric, her scream echoing through his head.

He had reached her first, the other two giving him a look of both jealousy and disappointment before they ran on, running to check the perimeter for whatever had caused the magic. They had all felt it, felt the rippling of time that only came from a Fae, the dratted beings that their father had enslaved centuries before.

They worked for him now, and feeling their magic only meant one thing.

Their father was close.

Jarron would have given anything to shift right then, to carry Ellie away and hide her in his cave in Spain, keep her there, keep her safe.

But he couldn't leave yet, they still needed to find the phoenix, and if their father was here they needed to do that soon.

His brothers could find the witch, find the child, and destroy the one thing that could give their father eternal life and continue his blood streaked reign.

Except, the witch had found him.

"Take him to my office, Ellie," The wrinkled old witch instructed to the girl Jarron held against him, the tiny little thing wriggling away and stepping right up to the powerful being that only stood a few inches taller than her.

Ellie faced the witch with a jaw so strong and defiant that Jarron instantly pulled her away from the older woman. Could she not feel the power rippling from the witch? This *Suvi* was powerful, Ellie had more guts than he had assumed if she was willing to go head to head with her.

"What is going on Suvi?" Ellie asked as she shook away

Jarron's attempted restraint. Her question was barely discernible through the pounding music that was echoing in the dark, sending the props and backstage scenery rattling. "He is a dra—"

"He is safe." Suvi cut her off with one wave of her finger, the action catching the attention of a few others who were openly ogling the trio now.

Their stares sent Jarron's instincts into overdrive. This was not a conversation, or a situation, that any bystander needed to be caught up in. Jarron sent a few a warning glance, keeping his dragon carefully restrained behind his eyes.

His brothers may be able to scare away any mortal with a glance, but his beautiful creature would only draw them in. Or at least it used to, his dragon was more focused on keeping Ellie safe than on drawing the others into him.

Unbidden by him, a snarl rose in his chest, sending a woman with long blond curls scattering. Her companion, the tiny little girl from the silks smiling brightly before she ran back onto the stage.

"Take him to my office," Suvi commanded harshly, her temper sending Jarron right back to Ellie, wrapping his arm around her waist as he attempted to pull her away from the witch, luckily this time she didn't protest. "I will find the others. Say nothing about your origins. Either of you."

The old bat's eyes dug into his, his dragon twisting uncomfortably at the power her gaze was infiltrating him with. Every word of her command was laced with magic, the power a heavy weight that pressed against his chest and made it clear that if he even tried to speak of such things he would be blocked.

He had been around witches before, but their skills did

not pass beyond casting simple spells with bones and reading tea leaves. This woman was different, every piece of her built upon a power so strong that he couldn't fathom how he had thought those other imposters to be real.

Ellie, however, didn't seem to care of such power.

"Then you will tell us everything," Ellie demanded.

The guts on this girl, she was as foolhardy as he was.

"You will obey me, child." Suvi's voice was a snap so dangerous that even Jarron stepped back.

Ellie, however, stepped forward, the sounds of drums and the smell of paraffin crowning her foolishness.

Jarron growled as his dragon did, pulling Ellie back as his hands wrapped around her, pressing her against him until he could feel the tense muscles in her back ease, feel her tiny body molding against his as he surrounded her. He lowered his head beside hers and faced the witch eye to eye, a snarl curling his lip and ripping from his throat.

His threat was clear.

He knew he could not take this witch, that he would die if he tried. But he would protect the girl he held until his last breath. Nothing could break through him to reach her. Just holding her in his arms cemented that fact, it breathed into him and fused against her.

She was his to protect. His mate.

The deep glare of his warning was broken as the witch began to chuckle, a deep throaty sound that rubbed against his nerves in all the wrong ways.

He wasn't one to feel the burning lash against his pride, it was more common that he was calming Killian from such tirades, but the way she laughed, the raspy throaty sound cutting like a knife, did exactly that. Jarron's growl turned into a glower, his eyes narrowing in a clear threat.

A threat that the old bat could care less about.

"You are still as glorious as ever, Ser Jarron," She said with a laugh, the words serving as a whip against his tense nerves.

Ser.

It was a title he had been granted many decades before, when his father was still caring of such formalities. He had known even then that the title was borne more from the king's pride at having his third born bred with such rarity.

But even then, it had not been used in the last seventy years. Hearing it now was a splash of ice against his spine.

"Do I know you?" The words choked in his throat, but it didn't matter, Suvi only laughed with that same throaty chuckle, and began hobbling away, calling back to them to meet her in her trailer.

Ellie twisted in his arms, her eyes wide in confusion, her own glimmering streaks cutting through the pools of brown in a light that was all too familiar.

It was not the first time that Jarron caught himself looking at the flames of her eyes in wonder, the fire so pure, so delicate.

"What kind of dragon are you?" Jarron whispered, leaning so close to her that he could see his words tickle against her eyelashes, the heat of his body coloring her cheeks.

She heaved at the proximity, the flames increasing before they were gone, drowned by a muddy brown pool that was just as beautiful without her dragon making itself known.

Wrapping his arm around her waist, he brought her closer, the music rocking louder as the smoke from whatever fire act was on stage began to swath around them.

Lifting her against him, Jarron felt her weight shift, every inch of her against him as he supported her with one arm, his free hand coming to rest against her cheek.

"Ellie," he whispered, her breathing picking up as his fingers began to trace his jaw. "What are you?"

Confusion colored her cheeks before she wiggled away from him, dropping to the ground like a cat before taking his hand and pulling him away. Smoke broke around her in dancing wisps of grey that along with her red costume, made her look more like the flame that he was sure lived inside of her.

"We have to get out of here," she said as she towed him behind her, exiting the darkness of the backstage and running into a brilliantly lit space full of padding and apparatuses that you would expect to see in a Olympic gymnastics facility.

"Hey, idiot!" A voice yelled from somewhere in the corner, the hard female tones directed at Ellie. "What are you playing at? Are you that dumb to try to—"

Jarron turned toward the shout, his eyes hard with warning as he warded off whatever beast had arisen to hurt her. This time, his dragon growled clear, and the girl shrunk away, her face rippled with fear, not a drop of desire painted there.

He would have done more, he would have ripped the girl to shreds had she continued, but Ellie ran through the tent, ignoring the girl as if she was nothing more than an irritating fly and pulled Jarron out of the bright tent and into the dark. The parking lot was dark, and thankfully empty on this side of the tent. They didn't stop, however, Ellie continued to pull him at a full sprint, the looming rectangle of one of the relos growing closer.

He had seen them when they had arrived, he had felt the faint whispers of magic emanate from them. Going into a circus run by a witch he had thought nothing of it. But now, as they raced toward the tiny building, the smell of magic growing stronger, he couldn't help but question why the magic was so strong, and what the witch was hiding.

The phoenix must be here.

The thought was brushed away as a wall of dust assaulted his senses as they burst through the main door. Thick metal clanked loudly against the opposite wall at their entrance, sending a tiny man behind a desk to attention.

"What in the--!" His shout was angry, but his face was angrier.

The tiny man's chair clattered to the ground with a bang as he stood, intent on shooing the pair out of the musty space.

"Take it up with Suvi, Alan," Ellie spat, continuing her race as she burst through another door, yanking the powerful dragon behind her. Her hand left his as the door behind them closed with a snap, plunging them into darkness.

The sharp sound of Ellie's labored breathing cut into the air and drowned out the ramble of the older man as he too left the relo, his door snapping behind him.

Her shadow jumped in the dark, the dim outline hardly visible to Jarron, even with the powerful eyesight of his dragon.

It didn't matter. He didn't need more than that.

He could feel her heat from here, feel the power that was hiding inside of her, it called to him.

Like a string on an old sweater, the line that somehow connected the two pulled against him, begging him to close the gap, to feel her warmth against him, to bring her into him.

She turned as though he had called her, the sliver of light that bled through the window falling over her face and casting her features in ribbons of faded blue. She looked even more beautiful in the subtle glow, her features perfectly cut even through the worry and confusion that lined them.

"What is happening?" She asked, her question clearly more for herself than for the man before her.

Jarron's heart melted at the despair in her voice, the cord that bound her to him growing taught as it pulled him toward her. Before he could reach her, she stepped away, her arms wrapping around herself as though it was her only source of protection.

The pose was so similar to how she was when he first met her, covered by the ash of her dragon in the steam room, that he felt warmth in his stomach twitch to life. His need for her growing in a different way.

"Ellie?" His husky voice rippled with concern, his hands still open to her as she began to shuffle through the room. His heart longed to grab her, to pull her into him, and for any other woman he would. Hold her, soothe her into submission with his powerful dragon.

But not Ellie.

Never to Ellie.

"What is going on?" She asked, turning toward him, her eyes blazing. It was beautiful. "Why do I want you so much?"

"Because your shifter has bonded to mine." He spoke simply, calmly, hoping that the very clear reality would be enough to calm her.

The bonding of mates was natural to many dragons in his kingdom, and to all shifters. One soul would pick another, the pull of their souls so strong that nothing could tear them apart. It was that connection, that love, that passion, that would tie them together as mates.

She surely understood what was happening without such an explanation. It was common knowledge.

Her reaction made it clear that she did not. Her breathing picked up, her lips pressed into a tight line as her feet shuffled, pulling her towards him as he pulled her back.

"You are my mate, Ellie," He said, keeping his voice calm as he tried again, keeping his palms up in a show of protection, of wanting.

"Mate?" she said, the word a stutter as her face twisted in the dim light, the blue shimmering over her painted skin, the lines of glitter she had placed there catching in the light until she looked like magic.

Even through the pain that lined her features, it made his breath catch, this beautiful other half of him.

"I am your mate, darling Ellie." Jarron said taking a step forward, his voice soft as he took her hand in his. Warmth spread up his arm at the contact. He suppressed a sigh as every muscle in his body began to calm, that same glittering magic he saw on her face rippling through his bones.

"So, you will protect me?" She said, her own sigh escaping as her muscles visibly relaxed.

"Yes. Always." He whispered, carefully moving her closer, not moving faster than she wanted. "A dragon will always protect his mate. I am your protector. That is what the old witch called our bond, although I have never heard it that way before."

Any trepidation she had melted away at his words, and she melded into his arms so perfectly it was as though she belonged there.

Mine.

The grumble of his dragon was clear in his mind, the

sound deep and familiar that Jarron didn't even flinch. Ellie did though, her almond eyes wide as she twisted in his arms, staring right into him, fear and awe clearly painted on her face.

Had she heard that? It was impossible, no one heard his dragon. In fact, he knew no other in his clan that could hear their dragon's voice so clearly.

It was only him.

The look on Ellie's face however, was making him question that validity.

Mine.

His dragon growled again, the word matching the raspy sound rumbling in his throat. Again, Ellie's eyes widened, her shock growing as she twisted against him, her fingers reaching toward his jaw, sending sparks of warmth through his nerves as her soft fingers made contact.

The growl turned into a groan as her hand wrapped around his forearm, her palm hot through his shirt as it ran up the skin, leaving a trail of fire behind.

"Yours," she said.

The sound was like music, soft and sweet, and for the first time Jarron did not want to lull her into his bed, but keep her in his life, safe and protected.

"I am so confused," she whispered in trepidation, snapping the calm like a rubber band. "How can there be three?"

The question was valid, but it didn't stop his dragon from sparking hot and angry. The creature didn't want to share, and Jarron didn't blame him. *He* didn't want to share.

"I don't know," he said, brushing his thumb over her back in a way that he hoped would calm her. "I am hoping the old witch can help us figure that out. I can't lose this. I won't lose you."

"Everything I have read has said only one. One mate. A unique bond," She said, her eyes catching the dim light.

"You have read?"

Everything about her phrasing was wrong. Although he could still feel the warmth of her fire against him, it twisted into a barb that pushed into his heart.

"I have never lived with..." she began, her eyes twisting to look anywhere but at him. "Our kind."

Our Kind. Reading about her *kind*. The barb became a warning light. Could it be possible that she knew nothing about herself, nothing about the amazing power she held inside of herself?

Her words, the fear that lined her face made it clear that she truly did not understand.

A rage erupted in Jarron that he was only barely able to control. This beauty, his mate, had been left in the dark her whole life.

No, he realized, she had been restrained her whole life.

"Has the witch been controlling you?" Jarron asked, his skin prickling in anger.

"No," Ellie responded quickly, the strands that had come loose from her braids falling over her face as she shook her head. "She and another dragon have been protecting me. There are..." she hesitated again, and his muscles tightened around her further, his skin so hot now that he was sure she could feel it. If she did, she said nothing. Her focus instead was drifting over the room, pulling from the window to what he could scarcely make out as a little table in the dark.

"What is it darling?" Jarron whispered, his finger soft as it dragged over her jaw and pulled her focus back to him. "You can tell me anything."

The battle was clear in her eyes, her mind rattling as she bit her lower lip. The skin bleached under the pressure, his fingers ached to reach forward and ease the tension, to rub his thumb over the soft skin, to feel her heartbeat through the fragile barrier.

"You can trust me," he whispered, knowing beyond a doubt that for the first time in his life the words might be true.

Her eyes were wide in hesitation before she spoke the words that cut so deep that any chance of control was lost.

"People want to kill me."

A deep growl rumbled in his chest at her words, his hands dragging up her arms and holding her so still that she had nowhere to look but at him. He was sure that the golden flames were visible in the deep charcoal of his eyes, but he let it shine, needing her to see his fury, needing her to know of his truth.

"I won't let that happen," His voice rumbled in a husky whisper. "You don't have to hide anymore. I, and my brothers, will keep you safe."

He said the words, and this time his dragon did not claim ownership. He did not rise in need and claim. He purred, he settled, knowing that it was true.

He and his brothers would protect her.

Perhaps the old bat was right, the thought settled comfortably, pooling between them in warmth.

"I cannot wait to show you everything that this world has for you." He pulled her into him, letting the heat from her skin meld with his. "To see your dragon, and meet the beast that is matched to mine. "

"I'm not a drag..."

Her words doused against his soul, a scream sounding in his head that never found voice. Before she could even finish, the door slammed open and her tiny frame was ripped from him. Killian's eyes were harsh as his teeth flashed white, smoke twisting through them.

Jarron barely heard it, his mind was trapped in the words she did not say, in the reality that he knew he should have been able to put together far before this.

"You're the phoenix."

13

ELLIOTT

Killian's hands were rough, although his touch was somehow soft.

He pulled me away from Jarron with a tug, tucking me against him as though I was a priceless artifact he needed to keep safe.

A very loud part of me wanted to melt into this new touch, into the new sparks of electricity that was running over my skin in lines of soul shivering pleasure. Like hell if that was going to happen, not after what Jarron had said.

And certainly not with the absolutely terrified look Jarron had fixed me with. His eyes screamed more than shock, they screamed with that 'oh-my-god-what-the-hell' look that made all those little sparks of electricity feel like stabs over my spine.

I was fucked.

I was so fucked.

I returned the look right back to him, trying with everything I had to beg him not to kill me right then. Jarron said he would protect me. He just promised that he and his brothers would protect me.

I was a fool to have believed that. His shock was already melting into a white hot rage. At least, that's what I thought it was. His jaw had begun to twitch and his eyes were now so dark that I was sure they would swallow full planets if given the opportunity.

"...You are lucky that old woman found us," Killian roared, his tirade finally registering over the panic inducing showdown I had been trapped in with Jarron. And even then, I was sure I only heard him because I had tried to escape his tight arms, his muscles holding tighter and pulling my focus.

"Are you alright, Ellie girl?" Killian whispered, the husky edge of his voice acting like cold water against my panic, and instead threatened to turn me into goo.

His warm palm pressed flat against the skin of my shoulder blades, sending a new wave of energy through me. Gasping at the sensation, I stopped my struggle, staring into the emerald green of his eyes, lost in that one little dimple as his mouth pulled into a curious half smile.

Forget the threat, I was officially goo, wrapped in fear, and mailed to hell.

All of the emotions blended together, twisting against heart and stomach until I couldn't help it, I began to cry.

I made no noise other than one stifled gasp, but I could clearly feel the warmth of the bastard tears roll over my cheeks, desperate to escape my tormented body and take every last drop of frustration with it.

"Let her go, Killian. You're scaring her," Drake pled from somewhere behind me. I hadn't even realized that he was here. Not that it mattered. I was still surrounded by dragons.

I was still going to get ripped to shreds, or skinned or whatever it is Zoe had taunted me with.

"Ellie girl," Killian tried again, his hand sliding down to

my waist as he lifted me against him, his frame so large that I felt like little more than a rag doll.

Maybe that's how they would end me.

I looked toward Jarron, my eyes welling with those hot ugly tears as I tried to pull myself together enough to plead with him not to say anything. To keep his overly handsome lips sewn shut.

His terror had melted however, although the shock was still plainly painted against the solid line of his jaw.

"Please," was all I said. The one word sounded pathetic and far too much like something a weak kid in a movie would say. But it didn't matter; it was all I had in me. Hell, I was amazed I could squeeze that one word past the rock in my chest.

It was enough.

Jarron's panic shifted slightly, his eyes lightening enough that I could see the glimmer of gold in their charcoal depths. They almost sucked me in.

Frozen against the comforting warmth of Killian's strong arms, hearing Drake's concern, seeing the light in Jarron's eyes; I realized that, all things considered, this wouldn't be a bad way to die.

Didn't mean I wanted it though.

"Please don't kill me."

My words were simple, calm, and full of every fear that had clenched in my chest. Saying them aloud lifted a weight and I took one shattered breath, hoping that it wasn't the last one.

"What is going on?" Killian asked, the husky whisper shifting back to rage. "Are you okay, Ellie girl?"

"Jarron?" Drake asked behind us, but I still didn't look away from the man in question.

"I need..." was all Jarron got out before the other two exploded in anger.

Killian held me so tight that I could feel his heart beat, the quick staccato pulse so loud that mine instantly tried to match it. Drake jumped between Jarron and I, posturing his larger brother with a terrible sound that rumbled my bones.

"I won't let that happen," Jarron said, his plea once again cut off by the growl of his brother, who didn't seem too interested in believing him.

Drake lowered himself further, his body hovering inches above the ground as his snarl lengthened, as his body began to smoke.

Holy--.

I tried to wiggle away from Killian, to escape his grip and make my own run for it, but with each movement his grip increased, until I was pretty sure I was going to be absorbed by his mass.

"Don't shift Drake," Jarron said, his voice lowering to a different kind of plea as his focus left me, drifting to the man on the floor who looked as though he was about to go up like a firecracker. "You'll only hurt yourself if you do. She is safe, both of you. I promise you she is safe with me."

Jarron stood on the other side of the office now, his body framed by the muted light of the window, the dim lighting from the lamp falling over him and pulling his handsome face into soft angles. The soft lighting sparked against the glittering gold that was spreading over his skin.

It was beautiful, and it chipped away at my fear, little by little.

"I'm not going to hurt you, darling," Jarron said, his intense stare shifting to me and taking a jack hammer to the last of my worry. "I am understanding why your shifter bonded to three, however. You have my word that we will keep you safe. All three of us. I will give my life for you, darling. We have been looking for you for a long time."

If I was confused by his proclamation, Killian and Drake must have been hit by a jackhammer. Killian stopped moving, although his hold did not loosen. While Drake didn't leave his predatory stance, the low rumble of his snarl silenced, his eyes wide as they flicked from Jarron to me, the innocent confusion bleeding into me and twisting against my spine in a pleasurable coil.

"She can't be," Drake said, his body unwinding as Jarron stepped beside him, the two staring at me as Killian kept me in his grip, his fingers hard little points of pressure against my spine.

It was like being hugged by a straight jacket. A really tight one, that wanted to kill you. He was certainly living up to his name.

My lungs were starting to burn, the strips of color that filled Suvi's office looking a little too glittery and blurred.

I pressed against him, desperate for air, for space, for a little bit of breathing room that wasn't filled with fear, or an unreasonable need to kiss them all.

Luckily, the knotted muscles of Killian's arms responded, releasing me from him. Too bad that meant sending me the two feet to the ground.

Gasping for air, I wasn't able to support my weight and crashed to my knees, the thin spandex body suit I wore pulling against the carpet.

"It can't be," Killian said from somewhere in the spinning oxygen-filled world, although I didn't bother to find him. I was too busy trying to stay conscious.

Drake reached me first, his arm wrapping around me as

he brought me gently into his lap. The rough calluses of his hands felt soft as he rubbed my back, electrifying my nerve endings and prompting air back into my lungs.

"Breathe, beautiful," Drake whispered, his voice low in my ear as he brushed the hair that had come free from the braids aside. "Slow breaths."

I wanted to tell him that that wasn't going to happen with me sitting in his lap like this, so close to his neck that all I could smell was the tangy scent of pine and rain.

I breathed it in, letting his foresty smell devour me.

"Good girl," he whispered, his lips brushing against my skin. Twists of pleasure ran over me and I let myself relax into him, giving my heart and soul what it wanted.

Well, at least part of what it wanted. What I really wanted was to wrap my legs around him and look into his eyes, taste him. Be kissed by him.

To know what it was to be kissed.

My breath shook with need as he held me, his hand pressing down my back and cupping around my hip making it clear he wanted the same thing.

"Breathe," Drake whispered as he pulled me toward him, making it clear he wasn't speaking to me.

Electric sparks infiltrated me, running over my skin as his breath ran over my neck. Hot, dangerous. As much as I wanted him, this was close enough, and didn't involve any exceptionally embarrassing acts of passion.

I sure as hell wasn't moving anytime soon, however.

"She can't be, Jarron," Killian whispered, his shock masked by my gasping breath. "She can't be the phoenix.

"I assure you she is," A familiar voice said behind me, Suvi's appearance adding a whole other layer of calm to the warm Drake-blanket I was wrapped up in.

"Now, if you are quite done attempting to strangle the girl I have spent the last twenty years protecting I assume we have some things to talk about."

14

ELLIOTT

The office was heavy with the smell of stress and fear. I could feel it press against my skin and drip from the gaze that each of the men were giving me.

Drake, amazement.

Jarron, a pride that I didn't feel like I deserved.

Killian, however, had fixed me with a look I didn't quite understand. It was full of determination, jealousy, and a brow so furrowed that he almost looked angry... or lost. Each emotion flicked on his face like it was on a timer, each expression lingering before it twisted to the next.

It was making me jump, this weird tirade of confusion that was aimed right at me. I doubt it would have been as bad if he didn't look quite so like he was going to jump out of his chair and carry me away.

Stifling a sigh, I sat back in the high back worn leather chair Suvi had sat me in, grateful there was a wide mahogany desk between me and the brothers.

I could only assume it was helping that the desktop was littered with even more bones and candle wax. I didn't know how magic worked, but I was definitely going to pretend they were wards or shields or something.

Even if all it did was keep me safe from Killian's furrowed brow that was enough.

Of course, I needed more help ignoring the way sparks of fire were crackling underneath my skin. It was taking every ounce of my strength to keep from vaulting over Suvi's desk, or shifting into a phoenix, or worse.

The heady sandalwood incense that always filled Suvi's office wasn't helping either, it mixed with the woodsy, smoky, minty smell that drifted from them and acted like gasoline on a flame.

Hot, beautiful, flames.

As if he could hear my thoughts, Jarron winked at me and I sunk further into Suvi's high back chair, my fingertips digging into the worn leather like handles on a carnival ride.

Maybe it was, my stomach sure was spinning like I was stuck on one of the dratted things. Spinning, tangling, just like Jarron and I on the silks.

I clamped my eyes shut, locking both his roguish smile and my delirious memories away.

"Knock it off Jarron," Drake snapped. "It is our place to help Ellie through this. You are making it worse."

His low warning bounced ominously around the small space, the protective tone soothing my frayed nerves, well, at least until the deep rough chuckle perked them right back up, sparks running over my spine as Killian laughed.

"Always the good little boy," he taunted with a snap. "It's no wonder you—"

"Gentlemen I am going to have to ask you to restrain yourselves," Suvi barked, the rough edge of her voice pulling my focus and my eyes snapped open to the three men. Their very different smiles sent me into three very different mind-numbing, heart-palpitating daydreams. Well, at least Jarron and Drake were smiling, Jarron with a low seductive grin and Drake with a roguish half-smile that sparkled in his eyes.

Killian was still taking a journey through his emotional gymnastics.

Look away, Elliot, you aren't doing yourself any favors.

Drake, Killian and Jarron sat on the other side of Suvi's tiny office, situated in the chairs that I had spent so much of my years pouting in, and even rampaging in a few hours before. While Drake was built with much more slender muscle, all three of them made both the chairs and the office look far too small.

All of them were still calling for me.

I swallowed, and put my focus on Drake, his kind eyes making the tension that much more palatable. I didn't want to run into his arms any less than his brothers', but there was something about him that wasn't as proprietary. It made me feel safer, somehow.

I didn't know how to explain it, but right then I didn't want to ask questions.

I was perfectly happy getting lost in the liquid brown of his eyes.

"You must calm too, dear," Suvi chastised, her voice calm as she stepped to the desk, blocking my view of the three of them and fixing me with a wrinkled grimace.

"Sorry," I mumbled, once again reverting to the tiny disobedient child I had been so long ago.

"No apologies. Just drink," Suvi demanded, nodding toward the bright blue tea she had brewed for me when we first arrived, saying it will help with my "bristling mating instinct."

It sounded much more eloquent when she said it,

although I thought "desperate need to bump and grind" fit just as well. I bit my lip and drank, the other three doing the same.

Although they had normal Earl grey.

"Why don't they need to control their *bristling mating instinct*," I asked, choosing to use her words and gaining a chuckle from Jarron. Drake nearly choked on his tea.

Killian didn't look away, but he didn't laugh either.

"Their claiming need is as strong as yours, but as you have chosen all three as your future mate, you are receiving triple the desire. Triple the need."

Coming from an old lady, the words didn't sound as dirty as they could, which I was grateful for, because staring at Drake was starting to do weird things to the pit of my stomach.

The lowest pit.

I swallowed, and instantly decided to drink more tea.

Suvi chuckled darkly, once again not helping. Let's add embarrassment to all the weirdness that was going on with me today. Ugh.

"Even then, these three boys have seen a total of six hundred years," she fixed them with a look, meanwhile I promptly dropped my tiny porcelain tea cup, sending a loud clink over the room.

"I expect better of them," she chastised them but I barely heard her, I was too busy bubbling over the bombshell she had dropped.

"Six hundred years?" I didn't even try to restrain my shout. At least I had the good sense to swallow my tea first.

Didn't stop both Jarron and Drake from cracking a grin.

"Combined," Drake emphasized, as if that helped.

I was still sitting with my jaw on the table, spluttering like a loon.

"Killian is the oldest, he has seen three hundred years on his own." Jarron provided, nodding to Killian who still did not look away. "I nearly two and Drake a little over a century. Don't let Drake's age or size fool you, his dragon is easily the largest of us all."

"It used to be," he muttered, his shoulders drooping before Jarron smacked his arm.

I looked at them curiously, waiting for someone to explain. When neither of them did, I sunk back into the chair, grateful when I didn't want to lunge over the desk with the smirk that Jarron gave me.

"You are dragons," I said, mumbling to myself as I took another drink of Suvi's tea, grateful only a bit had spilled on the table.

"You are a Phoenix," Jarron said, that same look of pride taking over his face.

"*The* Phoenix," Killian corrected in the same raspy whisper that ruffled my soul, his eyes burning into me in a ripple of heat, the anger all but gone.

I swallowed.

"What's the difference?" I asked, his correction gnawing at my bones.

"You are the only one, child," Suvi responded, before either of the others had a chance to respond.

"And I have *mated* to all three?" It was harder than I thought getting that word out, and even then it left a lump of coal behind.

"Bonded, dear," Suvi corrected, patting her hand against my shoulder like she always does. "It takes a little more connection to secure a full mate, so let's keep it at bonding for now shall we? Besides, I do not know what will happen if you mate your body and soul to all three."

Oh my god.

Had I suddenly been sucked into some kind of third dimension? Was Suvi going to give me the sex talk? Like hell if I was going to let Suvi give me the sex talk. I hadn't been close enough to a man for long enough to kiss one, let alone *sleep* with one.

Well, except for the last twenty four hours. But that hardly counted. I didn't even know these guys, I wasn't about to mate with them.

Yep. Time to put the brakes on that train, my mind was instantly filling with imagery of hands, and lips, and...

Stop it, Ellie.

"Yeah, okay, thanks got it," I mumbled out, before becoming hugely interested in my tea.

Thank god the dragons had the good sense not to laugh at me, or else I would have vaulted over the desk with the full intent of ripping heads off. Not kissing, just ripping.

Thankfully, the three of them had only caring and concern in their eyes when I finally got the courage to look at them, even Killian. Although, his jaw was a bit tighter than the rest.

I wasn't sure what I had done to piss him off, but I was really starting to get irritated.

"You have bonded to all three because of what you are, and what your shifter can do." Suvi interjected, thankfully deviating the conversation back into safer territory. "You have a hard path in front of you, child. You all do."

So much for safer territory.

"Please don't tell me there is some prophecy about me," I moaned, refusing to look away from Suvi, dreading any answer she was going to give me.

Luckily, she looked slap-in-the-face confused. Drake meanwhile chuckled.

"No prophecy," she said with a scowl, as Drake tried and

failed to hide a laugh. "These boys however, know what you are up against."

All of them shifted in their seats, backs straightening as Jarron's eyes faded to gold, his skin beginning to shimmer as a low growl rippled through the air. Whether it came from Jarron or Drake, however, I wasn't sure.

"Do I want to know what are we are up against?"

"Child," Suvi said, glancing at the clock on the wall as if it was counting down to some kind of explosion. "Tell them your full name."

I couldn't help but raise an eyebrow at that. I didn't have a full name. I had a first name. Nothing else. Not that I knew of. And they knew that. Well, kind of.

"My father..?" I began, Suvi nodding once in encouragement. "I was named after him."

It was just a name. Why was I having so much trouble saying it? It made no sense, but a dead weight had gathered on my chest, pressing against me until saying the one word was more akin to squeezing life from a toad.

Bulging eyes and everything.

"Elliot," I spoke slowly, not quite understanding what was going on, and understanding even less when all three of them jumped to their feet, the quick action causing me to jerk.

"The three of you have more at stake than keeping her safe," Suvi began, her calm tone running like sandpaper against my skin. I didn't know how she could be so calm when everything inside of me was a tight little knot. "She has a key inside of her to something that I believe could change the future of your clan, and of all the shifters."

"She was born of a dragon?"

"She was sired by one." Suvi clarified Jarron's question, as if that made it any better. I knew this, why were they acting like the world had cracked open? What was I missing? "And even without a prophecy, this task will take all of you to complete. You must keep her from your father, and stop him from discovering what is inside of her."

I could have sworn the air was sucked from the room. I couldn't breathe, I couldn't even stand if I tried. Everything was a heavy weight against my chest, so heavy, so still that it took me a second to recognize that time had stopped, that the air was that heavy.

So much for being safe.

So much for sexy dragons.

Suvi had called Jarron 'Prince' on the catwalk.

It all made sense now.

Forget being able to breathe, the walls were closing in.

Pressing. Swallowing.

I needed air. I would have to explain later.

It was either get air, or burst into flame.

I pushed my way through the weight of the world, taking one last look at the frozen men as I pushed past them, desperate to get to the door before whatever was stopping the world turned off again.

I had bolted from the door, through Alan's frozen office and out into the dry night air before the world had sped to catch up. The sound of panic and confusion overlapped through the thin metal walls as they popped back into existence and realized I was gone.

I listened to the mumbles, inhaling deeply as I tried to get my bearings.

"What the hell is going on, Elliot," a voice lit up the silent night, pulling my attention from the stars as I stumbled down the flimsy metal stairs.

There was only one person who called me Elliot.

Zoe was practically running through the dark toward

me, still in full costume and makeup. She had clearly run off the stage before curtain to reach me, the parking lot was still and quiet.

"They said you fell," She declared as she reached me, her hands tight as she held me out in front of her.

Two days ago I'd probably be okay with such concern, but I had had enough of being held, tugged, and panicked over.

"The Dragon King," I began. I had chosen the wrong words to start with.

"What about the Dragon King?" She shrieked as I tried to break past her, but her hands held on tight, the red fire of her dragon blazing in her eyes as she held me still.

I had never heard her voice so deep before, so full of anger, I could see flames lick behind her teeth, her skin bristling with smoke so fine that it looked like water against the liquid black of night.

The look should have been awe inspiring, but it did nothing to calm the panic that was attacking every nerve ending.

"His sons," I panted, shaking as the door clattered open and the deep impression of shoes against metal smacking against me.

Zoe's eyes darted from me to whoever had emerged from the relo, her eyes flashing with fire before she opened her mouth in a growl, and a line of pure fire exploded from her.

15

ELLIOT

"GET OUT OF HERE, ELLIE," ZOE SNARLED AS SHE PUSHED ME behind her, the dark sky streaking with fire.

I knew I should run. Listen to Zoe and take off into the night. But I couldn't. That string I had sensed before was pulling me back, right toward Killian and Jarron as they stormed down the steps.

I took one step forward, ready to jump between Zoe and the boys before I was thrown back by an explosion of flame.

Black fire burst from Killian's mouth, the black and yellow flames ripping apart the stars as I tumbled through the air, smacking against the hard parking lot with a thud that ripped both costume and skin.

Pain knocked against my bones as I skidded to a stop, heaving in both panic and agony.

I lay on the asphalt, costume torn, eyes wide as fire consumed the sky.

Maybe Zoe was right, I needed to get the hell out of there.

I ran as fast as I could, ripping my costume from me as

my skin began to heat, began to ripple, my phoenix desperate to escape.

To fight.

"No," I muttered through tears, or panic or whatever it was that was tormenting me. "We need to run."

The beast that lived inside me was much more optimistic than I was. I didn't know how to fight! Sticking around for this was not smart.

I didn't get very far before strong hands wrapped around me, swinging me through the air and pulling me against a chest that was pulsing with a thunderous growl.

"Stop Ellie," Drake snarled in my ear, the deep note rolling through my soul and twisting my frayed and confused emotions in a million different directions. "You need to stop. It's okay. I'm not going to hurt you."

"How can I believe that?" I raged as I tried to break from his grip, my hands beginning to smoke as I pounded them against him. He didn't so much as flinch, let alone let me go. "You want to kill me."

"I never wanted to kill you," Drake pleaded as the world behind him exploded with yellow flame, the echoes of mortal screams following right behind.

"I will never let anything hurt you," his voice was low as he pulled me into him, letting me beat on him as he tried to catch my gaze. I refused to look. I was too scared to look. "I gave everything to save you, when you were a baby."

His words buzzed through me, slowing my assault as my fists flattened against his chest, our eyes meeting. The warm brown sugar in his eyes hummed with flame as he looked into me, pleading, needing.

Honest.

His hands fanned over my back as the shouts from the battle increased, as the fire grew closer. The warmth of his gaze froze my fear as he held me against him, so close I could only see him, the lines of his face illuminated by the fire that was surrounding us

"I sacrificed my dragon for you, Elliot," He whispered, pressing his forehead against mine, the touch rippling through me. My phoenix rose at the touch, singing, no screaming to burst free and take him. "I would do it all again—"

Before he could finish speaking, he was ripped from my arms and thrown twenty feet away by Zoe, who now stood in his place, heaving, smoke flowing freely from both mouth and nose.

"We need to get out of here," she panted, her panic lost in the pulsing song of my Phoenix, the screaming need for the man who had been thrown from me.

"Drake!" I yelled, pulling away from Zoe's attempted restraint and rushing toward where he now lay in a heap.

Drake pulled himself up as I reached him, his eyes burning so red that even I backed away, suddenly terrified of what I had walked into.

Smoke billowed from both Zoe and Drake as she stepped forward, the asphalt burning around her.

"Get away from her," Drake bellowed as he stepped through the wall of smoke to face her, one hand extended toward me in an offer of protection.

I froze between them, unsure of where to go or who I needed protection from. I was caught like a deer in the headlights.

I wasn't the only one.

"Drake?" This time it wasn't me who had spoken, it was Zoe, the smoke and fire that surrounded her like a hell bound angel fading away.

"Oh my god. Zoe!" Drake's surprise was clear, but it was short lived.

He had barely gotten the words out before the wall of flame hit right into Zoe and burst her into the air, the girl falling end over end as I screamed, trying to catch her, to figure out what was happening.

I was ready to take off into the air and catch her in my claws when a deep throaty chuckle I recognized at once stabbed through the smoky air like a blunt knife.

Killian stood behind where Zoe had been, surrounded by smoke, his once pristine suit singed and smoking. His hair flowed freely around his face, streaming over his face until he looked like a mad man.

Anger and fear rippled through me like a bad cocktail, twisting my stomach and running up my spine in a ring of fire that ran over my skin in waves of golden flame, singeing what was left of my leotard. I let it burn, the heat traveling over me and catching in my hair in a crackling fire that lifted above me like a candle and a flame.

"Stop!" I bellowed as I charged the dangerous prince. A flicker of fear playing there before he laughed, the sound deep and mocking.

It cut against me, slicing against my heart in an open wound.

"She deserved it," Killian ridiculed, his bright green eyes flashing in the dark.

"No," I snarled, as the heat in my hands intensified, smoke seeping from my calloused skin.

It was the same as before, except this time I wasn't scared. This time I knew what to do. Or at least I hoped I did.

"You do."

I pushed my palms forward, not even sure if this would

work, or if it would just shoot a million pounds of bird dung at him.

Either would work, the fire that burned inside of me made sure that didn't happen, however, and ribbons of golden flame shot from me, streaming through the night and right toward him.

I didn't get a chance to see if the attack made contact, before a second set of arms wrapped around my waist, a wide body tackling me to the ground, and pressing my back against the course asphalt.

"Get off me!" I demanded, trying to fight the weight, desperate to get up and wipe that smug smile off Killian's face.

He deserved it. Arrogant bastard.

"Sorry, darling, that's not going to happen," Jarron spoke so calmly we might as well have been lying on a beach, not on the scorched asphalt of an abandoned parking lot.

"He hurt her!" I bellowed, sure that my words weren't making much sense.

"Calm down, Ellie," Jarron said again, letting more of his weight press into me as I began to fight him. "Drake won't let Killian hurt Zoe. *I* won't let him hurt her."

"Then get off me so we can stop him," I barked, the last of my costume ripping to shreds as I fought against his hold.

"I'm not going to let you hurt him, either. Believe it or not, this is how all our family reunions end up," Jarron said with a smile that froze me in place.

I stopped fighting. I stopped wiggling. Jarron lay on top of me with a sly half-smile, his hips pressing into me in such a way that I was surprised I could breathe, and not because of the weight.

"Family?" I asked as another cannon of fire erupted

above him, both the fire and the glittering light in his eyes numbing the confusion that was crippling me.

Before he could answer, the fire extinguished with a low hiss, the screams fading away as a ripple of purple light spread through the clouds, glittering through the inky sky like the aurora borealis. It was beautiful. Well, until one very old, very angry lady broke the silence with a snap.

"That's quite enough of that. That's no way to greet your brothers, Zoe. Clean up this mess while I disperse of the mortals."

I heard Suvi.

I heard Jarron.

But I sure as hell wasn't processing.

Drake knowing Zoe? Sure, they were both dragons, that seems probable.

But Zoe being related to the three brothers who had bonded with my phoenix? I didn't think fate liked to line things up quite so perfectly, but it seems that for me they were making an exception.

"Ellie," Jarron whispered from above me, the low murmur of his voice pulling me from my momentary stupor. "Are you okay?"

Hell no.

I had no clue what was going on. I was seriously starting to question my sanity.

None of the words made it to the surface, but they sure as hell screamed loud and clear for me. If I hadn't completely lost it I would have sworn Jarron had heard me. His face softened, his body compressing against mine enough that I could feel his warmth, feel the string that connected me to him tighten. A feeling of calm grew as his hand dragged up my arm, over my neck and against my jaw, his fingers tracing a faint line against my cheek.

I am pretty sure I forgot to breathe. Everything was frozen in a pleasurable shiver at the feel of the ice and fire in his touch, the twist of fire that was starting to build in my chest was sure as hell not helping.

My escaped breath shuddered as the tip of his finger traced the corner of my lips, my body melting into the hard asphalt, my heart racing as his eyes grew warmer, as he grew closer.

"Ellie," Jarron said again, his voice as heavy as the smoke that bathed the air, his breath a warm flutter over my lips.

Shit, I wasn't breathing again.

"Get off of her," Zoe snapped, kicking Jarron off me and sending him tumbling to my side, his hand still wrapped over mine protectively.

"Nice to see you too, Zo," Jarron grumbled, all warmth gone from his voice as he lay beside me. "I missed my big sis. I mean, last I heard you were dead, so this is quite a surprise."

Zoe gave him a glare so dark that it was swallowed by the inky night.

"Holy shit," I moaned, the loss of Jarron's weight ripping off the protective Band-Aid that he had smothered me with, everything coming back like a mother fucking battering ram. "Holy... no... oh god..."

My expletive filled ramble continued as I pushed myself to my feet, looking from an ash covered Zoe, to a singed Drake, to a surly Killian and finally to Jarron, who still lay stretched out on the ground, hands behind his head like he should be in a magazine, looking at me with wide dark eyes as a tiny smile playing around his lips.

He winked, I blushed, and then jumped three feet in the air as I realized why he was looking at me like that.

Between my near turn, to being thrown on to asphalt

and almost burned to a crisp I was once again, very nearly, back in my birthday suit. I shouldn't be concerned; seeing as it wasn't much different from the skin tight leotard I had been wearing. But if I was going to let my ass-crack, and other extremities, wave hi to the world I was sure as hell going to have a say in it.

I tried to cover myself but realized too quick that there were too many dragons, and too many angles to cover.

"Shit."

"Here you go, Ellie girl," Killian said with a low growl, his eyes swimming with apology as he handed me his slightly singed suit jacket.

I grabbed the jacket greedily, no matter how angry I was at him, or how hurt I was at the glare-fest he had been throwing at me, I wasn't prideful enough to reject a bit of modesty.

"Did hell freeze over?" Jarron laughed from the ground. "Did Killian's dragon actually give up part of his hoard?"

"Shove it, Jack ass," Killian grunted as he stepped toward me, intent on helping me into the oversized jacket.

He didn't get one step before Zoe blocked his path, still in the leather skirt and halter of her costume, although her long dark hair had pulled free and now billowed around her stern face.

"Not one more step Kill Joy," she said so loud that stepped back, right into Drake.

His hand wound around my waist as he pulled me against him, taking the oversized jacket from my hand and swinging it over my shoulders.

"You can't keep me from my mate, Zoe." Killian said, his eyes darting around Zoe to land on mine, the corner of his mouth twitching into a smile and sucking what little breath I had been able to absorb away.

"Your mate?" Zoe pirouetted she turned to me so fast, fixing me with a look so intense that I was worried she was going to spit fire. Something that I now knew was a real possibility.

"My dragon has mated to the Phoenix."

"Um, Bonded," Jarron corrected Killian from where he lay on the ground, it was clear he was enjoying the show. "You haven't mated with her yet, bro. And I have a feeling it will be a race to the finish line on that one."

Oh my god. Did he say that?

Talk about panty twisting nervousness. My stomach tied into one big knot as a rock the size of Jupiter lodged in my throat. I stared at him in bewilderment, only to have that knot tighten into a million trapped bee's with his well timed wink.

I hadn't kissed a boy let alone... yeah...

Ummm...

I am pretty sure the warmth that was consuming me wasn't just from the blush that was covering me from head to toe.

"Knock it off, Jarron," Drake said, his thumb rubbing against my back as the warm bubbling in my stomach tried to migrate. "She's not some diamond you can claim."

"Are you sure about that? She sparkles like one," Jarron said, his eyes melting into mine and making the bubbling warmth become more of a tsunami hell-bent on drowning me.

"Hey! How come the baby over there gets to touch her?" Jarron called, pushing himself onto his forearms. "We've all bonded to her, all of our shifters have been called to protect her."

"You've all..." Yeah, Zoe was about to spit fire.

Too bad I got there first.

"Can you all knock it off," I snapped, parroting Drake as I broke free of him, the guy chuckling behind me. I silenced that with one glare, he sure as hell wasn't off the hook either.

"I don't even know what is going on, you all don't get to claim me, let alone... sleep... with me." The word was devoured with my nerves, but I plowed on, I wasn't about to lose my steam now. "Up until an hour ago the only thing I knew for sure was that the dragon king wants to kill me. And now his sons want to ma..." My heart dropped like a rock, the blush that was already bathing me turning up to a solid tomato red. "I don't know you! Any of you!"

I directed that last part at Zoe, and although she flinched I didn't feel a least bit sorry. She deserved it.

"Calm, child," Suvi said, stepping through the dark to join us. Her power from whatever spell she had used to disperse the mortals still shining in her eyes. "I know it is a lot to take in."

"You lied to me too, Suvi," I spat, eyes shining with the angry light of my phoenix. The woman's lip twitching in warning. I ignored it. "You could have told me all of this... about mates..." Yep. Saying that word was proving to be an impossibility. "About protectors and why my name means something."

Jarron jumped up between Suvi and I like he was a human shield, but I pushed him away. Probably, a little more roughly than he deserved. What was it with this guy and trying to guard me from Suvi?

I realized I was yelling, I realized that my phoenix was dangerously close to the surface. But my anger was far too loud to even pay a bit of notice.

There was no going back now.

I didn't need him. I didn't need anyone.

"It's just a stupid name."

Tears burst from my eyes as I said it, my heart piercing, knowing it wasn't true. It wasn't just a stupid name. It was my father's name.

And judging by the men's reaction that meant something too.

Not that I knew what it was.

It was just another thing Suvi hadn't told me.

My breath hitched at the pain of the realization, ugly wet tears streaming down my cheeks. All three men stepped towards me in a need to protect me. To help me.

I could feel the need for them grow with each step, their kind eyes pouring into me.

But it didn't matter. I didn't want them. Not right then.

Maybe not ever.

"I don't know you," I said with a shudder, the words so broken I wasn't sure anyone could understand them.

It didn't matter either way, I bolted from them all, desperate for air, for freedom.

Before I could stop it, my Phoenix exploded in a burst of flame, and I soared into the night sky, leaving them all yelling behind me.

16

KILLIAN

"Stop Drake!"

Jarron rushed past Killian, tackling Drake to the ground as the younger dragon's skin began to glow in a violent shade of red. Killian knew that look, he knew what it meant, he could feel the same need to shift and take off into the air after her. But he knew better, his dragon was nearly as big as the practice tent, and would call much more attention to them than the beautiful creature that was now soaring through the inky black sky in a ribbon of brilliant red flame.

"Beautiful," Jarron whispered from somewhere on the asphalt below him, the man's face turned toward the glowing ribbons of color, all three of them staring at what had been a girl until a second ago.

He had never seen a phoenix before. Hell, he was sure that no one living had, other than the few of them who stood in the scorching parking lot. But seeing this, hearing the high notes of her song whisper through the breeze, he knew he would never forget it.

He had never seen something so beautiful.

Simultaneously, she was both swallowed by the night,

and shimmered like oil and flame against the ebony. Her feathers of gold, red, and shimmering purple faded in and out as she flapped her wings, making the massive creature look like a mirage against the sky.

If it wasn't for the flame, for the brilliant yellow and orange that burst from her at the shift and the colors trailing behind her as she flew, he wouldn't be certain that he was seeing her there at all.

But he knew it was her. He knew because his dragon knew, and the beast was bursting against his skin, threatening to rip him apart in his need to reach her.

To fly with her.

To be one with her.

His breath released in a shaky exhale as the pull grew, his skin heating, pulling. He stepped toward her, standing behind his three brothers as they sat transfixed, watching the glorious flight of the Phoenix before it was gone, swallowed by the billows of lavender smoke her flames released. The swirling tendrils cut through the night stars in a shimmering dance.

"Are you all going to stand here like slack jaw guppies all night?" Zoe asked from behind the men. Her harsh tone pulling through Killian like a whip. They all jumped, but Killian spun around, his eyes boring into his sister.

"Should we go after her?" Drake said from behind him, his worry clear.

Killian felt the same, his concern for Ellie was paramount, almost enough to drag him away from his sister.

Almost.

"She'll be fine," Zoe said nonchalantly. "She needs to cool down. She always comes back."

"And how can you be sure?" Killian retorted, letting his

dark eyes bore into the woman. Trying to ignore the need to attack her and take off into the night. He wasn't a fool.

There were easier ways to destroy Zoe if it came to that.

"Because I have been the one protecting her for the past twenty years," Zoe said with a flip of her hair, each of her words hitting with a hard knife's edge. "She does this all the time, and she always comes back."

Zoe looked the same as she had decades, and even centuries before. Just as lovely. The beautiful princess that his people still talked about in secret.

The one that they all preferred.

The thought made his blood boil even more, fire coating his tongue.

What he wouldn't give to attack her, to sink his teeth into her.

He probably would have if the powerful witch wasn't standing a few feet away.

"You are supposed to be dead," He muttered, his voice as hard as his jaw as he stepped toward his sister, letting his frame tower over her. Threatening her.

As stoic as ever, Zoe didn't even flinch. She simply lifted an eyebrow, staring at him even as he let the smoke puff from his mouth in a threat.

"Weren't you supposed to be king by now?" she countered, her dig perfectly placed. "It seems that neither of us are how we are supposed to be."

She smiled then, but the look was the same shimmering, powerful, glare that had grated on Killian's nerves for so long before he had disposed of her.

Or, he thought he had.

Screw it, he may not need to protect Ellie from this bitch anymore, but that doesn't mean he couldn't put his irritating sister in her place.

Killian let out one loud snarl, a snap of flame pushing between his teeth in a warning that would send anyone else running. Instead, Zoe rushed him.

Ash coated his tongue as he straightened his back, ready for her. Ready to let his flames roar from him and the black fire inside of him suck the life from her. He thought he had killed her before, he would make sure to finish the job this time.

"Hey, hey, hey," Jarron proclaimed, pushing his way between the two and pressing his hands against chest and shoulders mere seconds before they collided. "We've melted enough blacktop for one night don't you think?"

It may be a valid point, but his fingers still ached to rip her hair, or her head, from her shoulders.

"Knock it off will you, Kills?" Jarron barked as he pushed him back, sending Killian stumbling. "This is dangerous enough without you trying to murder everyone around us."

"I hardly think that killing someone who is already dead counts as murder," Killian said with a wave to the girl in question, his voice like thunder thanks to his dragon being so close to the surface.

"That was two decades ago, Kill Joy. That war is over. You won. Are you really going to hold that against me now?" Zoe retorted, hands on her hips as she stared him down. "Or are you more upset that I am alive and blocking your easy line to the throne? Nothing like your big sis showing up before your coronation to ruin your day."

She said it like it was a joke, some funny little quip meant to entertain. The quip, however, had too much truth to it and it sent Killian back to a low thunderous growl.

He had worked too hard, for too long, for his irritating older sister to come and destroy everything now. It was why he had been searching so hard for the Phoenix, to destroy his father's desire to rule forever.

Killian was born to rule. He was ready to save his people. He would stop at nothing to create that future. Blood suckers and sisters combined. No one could stop him.

"You are just another roadblock," He snarled, pushing past Jarron, ready to fight. Even one well-laid punch would help him feel better.

He didn't get very far.

Everything froze, before he could reach her. But it wasn't the same as during Ellie's act. Then, he could tell by the strong aroma of Fae that time was slowing, even if he didn't experience it.

This time, however, the world around him continued on as if nothing was happening, even though he was trapped in place. Not even Zoe was locked away.

"She is not going to fight you," Suvi said, her hand a glittering darkly as she held it toward Killian, the deep blue light growing brighter the closer she moved to him. "No one is going to fight you, Killian. As I told you before, we are all here under the same need. We are all taking the same journey. Your claim to the throne stands as long as we are together and the existence of your older sister is hidden. Even then, if that time was to come, that is a battle you and Zoe will need to fight. Right now, our focus is on Elliot, and keeping her existence a secret as long as is needed. It will take all of us to do this."

Killian dropped as Suvi's hand did, her hand releasing him from the awkward stance and sending him to his knees.

The foolish old woman was testing his patience. He could not trust her, and he certainly could not trust Zoe. If it wasn't for the power the old woman held he doubted his sister would be here.

A king would not let anyone, even a witch, live after the treatment he had received. This woman had treated him like a dog, and in front of two who had betrayed their kind.

He would show both her and Zoe what his role was. But now was not the time. No battle of flame or fists could get him there, especially with a witch of her power.

She was more than the fae that served him, and he would not forget that.

"What are you suggesting?" Jarron spoke softly, his arms crossed over his broad chest now that there was no need to stop a fight, although the side long glare he gave his brother made it clear that he knew the danger wasn't gone completely.

Jarron may be an irritating pretty boy, but he was the only one Killian trusted at his side, if only with his usefulness in harnessing Killian's temper. He would need that.

Drake, he could handle.

Standing near Zoe was testing his limits.

"Zoe and Drake gave themselves to save the girl who now holds your souls, I suggest that you calm so that we may follow the lead these two have set," the old woman said, as if that cleared it up.

Killian's temper flared again at the slight dig, but it was Jarron who growled that time, his fingers flexing against his equally as tight forearms.

"We have been searching for it... her... for years, witch." Jarron spat, his voice dark. "We may not have been there in the beginning, but we are here now. Sins can be forgiven, and we are doing our best to rectify ours."

The truth rolled through the night, or at least part of the truth did. They had been searching for the phoenix for years, yes, but not to save her. And certainly not to protect her. Their goal had been to kill it, to remove the chance of their father finding eternal life so that they could, in turn, remove their father.

Now everything was different. And Suvi knew that.

"Good," she said with a nod, her wizened eyes narrowing at Killian as though her gaze alone could dig for the truth.

He wouldn't put it past her.

Carefully keeping his dragon in check, he met her glare head on, his jaw tightening defiantly. "I have been told your goal is to overthrow your father. Is this correct?"

"That is what I have been told," Drake interjected.

Suvi gave him a nod of acknowledgment, but her focus was still on Killian, her ancient eyes digging into him with a steely eyed scowl. He had never known a glare to have a heat behind it, but hers did. It burned right alongside his fire in a heart-wrenching flame, his soul burning with guilt and a need to confess his sins.

Ah, she wasn't looking into his mind. She was pulling the truth from him.

He would like to see the old woman try. He would not let her break him. Thanks to Dabria, he was used to these tricks. He ground his jaw together as he faced her, the darkness of his dragon peering through his eyes as the creature made its own distaste known.

It did not matter how much he fought her power, however, Jarron broke first.

"Our father has been compromised, and the stability of our empire is under threat," he began, his voice a hollow monotone as Suvi pulled the facts out of him.

"You mean more than enslaving and abusing an entire nation? Or decimating over ninety percent of the non-pack shifters in the world?" Zoe snapped, her voice rising above the distant chatter of the last of the audience.

"From what I have heard, yes," Drake responded stepping closer to her and into the dull red and black glow that emanated from the circus tent.

"From what you have heard?" Zoe asked, not believing them, "so you haven't seen it for yourself?"

"How can I? While you were off pretending to be dead, I bore the weight of both our sins and have been banished from our kind. From all shifters! I am a scourge that none will even dare to be around for fear of his backlash." Drake exploded, sounding more furious than Killian had heard him, even Zoe stepped back. If it wasn't for his disappointment in the boy, he may have been proud of him for making the stoic former-princess wilt.

Both the title and her weakness made him smile.

"I trust what Jarron has said," Drake interjected before Zoe had a chance to jump in. "And as much as I hate to say it, I trust Killian. I know what they are feeling for Ellie. I feel that same. They are here for her, and for you. We have the same goal. None of us will do anything to hurt her."

Drake paused, running his hand through his hair as he looked back to the inky night sky. Killian knew what he was searching for. The stars were beautiful, but he knew as well as Drake did that those twinkling lights housed his heart, his soul, his mate.

But not just his...

Killian's heart twisted at the thought, his dragon rearing his head in jealousy. He may have attacked if it was not for what the boy said next.

"You of all people should understand that, Zoe," He whispered, his voice so low that you could barely hear it over the last of the crowds.

Zoe shoulders sagged, her face falling as agony ripped across it, the powerful facade she always held wilting away. But this time, instead of a wicked joy, Killian only felt pain.

When Alian's body was found in the square of the dragon's cave, black and gold stripes covering his skin, Killian had rejoiced along with so many others. The man had seduced the princess. Convinced the heir to run away saying that their dragons had chosen each other as mates.

Their father was certain the royal line to be exempt. And yet, here he stood, his heart pulling him far into the night sky, after a girl he had only met hours before.

His mate.

He couldn't even fathom how he would feel if he lost her, and he wasn't interested in finding out.

"She will be safe," Killian said with a growl, turning from Zoe without another glance. "I will protect that girl with my life, even if I lose her, or lose my crown, it will be worth it to me."

The words were a physical punch to say aloud, after so much work, and so much time, he could never have fathomed that he would give it all up so quickly.

He still wasn't sure.

But he knew that if it came down to it, he would for her. She was his and his alone, he would see to that in the end.

"I am glad to hear that," Suvi cut through his thoughts, her wrinkled face twisting into a smile.

"We may not have stood by Zoe at the start, we may not have seen the extent of the crimes our father committed then," Killian continued before he could think better of it, even though Jarron was giving him a look of warning. "But we saw. And we will overthrow the man who has caused so much pain."

"I believe that we can," Suvi said, shuffling away without anything further.

"Where is she going?" Drake asked in an uncomfortable whisper as they all watched her walk back towards the battered relocatable. She moved much faster than you would think with the hunch in her back.

"She's a witch," Zoe said with a groan, "She needs her bones."

This cleared nothing up, but when Zoe began to follow the old woman, the other three were forced to follow her right back into the trailer they had left.

Thankfully the little man had vacated his portion, but once they had entered the fabric draped corner that the witch called home he almost wished the little man was there to turn them away, like some kind of gatekeeper to the underworld they entered.

This was not the same room they had been in moments before.

The calm had left, leaving the room infused with a deep magic that shook his bones. A darkness spread from the old woman in a wave so strong it was calling to his own black soul. The very air was glittering, sparks of white and red floating through the air like falling stars.

He shouldn't be here. But he couldn't simply leave either. Instead, he straightened his spine, facing the witch without even a hint of fear on his face.

The old woman sat as still as bones in the same chair that Ellie had been in. He could still see the witch there, her skin as white as chalk, but he could still smell the lingering aroma of rose and lavender that was uniquely Elliot. The smell aroused his dragon, even as the creature reared up in fear.

The witch sat with eyes like the dead, staring through

him, seeing nothing but the mass of white her irises had become, the haunting things ringed with ebony. She was vacant, her body still, and if it wasn't for the wax covered feather she twirled in her hands Killian may have thought her dead already.

Everything about this woman screamed danger.

He had grown up with Fae, with their twinkling magic and flowers, and laughter. There was no joy in this magic, he clamped his jaw shut as his siblings slammed into his back. Gasps of panic echoed through the room as they each caught sight of the old woman, Jarron rushing her.

Well, until Zoe bustled passed the three and collapsed into one of the few chairs that were cluttered through the room. She sat in it so casually that it was clear this place was her home.

Or rather, where she had been hiding for the last twenty years.

"You should probably sit down," she mumbled, pulling one of the magazines on to the cluttered coffee table towards her. "She will be a while."

Before Zoe had even finished, however, the strip of monochrome in the old Witch's eyes faded away, back to a dull brown that dug into each of them in turn. Drake had not been paying attention, for he jumped to the ceiling when the old bat stared into him.

"The path that awaits you is difficult, but will lead in victory," she said, looking straight into Drake as he began to shake.

"Will we be able to defeat him?" Drake asked, his voice stronger than Killian had expected.

"You will be able to do many things once you are able to work together." There was more there than Killian wanted to admit, the vague wording grinding against him.

He wasn't the only one.

"I don't like where this is going." Jarron moaned from somewhere to his left.

"You must restrain your mating instinct boys," She said, tapping her teapot and sending the thing to brew. "I have restricted Elliot, but you three should also be aware of your needs. Mating is serious business."

Killian couldn't stop the snicker, the old woman couldn't control that. He wouldn't let her control that.

"I do not know if I can restrain my dragon to that," Jarron said honestly. Killian would have attacked him with the admission, if he did not trust the man. His trust did not allow his dragon to bark any less, however. "She is mine as much as she is everyone else's. I love her the same, and I know we all wish to be with her."

"No, Suvi is right," Drake rebutted, his voice shaking. "I feel the same. But running off to some orgy is not going to help anyone."

"Woah!" Jarron said, jumping to his feet. "Who said anything about an orgy, because I did not sign up for that, least of all with you two."

"Gross," Zoe cut in. "Can we back up? We need to make sure our focus stays on Ellie, and on keeping her safe. That includes dethroning the monster that created us. Let's get past that first. For you, but mostly for her. Trust me when I say you don't want to push her. Sex or otherwise."

Killian's dragon did not like that, but he did not push it away, either. If he was to abide by it, then his brothers would as well. Zoe was right, he had to control his instincts, they had no idea what a mating to all three would do to her, and if that was part of protecting her than so be it.

He would be with her in the end.

The thought, no, the promise of it, brought a smile to his face.

"I think it might be for the best," Killian said, his heart aching with the agreement.

Every muscle in his shoulders was tense as he looked to his brothers, glaring at them in defiance. For Drake, the message was easily sent, and the smallest of them backed down, dropping his gaze with a shake of his head. Jarron, however, met his stare head-on, his dark eyes nearly pure gold with the strength of his dragon.

Challenge met.

"Perfect," Suvi said, interrupting the staring match with a snap and handing Killian one of her many chipped cups.

He took it without looking, unwilling to look away from his brother just yet. The golden prince may bed most of the women, but this one he would not win.

"Because you will need your wits about you in order for this plan to work."

"What plan?" Jarron said, pulling his focus as he accepted his own cup of steaming blue tea.

"Destroying your father's kingdom," Suvi said with a grin that revealed a golden tooth, Killian was surprised that Jarron didn't make a jump for the glittering thing. "Not just him. But all of it."

"How are we supposed to do that?" Drake said, setting his own cup in his lap as he cast Zoe a glance that screamed pure fear. Killian barely restrained the chuckle. "We weren't even close to success last time, and then we had all of the fae on our side."

"Not all," Suvi said under her breath.

Her words were cut off by Jarron, who fixed her with a wink and smile. "You didn't have me, baby brother, and just you wait to see what I can do for you."

"Leave your pettiness out of this boys," Suvi scolded with a look. "We have an even better weapon. Although she will need some training."

"No!" Zoe nearly screamed, sending the contents of the cluttered coffee table into a scatter as she threw her magazine onto the hard surface. "You can't be serious. She is not ready."

"She will be fine," Suvi said calmly, drinking her own tea as she fiddled with the bones on the desk beside her. "The spirits have shown her safety. She is ready."

"Just this morning she cast the bones and showed her death!" Zoe was getting more and more hysterical, her voice rising with each syllable until she may as well have been screaming.

The sound, the reaction. It grated on Killian. How could he trust a woman so volatile?

"It could be death of another," Suvi said so quietly she might as well have been whispering. "I can see the path, and with everyone in place the future is clearer than it has ever been."

"How many peacocks did you sacrifice to get that answer?" Zoe scoffed, smoke drifting from her nostrils in curls and waves.

"What in the world are you two on about?" Killian finally interrupted with a snarl, unable to take it anymore.

"Suvi hasn't just been binding her phoenix from mortals, she has been binding her phoenix completely," Zoe said, still refusing to look away from the woman who was now grinning and leaning against the large mahogany desk.

"You mean..." Killian asked, trying to piece everything together. "How can she be binding her shifter, we saw her shift."

"And we were amazed when she did the first time.

Threw herself off a building and bragged about it the next day," Zoe said, finally looking away from Suvi to face him, her eyes meeting his in a non-hostile way for the first time. "She shouldn't be able to call the beast let alone shift."

"Damn," Jarron said with a sigh, leaning back in his chair. "My mate is fucking awesome."

Killian didn't think he could have put it better.

He also didn't think he had ever been more determined to win someone's heart.

If only he knew how.

17

ELLIOT

ALL THE WAY UP HERE THE AIR BURNED LIKE ICE IN MY LUNGS.

Every breath burned, the breezes cutting through my wings and as though they had been plunged into ice water. Everything was ice. A dark abyss of ice, surrounded by nothing but stars. The city was far behind, and any illuminated houses were so far below that they only added to the sparkling sea that I was streaming through.

A sea of ice and stars.

It was cold, and even though I could feel the burn of that chill, it was quickly swallowed by the burn of my flame.

The flames devoured the chill of the air into a hiss of purple smoke, adding it to the long trail of soot my phoenix left behind.

Flames. Smoke. Ice.

It reminded me of the boys. Each one matched me in their own way.

The thought was a stab right through my gut, and I called out, the cry of my phoenix mixing with my own in an oddly strangled note.

With every flap of my wings my heart pulled me back, my soul begging me to follow the string that was tethering me to the tent, toward the truth and lies and everything else I had left behind. Back to them.

I can't go, I sobbed to myself, knowing that in so many ways it was a bitter lie.

It wouldn't take much to turn around, to fly back to them and fall into their arms. To let them wrap around me, and hold me.

Ugh. Could I stop wanting them for one freakin' minute? I had flown away to get away from them, to breathe without smelling them, without wanting them. But it was worse here, worse in this skin, in the mind that desired them even more.

They are ours, Elliot. Go to them. The whispering voice of the Phoenix ran through my mind, the pulse of heat growing as the string in my heart tightened, pulling me away.

Before I could stop it, my wide wings began to twist, turning me to the side, cutting through the sky and sending me back towards them all.

Phoenix song rang out through the night, my heart swelling in eager pride at the movement. The bastard organ was betraying me.

Except that it wasn't.

I wanted this. Oh lord, I wanted this. Wanted them. Their souls, their dragons, their arms all tangled.

Crap.

I was soaring right back to exactly where I shouldn't be.

I don't know them, I pleaded, but the sensation of want and need grew deeper, my own mind battling right alongside.

I pushed left, my soul pushed right, and with a scream, sparks and flame exploded from the massive maw of my beak in a streak of red that shot like a javelin.

Holy shit! What in the world was that?

Shock froze my heart, even as I continued to soar forward, following the stream of red before it exploded in ribbons of fireworks and flame.

Holy, holy shit!

Less than an hour before I had watched flame explode from my best friend, watched smoke and flame explode from my hands, and now I was spitting bombs.

Could I go back to jumping off buildings?

No, I couldn't because everything had changed. It changed with three men, and their freaking gorgeous smiles.

I couldn't go back to what I was.

Because right then I was going forward, I was going home.

To them.

And it pissed me the hell off.

Keeping the beak of my phoenix snapped shut, I forced my wings down, steering myself away from the string, away from them. I wasn't ready. I would soar forever if I had to, just until I got my head of straight.

I mean, if I could, because doing that was going to be impossible. With every inch I moved away from them, an ache ripped through my bones, fire sparking over my feathers in golden waves.

Oh look, another new super freaky thing that I could do.

I hadn't made it more than a few strides before my phoenix began to turn back again, the two sides of me battling it out.

Light rippled through my feathers as I fought myself, my

wings twisted and spun until like an umbrella in a snowstorm, my wings crumpled, and I began to tumble back down to the ground.

Fire rippled through my feathers, smoke enveloping me as the cold air blanketed me, as the stars below me grew closer.

No, not stars, I reminded myself, *houses.*

I didn't even try to fight it, I let myself fall, watching feathers and fire fall behind me like a meteorite..

A falling star.

Give me time, I pleaded to the stars, as if I was speaking to them, and not to the beauty that was my soul. *I love them. I want them. I just need time.*

The words seeped into my blood, into my bones, into me. They pressed against me as my fire grew, a burst of flame seeping from the tip of every feather and with a bright spark, the stars vanished, the cold air was gone, and I was flying again, high above the stars on the earth. Nearly touching the stars above, hundreds of feet above where I was before.

I didn't know what happened, and I didn't know why, but I wasn't going to question.

I had had about enough of weird things happening.

Don't take too long, the whisper of my soul tickled my spine, my song following close behind as I unfurled my wings, and pulled myself around, soaring through the dark, and away from the tight pull of the string.

Away from them.

Through the pain in my bones, the aches in my soul.

I knew I had to face it, I knew I couldn't soar away forever, but I needed a moment, one breath of air and a moment to just be me again.

Because if everything I had heard was true, this may be the last chance I would get.

The last time everything could be considered normal.

18

ELLIOT

Zoe was sitting on my bed when I returned to my room shortly after midnight.

I was cranky, naked, covered in ash, and still very much desiring to be alone. Seeing her there was as far from a pleasant surprise as finding mushrooms in your mashed potatoes. Ew.

She looked up as I entered, expecting something from me. I wasn't in the mood to give her anything more than a glare and the hard slam of the door as I excused myself to my hot shower.

Cranking the heat as hot as I could, I tried to let the water melt away the angry tension that was still consuming my muscles.

All it removed, however, was the last of the ash that flowed down the drain in spirals of glitter, and possibly the top layer of skin.

It was good that I could take the heat, but it didn't stop me from exiting the shower looking like anything other than a freshly skinned and overly pink rabbit.

The mirror squeaked as I wiped the condensation away,

leaving a trail of water spots and a clear window to my olive skin and bright red hair.

Born of a dragon.

Fueled by a phoenix.

I wasn't sure I knew myself anymore.

I stared at myself the way teens do in movies, but instead of contemplating the size of my nose, or trying to imagine myself with freckles and blue eyes, I tried to calm my shifter down.

You know, normal teen stuff.

"It'll be okay," I told both of us, forcing anyone within hearing distance to believe it.

It seemed to work. With each slow breath, a little bit more of the gold heat of my flame began to leave my eyes, the fire slowly reducing to a tiny flare around my pupil.

Close to gone, still not calm. She was right below the surface, humming for answers, for the boys, for flight. For anything.

"Everything is going to be okay."

Well, 'okay' as far as being protected or mated or whatever to Zoe's brothers.

I scowled at the door to the bathroom through the mirror, the painted white slab feeling like some kind of portal.

Portal to answers.

Portal to men.

"Will you settle down?" I grumbled to my phoenix, the heat in my blood cooling as I wrapped myself in a towel.

Thankfully, this time, I could feel a low purr rumble deep in my chest.

I was going to take that as a good sign.

I had always talked to my phoenix, it's what you do when

you are six, alone, and filled with an alter ego that you can't tell anyone about.

And even if you do you would probably be carted away to some insane asylum, not like talking to my phoenix did me any favors. I was branded as weird for a reason.

The girl who talks to herself.

Suvi's spell kept most of my abilities locked away. I wasn't even able to shift until I was fourteen, and even then the old witch tried to spell away the creature like some sort of vampire banishment thing.

Not that I know if those are real, but at this point I was going to take everything on the internet like it was gold.

Because, you know... I have three mates now.

Before I could stop myself, I was scowling at the door through the mirror again, the gold flaring through my eyes.

"Fine," I said with a bit too much snap, knowing I couldn't put it off anymore. "Zoe. Answers. Guys."

My heart somehow managed to both twist and pick up tempo simultaneously.

Zoe was still sitting on my bed when I left the bathroom, fluffy white towel still secured around me. She sat up expectantly, something that did not help the song and dance number my heart was attempting to participate in.

"I'm back, I'm safe, and I didn't kill any villagers," I mumbled as I shed the towel and threw a long sleep shirt over my head, still refusing to look at her.

"Normally it's the dragons who kill the villagers," Zoe said, with the tiniest hint of a laugh.

"You aren't helping." The words ground through my teeth. "In fact, the only way I can see you helping is if you leave me alone."

Before I could do anything I would regret, I turned away from her, content to ignore her presence and instead rustled through the drawers in search of underwear. Anything to keep my hands busy, and not throw something.

Like this dresser. Or this really nice flat screen TV that was to my left. I didn't think either would be too difficult.

"Letting you embrace your angst in peace isn't going to help anyone."

"Well," I began, choosing a pair of white lacey things I had bought somewhere in Spain. "If I am going to embrace my angst, I would prefer not to do it with a complete stranger."

She looked at me as though I had slapped her.

"I deserved that."

Couldn't she at least fight back? Did she need to be so darn... agreeable? I grumbled, and tripped as I finished stepping into the fresh undies. Fuming, I turned to face the woman who sat cross legged on my king bed, the blankets around her mussed enough that I was sure she had taken a nap before I had arrived.

"What are you doing here, Zoe?" I asked, the last of my frustration pushing into my voice. "And don't say making sure I got home safe. I don't think I can handle being coddled anymore. I will be eighteen in a few days—"

"I'm keeping my brothers out of your room if you must know," she interrupted me, not making eye contact as she suddenly became very interested in a loose thread on her warm ups. "They don't like the idea of you being alone, and I don't like the idea of three strange men sharing your bed."

"Well, there's one thing we agree on."

"Can we turn down the drama a bit?" Zoe said, with a snap. I was obviously wearing on her patience a bit. Unlucky for her, I didn't give a damn. "I get it, you think we lied to you—"

"You *did* lie to me," I interrupted her, folding my arms

over my chest. Holding onto the dresser right then was not feeling like a good idea.

Throwing it at her may not be top of my list anymore, but breaking the darn thing in half was becoming more and more of a possibility.

"No, we kept scary things from you," Zoe said, as if that fixed it. It didn't. It just brought all of that rage

"Scary things?" I am pretty sure I was starting to sound hysterical. "I'm not five Zoe. And now, apparently I mate mated...bonded... whatever... to three..." hot dragons. I swallowed. "If you won't give me answers, I am sure one of them will."

I slammed the still open drawer closed with my hip and was ready to burst out of the room and find them, something that I was sure wouldn't be too hard with how my heart was pulling away from me, like some kind of sexy dragon sonar.

I didn't even care that I wasn't wearing pants.

"Stop!" Zoe yelled before I moved more than two steps, her eyes wide as she reached toward me, ready to launch herself off the bed. "Seriously, you have got to stop running away from me."

"Staying around you isn't helping," I stammered, taking a quick step back. "What else do you want me to do, Zoe?"

"Stick around and face your problems like an adult."

Ouch.

I could feel the sting of that across my chest, hot and ridged. Talk about the ultimate truth-slap.

As much as I didn't, and wouldn't, admit it – she was right. And I hated it.

Stuck as a mortal? Run off a cliff.

Mad you didn't get a role? Run off a cliff.

Meet three sexy men? There may not have been a cliff, but there was certainly a lot of running.

Except that wasn't entirely true. I didn't run from Suvi when she told me to go chill in my hotel room like I was a lost dog, and I didn't run from the guys until it became clear they were dangerous.

"I'm only running because I don't know what's going on," I said, the hard line of my voice quivering as the painful truth began to take its place. "All you have told me is to run. Dragon king? Run. Shifters? Run. You expect me to sense them, to know details about them, but you refuse to tell me anything. If you don't want me to run, then you have got to tell me what's going on."

I froze, the two of us locked in a stare as I tried to decide if I could trust her, and that alone was breaking my heart. Zoe had always been the one person I could count on, the one person I could trust.

Right then, all of that lay in shards on the floor.

I kicked my toe into the carpet, imagining little pieces of trust rolling over the low pile industrial rug like marbles.

I was doubting if any of them were going to go back together.

"What do you want to know?" Her voice was soft, and she wasn't looking at me, but those few words were like something of a miracle. A miracle that shown clear on my face, complete with open jaw and wide eyes.

This wasn't going to be like before, some rushed conversation in a dressing room. I would keep her up all night if I had too.

"Let's start with everything." I blurted out, wiping the fish-out-of-water look from my face. I wasn't going to miss this opportunity.

Her face fell.

"Let's start with the bonding," she offered in return. Ironically, that was the one thing I felt I had a grasp on.

She patted the comforter next to her, something which I stubbornly ignored, choosing instead to sink into the dated arm chair, arms folded.

"You mean that I bonded to three hot guys that so happen to be your brothers, and if I... ummm... sleep," did my voice squeak? I was pretty sure my voice squeaked, "with any of them then I'll be mated to them. Oh! And they also get to protect me from your wicked daddy who wants to kill me."

Zoe's jaw hardened, her arms folding over her chest as her nostrils flared in an exhale.

Yeah, I probably stole her thunder. Didn't make me any less smug.

"My wicked daddy wants to kill you so he can live forever and keep enslaving magical creatures and eating mortals for breakfast."

Well, that wiped the smug right off my face.

Damn. That was so much more than I had been expecting. If I thought I had a fish out of water look before, it was nothing to now.

"Eating..." Anything else I had been planning to say got stuck in my throat, trapped behind fear and what I was sure was bile.

"He is not a nice man, Elliot," Zoe said, her eyes digging into mine so intently that if I could move through the chair to get away from her I probably would have. "I wasn't lying when I said I would kill you before I let him get his hands on you. I'm not the only one."

"Noted," I said, grabbing the worn, yet decorative, pillow from the chair and wrapping my arms around it, like some sort of dragon shield.

"So it's a bit more than just skinning me alive, I take it?" I swallowed, and a tiny smile pierced the corner of her mouth. Yeah, that wasn't making me feel any better.

"Uhh yeah, just a bit. Your blood is magic. The phoenix grants you eternal life, and he wants that. He doesn't want to die, and he certainly doesn't want his children to take control of his kingdom. It took Killian and Jarron far too long to realize that."

Normally, mentioning any of those three would send my heart into furious palpitations, not this time, the deep growl in Zoe's voice had zapped it right out of me.

"Am I sensing some sibling rivalry?"

"No," she cut me off, "more like sibling irritations." Her focus burrowed to the door, as if the three of them were standing right on the other side, glaring right back. "But I think Suvi is right, with what is coming, it's good that you have all three of them. They are incredibly strong, and if they can figure out how to work together, there is no way we can lose."

I really didn't like the way she was talking.

"Wait, what are we losing?"

"You," she answered a little too quickly, and I jerked a bit, the word feeling like a whip against my back. "We aren't going to lose you."

I know she was trying to calm me, make some solemn promise or something, but it was hard to take it that way now that she wasn't sugar coating or hiding things.

"You said *we*. Does that mean you are including yourself in that?"

"There is no way in hell that I am letting you out of my sight," she said mischievously, leaning over the bed to me. "Especially with my three dumb brothers suddenly fighting their dragons over you."

"They are not..." I started, the imagery of massive battling dragons a bit too clear after what I had seen last night.

And I had never seen a dragon, just the flames of one.

I shuddered. Zoe noticed, and smiled.

"You do not want to bet me on that. Those three will fight over you," she teased, fixing me with a brow-raising smile that dropped right to my toes, an odd swooping sensation following behind.

Hearing her talk about them that way was sending me headfirst into a crazy hormone driven wonderland.

But not the Alice kind, the scary one where dragon kings hunt you and you want to attach yourself to some hot guy with eyes that burn like emeralds, or brown sugar or...

"You sound like a mom." I teased, determined to push my hormones back into reality.

"No, I sound like someone who fought too long and too hard to keep you alive. You may not have bonded to me," she continued, eyes blazing. "I may not love you like my brothers do, I may not be connected to you in the same way, but I am here for you. I won't let you face the beast alone."

Each word dug into me with all the strength and honesty that I had known from her. It was one of the biggest reasons she was my friend. Even past the shifters we hid inside of us, her sanity worked well with my flighty off the wall lunacy.

The last shreds of foolish anger that I was clinging to slipped away, the tension in my heart eased a bit, and I may have actually vaulted off the chair and onto the bed, taking the tall lanky dragon back with me.

"Oof," she grunted as we fell back onto the hard mattress.

"Plus, how can I be your mom if I am going to be your

sister-in-law some day?" She poked my side teasingly, but she might as well be poking a stone statue.

"Oh. My. God."

I may have yelled.

"It's not going to happen, Zoe," I said, arms wrapped over my waist as I stared at the ceiling. "Not only because of the..." don't say mating, don't say mating. "... marriage." That was so much worse, and Zoe's over exaggerated snort wasn't helping.

I exhaled, "But because there are three of them."

"I have done you an injustice not teaching you of our ways," Zoe said, sounding so much like an old guru that I would have laughed, if not for what she said.

"You aren't telling me that it's normal for female shifters to have three mates?"

"No, that one is all on you," she laughed, poking me again. "It's what you get for having a crazy strong shifter, and a crazy scary future. Evil dragon kings to overthrow or kill or whatever."

"Gee thanks." I was really starting to second-guess this whole knowing everything thing. Especially with how much Zoe was talking about the scary impending doom of my future.

"At least I am strong enough to face it."

That one was all for me, thankfully Zoe didn't totally call my bluff, instead she grabbed my hand.

"So are they," she began, the guru vibes growing. "Their dragon's had to see through Suvi's spell to even be able to sense your shifter, and even then they thought you were a dragon. When I look at you I only see a clumsy mortal. I only see your phoenix shine out of your eyes about half the time. I tend to tell by your scowl as to when she is peeking out."

"So you have been leading me on all this time?" I asked, sitting up on my elbows to look at her. Zoe, shrugged like it was nothing, the action making her face twist up funny. "You are the worst friend ever, Zoe."

I let my teen flag fly with that, flopping back down onto the bed beside her and folding my arms.

"Or the best," Zoe said, nudging me once with her elbow and sending me a quirky smile.

"Fine, best-friend Zoe," I said, pulling the pillow out from under my head and smacking her with it. "Tell me something."

"I enjoy mint ice cream, and chick flick binges, I'm looking for a man who can—"

"Tell me about my dad." I stopped her ramble with a whisper that might as well have been a hand grenade.

She stopped. I stopped. Hell, time might have stopped for the silence that stretched on.

"I will tell you anything within reason," she said, hitting me with her own pillow in an attempt to break the tension that was swallowing us.

Instead of fighting back however, I held on, pressing the squishy thing against me as I kept my focus on the rippling ceiling, my mind finding every dragon shaped squiggle there was.

"Why did they act like that when I said my name?" I spoke very quickly, before I lost my courage.

"How did they act?"

"They stood, staring at me like they were ready to bow down and offer me gold."

She chuckled, "that's probably because they were."

"Ummm I was kidding." I tried to force out a laugh, but it didn't work too well.

"I wasn't. You were named after your father," Zoe said,

grabbing the pillow I held and tucking it behind her head and settling in. "Elliot was something of an oracle to our clan, to all dragons. The strongest and oldest of the dragons, he began the relationship with the fae long before I was born and brought them into our fold. He was my father's beta. He was also the one to lead the coup to overthrow him."

"A coup?" I had seen enough of the world to know what that word meant, and that they never ended well.

Judging by the look on Zoe's face this one hadn't ended well either.

"What happened?"

Zoe pressed her lips together, pinching her eyes shut until two tiny drops of wet dripped down her cheeks. Zoe crying was as rare as rain in the desert; just seeing the wetness pressed painfully against my heart.

"By the time you were hatched, my father had enslaved the Fae and conspired with the vampires in an attempt to overthrow many of the shifter tribes of the world. Drake, your father, and I led about five hundred dragons, wolves, and fae in an effort to overthrow him. Up until a few hours ago I thought I was the only one who had survived. Your father died in that fight, I watched mine strike him down."

I flinched. I couldn't help it. Once upon a time, Suvi had told me he had died, but the knowledge had been numb and meaningless.

But now there was something in the way Zoe talked about it, that made it a bit more real.

That made him more real. Not just some guy that ditched his problem child.

Maybe I was loved.

Maybe I was protected.

"You saw him die?" My voice caught, the sounds tumbling out of my emotions as my own tears began to fall.

This time I didn't try to hide them, I let them fall, each one staining my cheeks as I met my father for the first time.

She nodded, "Yes, his last words were for you. Killian heard them, he was right there, holding Drake."

I didn't think anything she said could make me feel worse, but that did, and not in the emotional pneumonia I was coming down with, but in a heart stopping panic.

"Why was Killian holding Drake?"

Zoe shifted, the bed sagging under her weight as she exhaled with a sound that only spelled trouble. There was no way I could brace for what was coming.

"Killian and Jarron did not fight with Drake and I."

What the holy saint on a bicycle? No. Hearing that was like being struck by a battering ram, ran over my a million grandpas with walkers and given a stale candy as a consolation prize. My heart clenched, my phoenix screamed, and what little air that was in this room became as heavy as glue.

I was sure I had stopped time, but I didn't check. I lay still, trapped in the weird stunned silence until words finally returned, and my skin didn't feel like it was melting.

"They fought against you?" Each word hurt to say, the words painting a picture that I was fighting very hard to acknowledge.

"They did what they thought was right." Even I could tell she was trying to sugar coat it, and that didn't make it any better.

They had fought against Zoe. Against my dad. They had killed my dad. Worse, they had wanted to kill me and I was a baby or toddler, or egg, or whatever.

"So I was right to run," I said, each word as dead and

pained as I felt. "How can I trust they won't just feed me to the dragon..." that phrase didn't work very well in this context, it was way too close for comfort.

"From what they told me last night they have been hunting for you for the past few years, attempting to reach you before my dad does."

"So I can trust them?" I asked, looking away from the dragon-squiggle ceiling to Zoe, as she sat up so quick that I jumped.

"I need you to listen to me Elliot," Zoe said, her voice hard as she leaned over me. "Their dragon's have bonded to yours. Their hearts are yours. Just as yours is theirs. That instinct is strong enough that they can't do anything to stop it. I know."

"How—"

"Trust them," Zoe interrupted flopping back down on the bed beside me. "They are yours now. That, and they are good guys. Even Killian, I think."

I think?

"You aren't giving me much confidence."

"You'll see what I mean. Just do me a favor, Ellie," Zoe said, as she snuggled into me.

"Hmmm?" It was the only noise I could force to the surface.

"Don't have sex with my brothers."

Poke me and call me done. A few words and I was on high alert. I jerked violently as I was assaulted with a million heart pumping very much not PG images. Tasting Jarron. Kissing Drake. Seeing where Killian's tattoo goes...

Pinching my eyes shut wasn't helping expel the images. They were just as bright, my heart beat insanely loud. And warm... oh my god... how did I get so warm. I swallowed, crossed my legs, and forced every single image from my mind.

"Excuse me?" I said, my voice cracking.

"Don't get me wrong," Zoe said flippantly, thankfully ignoring to the hormone eruption I was trying to keep at bay. "They are good guys, but I don't know what mating with them will do to you, or them. For all I know your soul will explode in a million sparks of hormones."

Forget trying to force the images away, they were instantly gone. Just like my breath and that warm fuzzy feeling.

"I'm not quite sure what you are saying. Are you saying having sex with them, will make me explode."

She smirked. I was evidently missing something.

"I dunno, maybe it's a sibling rivalry thing, they already fight enough." She waved her hand into the air as she turned over, curling into the side of the bed like a disgruntled lover and quickly turning off the conversation.

Ugh now who is the angsty childish one?

"Don't do anything yet, okay?" She said as she turned off the lamp beside the bed.

Hint taken.

I wanted to say fine, but the warmth that was crippling me was telling me a different story.

There was something else there, something she wasn't telling, something she was hiding. And for once I was glad of it, all the something's she had already told me were bound to haunt my nightmares.

Add to that the impending doom of sex with the guys, and everything in me was nerves. Because, let's face it: I really, *really* want that. I want to be with them, I want to touch them and kiss them and lay with them. I want them. All of them. But knowing that I may never be with them in that way, was an odd realization that left a gaping painful hole in my chest, the sound of my heart echoing through the open forgotten spaces.

I listened to my heart pound, my mind dreaming of kisses and battles and every other *scary* thing Zoe had told me until the dragon squiggles in the ceiling began to move, and their distorted wings took flight with tiny streaks of fire charging before them.

It was all an illusion of my sleep deprived mind, but it didn't matter, it was beautiful, and it lulled me to sleep as well as the thought of the guys lips against mine.

19

ELLIOT

I was dying.

Okay, maybe I wasn't dying. But I sure as hell felt like I was being turned inside out, like some kind of demon from a bad 1960s horror movie.

Not that I was judging, but the 1960s was a bad time for horror. Especially German horror. I had seen that exact scenario in an old run down theatre in Germany when I was ten. I shouldn't have been anywhere near a movie with that much blood at that age, but I didn't speak German and there weren't many options between performances. Even then it didn't so much scare me as embed me with imagery of inside-out people and the aroma of booze.

One of which I had completely forgotten about until I woke up feeling like I had been steamrolled.

An inside-out pancake.

I didn't think it was possible for bones to ache like this.

"Oh my god," I moaned, trying to lift myself from where I had burrowed into the blankets. I barely moved. Even though I had managed to get my arm out from underneath me there was no way it was going to be able to support my weight.

My expletives were drowned by my pillow as I collapsed back into it, spine-rattling like a child's xylophone.

"I might be dying," I said to the pillow, as if the fluffy thing could hear me.

"You aren't dying."

If I could move, I probably would have jumped fifteen feet straight up, which would have been a feat seeing as I was laying on my stomach like some kind of bed slug.

That's what I was. A bed slug.

In my bone twisting pain, I had completely forgotten that Zoe had stayed over to protect my bed and my virtue from her brothers.

My stomach instantly become a knot. Couldn't the freaking sexual awakening give me a break for more than twenty-four hours? I wasn't asking for much, but judging by the way the treacherous organ was pulling my soul away from me, I couldn't count on it.

I was pretty sure if I closed my eyes and started walking I would run headlong into one of them.

"I am pretty sure I am dying," I moaned as I twisted my head toward Zoe, expecting to see her looking as disheveled as I felt.

But no, the girl looked flawless, like one of those yoga models you see in an "I just got up" Instagram shot that is way too staged.

Her hair was pulled into a perfectly messy side braid, not an under eye circle in sight as she sat cross-legged on my bed with a cup of coffee in her hand. A single bare shoulder was exposed through one of my too-big white t-shirts that I liked to warm up in. Thief.

I don't think I could ever make the tattered hand-me-down look that good, I might as well give it to her. Anytime I would wear it from now on would be substandard.

"Not dying," she said again as if that made it all better. "You are having man withdrawals."

"It's too early for jokes, Zoe," I grumbled, trying once again to pull myself up and failing.

"Not a joke." Even her teasing smile was flawless. "I've seen far too many dragons, and even some wolves, go through this. Although not as bad."

She took another sip, twerking her eyebrow at me as she did so. Nothing of what she was saying was making me feel all warm and snuggly inside.

"I am pretty sure I just have broken a bone." Or shattered one... or twenty.

Zoe's lips twisted curiously as she looked at me from over her coffee cup, her eyes sparkling with some kind of eagerness that I instantly wanted to smack off her.

"What?" I asked darkly, my voice distorted from the way my lips were sagging against mattress and pillow.

"This is the mates connection," she said, setting her coffee cup in her lap. "I have never seen it so bad you can't move, though. But it would make sense."

I glared at her in question, not interested in trying to talk into the pillow again. I didn't need to become more of a bed slug beside the morning queen.

"Triple the boys. Triple the skin-buzzing need. Your soul wants them, Elliot."

"Wants them?" I am amazed she heard that through the pillow. "How can I want someone I don't even know?"

She nodded, "Contact, connection, you are having withdrawals from your mate. Or bonded pair since sex is off the table. You know the drill. I've seen you scour those teen fandom sites before. You can't not be around them. So, you are going to have to get to know them."

I groaned, she smiled, and took a drink of her coffee. Like hell if I was going to let that be a thing. My body needed the boys? Nu-uh. My body needed coffee and a workout.

I mean, I wouldn't say no to a hug. Or to a hand...

I groaned louder, I was not going to dive back into the rabbit hole. Not today. Wanting them? Yes, sure, I could go for that. Needing them to touch me or something so I could feel normal? I was so not okay with this.

"Or... I just broke a bone." Saying it louder would obviously make it real. Zoe, however, didn't seem to agree with me. She chuckled and leapt from the bed. Hopefully to grab me a cup of coffee. I was going to need it.

"Just remember no sex."

"Wow, thanks Zoe. Because I needed that reminder. Again." And also the overdrive of butterflies to make a reappearance. Luckily, I blocked any of those heart-pounding fantasies from taking over before my bed slug turned into something a bit more active.

Determined not to let bonding, mating dragon-men become the ruler of my bone health I began pushing myself up, gritting my teeth through every agonizing motion. I was determined not to let her hear a peep. I would drink a whole gallon of milk if I had too.

I was going to kill the bed slug right now.

Arm shaking, I propped myself up like a camera tri-pod and shifted my weight until I leaned against the headboard like a piece of crumpled origami, head twisted somewhere below my armpit.

Well this was awesome.

As flexible as I was, I wasn't uncomfortable, well, other

than the bone splitting "I need my men" pain I was trying to ignore.

Even with that I was sure I looked like something out of a horror movie.

Forget the inside out pancake people, I was a twisted zombie from hell.

A very stuck twisted zombie from hell.

Sure enough, the second Zoe turned from the tiny kitchenette to face me, she shrieked, jumped, and promptly dropped the two cups of coffee she had poured, sending brown liquid to splash over her, covering the hem of my shirt.

I would have laughed if I was able to get any air into my lungs; and if I wasn't mourning the loss of my coffee. I really needed that.

"Oooo," I taunted her, my sarcastic scoff nowhere near frightening.

Zoe's fear melted to humor and she broke down in a fit of giggles, coffee stains forgotten as she rushed to help me out of my predicament. Which was good, because I was starting to be concerned that my head was going to pop off with the pretzel I had gotten myself into.

"I'm going to have to call them, you know," She said as she leaned me against the headboard, making me feel very much like a toy that had lost its stuffing.

"Don't you dare," I threatened, even as my heart thundered a resounding 'yes!'. "I am ninety percent sure I can power through this. I just need coffee, some protein, and a good run."

"You can't even lift yourself off the bed and you want a 'good run'?"

"The coffee will wake me up." Lifting my chin, I looked

her dead in the eye, putting as much smug determination into my eyes as I could.

Unluckily for me, Zoe saw right through it.

"Don't make me knock you over."

"You wouldn't dare!" The wicked look in Zoe's eyes returned before I could finish speaking, her sharp little forefinger poking into the tender flesh of my shoulder, pressing, threatening.

Little by little, pushing me over. Like a freaking tree in the forest.

"I'm calling my brothers."

I flopped over before I could protest, sending me back into the pillow as a knock reverberated from the door.

"Open up, Zoe," A rough voice that I recognized at once rippled through the heavy wood door and I instantly found myself filling with both need and a weird belly rumbling fear that I hadn't experienced before.

Fear and Desire. They tumbled together as I lay there, unable to move, as the man who was there when my father died stepped into the room.

I swallowed, Killian looked as amazingly hot as his sister did in the morning. Except with him it was more like mouth watering attraction.

I was pretty sure it was morning, not that I had seen a clock or anything. It smelled like morning. The damp air from the partially opened window twisted with the smell of rain and dirt, the smell combining with that dim yellow light I had come to associate with this place, the dull light of dawn as the sun spent hours trying to clear the mountains that surrounded the valley.

It was morning, and Killian was still dressed as though he was going to a dinner party. He had, however, lost the full four piece ensemble I had seen him in before. Instead, he wore a light grey number that was perfectly laid over his broad shoulders, tugging over his arms...

My heart flickered. Damn it. Fear and Desire was right. I could still feel the pain of what Zoe had told me, but I still wanted him.

"Elliot!" He said with that same warming rumble as he rushed me, kneeling on the floor so that his face was nearly level with mine, those glittering eyes melting right into me. "Are you okay?"

So much for a mate's connection. The way Zoe spoke about it I had expected the guys to be invalids themselves. But no, Killian walked in as if it was nothing.

"How come you get to walk?" I said through the pillow, my voice so muffled between squished lips and overused feathers that I wasn't sure he had heard me.

It didn't matter if he did. He could have heard gibberish for all I cared, all worry was wiped from me with the look he gave me.

With the smile that blossomed over his face.

I had seen him smile before, but then it was a dark teasing grin that rumpled me in all the right ways. This one boiled through me, the warm grin bleeding into his eyes and making him look... dare I say it, happy?

"Good morning, Ellie girl," he whispered, pressing his hand against my neck, letting his thumb softly trace the skin there.

If his touch was like fire before, that intensity was swallowed in the waves of energy that were pressing into me. Devouring me like a soft blanket that you want to wrap up in. Heat radiated through my muscles, pressing into my bones as the crippling pressure began to leave, as the pain began to melt away, and I began to melt away.

I couldn't turn off the voice in the back of my head,

warning me to stay away, but I couldn't stop myself either. I leaned into his touch, a soft whimper rattling in my chest. He smiled at the sound, and leaned closer, so close that I could smell the smoke and mint aroma that usually followed him around.

"Is that better?" He asked in that signature husky whisper.

I couldn't find it in myself to nod, but it must have been clear in my eyes because he smiled and leaned closer, pressing his forehead against mine. The brilliant green of his eyes soaked me before he closed them, sending another wave of energy over me, and another low moan escaping from my lips.

"What are you doing?" I asked, glad when the question was more air than pillow.

"Connecting with you," a voice that was as familiar said from behind his brother.

My eyes popped open, half expecting to see Jarron had taken his brother's place, but it was still Killian's green eyes, still that soft smile that made his face light up in an entirely different way.

"Feel better, Ellie girl?" Killian asked as he began to pull away, the soft light in his eyes fading with every inch he put between us.

I nodded numbly, my heart pulling in a million different directions as I watched him go, watching the light in his eyes fade back to that same scowl I had seen last night.

Yes, I felt better, my bones didn't feel quite so much like they were going to splinter and fall out of me. But seeing Killian's face darken into the same scowl twisted my emotions in a different way that was almost as painful.

"Good morning, darling," Jarron said as he stepped behind his brother, his arms full of what I recognized at once as a bed tray. Not that I had ever been served breakfast in bed, but I had seen it in movies. Seeing the tray here, however, was confusing, and my mind instantly jumped to some sort of last meal scenario.

I probably would have panicked and run if Zoe wasn't grinning behind the two men, her arms folded over her waist as she watched us.

It was definitely going to take some doing to trust these two, and not because I had been inundated with "all the dragons want to kill you" stories as I grew up. But because of what Zoe had told me.

My heart was telling me that their past wasn't a problem. I was having a hard time getting my mind to cooperate.

"Good morning," I said, final able to push myself up into a sitting position that didn't leave me looking like a deflated rag doll.

Although my muscles were more akin to something stolen out of a creaky old man, I was able to move with limited pain. Muscle pain I was used to, and that seemed to be all that was left. And that could very easily be from the rock climbing, running, performing without warming up, and falling to my death that was last night.

Oh, and a fire-spitting battle between four dragons.

Yesterday had been a doozy.

"Where is Drake," I asked.

"He is with Suvi," Killian said, the same frustration on his face echoing in his voice. "He is waiting for you, you will see him soon."

Talk about vague and unhelpful, but right then I didn't care. I was happy to be sitting, even if my muscle aches were getting worse by the minute.

I moaned a bit as I settled against the headboard,

rubbing my shoulder in such a way that I instantly gained a look of concern from Jarron.

"I'm fine," I said quickly, as the blonde model pushed his brother aside to place the tray before me.

Glasses clinked and the smell of bacon, coffee, and syrup assaulted me, but I didn't even get a chance to bask in what I was sure was some kind of perfect display. I couldn't pull my focus away from the darkness that was Killian. His eyes narrowed to his brother before he stepped away, hissing something to Zoe as he stepped to the other side of the bed.

Oh lord, could my heart get any more tangled in barbed wire with this one?

"Forgive me if I don't believe you," Jarron said sweetly as Killian sat beside me, the mattress shifting as his weight pulled me toward him. "But worry not, we can fix it."

Killian caught me before I fell side long into him, his hand hot against my exposed shoulder as he helped me back up. The bright green of his eyes glittered as he carefully pulled my t-shirt back into place, smoothing the fabric as that roguish half-smile gleamed at me. My skin prickled at his touch, my phoenix screaming in need as she pressed against my heart, her song echoing in my ears.

"Beautiful," Killian whispered, the single word smothering the last of darkness that lived in him, revealing that same calm as before.

"I have never heard anything like it," Jarron said, sitting on the other side of me and shifting the bed again, sending me flopping a bit in his direction. "Is that your song, darling?"

I could only nod, still lost in the jewel bright shine in Killian's eyes.

"I have heard of the phoenix song before, but I never

expected it to be that..." Jarron's breathy awe faded as he closed his eyes, as if he was losing himself to the still lingering note.

Yes, it was beautiful, but I had never seen someone react that way before, hell I had never seen someone react at all, my song was hidden. My song was forbidden. But they could hear it, and they loved it.

If I ever needed to fly without the use of my wings, I was pretty sure I could accomplish it right then and there.

Jarron's hand wrapped around mine, his awe as brilliant as his brothers. Their sister, however...

Zoe may not look angry, but she sure as hell wasn't basking in the phantom song like Jarron was.

"What?" She asked with a laugh, throwing her arms up in that exaggerated way. "Don't look at me, you know you are nothing more than a boring mortal to me."

"She is nothing near a boring mortal," Jarron sighed.

Zoe rolled her eyes in frustration, although I was more likely to melt into him, and not because my sore muscles were making it hard to sit like a person who had, you know, bones.

"You really can't hear that?"

She shook her head. "Nope, and all I saw was your naked behind disappearing in a puff of light last night, so don't expect me to join Jarron's awe inspired rant about how beautiful your phoenix is, because I can't see it. Besides I heard it all last night."

I was going to choose to ignore that last part, but if the way Jarron was looking at me with those dark charcoal eyes was any indication I was going to hear it all anyway.

"I still can't believe that you have been leading me on all this time." Yeah, my shoulders may have a sagged a bit. I was trying not to take this personally, but damn it was a bit of a blow to my pride. "All this time, here I thought I was some kind of force to be reckoned with. That I could take you in a fight."

That time, they all chuckled, even Jarron who was still looking at me with puppy dog eyes. Forget a blow to my pride, they might as well drown it.

"I wouldn't try that, Ellie girl," Killian said, his hand patting the blanket next to me. "I don't think you could take her."

"She might," Zoe said, her eyes only on me, even though both guys were now staring at her. I wished she would look away, the fire was clearly back in her eyes, but it wasn't in the anger her dragon usually brought. This was different, this was eager. "We won't know what she is capable of for a while yet."

"Should I be concerned?"

"Only if you have any plan of trying your luck on defeating, Zoe," Killian said, misunderstanding. His tone was eager for a battle, and here I was concerned I was going to spit more than exploding javelins. Luckily, Jarron caught my meaning and gave me a helpful shake of the head, that I was going to take as meaning I wasn't going to start exploding buildings with a scowl.

"Even if you want to," Killian continued, oblivious to any exchange. "I would defeat her before she did any damage. I have before."

Zoe smiled a bit and gave him a look I didn't quite understand before turning back me.

"Duel to the death or not," Zoe said, her choice of words not helping to calm the twist of fear that was rampaging through my shoulders. "You haven't seen my dragon. You haven't seen any dragons. For all you knew we are some kind of furry snakes that let people ride on their backs."

I didn't flinch, but I sure as hell gave her a look. The boys didn't know what she was talking about, and I would prefer to keep it that way. I had watched that movie a ton as a kid, it was on one of the hotel cable channels when I was about eight, too young to train all day, and not old enough to be left alone. So it was movies on the battered old set that traveled with us for training playback.

I had watched it so much that I was certain Zoe's dragon was in fact, a fun-loving snow white furry beast with glittering scales.

She had told me how wrong that was, but I think last night was the first time it had really sunk in. Dragons were fucking scary.

"That is by far the most peculiar thing I have ever heard," Jarron scoffed, and Zoe earned herself another look. "I wouldn't let anyone ride on my back, well except my beautiful Phoenix."

And I was officially back to melting into those beautiful dark eyes that I was sure would go on forever. I probably would have if Killian hadn't snorted so loud that I jumped.

"Watch yourself, Jarron," he said, his voice grinding through gritted teeth.

"I would have to agree with Killian," Zoe said, pulling Jarron's focus right to her and thankfully releasing me from the spell. "Shocker I know."

Jarron laughed, Killian grumbled, Zoe folded her arms over her waist again and I was left looking between them all like I was trapped in some kind of Olympic ping pong competition.

"Care to explain?" I ventured, earning myself another snort from Killian and a worried expression from Zoe.

"Not today, darling," Jarron said, pulling my focus as he

ran his fingertips over my arm, the soft pads trailing fire over my skin.

I gasped. Like, a loud audible and totally embarrassing gasp that I was sure they could hear half a mile away.

When Killian had touched me it had been smothered in a warm blanket, wrapped up in him and ready to let him take me away. Jarron's touch was like a live electric wire that rippled through my muscles, filling me with a power that made my back arch.

Eyes snapping open to his, shock and confusion plagued me as his touch left, taking the electric storm right with it. Although it left the lingering song of my phoenix behind. I hadn't even realized she had reacted to that, I had been too caught up in the heat to notice.

"Better?" He asked, the smoldering darkness of his eyes threatening to pull me back into him.

"What do you guys have? Magic hands or something?" I asked as I stretched my neck and arms, nearly every muscle pain that I had woken up with evaporated.

There was still a lingering ache, and I had an idea on who could fix it.

"No, they are your soul's connection," Zoe said, a touch of frustration in her voice as she pushed herself away from the dresser she had been leaning on. "Mate's connection, remember?"

Damn it. It was a real thing and based off what I had felt, it wasn't something I could just battle through. Not that I wouldn't try.

Great. Forget puberty, I apparently had a dragon addiction.

"Well, as much fun as this has been, I need to go get dressed, wash the coffee from my legs and get to warm up. Just as you do." Zoe looked at me pointedly, the look making it very clear she wasn't lecturing me about being to the morning grump on time.

No sex, yeah. I got it, Zoe.

I was clearly being given a trial run from an overprotective parent.

The remains of both warm blanket and electric storm were making it very clear that I did, in fact, *not* have it. And we were even missing a guy. I was so dead.

"And drink your tea," Zoe said with a nod toward the tray that I had forgotten about. "You need to get your mating instincts under control."

"Don't say it like that," I moaned, as the door slammed shut behind Zoe, earning me a chuckle from both Jarron and Killian. The two sounds completely opposite from each other. One high and joyful, the other dark and dangerous.

Both rattled through me and brought back the onslaught of butterflies.

Right. Tea. Right now.

I refused to look at either of them and instead grabbed the dainty little teacup that had obviously come from Suvi's office, chugging the blue stuff like it was the key to life itself. Judging by the way it instantly smothered the flames that having these two so close to me was doing I would have to say that that wasn't too far from the truth.

Tea mostly consumed, I was finally able to take stock of the array that was before me, bacon, overly rubbery eggs, and a way too fluffy pancake smothered in strawberry goo. It was all clearly from the hotel's continental breakfast, but I didn't care. They had not only brought it for me, but they had braved the scary pancake making device for me.

I had first seen those in California, and even after nearly six months of being in that states I was still terrified of the contraption. Not because of burns, but because the thing seriously looked like it would suck me onto its conveyor belt of doom and perform some kind of medieval torture on me.

No thank you.

This one, however, looked great.

"Thank you," I finally replied, setting the tea cup down and cutting the silence. I was going to pretend I didn't notice them staring at me while I drank my tea.

"You are very welcome," Jarron said, leaning in close as he inspected the dish again, as if needing to double check that the rubbery eggs hadn't migrated on to the pancake. "I tried to get you lots of protein. I am not aware of what Phoenixes eat, but Drake said that athletes need protein. He even gave us some powder stuff to put in the pancake. So it should taste like a chocolate chip cookie."

He said it all very fast, very excitedly, and so close to me that I didn't care so much as to what he put into the pancake as I did being able to breathe.

"Will you give the poor girl some space, Jarron," Killian barked from beside me, the mattress shifting as he did. Jarron didn't need to be told twice. He took a quick step back and sat down near my feet, although his eyes never left mine.

I swallowed and began to cut my pancake into manageable pieces, part of me worried how the strawberries and chocolate chip protein powder were going to mesh.

"Excuse my little brother," Killian said, his emphasis so clear that I couldn't help but chuckle. "He's always been a bit of a ladies man, he doesn't seem to know what to do with himself."

The growl from the foot of the bed was unmistakable and I looked between the two of them, suddenly worried for the safety of my bacon. I stuffed a whole piece in my mouth before Jarron could respond, making me look like a gerbil.

"Threatened are you?" Jarron said with a laugh, giving me an exaggerated wink. "I may not have been idle while waiting for our girl, but now I know how to make her exceptionally happy."

The bacon was officially forgotten, well, except for the fact that I was now choking on it and hacking like an old woman with lung cancer. Cute. I stifled a hack, while Jarron gave me another one of his wide smiles.

They were quickly becoming my favorite.

"Our girl," Killian repeated, his voice harsher than I think I had heard it. "You speak as if you know how to please a woman and not just charm her into submission. I believe that if any choice has to be made that is a battle I am sure to win."

And my mouth was back to hanging open. My heart was going a million miles an hour, thanks to the tea I was pretty sure it wasn't because of my 'mating instinct.' Not that it made much of a different. I was still violently blushing.

"Ummm," I began, my voice so soft that part of me hoped they wouldn't hear, instead they both turned to me with varying expressions of humor. The glittering mischief in their eyes wasn't helping.

Okay, now I saw the family resemblance, and it really wasn't helping to calm the heart palpitations they were giving me. Time to steal my courage and set some boundaries. Bonded to super hot dragons or not, I wasn't going to let them put me into submission. Ew. Thinking it made me cringe, which they noticed.

"Can we perhaps not plan on pleasing or charming me?" I said, grateful when my hormones didn't get the best of me and I could get the words out in one shot. "I mean, I would like to get to know you first, if you don't mind."

"Oh, Ellie girl," Killian soothed from beside me, his hand

soft against my shoulder. "We would like that more than anything."

Damn. His face was soft again. Don't melt.

Don't melt.

"Why do you think we got up at such an ungodly hour to be here?" Jarron said, the sound of his smile infecting his voice and thankfully pulling my focus. "We faced mortals and weird breakfast food for you."

I quirked my eyebrow. I didn't see how that was some kind of life-endangering feat, but seeing as they were both giving me solemn nods, I was obviously mistaken.

"Do dragons not eat breakfast foods?"

"Let's put it this way," Killian said, his fingers sliding down my arm to my elbow. "We like protein too."

He smiled, flashing his bright white teeth and I couldn't help it, I flinched. The thought of those teeth biting into anything, especially me, was most unpleasant and brought the story Zoe had told right back to the surface. The dragon king murdering mortals, and these two standing right by his side.

I pushed the need to run away, Zoe had said they were safe, and I was going to trust that. Sure as hell didn't mean that I wasn't going to get to the bottom of this.

"Don't worry, darling, he doesn't bite." Jarron was trying to be funny, but I don't think anything he could have said in that minute would have been.

Killian's expression began to darken again, his eyes digging into me and sending a shiver down my spine before a gentle buzzing pulled me from the prison of his gaze.

The anger did not leave him, but it was no longer directed at me, but rather the tiny box in his hand. He gave the cell phone a dark look before looking up to Jarron with the same expression.

"What is it?"

"Elliot," Killian said, the use of my full name prickling my skin. He was close to me again, his eyes pulling at mine, pulling at me. My breath caught and his lips twisted into a half smile, revealing his dimple. "I have to go, but I will return the moment I am able. Please stay with my brothers. As foolish as they are, they will keep you safe."

I didn't even get a nod in before he leaned towards me, his hands soft against my neck as his lips pressed against my forehead. My skin prickled, a warmth washing through me as I leaned into him.

Before I reached him, he was gone, the warmth that had taken up residence in the pit of my stomach the only memory of my first kiss. I wasn't sure if it counted, but I was going to claim it. That warmth, the feeling of wet and wanting.

That was mine.

I would never have assumed it would come from him. He seemed to be scowling at me more than wanting me, but right then I felt very much wanted. It only made me want to crack whatever anger was inside of him more.

It made me want to know him.

My exhale shook in a sigh as it exited the earthquake that was my body, my focus still lingering on the door Killian had fled through. He didn't even look back.

"It would figure he would steal the first kiss," Jarron said with a laugh, the hidden frustration on his voice popping the euphoria bubble that I was content on riding.

"I hardly think that counted." It did. It *so* did. "It was a forehead."

Terrible liar that I was, I was pretty sure Jarron could see right through it. Or, at least he would have if he wasn't leaning so close, his focus only on my lips.

"A very beautiful forehead."

I shot Jarron a look, starting to understand what Killian meant when he said he would charm me and moved both my blankets and the tray off to the side. There was no way I was going to let myself get stuck in some kind of sibling rivalry, even though I was very aware I had already been thrown in head first.

"Anything Killian can do, you can do better?" I sang, earning myself a smirk from the man in question.

"Something like that."

"Well do yourself a favor," I said, thankful when I could stand without issue and balled my shirt over my breasts in an attempt to give myself some kind of modesty. "Don't hustle to get to the finish line. I am not something you can conquer."

First stop, dresser and clothes.

"Oh, darling. I won't think of it," Jarron said as he spun around on the bed to face me, every bit of sincerity lining his voice. "My dragon is yours, and you are mine. I plan on being by your side for all of your life. I have time. And I will give you all you desire when you are ready for it."

Nervous energy rampaged through me and I opened my mouth, ready to thank or gush or snap or something, but instead, I huffed and turned to my drawers desperate for clothes. Who knows, maybe I would find my spine in the bottom of my t-shirts and leos.

"Rest assured that I will capture the next kiss, darling." So much for no conquering. I didn't want to see how deep this sibling rivalry would go.

"You guys can't help yourself, can you?" I said, settling on a t-shirt with a German band I liked on the front. I almost stripped and pulled on the shirt. But thought better of it at the last minute.

I was nowhere near ready to take off my shirt in front of him. Even if I was wearing a bra. Which I wasn't.

I bundled the shirt against my chest more, as if that mattered, he was behind me and couldn't see me anyway.

"It's hundreds of years of rivalry," he said with a dark chuckle. "It's built into our blood."

"Oh, is it?"

He nodded, "the only question is, which am I going to kiss first."

"Excuse me?" I questioned as I continued to rifle through my drawers in search of a pair of pants. I really needed to be better about folding my clothes.

"Will I kiss the very beautiful forehead, or the very beautiful behind."

I froze, embarrassed heat rippling over my skin. I had forgotten until that moment exactly what I was wearing, and thanks to the way I had pulled my shirt up, he had a great view of the very white, very lacey Spanish underwear I had thrown on last night.

Oh, fu--.

Before I could move to cover myself, Jarron was there his fingers soft against my shoulder blades as he turned around to face me. His face was kind, too bad I was already bristling.

"Let's get one thing clear," I said, a little bit too much snap in my voice. "I heard what you said last night, and this is not some kind of race to my bed."

I guess I had found my spine in the drawer after all. Well, until his soft fingertips began to trace a line over my skin.

"Don't worry," Jarron said, his hand warm as it ran down my arms, only leaving to tug my shirt down and give me at least a faint illusion of modesty. "Suvi made it very clear we weren't to mate with you, and I will hold to that as long as possible."

"As long as possible?" I choked, my chest tightening as his hand came to a rest against my hips, pulling me closer to him. So close I could feel his hips against mine, so close I could feel his heat as his hand moved around to my back. Holding me against him.

Pressing me into his heat.

"Mmhmmm," he mumbled, leaning down to run the tip of his nose across my jaw, over my cheek, that same growl I had heard before rumbling through my mind.

Mine.

I shuddered at the sound of his dragon, at the power in his touch, at the heat, at the way he pressed his cheek against mine. At the way he whispered in my ear.

"Because it's going to be very hard to keep my hands off you if I keep seeing you like this."

20

ELLIOT

My heart was as loud as a Japanese drum as I got ready for the day, throwing on what was possibly my least revealing leotard. And yes, it took me some time to dig through my drawers and find it.

Not that I was some kind of a floozy, but leotards with cut-outs and mesh and back patterns were so much more fun to wear than this yard of spandex.

The high neck cut leo was a deep green, it had to be dark so as not to turn me into a Christmas Tree, what with the red hair and all. Forgetting the fact that tights, leo, and shorts were skin tight, it was possibly the most modest rehearsal uniform that I owned.

Modesty had never been high up on my importance totem pole but being around Jarron was quickly making it a necessity. Especially knowing that Drake was planning on meeting up with me at rehearsal.

I was going to be a freaking Amish pilgrim if that's what it took to get myself under control.

That and blue tea. I didn't care if it turned me into a bright blue monster, I would bathe in the stuff if I needed to.

Jarron escorted me to the annex tent shortly after I had emerged from the bathroom. Part of me had hoped for a look of disappointment in my leotard choice, but instead, he smiled appraisingly and tried to pull me into him. His fingers were fluttering on my hip like little Eskimo kisses. Soft. Hesitant. Needy.

I would have lost myself in his touch if I didn't have Zoe's voice rumbling in my head.

She was almost worse than a chastity belt.

A fire-breathing chastity belt.

Ouch. Good god, the imagery of that was about as bad as when you Google with safe search off.

Sidestepping Jarron and his fluttering fingers I pulled away with a smile and retrieved one of my many hoodies. This one a black thing from South Africa. The fabric may be thin, it didn't get cold down there after all, but it was better than nothing. Wearing any more than that in the desert would lead to some very curious looks.

So would using bubble wrap as a dragon shield, but I had a feeling that would truly brand me as a weirdo.

Not that I was against it.

Bubble wrap wasn't off the table, especially when he slipped his hand around mine when we are about halfway across the sweltering blacktop. Not even ten in the morning and the sun was attacking. I could probably put up with it better if there was any chance of a cliff to dive from.

"Mmm, if that's the smile I get for holding your hand, I cannot wait to see the grin I get for--"

"For what?" I interrupted, the chastity belt-tightening, just like his hand. His thumb drawing circles over my wrist. "Hopefully something that doesn't involve..." sheets. beds. tangling of limbs. I swallowed.

"Involve what?"

"Dragons?" Yep. Totally came out as a question.

Good thing Jarron didn't care. He grinned wider, flashing his bright white teeth and revealing his beautiful dimples.

"No, I can't wait to see your smile when I show you my hoard."

I stopped in place, dragging Jarron back when he failed to follow suit. Hoard. My mind instantly went to a group of people with pitchforks, but I wasn't dumb enough to think that's what he was talking about. I had heard him say something about it last night, but in the height of people spitting dragon fire, and dragon kings, it hadn't clicked. Teen YA may be my only insight into the world, but it was far more accurate than I had assumed.

"Your hoard?" he smiled at my ridiculous slack-jawed shock and pulled me toward him, continuing our journey toward the white tent that the rest of the performers were streaming into after a carb loading breakfast.

"Yeah," He said, broad smile still in place. "I am not going to ruin the surprise, but I have a feeling you are going to like it."

I tried to smile, but it didn't quite take.

"Don't dragon's hoard like jewels and things?" I asked, thinking back to a very specific book I read about four years ago.

It featured a dragon with rippling muscles and a particular set of twerking eyebrows. I hadn't gotten very far, and before I finally had to chuck the book in the river I was blushing so hard I couldn't see straight, but I did remember his hoard.

A cave of diamonds, glittering like a million facets of the starry sky. The image had stuck with me, a little secret part of the world that I would never fit into. Something beautiful that I could pretend was part of me.

Having Jarron here, having his warm hand in mine, was making me rethink that.

"Do you keep it in your cave?"

This time it was his turn to stop, but instead of me casually slowing down, I slammed right into him. "Oof."

"Elliot," Jarron said with a chuckle, turning around to face me as I rubbed my nose. The poor thing was going to bruise after that collision. "I'm going to have to ask you to never say that again. Unless you want me to start breaking out the 'that's what she said' jokes."

I scoffed. Really? That's what she said. I think we could do better than that.

"Why? Aren't you going to show me what you keep in your cave?" And yes, I said it with every drop of seduction I could muster. May not be much, but it did the trick.

Normally my sass would earn me a chuckle and a glare from Zoe, the loud snort that came from Jarron however, was nothing close to what I expected.

It was like the sound a pig with a head cold would make when trying to swim through Jell-O. It was so loud and so unlike the pretty poster boy that I couldn't help but laugh.

"I'm not going to show you, or visit, any caves, for quite a while, darling," Jarron said with a wink, "Besides, the cave you are thinking of are no longer what dragons call home. Well, not many of us anyway. I can only think of one and he has always been considered a bit odd."

I think my whole world of education from 'the Online School of Shifter Lore' had come to a crashing halt.

"What do you mean you don't keep your hoard in a cave?" I shrieked, earning me a look from one of the techs, his eyes flashing with such blatant curiosity that I wanted to smack him. Instead, I smiled brightly and waved.

I don't think I had seen someone move so fast in the opposite direction before.

"I mean that we don't keep our hoards in caves, and even then our caves are more like elaborate hi-tech cities cut into a mountain," Jarron said, tightening his hand around mine and continuing to lead us toward the tent.

The techy gave me another slack-jawed stare as his head practically did a three-sixty to gawk at the two of us. I gave him another smile, or rather another glare-filled warning look.

Eyes forward, Caleb. Mind your own business gossip queen. Ugh.

Maybe walking with Jarron to the morning grump was not the best idea. Add to that our currently intertwined fingers and I might as well have been sacrificing myself to Stacia and the gossip gods.

As nice, and comfortable, and warm as it was, I pried my fingers from him, choosing to gesture widely to cover the separation. It probably would have worked too if I was talking about rabid hummingbirds, and not, you know... caves.

"So if you don't put your piles of jewels in a cave, where do you keep it?"

"You really want us to hoard jewels, don't you?" He asked, shoving his hands in the pockets of his perfectly tailored and possibly too tight jeans. Not that I was complaining. I nodded eagerly to his questions. "Poor Killian is going to be heartbroken."

He laughed as if he had told the best joke ever, the sound a little less like a drowning pig and more like the deep grind of the engine. But sexy.

A sexy engine. Yeah, that made sense. The sound was doing weird things to my brain.

"Am I missing something?" I asked, shoving the electrical hormone tornado to the side. Jarron gave me a sidelong glance, the gold in his eyes reflecting back to me as the sun began to clear the mountains.

I had seen the color last night, when we were dancing in the silk, but somehow in the sun, it looked different, like little pathways to his soul.

"How is that you have lived with Zoe for your whole life and know nothing about dragons?" He asked, disrupting my illegal soul searching.

"Lived, yes. We weren't friends until about four years ago," I said with a shrug, suddenly wishing I had my own pockets to put my hands into, if only to give them something to do. Stupid women's clothing. "Before that she was so old, and beautiful, and she was always with Suvi..."

"So you were alone?" He asked. I didn't miss the sad little undertone there, the sound pushing my hackles up.

Yes, I was alone, because I talked to my shifter, and was Suvi's weird niece whose parents had 'died in a house fire'.

"I had my phoenix." It was the only answer I could give him right then, and even then it was a whisper, and not only because we were now only steps away from the tent, and from a million ears and eyes that were trained right on us. The girl who had fallen from the ceiling, and that weird guy who had somehow, magically caught her.

"Well, I have news for you beautiful," Jarron said, pulling me to a stop, placing us right in the middle of the straggling performers like a rock in a river, leaving the last of them to flow around us. "Not only are you not alone anymore." He smiled shyly, the tiny spark of a smile igniting that fire in my heart again. "But I am going to show you everything you have been missing. And we are going to start with my hoard."

"You mean that pile of trash you keep in the shoebox under your bed? No one wants to see that."

The slivers of gold in Jarron's eyes faded away, drifting back to the dark charcoal that was equally as devouring. I probably would have gotten lost in them if I didn't recognize the voice and instantly fall into the weird anxiety-ridden eagerness. I hadn't seen Drake since last night, and now, with my head full of images of Killian holding Drake down. Hurting him.

I swallowed, instantly opting to corner Killian about it all later. I wasn't going to be able to let it slide.

"It's not trash," Jarron growled, a low rumble rippling from his chest. The sound was so surprising that even though his face was spread into a playful smile I stepped back. Away from the mischievous grin that had taken over his jaw, and the ebony black of his eyes that were thankfully not looking at me.

I was pretty sure I would wet my pants if it was.

"It's better than those rocks you try to say are precious," Jarron prodded playfully, as Drake came up beside me, wrapping his arm around my waist and pulling me into him. The warmth from his skin radiated like a hot water bottle and I sighed.

Oh my!

His touch was like a firecracker inside of me compared to his brothers. The sliver of skin that pressed against my bare elbow was sending little sparks of fire through me, the heat igniting in explosions over my spine. Before he crippled me with his orgasmic touch, he moved away, pressing his palm over the thin fabric of both hoodie and leotard. Not that it helped, I could still feel his heat, although now it was more like a tease for what was waiting for me.

So much for Suvi's tea. I was going to have to fight this bristling on my own.

"Oh, they are precious, brother, but I am afraid I am only going to share that secret with Ellie," He twisted me in his arms then, turning me to face the man that was so different than his brothers. "We will have to let her decide who she desires more."

I swallowed, once again lost in that liquid sugar of his eyes. Oh lord, they were going to be the death of me.

"Don't you mean decide whose hoard she desires?" Jarron asked with a laugh, thankfully Drake didn't look away.

"Maybe. I'll let you figure that out Jarron," Drake said with a smirk to his brother, his touch softening as he stepped away a bit, as if I needed space to breathe or something, which I might.

"Now," Drake continued, thankfully ignoring any gaspy inhale that I was currently trapped in. "I know I asked you to coffee yesterday, and while it's not the date that I had hoped for..."

He lifted his right hand, revealing a small cardboard carrier and two cups of coffee, the tall white to go cups steaming lazily.

"Zoe said you take it black." He said with his trademarked crooked grin. "Which is lucky, because that's how I take it, too."

Oh god. I could kiss him, well not really. But after the tea this morning I hadn't been able to eat more than a few slices of bacon, and some eggs. While good, it would never hit the spot. Not like this dark concoction of the devil's bean. Its aroma was already pulling at me. Addicted? Sure. Happily. I couldn't grab at it fast enough, that pastry he had brought along with it was icing.

"Oh my god, thank you!" I shrieked, instantly taking one deep chug of the beautifully bitter brew.

One benefit to hiding the hottest heat in the universe inside of you? I didn't have to wait for the coffee to cool down.

"I needed that after last night," I sighed as I emerged from the cup. "You are my hero, Drake."

"Hey!" Jarron said, muscling into the small gap that separated Drake and I. "I bring you a full breakfast, complete with that powder stuff and Drake is your hero?"

I froze in place, the cup millimeters from my lips. All I could smell was the bitter coffee and all I could see was the bitter, yet triumphant, smile of two brothers.

"This is going to be a thing isn't it?" I grumbled before taking another sip.

"Ignore him." Drake said, giving his brother a look although he did not take another step closer. "How did you sleep, Elliot? How was your flight? Do you feel any better? I know it's a lot to take in, and we will help you through it, I promise."

My jaw could have very easily detached from my jaw and fallen to the ground like one of those ridiculous cartoons.

First Jarron offers to tell me everything there is to know about dragons and now Drake is not only asking about my flight but making sure I was feeling great. This must be an ulterior dimension or something.

"I'll take that as a yes," Drake whispered, carefully brushing a few strands of my tomato red hair off my face, the heat from his hands the only thing I could feel. "I'll answer any question you want at lunch--"

"Well, maybe not *any* question," Jarron said, neither of us turned.

"But first, Jarron and I need to go meet our new co-workers." He smiled brightly at me, his eyes lighting up as the thin pull of his dimple pulled beneath the rough growth of a beard.

I, however, might have been hit by a truck.

"New co-workers?" I asked, my voice catching as I looked between the two of them.

"Yep," Jarron said brightly, stepping up to me until I was effectively trapped in a dragon sandwich, which I was also perfectly okay with. "We are your new silks partners, whatever that means."

Whatever that means? It means ultimate trust, and so much skin touching, and eye contact. In a nutshell? It means I am in trouble.

Damn.

21

ELLIOT

Walking into the tent with two of the hottest men known to man flanking either side of me was possibly one of the most triumphant moments of my life.

And the most embarrassing.

Every eye was on me, the people I had performed with for years not even trying to disguise their shock, or their gossip.

"Isn't that the guy that caught her last night?"

"They probably don't trust her to perform on her own anymore."

"How could they let her back on stage after that?"

"What is she doing here? And why in the world are the new guys with her?"

That last one was from Stacia, who I gave a very open glare before winding my arm through Jarron's, knowing that he would react the way I wanted. He didn't disappoint.

He threw his arm around my shoulder, pulling me into him and pressing his lips against the top of my head. The soft touch bristled through my head, the heat of his breath running over my skin in a wave that was far too perfect to be accidental.

"Doesn't count," he groaned, sending more heat through me.

I shivered as the heat rose to what could easily be considered a burning level. My phoenix pressed against me, letting out a note so loud and so pure that I was surprised that everyone hadn't heard. Jarron, however, looked down at me, those shining golden strings overtaking his eyes.

I pulled away from the blonde god, only to be met by Drake who was looking at me with the same look of awe that Jarron and Killian had given me the first time they had heard my soul's song.

"I take it you heard that?" I asked as we found seats in some camp chairs far too near the front for my liking. That's what we get for being so late, we were now on display for everyone.

"It's beautiful," Drake whispered, his fingers hot against my shoulder.

The whole world didn't seem quite so scary and alone anymore.

"If you guys keep giving each other puppy dog eyes I am going to have to sit between you." I jumped at the voice, sending little drops of coffee over my lap and settled back into the chair, turning not to Jarron who was looking entertained enough to have been the culprit of my embarrassment, but to Zoe, who stood over us with her hand on her hip.

"God, you look like a mom," I teased, taking another drink while her lip curled in shock.

Both Jarron and Drake tried to hide their laughter. They failed, which only fueled Zoe more.

"You need some of those high-waisted butt pocket jeans."

It was a blatant prod, if not for the fact that I knew she would rock them, especially given that her current jeans and t-shirt look was nearly perfection. The benefit of having legs as tall as I am, I guess.

"That's it," Zoe said, the fire clearly sparking behind her eyes. "Move."

Drake didn't hesitate before he was on his feet, shuffling one flimsy chair over and leaving Zoe to sit next to me.

"Nice to see you not looking like a slug," she said as she sat down.

I knew I looked like a slug.

"I'm going to go with caterpillar," I countered defiantly, sipping my coffee. "They are cuter, and then there is that whole butterfly transformation thing..."

"Drake will have to bring you breakfast tomorrow so he can see you before your transformation," she teased, before turning toward Suvi as she walked up to Alan. The aggressive side eye the old lady was giving her made it clear that they had been chatting before this.

For once I was glad not to be included in their old biddy's club.

"I think I'll pass on that," I said as Suvi called everyone to order. "I'll power through it better tomorrow."

Zoe snorted a bit too loud for the hush that had taken over the crowd, which was awesome, because now any eyes that weren't focused on us were. So basically just Xi, the girl may be the only one naive to the hunks that had escorted me into the tent.

Oh, to be thirteen and oblivious again.

"You can't power through it," Zoe scolded as Suvi began her usual morning announcements.

"Watch me."

The sidelong glare I was now receiving from Zoe made it

clear she knew I was full of crap. Which was fine because I also knew that I was full of crap, except mine was more of the scary determined kind of crap. I would fail, there was not question, but I would sure kick some trash getting there. Having Killian and Jarron see me like that was one thing. I didn't think I wanted Drake to see me that way. Vulnerable. Broken.

I don't know what it was, but there was something in the way he looked at me that made me think he had seen enough of that. I didn't want him to think I was something that needed to be fixed or saved.

I wish I understood why. My phoenix sensed it more than I did, her sadness was as strong as mine was I leaned over Zoe in an attempt to reach him, his eyes soft as they fixed on mine.

Soft. Kind. Warm enough to melt into.

I needed more tea.

I don't think I had ever sat back faster. Which was a problem because those chairs had seen far too many butts, and far too many not so careful acrobats.

My back slammed into the fabric, which ripped with the sound of an unfortunate fart and the thing crumpled around me. Metal and fabric folded against my limbs like a broken umbrella and I lay on my butt, in the middle of the tent, my hands and legs sticking above me like tentacles.

Yep. Just my luck.

The tent erupted in laughter as multiple sets of hands jumped into action, Drake pulling me up and into him, as Jarron promptly snapped the metal of the chair in two. Luckily the things were flimsy anyway or someone might think something of him bending and snapping metal into oblivion.

Like me. And the wide eyed stare I was now giving him.

"Are you okay?" Drake asked, holding me against him as he led me over to his chair.

So much for him not seeing me in a compromising position. At least it wasn't my butt up in the air. Although I had a feeling that would happen before too long.

"Here, sit," Drake said softly, his hand warm through the fabric of my clothing.

Let's just add to the blush that the great chair debacle of the twenty first century had given us.

"I think I have sworn off chairs," I mumbled as I collapsed to the ground, choosing instead to lean against Zoe's legs; although Drake's legs looked much more comfortable.

I must remain strong.

"Well, since Elliot has begun the introduction, I would like to introduce you all to the newest members of our troupe. Many of you may have heard of Drake Cuelebre. The celebrated rock climber is currently rated third in the world and has most recently completed his third free climb of El Capitan in Yosemite national park. Just last month he competed in the International Olympic Exhibition in Beijing where he placed first."

I think with every word she spoke my heart thundered more and more.

Why, yes. Yes I had heard of him. That free climb was one of the most deadly in the world, and he had done it three times. One of them happened last year. I would never forget it, we were in Australia at the time and his name was everywhere.

Now, he sat behind me, casually twirling a strand of my hair through his fingers.

And now, I guess, he was going to be my partner.

No, my heart reminded me, my Phoenix screaming in indignation.

My mate.

He was my mate. One of the three.

Don't turn around. Don't turn around.

I couldn't stop myself. I turned around, looking as awe stricken as everyone around me. For once that soul twisting half smile had no effect on me. There was too much shock melting it away.

"Famous some?" I tried to tease, but it came out more as a gasp and a squeak.

"I wouldn't say that," He whispered as he nervously dragged his hand through his hair, giving a not so happy wave to Stacia who was trying to get his attention. "More like bored."

I raised an eyebrow at him in question, but before he could answer Suvi was continuing, yelling over the chatter that was rippling through the tent like a thunderstorm.

"He and his brother, Jarron, will be joining us in a new aerial act alongside Elliot. You may have heard of, or seen, Jarron's appearance last night, it was quite the feat if I do say so myself."

Jarron laughed loudly at Suvi's appreciation, waving to a few of the other cast members and sending some of the younger females into what I am sure would have been classified as swooning fits a hundred years ago. Jarron smiled wider, Zoe meanwhile rolled her eyes from where she sat next to him, smacking him hard on the bicep.

"What?" He mouthed to her, but even I was giving him a look, an angry scowly look that I was pretty sure was not coming entirely from me.

Jealousy bubbled like some kind of alien life form that was threatening to erupt. I could taste the bitter heat of the putrid emotion on my tongue, my heart boiling in an energetic orchestra right behind.

I was one step away from taking down Stacia, her friend, and the poor trapeze flyers in one fell swoop if I needed to. Luckily, Jarron caught sight of the daggers I was currently throwing at him and slunk back down into his chair.

I wish it was enough to stop the rampaging heat from escaping, everything in me was on fire. One glance at my hands showed me how close that was to being true.

The same smoke was seeping from my skin, rippling over the calloused palms in agitated waves.

"Shit," I moaned and tucked the appendages under my legs.

"Make sure to welcome our new arrivals, but give them space to train, their act will be debuting very soon and they don't have a lot of time."

Everyone nodded, murmured, and started to break camp as a whole hoard of people made a beeline right for Drake. I however, was trapped on the floor, locked in place under Zoe's gaze.

"You don't seem too surprised by that," Zoe said, dropping to the floor and asking for my hand.

Of course she saw. And she wasn't the only one, Jarron was right there, his touch already sending electric waves through my muscles as he gently coaxed the renegade appendage out from its hiding place.

"You aren't used to controlling your shifter are you?" I wasn't sure if it was a question, or a statement. Either way, his voice surprisingly soft.

Soft as his fingers as he began to drag them over my palm, shooing away both smoke and agitation.

"I'm used to hiding my shifter," I said, stoically keeping

my voice hard and straight, despite the way my breath was catching. "Never let her out. Never let anyone see."

"Darling," Jarron said, his fingers leaving my palm to run down my jaw, pulling my focus back to him. "You never have to hide with me."

It was one of those moments where the world drifts away as everything around you melts into oblivion and the only sound is the steady breath of the man who has captured you. The quick beat of your heart in your ears. I would have sworn I had stopped time, gladly sitting to get lost in the black holes of Jarron's eyes. Well, that was until Zoe moaned, sighed, and shoved him out of the way.

"Stop being disgusting," She grumbled, giving Jarron a look as he dramatically flattened himself out on the floor. "We have work to do."

She didn't wait for his dramatics to end before she stormed away, leaving me sitting confused, and Jarron laying on the floor like some kind of model on a romance cover. All he needed was the open shirt.

Ugh. I didn't need that image. I had seen him shirtless and putting two and two together was messing with my internal organs. I didn't know how much more my heart could take before it burst out of my chest.

"Nice to see that Zoe is the same," Jarron grumbled dramatically from where he lay. "After last night I was beginning to think she might actually enjoy being around me."

"Have you two never gotten along?" I asked, knowing that it wasn't as deep as that, but I was curious.

"That depends on what you mean by never." Jarron sighed, staring at the ceiling with such intensity I almost turned to see if there was a dragon there. "We didn't leave on the greatest of terms."

"I know. She told me some of that last night." My stomach twisted at where this conversation was heading. I wanted more information to the bombshells Zoe had dropped last night, but sitting here surrounded by at least five performers who were trying to find a way to break in on our conversation was probably not the right venue.

Jarron's focused dropped from the ceiling fixing me with a curious side glance, "What did she say?"

"Not much," I answered quickly, preparing to side step. Gregor was paying way too close of attention.

I shrugged like it was nothing, something that Jarron clearly wasn't buying. He sat up and fixed me with a look that would have been handsome if it wasn't for the fire behind his eyes. He didn't need to call bullshit to say it, I was hearing it loud and clear.

"Hmmm," Jarron said, that darn sonar my heart always had on him telling me he was scooting closer, and instantly moving into overdrive. "Your apprehension of Killian and I this morning is suddenly making sense."

I guess I had been more obvious than I thought. I suppose when the only two emotions you have are "I'm going to jump you" and "I'm scared of you," you are going to tell when something's up.

Note to self: drink the tea first tomorrow.

"Darling," Jarron whispered, the brush of his hot breath over my cheek pulling my focus, the man now sitting so close that our knees were touching. "I know it is no excuse, but we did what we thought was right, and once we realized our mistake we have been working to correct it. I know Killian will make it up to you. We will both prove our worth, as well as our regret towards our choice. We will make this right, we will protect you from our father, dethrone the man who gave the order, and give our lives for yours if need be."

I could scarcely breathe as his hands wrapped around mine, as he moved closer, as his eyes grew so dark that they were all I could see.

Dark little abysses that were sucking me in. But not in passion. In fear.

It was as if my soul knew what was coming, and she was doing everything in her power to protect me from the pain.

"We owe you that," he continued before I could say anything. "I owe you for what I have done. I never should have followed the order. I never should have taken your father's life."

Nothing could have protected me from that.

It was a miracle I didn't slap him. That I didn't scream or run.

I couldn't move. I felt heavy. Like a weight I never knew I had been carrying around collapsed right on top of me. Zoe hadn't told me he had been the one to kill my father. But right then I couldn't find the words to tell him that. I could only sit there and cry.

22

KILLIAN

THE AIR FELT MUCH HEAVIER TO KILLIAN THAN IT HAD BEFORE he had left home to meet with Jarron. It could have been that the hot dry air of the Midwest was like flying through sand compared to the liquid humidity of Spain, where the moisture was so dense he could feel the air press against his skin. Killian was sure, however, that the weight on the air came from the same weight that had taken up residence in his heart.

A vast empty hole that could only be filled by something he had left an entire ocean away. The thought of her made his chest tense, his bones ache with a low moan that try as he might he could not push away. He longed for her, and no matter how beautiful Spain was this time of year, it could not make that need of her dissipate.

The sharp mountain breeze blew behind him, pushing him deeper into the long dark cave, tugging at the strands of hair that had come loose from his bun. The icy chill whipped at the untucked white shirt of his suit as he attempted to button it so as to transform back into the hardnosed prince he had left as. It was proving to be a feat, seeing as each step was opening the hole in his heart until it was a crevice.

He would do anything to protect her. But he had others to protect as well. His people. Many of them didn't know the danger they were in, didn't know what was happening in his father's high court. Even without Ellie, he has a duty to them to finish this - to kill his father.

Ellie's existence fueled that need even more.

He still wasn't sure if his brother's existence in this equation was a complication or a benefit to that plan.

Thank god he had left the jacket with Ellie, it was something to keep her safe and warm, and to keep her wrapped in his scent, lest his idiotic baby brothers try to do something in his absence. He may have a job here, but he wasn't about to let those two fools take over the girl he had claimed.

Leaving the jacket there, however, had created a few more problems. He needed to replace the jacket before anyone noticed it was gone.

He was known for his suits, and while most dragons kept their hoards concealed, Killian wore his for the world to see. If one of his subjects saw him without a vital piece of his hoard there would be talk.

He had risked a lot by leaving Utah as late as he did, and his father's frantic phone call from the morning had only put him more on edge. But he needed to see Ellie, he needed to hold her, to soothe her through the pains that their connection had caused her. And even though he was sure he would hear it from both Jarron and Ellie, that lingering kiss was a gift to her. A memory he could hold with him as he danced among the wicked here. It would have to be enough to tide him over before he could return to her.

At least he hoped so. He had no idea when he would be able to return, or if he would be able to contact her before he could. The kiss was all he could do.

Killian straightened his collar and walked deeper into the mountains of Montserrat, where his kind had first banded together as a clan many centuries before. It was late enough in the day that most had resigned to their individual caverns until sunset, leaving the long entry corridor silent and filled only with the occasional flicker of a lamp in a window.

In the distance, the dull glow of the main square called to him, prompting him to pick up his pace as he scuttled past the homes of the wealthier dragons that were carved into the rock.

The closer he moved toward the square, the more ornate the carvings around the entries became. The centuries-old mosaics and perfectly created spirals blended into the stone, in designs that even in the dark appeared to be dancing. Each one was more intricate than the last as the families one-upped each other.

Centuries of pride. Centuries of mortal stonemasons captured and killed. The thought had once filled Killian with pride, now it only brought a scowl to his brow.

A light flickered to life in the cave behind him and Killian picked up the pace, turning a corner of the long stone tunnel before it opened up into the large multi-storied heart of the Dragon City.

Rydaim.

The city was as old as time itself, although it had come a long way from the legends of the first dragon who had dragged his mortal capture up to a crevice in the ancient mountain range and took her for his own. For centuries following, dragons lived apart, fighting over lands and hoards and maids and who knows what else until Killian's great, great, grandfather, Belin, brought them all together.

It was all lore of course, but his family revealed the story as truth and placed a crown on their head regardless. for centuries they had ruled over the ancient city. Over the dragons. Over his home. Even with all the scars that were hidden in the rock, it was still his home.

Just walking into the massive courtyard healed the hole in his heart, if only a little, although he would not let it show in his face. He kept his jaw hard, his eyes impassive, and stepped over the stone toward the imposing stone fountain that sat in the very center.

Three dragons, wings spread, teeth bared, all stomping and gnashing on the bodies of mortals. Water poured from the stone as if it was blood, streaming from the largest dragon's mouth in what was supposed to be fire. It was a violent show of power and he hated it. If only because he remembered what it had been before.

A girl and a dragon, intertwined as they stood side by side. Water flowed from the palm of the girl in a show of the life-giving magic of the Fae. The woman's face was beautiful and even in stone her eyes had sparkled. Many said she was carved into the eternal spring of the dragon city for a reason, but any story that went along with it died when his father melted the stone to nothing, destroying the Fae alongside.

Sometimes when he slept, Killian still heard the screams of the massacre, saw the tears of a child that he had destroyed without a second thought. The fountain had been wiped away in one day, and so had the freedom of an entire race of people.

The King had rebuilt the fountain, and the city. Building a new story and a new future right along with it.

The fountain was only one piece of the massive city, only one show of the power and danger that lurked here.

Funded by the pride and hoards of centuries of his kind, the city dripped with wealth and conceit. The stone of each storefront was polished, the pathways that connected the high rise homes and stories of apartments dripped with flowers and jewels. Buildings surrounded the fountain with facades of marble, granite, and in some cases diamonds. Above it all, the King's quarters glittered in a million colors that overlooked the large stone square like the eye of a God. The thought would seem silly, if so many didn't already believe it to be so.

Their God, King Ceres.

Heart pounding, Killian glanced to the wide stained glass window that covered much of the ceiling. The massive thing glittered above them like a discolored sun. The mosaic his father had added to it two hundred years ago burned bright, showcasing his hopeful future: the death of mortals, and the rise of dragons to both destroy and devour the subspecies.

The image made him cringe, but not because of the contents, because the light meant that his father was awake, and waiting for him.

"Bloody hell," Killian swore, and quickly diverted his path so as to take the outlying streets of the city on his way to his home. His father wouldn't be able to see him here.

Compared to the beautiful town square, these streets reeked of the secrets that his father tried so hard to hide. Refuse of garbage, of life left forgotten.

Huts of stained cloth and broken stone were pressed into every crevice, cans with tiny flames set near each one, like little beacons of hope. Although what hope they were going to find here he had no idea.

There was nothing here but misery.

"Please sir," a tiny voice called out from the shadows, the wide green eyes of the child peering at him through the dark. The color was so close to his own... they could have been beautiful, but he could tell at once that all the life had been sucked out of them. All of the magic. They were as dead and dull as a dying grass. "Do you have any bread?"

She reached forward, her long fingers thin enough that he was sure they would break without too much effort. Each part of her skin was covered with dirt, blood, and who knows what else. But it wasn't the filth that he looked at, it was the long jagged scar that ran up her arms, from wrist to elbow, the skin not quite healed right.

The mark of a Fae whose magic had been pulled out of them. A Fae who would not yield to his father. Now, this child and all the others who lived in these hovels were nothing. They barely even had value as a slave.

"Child," Killian said, turning to her as he began to search his pockets. But it didn't matter, the girl took one look at Killian and let out a long low whistle before she vanished, the shadows swallowing her as if she was one of them. The flickering light of every single makeshift lantern vanished with her, plunging Killian into darkness. He twisted in place as the echoes of feet shuffling against stone broke through the dark, turning toward the last of the frantic whispers as the Fae disappeared.

The Forgotten.

When he was a child the sound of the vanishing Forgotten was terrifying to him, the shuffle, the whimpers that echoed from the dark. The sounds were almost like a whisper before an attack, but the attack would never come. The people were too broken, too trapped to even try. Now, the sounds of a hundred lost souls only cracked against his already broken heart.

He could say nothing to bring them back, so he only placed the coins from his pockets against the grime covered sill where the child had been hiding and sprinted down that alley, running into the servants quarters of the massive estate he shared with Jarron.

"Callay!" He bellowed into the dark, the second the door had shut. The single word ignited in a spark of light that spread and grew as more and more lights began to ignite. "Callay! Wake up!"

Killian didn't wait, he charged through the servant's halls and into his kitchen, grabbing a roll and some meat from the fridge before Callay finally caught up with him.

"Master!" The tiny girl shrieked as she entered the white marble room, her long silver hair streaming behind her as if it was suspended in a gentle breeze. Her eyes glimmered in strings of the lightest blue when she saw him, her smile spread wide. The drab grey uniform did nothing to smother the light that glimmered from both her hair and eyes. He remembered when she first was assigned to him, her skin had a gentle glow to it, that was gone now.

Most of the serving Fae lost their shine months after training. Callay still clung to some of hers.

"You were supposed to be with your father hours ago! What are you doing here?"

"Running late," Killian said from behind a mouthful of roll. "I need a new suit."

"I can see that," The girl replied with a grin, bouncing on her toes before snapping her fingers and producing one of the many that Killian kept in his room. It was a dark grey three-piece that Killian loved, and his dragon adored. An appreciative growl rolled through his belly at seeing it. "How did you lose that jacket? You love that jacket!"

"When was the last time you left food for The Forgotten?" Killian said, carefully sidestepping the question.

He may trust Callay, but the location of his jacket and the existence of Ellie was not something he was willing to share.

Even if she wasn't the Phoenix, the knowledge that his Dragon had taken a mate could end in disaster if his father was to catch wind of it. And Dabria's interference from yesterday had already put him on edge.

"Last week," Callay said softly as she produced another roll and held it out to him. "There have been more patrols the last few days and my contact hasn't been by."

Killian raised an eyebrow, shoving the roll in his mouth as he began to shed his pants, swapping them out for the beautiful grey linen. "Did you say they were from Jarron? They always take it if you say it is from the *golden prince*."

Killian scoffed at the ridiculousness of that truth, the title may be ridiculous, but it suited his brother, and somehow it always got him exactly what he wanted. Any humor was lost in the look on Callay's face, however.

"There have been more patrols," she repeated, her eyes growing wide as she handed him his jacket, the fear and shock that was lining her face sending an iron barb through his heart. He had known the girl since she was sworn in as his slave at the age of eleven, and he didn't think he had ever seen such fear in her eyes. Not even in the brutal training that the enslaved Fae were forced to endure.

Quickly zipping his pants, he spun around, sure that his father, or even worse, Dabria, was behind him. His hands grew heavy at the prospect, the dark power that was in him pulling to life as the air grew cold, his dragon sucking all the fire and warmth from it.

No one was there. It was only the two of them in the massive kitchen, the only other movement coming from the glitter the reflected off the wide white granite countertop, little pops of light that hit against the dark stone walls. If only that was enough to calm the panic was tightening through Killian's chest, his dragon screaming to run home and protect Ellie.

Home. He was home. What a curious thing for his dragon to think.

For his heart to want.

Killian shook his head, banishing the confusing emotions and turned back to Callay, his green eyes darkening as he pushed the emotions away, leaving only the frustration behind.

"What is it Callay?" Killian growled. The sound tumbled over the stone, reverberating back to him in a roar that would have made any mortal jump.

Callay, however, met his glare head on.

"Master," she began, the never ending flow of her hair picking up in her agitation. "Parris is here."

"Shit."

White hot rage ripped through his muscles, pulling him every which way as he grabbed the vest and the jacket from the tiny Fae, nearly knocking her over.

Parris. The immortal bastard had been slowly grooming his father for the last hundred years or so, although he and Jarron had not caught on to his plan until a few years ago, when the Vampire's desire for the Phoenix was revealed and the true danger for all Dragons became clear.

His father had enslaved the Fae. His father formed an alliance with the Vampires. His father had squashed shifter packs all over the world. If Parris had his way, however, he would rule beside the dragon king, bringing thousands of his progeny alongside. Perfectly placed for a coup of another sort.

Millions of Vampires. Thousands of Dragons. Even with the Fae at their side, no king would favor those odds.

Killian was determined to overthrow his father and stop this madness before it was too late. It was why he had begun to hunt for the Phoenix in the first place. If he could remove the beast from his father's grasp, and take the fire for himself it would be an easy task to overthrow the old loon.

His bond to Ellie may have put a wrench in that plan, but he could still overthrow his father. Hopefully, before whatever nonsense Parris was planning was thrown into play.

"How long has he been here," Killian grumbled, his fingers stumbling over each other in an attempt to fasten the vest correctly.

"A few hours," Callay whispered, lifting herself on tip toes as she smoothed the expensive fabric, trying to wipe away a tiny bit of fluff from the vest before holding the jacket up to him.

"Shit," Killian swore again, inadvertently looking up toward the massive royal chambers above them. He may not be able to see them from inside of his kitchen, but that didn't make them any less imposing.

"I need you to get a message to Jarron," Killian barked as he checked his reflection in the shining surface of the refrigerator. "Tell him the bastard bloodsucker is here and to stay with..." he faltered, unsure of what to say. It may have seemed childish when Jarron had suggested it earlier, but the use of a code name would do well right about now.

"The Eagle?" Callay provided, giving him a knowing smile that stopped his heart.

Killian tightened his jaw, his eyes darkening as he stepped closer to the girl. But she didn't back down, she didn't flinch. She stared at him with wide eyes and a smile hidden in the corner of her pale lips.

"It's a code name," she said as if that settled it. It only flared his agitation more.

She knew.

She had to know. The look in her eyes screamed it, Killian would have to hope that the darkness shining from him screamed nearly as loud. Her lack of flinch or fear was not very reassuring.

He couldn't say anything here. Even for the king's oldest son there were too many ears, too many dangers.

"You need to go," she finally said, her voice firm as she placed her hand against his chest, the low tingle of her magic rushing through his veins. "You need to keep her safe."

Her words echoed in his head as her power grew, one final snap of fear hitting against his spine before he felt as if he was being pulled through a tube. A glittering, heat-filled tube. When he had been a child he hated the joyful warmth of the Fae's magic, the subtle pain that each 'trick' left him with. Once he began shifting, however, he knew better than to complain.

If shifting into his dragon was agony, this was nothing more than a slap on the wrist.

Now, after having felt the water bottle warmth of being near Ellie, Callay's magic felt nearly as familiar and wanted.

"Killy!" The screech hit his ears before the massive throne room had fully come into focus, the rush of air and the scent of blood hitting him hard. His stomach spun even as his head began to settle, the high carved arches the lined the walls slowly solidifying.

The space was massive, big enough for a dragon, and judging by the freshly charred bones that were piled at the base of each carved arch, his father's beast had recently made an appearance.

"I was beginning to wonder when you were going to show up, handsome." Dabria crooned, the sugar sweet voice feeling like acid against his twisted stomach. "Your father and I were worried."

Keeping his face impassive, Killian straightened, tugging his jacket into place as he turned toward the woman's' voice, toward the smell, although he knew what was there.

His father was framed by the stained glass he had seen from a hundred feet below, the dying mortals glittered in the glass behind him, the scene so intricately created he could hear their screams. It sent a twist over his spine.

King Ceres sat on the large throne that had been there for centuries before he was born. The massive thing was carved from the darkest stone in Africa, glittering diamonds peeked out from the teeth and claw marks that covered the surface. The deep gashes were the only remains of a million pack battles as dragons with more guts than brains tried to defeat the old man, and the equally as ruthless men that can before him.

Killian may have the brawn, but he also knew he could not defeat his father in a battle. His sister had already tried that. So had the man whose carcass sat at the foot of the throne, it seemed.

"I am glad to see that you did not drown in the sea," King Ceres said with a voice like sandpaper, the sound grinding on Killian in all the wrong ways. His spine straightened at the sound, at the hidden laugh and taunt of failure that always lined his father's voice. The muscles in his back zipped together as though someone had nailed him onto a string.

"I may not have drowned, but those poor fishermen who caught sight of me have breathed their last," Killian lied with a low laugh, the king joining him with a loud guffaw that was only broken by the ripping of flesh as the old man took another bite from the appendage he held.

The king was large, nearly as broad as Killian, although what he was missing in breadth, he made up in height. He towered over everyone, his glare a deep scowl that ripped into any lie. Or so he thought. Although his grey eyes matched his hair now, it didn't make him any less imposing.

"Come join us, Killy," Dabria crooned from where she was perched on one of the armrests of the throne, leaning over the king like the whore she was. Her eyes dug into Killian, a seductive smile twitching on her lips as she reached over the king, her long fingers pulling a strip of meat from what his father was trying to pass off as a meal.

Killian's dragon growled hungrily at the smell of blood and meat, his lungs twisting in warmth as the heat from his flames began to coat his tongue with ash. His hunger grew as Dabria taunted him, her lavender eyes sparkling with ice as she licked her fingers, blood dripping bright red over the ebony of her skin.

"Don't be silly, woman," Ceres said through a mouthful of mortal. "Does he look hungry to you? My son has feasted on the flesh of fisherman! The mortal fish of the sea!"

He ended with a laugh, the boisterous sound rattling the bones that lined the throne room. Reluctantly, Killian joined in, forcing out the loud sound that if he had to guess by the smug look Dabria was fixing him with, she saw right through.

As long as she didn't peer any deeper.

Before she, or anyone else, could call him out, the large stone doors of the throne room opened with a low grind that rattled both stone and bone. Dabria looked up eagerly, Ceres jumping to his feet as he rushed toward the newcomer, the left arm of the mortal forgotten at the floor of the throne's dais.

Killian didn't need to turn around to see who had entered, he could feel the icy cold of the undead in the air long before the doors had closed.

"This, my dear, is the chamber of the Dragon King." Parris's voice slithered over his skin, the chill of it threatening to extinguish the heat that his dragon was now burning. He could feel the creatures hatred and anger rise alongside his own, burning in need to escape, the rip the head off the undead monster.

Killian dutifully restrained the growl of his dragon as he turned to face the leader of the Vampires.

Parris was dressed in his usual all black, the tight-fitting jeans and t-shirt perfectly accentuating his lanky, trim frame. His leather jacket was vintage and fit the bad-ass college kid look he was going for. Different decade, same image. Attractive youth, luring beautiful woman into his bed, and their flesh beneath his teeth. Judging by the body near the throne, and the beautiful brunette he had escorted in, he was working overtime.

"Ahhh..." Parris crooned, brushing his blonde hair back from his pale skin and fixing his blood shot eyes on the only thing that stood in the way of what he wanted. "The prince has *finally* arrived!"

Parris fixed Killian with a scowl that was easily missed by his father, the mans hungry eyes were locked on to the beautiful mortal Parris had brought. Ceres smiled at the girl, his nose trailing over her hand as he kissed her skin. He could practically hear his father's dragon breathe her in. Taste her scent.

Killian's scowl tightened against the vampire, the blood sucker meeting the look head on. What his monster wouldn't give to rip the man's head from his shoulders. To destroy him and his little games. A beautiful mortal was just what a dragon king needed to satiate his desires, get him drunk on mortals and pull him deeper into his trap.

Normally it was a game that Killian would gladly play, the pull of tangled flesh one he wouldn't pass up, even once he knew what Parris was up to. Not today.

"I could have brought you your own mortal to warm your bed if I knew you would arrive in time," Parris said smoothly, the man smiled as he let his teeth flash, the large fangs gleaming in the dim light. Killian didn't so much as flinch. He folded his arms over the wide barrel of his chest and lifted his chin.

"I can find my own whores thank you very much," Killian said with a glare, taking a step toward the vampire, who thankfully stepped back. The powerful immortal wasn't usually one to let Killian posture him that quickly. But he wasn't going to ask questions. "I am here to speak to my father."

Ceres perked up at that, his grey eyes flashing as he turned from the woman who was practically falling between Dabria and the King. She clung to Dabria, letting the powerful female kiss her as the king ran his hands over her curves. The mortals motions were making it very clear that the vampire had already feasted from her, and the lack of blood was inebriating. He might as well have drugged her.

"We can speak later, Killian," Ceres grumbled as he ran his finger over the woman's shoulder blade. His finger pressing into her flesh as he brought her closer. She stumbled into him, giggling as she tried to pull away, but the king held on tighter, the grey in his eyes filling with flame. "Won't you stay and share this gift with me?"

His father didn't wait for a response before leaning into the woman and locking his lips with hers. His weathered hand dragged up her back lifting her shirt as Dabria began kissing the woman's neck, her eyes digging into Killian's.

Kissing, licking, devouring. It was clear she was trying to get a rise. But Killian barely even moved. Locking his jaw tight, he scowled at the pair, a vein pulsing in his neck as he blocked his mind, and hopefully Dabria from it.

"Want to share, Killian?" She crooned, stepping away from the woman to Killian. "And then, I'll share something else with you."

The needy hunger of his dragon was doused in the icy chill of her dragon's flame. He swallowed, trying to push away the heat of his rage that having her so close to him was filling him with. It was so much worse than in the hallway. Then he had only felt the need for the unnamed girl.

Now, he had heard Ellie's heartbeat, he had felt the warmth of her skin. He had connected to her, his dragon, his heart, his soul. Ellie was his, and having Dabria take that place filled him with a rage so strong he could feel the acid on his tongue.

He pushed the thoughts from his mind, locking his heart down lest Dabria get a whiff of where is mind was.

"I don't like to share," Killian growled, letting the frustration of his dragon out as his eyes began to grow dark, the creature pressing against him in agitation. "And it looks like you have already given yourself to someone else today."

Killian gripped her forearms, pushing her away from him

as slow as possible so as not to throw her across the room. As much as his dragon wished it to be so, he could control himself better than that. Letting the heat from his dragon burn her skin, he gave a not so subtle glare towards his father who was now carrying the tipsy woman to his throne.

"Is this about your mortal whore?" Dabria taunted, raising her voice with a snap that caused Parris to turn his head, his eyes narrowing at them. "You have shared me enough. And I will share you if I have to. I would love to show your whore what dragon fire can truly do to skin."

She smiled, the ice in her eyes flashing dangerously that Killian's need to smash her skull into the rock was only growing. He could not rise to this, he couldn't not give them all away.

"None of your games, Killian." She crooned. "Bring your hooker here and we can burn her together."

Dabria reached up, her blood-streaked finger tracing the line of his jaw, moving down toward his chest. Her ice trailed behind the touch, sending a shiver down his spine that she clearly misread and she took a step toward him, her hands reaching.

She didn't get far.

Killian pushed her away from him, keeping his hands against her shoulders as he ripped his focus away from the still staring Parris, the scarlet glare of the vampire setting him on edge. He didn't like the look. They knew too much already, and with what Callay had said, he was suddenly wondering how much they knew, and how much danger he was truly in.

His instinct was to shift and break through the roof in an effort to reach Ellie, to protect her from whatever evil was here. But the witch had made one thing clear before he had left: His father could not know of Elliot's existence. Which means everything had to go on as normal.

He would draw the line at sleeping with the social climber, however.

"I don't like filth on my suit's, Dabria," he sneered from behind clenched teeth, knowing that the excuse was flimsy at best. It didn't matter, though, the threat in his voice was clear, the low rumble slamming against her and turning her lust filled eyes to the angry heat that was so common for when she didn't get her way.

"Send me a message when my father's appetite has been satiated," he said, taking a step to the door, well aware that Parris was still following his every movement.

He needed to get out of here and to a phone, to make sure she was safe.

"I am not your father's messenger," Dabria spat, stepping in front of him.

"Actually, Dabria," Killian said, rushing back to the woman whose eyes were now throwing daggers into him. He let each one hit, his smile widening as they bounced to the ground. Useless. "That's exactly what you are. Don't let your place in my father's bed fool you into thinking you are more than that. A messenger. A servant."

Dabria's eyes widened, her jaw dropping as Parris' snicker echoed over the stone. He may not be watching them anymore, but he was very clearly paying attention.

"I am not your servant. And you have welcomed me into your bed enough," she sneered, grabbing his arm and pulling him back toward her. Her mouth was open, ready to yell, to bait, but any further battery stopped short with the tight grip of Killian's hand around her arm.

"I can do better," he said, stepping past her to the pale

man who was now watching his father devour the woman with a look of hunger in his eyes.

"Parris," Killian said with a snap, but even the low rumble of his voice didn't turn the man's focus. "I am assuming you will be here for a while?"

"As long as it takes to fulfill your father's desires. I am at his command," The little man said, finally turning to Killian, his deep red eyes digging into his before glancing at the still fuming ice dragon. "And yours as well, your majesty. If mortals are what you desire, I can bring you the most eager women you have ever seen."

Killian couldn't help but smile at that, not because of the woman, but because of the truth behind it.

Even with what little Dabria had seen in Utah, they still had no idea.

"I would like that," Killian lied, his heart and dragon screaming in agony. But it was worth it, a tiny price to keep her safe. "Bring me a few."

Parris may think he had the upper hand, but Killian had something that neither of them knew, and neither of them could control.

Not that he could either, but keeping her safe could very easily lead to the death of the king.

And then Killian could take his throne.

23

JARRON

I<small>T</small> <small>WAS LIKE WATCHING HER THE FIRST TIME, HER BODY</small> twisting, moving, dancing through the air so gracefully that it was obvious she belonged there.

That her home was there.

Jarron sat, transfixed, on the edge of the mat as he and Drake watched her, a spin, a twist, and a drop that had him running. If it weren't for the mat he would have, even Drake jerked forward, but she caught herself at the last minute, the silks having wrapped around her so securely that it was clear she wasn't going anywhere. That was, until with one quick motion it all came undone and she hovered in the air with the silks wrapped around her arms, extended out like some kind of angel.

An angel.

That's what she looked like.

Jarron recognized that move from last night, and it had the same effect on him then as it did now.

Pure, unblistering awe.

Sitting there watching her he could feel his connection for her growing. His love. His need to protect her. Just like last night, when he had recognized her for the first time, that pull grew from the pit of his stomach, begging him forward. He had tried very hard to sit still, to look as impassive as possible, but now without Killian here he didn't feel the same need to hide it.

So, he smiled as she spun, sprinting toward her as she landed, a wide grin spreading over her face.

He didn't move fast enough.

"That was amazing, Ellie," Drake said as he reached her, his hand soft against her shoulder, a burst of jealousy twisting against Jarron's spine.

"Thanks!" Ellie was beaming, the bright light of her shifter glowing in subtle flames behind the brown of her eyes, like light through a stained glass window.

The light seeped into him, and Jarron felt his dragon rise to greet her phoenix, the golden heat of his flame consuming both chest and belly. He couldn't help himself, he wrapped his arms around her, crushing her against him as he lifted her tiny frame off the floor. She felt so small against his bulk, he could have held her there forever. Perhaps he would have if it wasn't for the knowing smirk Drake was giving him.

Suppressing a laugh, his bothersome brother toasted his coffee to him, the white paper cup a silent mocking tribute. He would have loved to knock the kid out of the way, but there were simply too many people watching their pseudo-rehearsal for that to happen.

Besides, Ellie had made it clear she had quite enough of their bickering for the day. If she thought he and Killian were bad, she didn't want to witness the trouble that he and Drake could get in to. Even with the kid being banished to mortality for the last decade, nothing had changed.

Jarron gently placed her back down on the floor and the

girl took a quick step back, brushing her hands against her leggings and she looked down, unwilling to make eye contact.

His heart sunk, all of the liquid energy that was consuming him draining as fast as the blood from his face.

It was the same. The same look of confusion, the same cold fear.

Same as when he and Killian had come to her room that morning, rushing to her side after having woken with the most intense body aches he had felt in almost a century.

Having Zoe stay with her had been a mistake. Their past was a story he should have been able to tell, her confusion and discomfort had made it clear it had been done for him.

Her reaction to his apology for his hand in killing her father, however, made it clear he may have misjudged.

Ellie hadn't known that it had been his fire to kill her father.

He would have to find a time to talk to her, to explain.

"Alright," Ellie began hesitantly, pushing some of her hair out of her face, before focusing on Drake. Something Jarron's dragon did not appreciate. "We are going to start with foot locks and a cross back straddle. That will give us an opportunity to learn base work."

Jarron's heart sank, none of that made sense, and he was sure his confusion was clear on his face. Drake, however, took a sip of his coffee and nodded like he knew exactly what was going on.

"Do not tell me you understood that," Jarron said disparagingly, fixing Drake with a look. But his bastard baby brother only laughed.

"Circus is good cross training."

Wonderful. He always prized himself on being better

than his brothers at everything possible. Of course the one thing that Drake would best him in was this.

The thing he needed to master to impress her.

"Great," Ellie said with a clap of her hands before bounding off to untie the long strands of multi-colored fabric that had been tied against the canvas wall.

"Just because you are a world famous climber doesn't mean you get some kind of free pass." Jarron grumbled as Ellie released streams of baby blue fabric, the sails flowing through the air like water.

"Oh, no free pass here." Drake said with a smile, his focus still on the beautiful girl. "I stayed up all night watching videos. May have snuck into the tent about one a.m. to give a few things a shot"

Jarron's jaw dropped. It's a good thing this wasn't a competition, because both of his brothers seemed to have it out for him. Drake becomes a master circus performer overnight. Killian sleeps outside the girls door. And Jarron? He, the idiot that he was stayed up half the night dreaming of Ellie and watching cartoons, ignoring texts from the half dozen other dragons that he had been perusing.

Never mind. This was a competition, and he needed to up his game.

"Alright, pick a silk and let's get started." Ellie proclaimed, bouncing on her toes she was so excited. Her enthusiasm was contagious. Well, it was, until after more than a dozen tries and Jarron was still stuck with fabric tangled around his foot.

Meanwhile, Drake had mastered the lock and was now working on what Ellie had called an invert, and Drake had named a curse that should not be repeated.

He should have been able to find solace in the fact that Drake was struggling now, too. Except that he was already so far ahead of him. More muscles did not exactly translate to greater success here. He may be able to hold himself up, but twisting a long strip of fabric over and under your foot with perfect dexterity was certainly not happening.

"How is it going?" Ellie asked, sinking down onto the mat where Jarron had collapsed, flat on his back, his left foot still tangled and hovering about a foot off the ground. "You can take a break if you want."

No rest for the wicked, Jarron thought, but instead he smiled and turned toward her. "Nah, I'm determined to get this."

"I can see that," she said with a quirk of her eyebrow, "Or are you determined to beat Drake?"

She smiled, that beautiful light shining behind her eyes again. It twisted in his stomach, taunting him that the look was more for his brother than for him.

"Maybe it's a little bit of that." He forced a smirk on to his face, the look sunk into her, having the same effect that he had on so many others.

She smiled, blushed, and turned away a bit.

"Well," she whispered as she scooted down to his foot, lifting it as she slowly began to feed the silk through the weird knot he had trapped himself in. "Let's untangle this and try again."

He watched her work, watched her soft hands as she carefully manipulated the long strands of silk. Her fingers were so careful, so controlled, that it was almost like a dance of its own. Watching her perked up his dragon, pulling him toward her.

Always acting before he thought better of it, Jarron sat up, his hand soft as it pressed against the bare skin of her shoulder, the touch sending a rush of warmth through him, the heat flared as she turned to look at him.

"I meant what I said," he said softly, before his better judgment had a chance to catch up with him. The middle of the crowded tent was probably not the best place for this conversation, but it didn't matter. He was already in it.

"It doesn't matter Jarron," she replied, although her tone did not reflect her words, the once tender actions of her hands speeding up and jostling his leg around. "I didn't even know him."

"He was your father, Elliot," He said, the use of her full name cutting through his heart, especially considering the context. "And I knew him. It matters."

"Does it matter now that you know me? Or did it matter the moment the blade left his skin?"

He cringed, unwilling to acknowledge how close to the truth she was. Although the blade was part of him. The talon was still stained with blood.

He may regret it more, having bonded to her, than he did when it first happened, but the regret was still there.

"I've regretted it every moment," he said honestly, his heart clenching painfully with the memory, even the warmth from her close proximity could not quench the pain of it. "And Killian and I have spent the last five years looking for you."

Now was not the time to tell her that they had planned on killing her. There would never be a good time for that one to come out.

"But you didn't know he was my father..." she whispered, she had completely stopped trying to untangle him by that point. "You still killed him."

"My father commanded me to," he said, well aware the words were nothing more than an excuse by that point. A foolish excuse. It didn't matter what his father said, he still chose to follow him, he still chose to end Elliot's life.

He could have walked away. He didn't. And it had haunted him every day since then.

She sat by his feet, her back to him as she watched Drake attempt the invert again, before coming down and untangling himself from the silk as if it was nothing more than a jacket he had put on the wrong way.

"I don't understand why you fought with him," she whispered, her eyes glistening as she finally turned to face him.

A lump the size of a soft ball had lodged into his throat, his foolhardiness at entering into this conversation evaporating.

"My father is not one who is easy to defy," he grumbled, just mentioning his father sent a darkness over his heart.

It had been years since he and Killian had spoke about that night aloud. Spoken of the last battle, and of all the carnage, and the backlash that happened against the Fae. It took them years to see it, to begin working against him, but it was never enough.

Even now, saying it to her, was more of a string of excuses that she was caught in the middle of. He didn't know how to make her see. Judging by the darkness in her eyes, he wasn't sure it was possible.

"You and Zoe seem pretty scared," she said, looking toward the large flap of the tent that had been pulled open, revealing the troupe of fire eaters who were dancing around each other like some kind of leather clad spiders. "She won't tell me anything about what happened either."

"She faked her death to get away from him," he said, as if that somehow made it all better.

There wasn't a drop of understanding on her face, however.

"Are you going to fake your death now, too?" she asked,

glaring into the fabric as though it had wronged her somehow. "Will you disappear along with me?"

"Anything to keep you safe." Jarron whispered, reaching forward and turning her from the knot.

His fingers brushed over her skin, that same warmth rushing through him as his dragon purred contentedly inside of him. He let the sound out, let her hear as the glittering creature inside of him spoke aloud again.

Mine.

This time the single word did not have the same effect it had in Suvi's office, instead of awe, her eyes grew wide in fear, the pupils shaking as she stared at him.

"I will always keep you safe," he promised, his fingers smoothing over her skin as he tried to wipe away the fear that had taken over her heart.

It didn't work.

"Maybe I don't want to be safe." She said, twisting away from him to tug and pull at the fabric, her motions angry. Almost as if she was desperate to get away from him. The thought pulled roughly at him. "Maybe I am done hiding. Maybe I want him to pay."

"You don't know what you're saying." Jarron said honestly, his voice growing dark.

"At this point, I don't care," she hissed giving the fabric a tug and releasing his foot, the slightly numb appendage hitting the ground with a thud.

She didn't even give him a chance to respond before she jumped to her feet and sprinted back to where Drake was.

His heart pulled toward her with every step, his dragon snarling as Drake pulled himself into a perfect flip. His toes were even pointed as he hung upside down in the fabric like a monkey.

The ache in Jarron's chest grew louder as Ellie reached

him, wrapping her hands around his before lifting her feet, hanging from his hands for a moment before he dropped her, clinging to his left shoulder.

His ache turned into a stab and Jarron turned away, unable to watch anymore. The regret in him was so strong that he might as well be swimming in it.

For what he had done to Drake, and for what he had done to Elliot, even if he had not realized how it had affected her life until now.

Drake had been able to forgive him. He could only hope that Ellie would be able to as well. He would have to cling to that, otherwise, both he and his dragon were headed into centuries of pain and a long, slow, soul crushing death.

He didn't want to test the limits of how long a dragon could live without its mate. But he would if he had too.

With a heavy sigh, he pushed himself up from the mat and slunk away to the spigot near the door where several others were refilling their water bottles. Among them was the blonde woman he had seen yell after Ellie last night, and who was already trying to put the moves on both he and Drake. Normally, he would flock to such attention, his dragon had always loved to play with a mortal. Part of it, he was sure, stemmed from how he was raised. There was always something delicate and gentle about them.

Easy to break.

Not the like the dragons he knew. Females like to bite and scratch.

That was, however, before Ellie. Ellie had zapped all of that out him. He only wanted her. In fact, every step he took toward the seductress that was currently making eyes at him was another nail against his soul.

"Hi there," she said, the moment Jarron had moved within ear shot. "I'm Stacia."

Her accent was thick, and Jarron recognized it as once. The wide majority of the vampires that visited his father's throne room were from Russia or the former Yugoslavia. He would guess she was as well.

"Hello Stacia," he said, surprised that there wasn't a hint of flirting in his voice. That might actually be a first. "Nice to meet you."

"You as well," she said through teeth so white they might as well be glowing. "We are glad you are joining us."

He didn't respond, but he was not foolish enough to think that was the last he would hear from her. He knew her kind too well.

"I'm a contortionist and a tumbler," she continued without prodding, shaking her ass enough that he could tell she was trying to showcase something, although what he wasn't quite sure. "I swing for Ellie, you know, play her part when she's been out too late to make it to the performances."

She hesitated, watching him for a response, interest, something. He was sure that a week ago he might have greedily given into those hips, but not right now, and especially when he had no idea what she was trying to get at.

Instead, he gave her a smile and went on to fill his water bottle in peace.

Well, or the illusion of peace.

"She's out a lot," she said without prodding. "Late nights. Visitors in her hotel room and such."

Ahh. That was her game.

Like a cat with a mouse, bullies always wanted what their supposed nemesis had.

"That was quite the catch you made yesterday."

So predictable.

He had had quite enough of small town espionage in his life to be fooled by this girl's game. In fact, if she played it any more plainly he might as well have named her cellophane.

"Yes, well, it was meant to be a surprise, of course. My brother and I have been training with Ellie for quite some time," Jarron finally responded, giving her a faint smile, but his heart wasn't in it.

Instead, his heart was actively pulling him toward Ellie, who was now inspecting the long tattoos that covered Drake's shoulder and arm, the dark lines perfectly covering the scars that remained there.

"I doubt that," Stacia purred, stepping close to him, not that Jarron noticed.

He was still looking at the two of them, his spine twisting as the regret grew, part of him wondering if Drake was going to tell her what happened, or if he would lie. He knew the boy well enough that he could only assume that any story he would tell to be about climbing, and not what really happened.

They couldn't keep it from her forever. If they were to keep her safe, if they were to defeat their father. She would see Drake's dragon eventually, and then she would know.

"What do you say?" Stacia said, pulling his focus away from the pair as Ellie began to show Drake another move, her hand pressing gently against his good arm as she moved him into position.

Jarron's dragon stirred in jealousy, his stomach jumping right alongside.

"I'm sorry?" Jarron said, finally turning back to the girl who was carefully trying to mask her displeasure. Too bad anyone could see the hatred behind her eyes, the look darkening what he was sure was a normally beautiful face.

"I said," she scoffed, stepping closer still and placing her palm against his arm. His muscles tensed at the touch, although not for the reason she assumed judging by the gleam in her eyes. "That if you ever want to catch someone else I have a few ideas, and I promise no competition."

She smiled then, holding herself against him before she looked away, her dark eyes making a laser focus right to where Jarron's heart was stitched to.

He followed the gaze unwillingly, his dragon growling in expectation.

The two stood side by side, Ellie laughing at something he said while wrapping his good arm in that same locky-thing she had done to him on stage the night before. But, instead of the panicked motions he had experienced, she was kind, gentle, smiling brightly as she showed him how to hold his shoulder.

And then they jumped, hands clasped, other hand bound, and spun around each other like a Cathcrine wheel.

Just as he had with her.

As much as it stung him, seeing his brother take his place, Jarron had to admit that his brother was graceful. As the shortest of the two he matched her better, their movements were more in line.

A low roar echoed from his throat, although this time he wasn't sure if it was him or his dragon that made the noise.

"I don't like to share either," she whispered, giving his arm a squeeze before stepping away, letting her hips sway enticingly.

Jarron barely saw her leave, he barely cared, he was currently trapped watching Drake hold Ellie so close that no light could seep between them.

Only Drake's bare chest and the thin fabric of her leotard.

He thought he was okay with it. He thought his dragon was okay with it, but seeing the two of them like this, was flaring a rage that he hadn't felt in centuries.

Ash filled his mouth as his dragon snarled so loud that several people turned their heads.

He didn't even turn. He made no apologies. He just stared at his brother, stared at her.

Wanting her.

Needing to claim her first.

She had asked him not to make it a competition, and he knew that he wouldn't. He would gladly share her. Love her. Protect her. Please her.

As long as he got there first.

He was one step away from lunging between them and carrying her away like so much of his hoard, when his phone buzzed in his pocket.

One glance at the screen took any pillaging need right out of his wings and left him filled with dread.

It was from Callay.

"Parris is here. Father is drunk."

Shit. They may have less time than he thought.

He didn't even say goodbye before he left.

24

ELLIOT

"Again."

Yep, I was going to punch her. Fist to the face. I didn't care if she was a dragon, and if Jarron and Killian didn't think I could take her. I was mad enough I was pretty sure I could figure out how to pin her to the ground. This was getting ridiculous, we had been at this for hours, my body hurt, I was hungry, and Zoe didn't know anything about silks rather than how to say 'again' *again*.

I didn't even try to restrain my glare, "What did we do wrong this time?"

I fixed her with a glare to drive home my point, but she wasn't even looking at me, she was staring at the entryway to the tent, the heavy canvas gently waving in the breeze. With as drenched in sweat as Drake and I were, the breeze looked inviting, at least it would if it wasn't a hundred degree blast of heat.

I was hot enough.

"Zoe!" I barked, pulling her focus right as Drake came to the ground beside me, chest heaving in an attempt to catch his breath.

Zoe shook away whatever thought had trapped her and went back to the clipboard where she had been studiously taking notes of everything I had been teaching Drake.

"That last part could have been smoother. Ellie, can you keep your leg straight before he grabs you ankle? It would look..."

"No," I interrupted her with a snap, folding my arms over my chest as I sent her an icy stare. "If I do that we run the risk of hyperextending my knee. When he is more confident in grip strength and my flexibility we can, but for right now it's safer to keep the knee bent until we reach the position and then extend it. It will help him build muscle strength on that arm as well."

The words came out in a rush, each one tightening in Zoe's jaw as I systematically, and very purposely, reminded her that she knew nothing about my discipline. Without even meaning to, I popped my hip and fixed her with a glare that furrowed in her brow and sent Drake into a poorly disguised chuckle.

Don't prod the dragon, my ass. She may be older, but like hell if I was going to let her think she could boss me around. Drake and I had been practicing this routine for the last week, running it non-stop since the day Killian had left.

Jarron was supposed to be the swing for Drake, but the guy had been as absent as their oldest brother. I think I had only seen him twice since the day everything exploded, and even then he was more interested in watching me in the silk than being in it. If I didn't know any better I would say his first time up scared him.

Everything had gotten much better since then, and my bristling mating instinct was under control thanks to Suvi's tea, but with so much time away from the other two, I had been left with a massive hole in my heart that Drake could not quite fill. Not to mentioning the lingering ache in my bones and muscles. I was all ripped and pulled, and grumpy.

Drake tried to soothe the pain away, but I still felt ripped open from my heart to knees, the torn ragged edges pulling me toward the parts that were missing. A whole ocean away. Yeah, I may not know exactly where they were, but I wasn't an idiot.

The sons of the dragon king still had a role to play.

Sensing my discomfort, Drake's warmth washed over me as he took a step closer, his hand soft as he ran it over my bare back, the contact leaving a glittering trail of energy behind it.

I restrained the shiver. Judging by Zoe's smirk she saw it anyway.

"Isn't Ryn waiting for you or something?" I asked before Zoe had a chance to find her tongue. "You don't want to let your act slip while you are busy trying to learn ours. We are getting close to being ready, and then you can see it and tell us how awesome we are. But you know you don't know enough about this stuff to help."

I fixed her with a smirk, poking enough on her ego that the bossy facade slipped away and she smiled.

"And, sis," Drake said from beside me, wrapping his arm around my shoulder and pulling me into him. "If you are worried about forbidden mating I will have you know that I am pretty sure Blondie over there will make some snide remark to stop anything from happening."

He gave an exaggerated nod to Stacia, who had been not so subtly watching us for the past week. And stalking Drake. And following him around like a lost dog. And inviting him to dinner. And inviting herself to ours.

Ugh. I shouldn't think about it. Watching her wave to him and bat her ugly bedroom eyes... Speaking of punching.

Drake pulled me back, wrapping his arm around me tighter as he pressed me against his side. I hadn't even realized I took a step forward.

"Down girl," he mumbled, twisting toward me until I could feel his hot breath run over my skin. He was close, not close enough to kiss, but the slightest turn put him right in line with me, his melting eyes all I could see.

"You know I am no one's but yours, Elliot."

As if his melty warm eyes weren't enough to send me into convulsions all on their own, his swoony comments were certainly giving me a run for my money.

Stay strong, Ellie, don't collapse into his incredibly strong and sinewy arms.

I couldn't help it; I took a step towards him, my hand lifting to flutter over the long lines of the tattoo that covered his arm. The sharp angles of his bizarre tribal tattoo were almost as familiar to me now as his eyes. His face broke out into a soft smile that tickled my muscles and warmed my stomach. Soft pleasurable waves...

"Really?" Zoe scoffed from where she sat at the edge of the massive crash mat. The sharp tone of her voice promptly popped our bubble and I stepped back, sure that the look of guilt was clear on my face. "I highly doubt you will be able to control yourselves. Can you at least save it for the act?"

"Goodbye, Zoe," Drake said with a tone that was very near boredom.

Or at least it would have been if he wasn't so irritated.

"Fine, fine," Zoe said with a wave of her hand, setting the clipboard down like it was some kind of peace offering. "Just do me a favor and don't *connect* too much."

I blanched. Really? All she was missing was air quotes.

Her emphasis was not helping. Neither was her brother, who instantly grabbed me and spun me into a low dip his nose tickling against mine.

"Do you mean like, this?" he asked, his arm strong against my lower back, his fingers tight as they wrapped around my waist. "Or do you mean when I catch her in that epic drop?"

He smiled at her, she groaned, and I couldn't help but cringe. It wasn't an epic drop yet. We hadn't landed it more than twice in a row.

"Both," Zoe said, her huff melting into a smile before she took off toward the still waving canvas flap, the lingering smell of paraffin oil following behind her.

"I'm going to hear about that later, you know," I said, stomach twisting as I watched her go.

"Nah," Drake said with a wave of his hand. "If she's going to guilt you over her butting in then I'll talk to her. She can't get mad at her adorable baby brother."

Drake fixed me with a wide grin as he grabbed our water bottles, tossing my bright red canteen at me with a wink.

"You can't expect that to work," I said through a laugh, quickly taking a drink. I could practically hear my muscles sigh in thanks for the liquid gold I was giving them. "Puppy dog eyes are for five-year-old girls and..."

"Baby brothers," he interrupted, before I could go any further.

"I don't think you qualify as a baby brother once you a hit a *certain age*," I taunted. Thank god I was used to Zoe being several hundred years older than me by now, or being so attached (and so attracted) to Drake and his brother would be weird.

That and years of getting all my information about shifters from the internet. You know how many teenagers fall in with immortals? I'm part of a percentage now. At least I am almost eighteen, I'm an adult in most countries.

So, totally not weird.

"Not with Zoe," Drake said, licking drops of water from his lips. "She has more of our mother in her then she would like to admit."

I froze, mouth open, the water bottle a good six inches away from my mouth. "Your mother?"

Don't know why that sidelined me so much. It's not like she didn't have a mom, everyone had a mom. Hell, I had a mom somewhere in the infinite cosmos. Although no one knew who mine was, so that made her decidedly dead and unimportant.

But Zoe? Drake? Jarron? Killian? They obviously all had a mom. You would think that after so much time with Zoe I would have heard something.

"Yeah, Firane." Drake said with a shrug, no longer looking at me as he carefully began to rearrange the water bottles. Which apparently needed to be in a perfect 90 degree angle from each other now. "She was a firecracker. Powerful. Brave. She stood up for what was right."

"That sounds like, Zoe." From what I knew about whatever war had led to me hiding and Zoe being fake-dead she stood up for something right.

Her brother? Not so much.

The thought infiltrated me like a battering ram and I controlled the cringe.

If I even saw Killian again I knew I was going to nip this in the bud. Should be a fun conversation.

'So I heard you wanted to murder me as a baby, tell me, are you still in the same camp?'

Awesome. It was going to be awesome. I grimaced again

and that time Drake caught the look, giving me a raised eyebrow that pulled his dimples into near perfection.

"You okay?" Not with you looking at me like that.

"Yeah," I lied, because honestly, I wasn't wanting to get into the whole thing with Drake, no matter how much I had begun to feel comfortable around him and --ummm--- like him. Jarron and Killian were the ones I needed to hash it out with. "Let's try the trapeze sequence again."

Drake gave me a look that clearly said he didn't believe me, but thankfully let it slide and instead jumped to his feet and lead the way back over to the bright red silk we had been using for rehearsal.

It was one of my favorites, if only because it matched my hair, which I promptly resecured in a scrunchie. While I could normally perform with my hair down, having long strands of red fly in Drake's face seemed like a distraction he didn't need.

Grabbing my hand, he pulled me toward him as he gathered the long poles of the fabric beside us, spreading it in the wide sails as I had taught him for the opening climb.

It was a hand over hand deadlift, performed by gripping the edge of the wide strip of fabric. It was one of the hardest climbs I knew of, but with his climbing skills he had mastered it easily. Which, I am not going to lie, was super hot.

This time, he wasn't climbing however, he moved the fabric around until it surrounded us in a wide cocoon, blocking us from view.

"Are you sure you are okay, Ellie?" He whispered, the fabric moving closer as he weaved his arm around me, bringing me even closer.

So close I could feel his hips against mine, so close I

could feel a burning heat radiate from his chest, soaking into me like a hot water bottle.

"Yeah," I whispered, having way too much trouble getting the single word out. "I think I just need to talk to your brothers."

His face screwed up at that, a cute little cluster of wrinkles appearing between his eyes. I reached up to smooth them, unable to resist gently pressing the deepening lines away. As cute as it was, I didn't want him worrying about me. I was ninety percent okay talking to his brothers on my own.

Okay, maybe it was more like seventy percent, but it was a solid seventy percent. But it was growing, especially with the way Drake had begun to shiver beneath my fingers, that low roar I now recognized as his dragon rumbling in his chest.

I was totally having trouble breathing right then. If I wasn't acutely aware that Stacia and the rest of the cast were behind the thin veil of fabric, I might have been tempted to make the gap between us even tighter.

Darn it all. As much as I hated it, Zoe was right, tea or not, controlling myself around him was becoming more and more difficult.

"If it's about what I think it is, you should wait," He whispered, the soft tips of his fingers circling over my spine as my own touch wandered to his hair, the closely trimmed shag on his neck as prickly as the growth on his face.

O.M.G., breathe.

"Wait for what?" I said, forcing a laugh into the breathless question. "You mean like wait for them to come back."

I tried to smile, but I don't think it worked. I probably

looked more like I had drunken sour milk with how he was looking at me. Pity wrapped in worry.

I hated it, but I also understood it.

I mean, he saw the agony I experienced every morning. He saw the way my bones ached, and my muscles throbbed. The pain grew a bit more every day that Jarron and Killian weren't there, the aches never truly leaving. I hated that I needed them. I also hated that I couldn't have them with me right now. The two conflicted feelings were nestled in a deadly tango of mistrust that stemmed from some mysterious past that I wasn't sure I could ever understand.

It's like being in love with the devil, you know he has a heart, you just need to stop being afraid of the horns to see it.

But Drake, Drake wasn't a devil.

"I mean, wait until you are ready." He said, his eyes melting me, warming the air between us as they began to spark with light. "Everyone has sins in their past, it does not make them bad people. But if you want to hear it, you need to be prepared to listen, to understand, and possibly forgive."

Pulling my hand away from the rough prickle of his two-day beard growth, I tried to step away, hard as it was. Not that Drake would let me go anywhere.

"Jarron said he killed my father," the words were out before I could stop them, stabbing against the calm comfortable air like a blunted knife.

Drake pressed his lips into a tight line at my confession, the light in his eyes doused with red as a hiss of air pressed between his teeth. The look was not helping the axe murdering I was doing to our safe space.

"Jarron has done many things he regrets, to many people he loves," Drake spoke softer than I expected, given the harshness in his eyes. "Including you. He is yours, as I am. As Killian is..."

I jerked a bit, the movement cutting him off as I tried to step away again, but he held on, stepping closer as he leaned in, his soft breath whispering over my cheek as he spoke.

"Your phoenix has claimed all of our hearts, but their good was there before you came along, you will see." He pulled away then, the darkness that I had seen in his, having melted away.

"They are there for you," he whispered, leaning in until forehead rested against mine, his eyes fluttering closed as heat radiated from the contact. My phoenix bristled, pressing so hard that I gripped his thin tank top tighter, desperate for something to hold on to.

"I am there for you, Elliot." He hesitated, his breath catching as his eyes flashed to mine. Digging into me. Sucking my breath away from me. Damn those eyes. They ruled me.

I sighed, long deep and loud enough that Drake smiled, that dimple popping up.

"I am quickly falling in love with you."

His shirt was suddenly not enough to help keep me upright. A second ago, I could have melted into him. But no, he had to go ahead and drain the blood from my face. My heart may have been doing somersaults, but my Phoenix was practically throwing a house party.

Did he really say what I think he said? I had yet to kiss him, to kiss anyone. And he was... and I was...

"I..." Oh my god, I didn't know what to say, or even if I had the guts to say the words that were pressing against my chest dying to get out.

I wasn't ready.

It didn't seem to matter that I had no answer, his grip around my waist tightened, pressing me against him as his hand began to trail up my back, over the fabric of my leo, toward my revealed skin.

I would not gasp, I would not gasp.

My willpower was shot, the second the rough calluses of his hands touched my revealed skin, a loud hiss escaped me. My Phoenix was already awake, but now my soul was right there, pressing against my skin, swelling in my heart, shining from my eyes.

So bright, I was sure he could see it.

"Beautiful," he whispered, his breath hot over my lips as he leaned in closer, his hand moving over my spine to cup around my neck, pulling me closer still.

My skin prickled under his touch, stomach twisting in need as I tried to move closer, realizing I was close as I could get without...

"Drake," I whispered, barely able to get the word out past the massive pressure that was building in my chest. Past the need that was trying to slam me closer to him.

"I know," he sighed in return, his breath running over my skin as he moved closer, his lips so close to my cheek that I tensed, expecting the kiss, wanting it more than anything.

Before I could ask, before I could turn, he was gone, his hand leaving a chill behind my skin as the heat vanished, as he vanished. The silks swirled around me as he began to ascend, pulling himself up on the tiniest sliver of fabric, his legs dangling below him.

The muscles of his arms and back pulled and rippled as they worked, as his inhuman strength easily lifted him eight feet in the air, his moves confident as he began the routine we had run through a hundred times by now.

Reaching his destination, he rolled back in a perfect

pike, wrapping the silk around his arm in a lock like I had done to Jarron on that first day.

From locks to a pike, to a wrap, to an extension. He moved through the motions smoothly, swimming through the silk as though he was swimming through air. As familiar with them as he was with flying.

Seeing him there made me want to see his dragon, to fly by him. I had no idea when, or if that was going to happen, but for now, this would have to do. Besides, if I thought he was hot before, it was nothing to now. I had no idea how amazingly sexy a man could be in silks until this moment.

Drake spun in the silks to an invert, the silks crossed over his back in a straddle that made the perfect base, his hands extended down to me.

Desperate to reach me.

I was pretty sure that right then if I jumped I would reach him. Float right up and into his arms. While I am sure it would give our act the pizazz that it needed, I also didn't need to give Stacia anything more to freak out about.

Not that I could see her, not that I cared. We had run this routine a million times, but this time it was different. The world felt different. He felt different.

I swallowed, letting the buzz of energy consume me, and climbed the silks to him. Dancing through the silks, my hand wrapped around his wrist, our hands interlocking as he lowered me below him, hovering ten feet in the air.

His hands around mine were the only thing keeping me airborne.

Keeping me safe.

I twisted back as rehearsed, eyes locking with his for the first time in the last few minutes. I nearly fell.

Like dropped to the ground in shock. Beautiful, beautiful shock.

His eyes were full of fire and flame, the melted brown sugar consumed by a light the color of burning embers, like the hottest coals in a fireplace. His gaze smoldered into me, sucking any breath that I had hoped to take out of my chest.

I was supposed to move into the first flip and I waited for him to swing, but instead he bent his arms, slowly bringing me to him. His eyes burned the closer I got, my own bending until we were at eye level, him hanging upside down, and me hanging from him.

"I love flying with you," he whispered when I was close enough to hear him. "This is the closest I have gotten in years, and I am glad it is with you."

I couldn't find the words to respond, so, like a loon, I stared at him, my eyes wide as he brought me closer, his lips soft against the tip of my nose.

It was the tiniest of touches, but it might as well have been a lightning strike. Energy ran through my body in ripples, shivering through my muscles as he began to lower me, letting me hang below him again.

"Ready, Elliot?" He said from above me, running his fingertip over my wrist to get my attention.

"Yeah," I said, screwing my focus back into place.

Yes, I was all sorts of woozy, but considering the amount of adrenaline that was now running through me I had a good feeling we were going to land the ending. Like nail it to the wall and call it art.

"Yeah," I said, again, more determinedly, and began to swing myself enough to give myself the momentum that I needed for the first flip.

Drake matched me move for move, releasing me with perfect time for me to flip twice and grabbing my arms again.

Another swing, another flip, and this time I caught my

feet on his shoulders. His hands were strong on my waist as I bent back, rotating to a superman. He held me tight before, with a tap against my waist he released me and I twisted down.

Over to the left, into a pike. Up and over, triple barrel. We had run this portion of the routine so many times that we had mastered every move. Knew every drop, and every twist. It was perfect. I trusted him beyond anything, I knew he wouldn't drop me. I knew he had me.

Even without the whole mating-bonding fiasco, I started to understand the look that Ryn and Zoe had. Understood why the pole teams were the way they were. I felt, for the first time, what it meant to be part of an act, and not just performing one.

I knew what it meant to not be alone. To feel safe. Confident. Free.

Drake swung me to the side, and I spread my leg, catching his in mine and swinging myself up on top of him. Holding the long poles of the silk, I lifted into a split arching my back before I dropped, the same as I had off so many cliffs, so many buildings. The same as I had at least fifteen times today.

The final move. That last drop.

My heart pounded, my hands reached, his fingers grasped for my wrist as mine did for his.

And like all the other times, I felt the fingers of his weaker arm begin to slip, and myself continue to fall.

I twisted through the air, pulling myself onto my back as I prepared to land on the soft mat.

Instead, strong arms wrapped around me.

The heavy aroma of mint bathed the air as deep green eyes pressed into me, the strong arms holding me beneath them.

"I guess it's my turn to catch you," Killian said with the deep voice that awakened every single feral instinct in my phoenix.

Like a tickle you enjoy, or a hand in the right place, his voice did weird things to my body, and I tried to move away. Well, until his hand pressed against my arm in an attempt to help me down.

The skin of his palm was icy against my sweaty forearm, but it couldn't have felt more like fire. Well, more like a freaking explosion. I clamped my jaw down as a scream tried to escape, leaving a sound of pure pleasure to filter past my lips. He smiled at that, his own euphoria shimmering through the streaks of dark fire that was taking over his eyes.

I shouldn't like that. I shouldn't like the touch. I shouldn't like the smile. My brain was screaming in confusion, but my heart, my phoenix, my bones were dancing in a pleasure that was very nearly crippling me.

Well, maybe it was. Chances were high that if he put me down I would collapse to the ground. Everything about me was jelly. I was absorbed in him, in whatever power he was filling me with.

It had been over a week since I had seen him, and right then I knew that I never wanted to be without him again. Scowl or no scowl. I hadn't realized the pain, the odd hole that I had been left with could be filled so completely. With just one touch.

I wrapped my arms around his neck without thinking, burying my face as his massive forearms pulled me into him.

Killian sighed as he held me against him, the sound so deep and needy that I almost lost my head again.

"I missed you, Ellie girl," Killian's rough whisper tickled

my ear, his long curls covering my face as he gently pressed his lips against my cheek.

Yep, I moaned again. I fucking moaned. Unfortunately for me, the sound did not go unnoticed, and it wasn't by Killian.

"Common, Kills. You gotta at least give the rest of us a chance before you woo her away," Jarron said from right behind me, his palm warm against my back, sending more warm tingles through me, sparks sprinting through my muscles like they were running a marathon.

I was going to need a freakin' tea IV. I was sure the rampage of emotions were from not having seen them for so long, but if one touch was going to turn me into a pubescent jackrabbit, I was pretty sure I couldn't survive two at once.

I wiggled out of Killian's arms before I completely lost myself in their euphoria and was able to keep myself standing, and probably only because Drake was there to catch my wobbling ass.

"How was Rydaim?" Drake asked as he set me back on my feet, Jarron quick to step in and wrap his arms around me.

Even with the awkwardness there, I didn't step away. I let myself fall into him.

"Cold, dark, and full of lies," Killian said with a growl, the harsh tone in his voice rampaged through the glitter that being around them was giving me. I gave him a look in question, but he wasn't even looking at me.

"Sounds about right," Drake said with a bark, his voice darker than I had ever heard it. "At least from what I remember."

The magical joy-bubble that filled our space had popped.

"What is Rydaim?" I asked Jarron, whispering through the tension.

"Where we grew up," he returned, and suddenly the fear and anger that was infecting the air making sense.

"So home?"

"No," Jarron said, giving me a smirk as he pressed his palm against the side of my face. I resisted the urge to lean into his touch, to breathe in the scent of pine that always emanated from him. "This is home."

25

ELLIOT

Jarron said nothing as he began to walk me back toward the hotel, his hands plunged into his pockets as he kicked at the gravel in the parking lot. It scattered before us, the tar slicked surfaces reflecting the light of the moon as it peeked through the clouds.

The three of them had sat on the front row during my act, the awe shimmering in their eyes as I spun and tumbled through the air. It was different, somehow, having all of them there and not just Drake with his ever present smile. The nerves were higher, my heart practically jumping out of my chest as I remained hyper focused on the moves.

I could never be sure, but judging by the way both Jarron and Killian were white-knuckling their chairs at the end of my last drop they were ready to jump into action lest I fall again.

No falling.

And not because I had my head on straight and wasn't clamoring over myself to jump into their laps, but because time stayed perfectly and solidly in place. Which was good because I had enough to worry about.

Like Jarron staying the night with me.

I had gotten used to Drake being there, lounging on the tiny couch as we chatted well into the night, and crawling toward me when neither of us could move in the morning. But Killian needed to talk to Drake, Zoe, and Suvi about the wicked kingdom he had returned from. Which left me with Jarron.

Who I hadn't spoken to since his confession of a week before.

Drake was right, I needed to talk to him before I put some fence around him. But I had expected that to be a week from now, not minutes. Judging by the way I wanted to both run away, and into him, that fence might already be there.

I sighed roughly and wrapped my arms around my waist like I was trying to keep in warmth, which was ridiculous because it was nowhere near cold. Even if I wasn't a walking talking radiator the air was probably near a hundred, with the sun down. I didn't want to know what a real desert felt like.

There were far too many trees here for it to be a real desert.

I may be nervous and jittery, but that didn't stop my phoenix from nestling against my heart, thundering in joy at Jarron's very presence.

"Don't you need to be at this meeting?" I asked when we had made it about half way across the parking lot. "Or, better yet, don't I need to be at this meeting?"

"Nah," Jarron said, shooting a wide grin my way, "It's all boring war planning."

Boring and war were never words that I would have put together, least of all when concerning the wicked dragon-man that wanted to eat my bones or something. I still wasn't totally clear how that whole 'steal your life force' thing would go down. But that one I might be okay with being in the dark about..

"Do you wish to help them decide on a plan of attack?" Jarron asked, his tone making it clear he didn't quite believe it. "I thought you would want to stay out of hearing about all the dangers of the world."

"They've kept me in the dark most of my life. I'm kind of over it." I said honestly, casting him a side glance. "Drake did fill me in on the basics. And Zoe..."

I drifted off, letting the night swallow my words, except that the words seemed more like a spotlight than a wisp of smoke I could ignore.

"Just make sure I know before we head into an attack," I finished lamely, the dark chuckle that burst from Jarron couldn't have been more clear that he didn't believe me.

"Consider it done." He tried to smile, but even in the dark I could tell it didn't quite reach his eyes.

Jarron walked as close as he dared, or rather, as close as he could without bumping into me. He was watching me carefully, his dark eyes looking nearly non-existent in the dim moonlight, except for the little golden lines that were pulling me into him. But that may also be a trick of my phoenix, who was practically purring with the look he was giving me.

Come on, girl, I've pulled myself together, now it's your turn.

I wonder if Suvi had a stronger tea, specifically for my shifter. I still hadn't taken the IV off the table.

"Is there anything else you want to know?" He asked as he opened the door for me, holding his arm out in an exaggerated escort.

I gave him a side glance as I passed him, not quite sure

what I wanted to ask. Or even if he was talking about the war meeting that the others were in.

He could see the elephant in the room as well as I could. Or rather, the dragon. I was pretty sure the dragon had eaten the elephant long ago.

"I want to know why?" I finally answered as I pressed the button for the elevator as two other joyful performers joined us.

Talk about the worst timing ever. Jarron greeted them joyfully, learning names and performance places and even favorite foods in the time it took to load the elevator and rise to the fourth floor. I couldn't find it in me to respond, my stomach was twisting with the question that lingered in the air, pressing against my chest until it was hard to breathe.

"I look forward to getting to know you," Jarron said genuinely as the elevator door slid closed, leaving us in the beige hallway, and the two of them to continue their journey to their room.

"They were nice," Jarron said into the silence, the quick subject change only adding to the tension that was now so heavy in the air I could taste it.

"Don't you think they were nice?" Jarron asked as we walked down the hallway, the sound of our shoes against the carpet echoing like muffled drums of a countdown against my heartbeat. How could he be so oblivious? Couldn't he feel that weight against his chest?

With the look he was giving me, still expecting an answer, the answer was clearly no.

I could only nod, the single beat plunging us into silence as we walked the last few steps, leaving only the electronic beep of the door to keep us company.

"I didn't know any better," Jarron said from behind me the second the snap of the door filled my tiny hotel room.

It was like being kicked in the balls, or I assume it was. The unanswered question had built into wall and with one swift kick he answered.

"I killed him because my father asked me to and I didn't know any better."

"You told me that before," I gasped, my voice caught in my throat as I stood still, frozen in the tiny hallway that led to the living space. I knew the bed, the dresser, the TV. I knew everything that was in front of me, but I couldn't see it. I might as well have been frozen in ice with the blur that I was looking into.

"Yes, and I know it is no excuse," He whispered as the lock slid into place, the grind of metal against metal ripping over my spine. I shivered, the sensation crippling me as his hand against my shoulder gently prodded me to face him.

Taking one deep, cleansing breath I complied, well aware that both my chest and my hands were shaking. The shake didn't get any better as I faced him, as he intertwined his fingers with my own, his tears falling over my skin in little pricks of boiling heat.

"Killian was a child when Rydaim fell." Jarron said, his voice cracking through the tears, pain clear in his eyes. I stared at him, stuck behind his words, not sure where this was going, not sure if I was ready to dive into this, but knowing I couldn't stop it either. "He was little more than a decade old the day our father enslaved the Fae that Elliot had brought into our clan. They were your father's friends, they trusted him. We had lived in harmony, until the king massacred them all. Killian remembers the blood. He remembers the screams. He was a child, and he loved his father. He fought with him and destroyed thousands because it was all that he knew. It was what he was told was right. I was raised after their enslavement. It was all I knew. I didn't know any better. It was our truth. We had been told they were born to serve us, we had no reason to question."

Jarron paused, his shoulder sagging as he looked down to our hands, his thumb moving over my skin, leaving a trail of glittering heat behind. I would have shivered at the touch, if I wasn't so frozen by his words, frozen by the pain that was dripping from him as hard and as fast as his tears.

I had never seen him like this. I didn't know him well, but the fear that pressed through his dark eyes let me see him more than the others. I saw him. The real him. The dark depths of his eyes cracked with the depth of him, not a sliver of glitter present. There was only pain, only regret. It sucked the breath from my chest and my knees began to buckle, my own pain boiling right to the surface.

"Zoe was almost a hundred the day Rydaim fell, she knew better, and she fought our father before the first of the magic was cut from the little sprites. She fought to help them for years after. She and Elliot. I didn't know of Elliot's role until years after he was gone. Years after I knew the truth of what had happened." Jarron continued, his hand tightening around mine as he led me into the living area, nodding to the tiny couch Drake usually slept on.

I didn't hesitate to sit, I wasn't sure my legs could keep me standing for much longer. I sighed as I sat, but not in comfort, the unforgiving cushions felt twice as hard against the rigidity that was taking over my bones.

"She asked me to fight with her," Jarron whispered as he sat beside me. "She asked me to stand with her and Drake, but I didn't know any better. I had been raised to think the Fae inferior. I didn't know them besides as my slaves. I didn't see..." He paused his voice catching, the last of the wall he had been trying to hide behind crashing down as he fell forward, his fingers wrapping through his hair as he pulled and tugged at the strands in agony.

His sobs ripped through the air, pulling me toward him. Begging me to reach for him, to hold him, to comfort him. I wanted to, or rather, my phoenix wanted to. I couldn't find it in me to move. I sat as still as the breaking heart that was pulsing in my chest.

I knew where this story was heading, and just like the steps that counted down to the room, each echo of my heart beat pulled me towards where I did not want to go.

"So you killed him." It was a statement, the hard finality hitting against Jarron's soul and the over confident man collapsed more. His chest shaking as he struggled for breath, his sobs fading away.

"My father commanded it," He said with a shaking gasp, the words fighting past his tears as he sat up to look at me.

I didn't know my father. It shouldn't matter, except it did. It mattered because it was still my life. It mattered because I needed to trust him, both he and Killian.

I needed to know both in order to be able to put my life in their hands. Something I was still delusionally trying to convince myself was still a far way off.

"My father said Elliot was a traitor, that he had evacuated several Fae for his own personal uses. But the Fae belonged to my father, stealing his property was punishable only by death," his voice caught, his eyes dead and far away as they peered into the dull glow of moonlight, seeing something I could never understand. "I thought it was right. I was told they all belonged to my father. But people cannot belong to other people, just as you cannot belong to me, or Drake, or Killian. We love you. We do not own you."

His words lingered in the air, but I sat, still frozen in his pain.

"Your father saw that," he said before I could gather my thoughts. "He was saving them from the beginning. He saved them while he taught me as a boy to fight them. He saved them when he would take Killian and I on hunting trips, and teach us to spar with swords like the mortals did. He brought the first Remington home, and we laughed at the silly mortals weapon as we hit cans off a fence. Racing the gun with our fire. Elliot's fire was the fastest. And even then he saved them. He was good from the beginning. I should have seen it then."

The memories hung in the air like fireflies, they glowed in my mind as a picture of a man I never knew blossomed before me, and for the first time I think I actually truly missed him. Every time I learned something new about him, it pressed against my heart in a loss that I didn't understand. But Jarron's memories, they were so real. My father was so real.

It was almost like I knew him, just a little bit. I didn't know what I had missed, not having a father. But now I was starving for more.

"How did you know?" I finally asked, refusing to look away from him, "How did you know the king was wrong. You say you didn't know. But what made you know? When did you see?"

The question ended lamely, but luckily he didn't call attention to it, he just smiled sadly, taking my hand and tangling it with his own.

"Callay."

I wasn't quite sure I heard him, "Collie? Is that a person."

Jarron nodded, and I felt the hot heat of confusion and jealousy rise up. Thankfully, I easily restrained my phoenix that time.

"Callay is Killian's... she works in his house," Jarron said stiffly. I was pretty sure she didn't voluntarily work for anyone judging by the hesitation there, but I wasn't about to call attention to it.

"She is a Fae?" Another nod. "What happened?"

This time he shook his head, his shaggy hair swinging over the tips of his ears, "Nothing good. Killian saw it first. He had to convince me to see, luckily I am not as bull headed as he is." He tried to smile, but the false joy didn't quite take, so he plunged ahead, talking fast. "She has worked for him for years, always devoted. She was one of the first to pledge herself to service. She won't even admit what happened."

He stopped, as if that was it, answered, sealed, and finalized. But I only heard holes. Holes that gnawed on my soul, twisted through my spine and left me wondering.

"What happened?" I asked again.

"Our father... He used her and gave her child to a... man..."

His voice caught, and he looked away again, although his hand held on tight, like I was an anchor in a sea of pain. That time I felt it right alongside him. The pain, the anger, the determination.

"I will help you fight him," I said, the words tasting like salt against my tongue, even as my phoenix sang in joy at the promise, at the truth behind them. Except it wasn't truth, not completely. "We will defeat him."

That was the truth, and it felt powerful. More than that, it felt terrifying, and my tears rose up to join his.

Our tears fell, but they were no longer quite as hopeless. They didn't drip with pain, and for the first time since we had left the tent, the deep charcoal depth of his eyes glittered in the dim moonlight of the hotel room, the sparkling lines that drew me into his soul.

Except they weren't lines. The fire of his dragon blazed in the brightest gold, the darkness in his eyes encompassed by flames so bright, so brilliant, that I couldn't stop the gasp.

It was his soul, his dragon, I could see it, and it was beautiful. I bit my lip as I leaned into him, my free hand lifting to his jaw, the muscle clenching beneath my fingers.

Ellie.

The voice was a strong rumble inside my head, the same voice I had heard before. The same rumble of want. Except this time I could see it in his golden eyes, I could feel it in the heat of his hands.

"Jarron." The word swallowed the last of the pain, any residue slipping away as he smiled.

I didn't stop him as he leaned in, I didn't stop him as his hand lifted to cup my neck, as his breath brushed over my lips. As his made contact.

Soft. Wet. Warm.

Fire rippled through every muscle as his lips pressed against mine. His fingers, burrowing into my hair as he brought me closer. Heat rippled deep into me, pooling in my stomach as his hands gripped my hips, pulling me into him, lifting me onto his lap.

I didn't protest. I wasn't sure I could if I tried. I just clung to him. My arms wrapping around his neck as I kissed him back, as I sighed at the feeling that I had been waiting my whole life to experience.

"Jarron," I breathed, letting my fingers tangle in his hair as he brought me closer, his tongue darting out to taste my lips.

Shock sparked in the back of my neck at the heat, and the fire that came alongside and my eyes jerked open, only to have every drop of passion and need evaporate.

"Jarron," I heaved, fear taking over as I jumped from his

lap, holding my arms out in front of me as flames the color of molten gold rippled over my skin.

They looked like ripples in a pond, dangerous, scary as shit ripples in a pond. They moved up from my hands, burning away the sleeves of my jacket in little puffs of smoke.

"Jarron," I said again, begging for help as I watched the flames grow closer. "Did you do this?"

"No, this is you," He nodded his head, eyes wide in his own panic as he stood, his hands out in front of him like I was a bomb that he needed to diffuse.

Maybe I was. I didn't know anymore. Right when I think I had a handle on this whole phoenix-dragon-mating-bonding crap, something else happens that turns me into a ticking time bomb.

Literally.

I didn't think I could take it anymore.

"What is happening?" I nearly screamed, shaking my arms in panic, willing to do anything to get the flames to go away. Instead of extinguishing like matchsticks the fire flew from me in balls of molten lava, sparks and embers falling from them as they soared.

Right into the wall, the TV, and the bed, the last of which exploded in a burst of flames that shoved us back, me into the now destroyed TV and Jarron into the wall.

Still, the flames burned.

No, no, holy freaking no. This could not be happening. I resisted the urge to shake the flames away again, and frantically began to blow on them as they crept up my skin.

I could have sworn my phoenix was laughing.

"Fix it, fix it, fix it," I said to no one imparticular as Jarron grabbed the blanket and wrapped it in on itself, and practically threw the still smoldering cloth into the bathroom.

Still I blew, looking ridiculous as I lay on the floor huffing and puffing on my arms. One minute I am kissing one of the hottest guys known to man, and the next burning down a hotel.

How is that for a first kiss story. If only it was even remotely funny.

"Darling," Jarron breathed as he kneeled before me, his eyes still glowing gold as he looked at me, his hands extended. He was calm, gentle, and there wasn't a drop of fear in his eyes.

No disappointment.

No shock.

Just pure golden affection.

"Breathe, darling," he said again as he scooted closer, cringing as he pressed his hands against my still burning flesh. It was clear it hurt, clear it burned, but he said nothing. He kept his eyes on me, bringing me into him.

"It's just your phoenix," he whispered, "And your phoenix is beautiful."

"Even when it burns you?" I asked, watching my arms as the flames began to extinguish.

"Even when it burns me. But I think Zoe was right," he continued with a grin, that same heart stopping smile burning through me.

"I think we may need to control our bristling mating instinct. Because you may actually explode."

I didn't even try to restrain the groan.

I hated when Zoe was right.

26

DRAKE

Suvi had fired up her pipe before she had even sat down all the way, the long tendrils of liquid green smoke trailed from both pipe and mouth as she brought it to life, and the scent of sandalwood, stone, and something else Drake couldn't place became a wall.

Zoe had promised him that he would get used to the witch, and to her strange habits, but Drake was beginning to think that was impossible. Well, at least until she stopped smoking a dead skunk, or whatever she shoved into that ancient wooden pipe."

"Do you have to smoke that?" Killian asked, his dark eyes digging into the pipe.

Ahh, something that Drake and his brother could agree on, not that that he would ever admit it. Trust did not come easy, and they were just beginning to test that fragile relationship.

"Yes, your royal highness," Suvi said, continuing to nurse and puff on the long stemmed tube. "Yes, I do. It's good for my old bones if you know what I mean."

She gave him a smile and wink that broke through his

stony exterior and left him looking dumbfounded from where he stood in the middle of Suvi's office. Zoe laughed, at either Killian's expression or Suvi's response Drake wasn't sure. Before he could even venture a guess, Killian's stony mask snapped back into place as though it had been slapped there. Flinch included.

Perhaps this wouldn't be quite so bad, Drake thought and sat back into one of the over worn chairs he and Zoe had claimed.

"You should try it sometime," Suvi continued, taking another puff and blowing the smoke in his direction. "Might do your old bones some good too."

Killian's scowl deepened and this time Drake was not as successful at withholding his chuckle. The accompanied pig-snort sound resulted in him getting quite the look. Drake met the stare head on, his dragon bristling under his skin in hope of attack.

He pushed the creature down, knowing that no matter what happened, he could not let him escape. Restraining the dragon had gotten significantly easier over the last few days, but he wasn't about to broadcast that to the world.

"Might do your old bones some good too," Killian said with a sneer, the look directed right at Drake.

Drake let the anger boil, his dragon growling loudly, even though he was kept perfectly controlled.

"I think we have had quite enough of that," Suvi said, filling the office with more smoke. "You have asked to speak to us for a reason, Killian, and I for one am growing impatient at waiting. I am assuming that since Jarron is not with us he is apprised to what is coming?"

"You would be correct," Killian said with a solemn nod, all sign of his combative nature vanishing. "He is with Elliot. I know none of us feel safe with her being alone yet, and after the week I have had in Rydaim I would have to suggest that it become the rule."

Every word plunged Killian deeper in the controlled powerhouse that Drake had glimpsed. It was unnerving. He had grown up with this man, with his temper, with his callous nature. It was all he had seen in him the last few days, but somehow it had vanished. His irritating older brother appeared to be, as much as it disgusted him to admit it, a prince.

One glance at Zoe, and the narrowed glare she was giving him and he knew he wasn't the only one being slapped around.

"And how is Rydaim?" Suvi asked, taking a puff of her pipe, seemingly unaware to Killian's Jekyll and Hyde act.

"It is as it has been for the last two hundred years," Killian said, the dark warning in his voice returning enough that Drake flinched, but not in fear. His brother was disgusted. It seems he was full of surprises. "The underground persists. The slave trade has grown into a human and Fae trafficking ring that as much as we try Jarron and I cannot seem to infiltrate enough to shut it down. The Forgotten have grown, and after the purge of the tunnels a few years ago..."

Zoe shot to her feet, the action causing Drake to jump even as his heart sunk. This news was not new to him, but it didn't hurt any less, it didn't make his dragon hiss in anger any less. His mouth grew hot at the memory of all the friends both he and his beast had lost.

The underground caves were where their attempt to overthrow their father had started fifty years ago. He had been a child when he had fallen through the cracks and discovered the Fae city hidden underneath their own, when he first started to understand the injustice his father had caused. It wasn't until Alain's death that Zoe gained the courage to rise up against the man who had made it clear his daughter would not ascend the throne, as was the custom.

She had too much good, and there was no better option than for him to remain in control forever.

She would save them all, and all Ceres knew was death. Hearing of the purging of the tunnels and all the death that followed had actually fueled his decision to help his brothers.

"What do you mean purged?" Zoe asked, her voice catching.

"I mean that Parris sniffed them out and he and his harem feasted on their blood for a year before the life was drained from them. Taking the last of the pure Fae magic with it," Killian spoke with such darkness that Drake could feel it press against his soul.

That he hadn't heard, and he sunk into his chair as Zoe collapsed into hers.

Parris. The vampires.

His father had struck a truce with them when Drake and Zoe first rose up against the king. It was one of the main reasons they lost. Fae blood does weird things to Vampires when they feast upon it.

The memories still haunted his dreams.

"What are the vampires still doing in Rydaim?" Zoe asked, her voice hard as she looked from Drake, his dragon pressing painfully against his skin at this new piece of information. Judging by the fire that was igniting in the dark of Zoe's eyes, he wasn't the only one.

"Currently?" Killian clarified, straightening his jacket and refusing to make eye contact with any of them. "Getting father drunk on the flesh of mortals, priming the man to fall so he can take control of our kind. Although how he plans to do it, and what he hopes to gain, Jarron and I cannot figure out. Besides using our information to reach the phoenix first, we are at a loss."

For the first time Killian actually looked concerned, his brow furrowed, his eyes dark. While it may be wishful thinking, Drake was sure that he saw the powerful man's shoulders droop. Killian had always been the spitting image of their father, his blood and soul in line with the tyranny that their line favored.

All that had somehow vanished.

"So there is more than father that wants Ellie's fire?" Drake asked, his dragon grumbling protectively at the very idea. Killian only nodded in response, the simple head nod making him want to run out of the room and glue himself to his beautiful mate. He barely stayed in his seat.

With the way Killian still stood, his fingers fidgeting with the hem of his expertly tailored jacket it was no wonder he had wanted Jarron to stay with her.

"If the vampires are searching for her, we may have already lost, they sneak through the dark like maggots," Zoe snapped, her fingers digging into the armrest of the chair as she leaned forward. "They may have found her already."

"They have not," Suvi said, lazily smoking her pipe as she looked at something far behind us.

"You don't know that, Suvi," Zoe countered, but the old witch stopped her with a single look.

"I know," she said, looking so determinedly into Zoe that Drake was sure he had missed some secret. Zoe, however, looked just as confused.

Drake looked between them, waiting for silence or knowledge to break, Killian broke the silence first.

"They haven't found her," Killian said, as if it settled it, "If they had Parris would have made a move. As it is he is still bringing father virgins for his bed." He scowled, his disgust clear. Drake did not hesitate to join him. "I am concerned that this new threat, this new battle will stretch us too thin. We are only four dragons, a witch, and a bound phoenix, we cannot hope to defeat an army of the undead."

"We *cannot* defeat an army of the undead," Zoe clarified, as if that made it better. Drake shot her a look, they were facing the impossible, and her logic was not helping.

He was suddenly very glad that Ellie was not here for this. The girl was still coping through the fact that he and his brothers had bonded with her. This would only be gasoline to an open flame.

"We can defeat them all. It is the same battle, and the same enemy," Suvi said, her pipe now sitting forgotten on the desk, smoking lazily as it fumigated the room. "Nothing has changed, but we must be aware of the snake. I know Parris well, I met him when he was a weakling seeking medicines for his thirst. A newly turned immortal disgusted with his fate..."

Her voice faded off, her eyes glossing over with a haze that caused Drake to jump. It was the same as last night, except there were no bones, and no dancing stars. Didn't make the empty look in her eyes any less discomforting. He pushed his back into the chair, attempting to ground himself. Or, at least move away as much as possible.

"Parris is more than a snake. He is a disease," Killian growled, the disgust clear as he began to pace, his eyes continually darting to the door as if he expected the greasy man to appear. Drake squirmed in his chair, snake or not, he did not look forward to facing the demon. "We cut off the head and he will be gone. I need to get close enough."

"You cut off the head of this snake and a million more

will appear," Suvi said, placing the pipe back in her mouth as she cleared her desk, opening one of the drawers with a loud squeak. "The only way to defeat this monster is to gnaw your way from tail, and swallow him whole from there. Catch him before he wriggles."

There was something in the eager joy in the old woman's eyes that made Drake's dragon lift its head. The beast pressed against his heart as he tiniest of flames began to fill his mouth. It was a comforting feeling, if only because he wanted to destroy the vampire as much as his dragon did.

"So how do we find the tail if the tunnels have been cleared and the underground removed?" Drake asked, sitting on the edge of his seat, ready to jump up and do the deed then if he could.

"It is still there, we just don't know where." Killian said, stopping his pacing to lean against the wall of Suvi's office, the motion sending a ripple of air through the fabric she used as wallpaper. "Jarron and I have been working for the past few years to try to infiltrate the underbelly of Rydaim, to find allies and stop Parris's infection before it grows to something we cannot stop."

"And what have you found?" Suvi asked, pulling a handful of what appeared to be bones out of the drawer and throwing them over the desk with a clatter.

Drake tensed, expecting the office to instantly fill with stars. He wasn't the only one, Killian stepped back with a jolt. Meanwhile, Zoe looked right at home. Well, at home as you could feel when surrounded by talk of war.

"We have found a few allies, and made contacts that will allow us to bring them food when Parris and his vampires aren't roaming," The last few words came out with such a darkness that Drake flinched. Good old Killian wasn't lost forever it seemed. "We are hoping that the kindness will show willingness and we can find a few to stand with us."

Drake was nearly bowled over. How in the world could his angry, gruff brother be doing something so... good. He scoffed at the impossibility. Zoe beat him to it.

"We had thousands of Fae with us and we hardly made a scratch on you and your precious daddy," She mocked, the heat in her voice shimmering through the air around her like a mirage. "A hostile takeover will not work."

"Spoken like a true dragon," Killian said, looking right at his former enemies with a gleam of excitement in his bright green eyes. "Brute strength will not win, just as Suvi said. It is why you failed. What we need is a revolution."

Killian's excitement, his sense, his power. It all infected Drake and made him ready to jump up and pledge to the cause. He wanted to, it was what he had wanted for years. But now there was something more precious than that. Something that threw more than a wrench into this. It threw a mother fucking bomb in.

"Killian," Drake ventured, his dragon raging as he addressed his brother, the sound a warning purr as the powerful dragon turned toward him. "What about Ellie?"

"This is the only way to protect her, Drake," Suvi said, answering the question before Killian had a chance. It didn't matter who the answer came from, it still twisted in Drake's gut. "Sometimes we must fight for freedom. Sometimes safety does not lie in hiding.

The sentiment was true, but it bristled against Drake like a bed of nails. he had not hid, he had fought, and he had paid the price. After that, what choice did he have? A single dragon cannot make a difference. He would need the use of both wings to even try, and that was a distant memory.

"Where do we begin?" the old lady asked, concealing an eager grin as she threw her bones, placing the pipe back in her mouth.

Drake wasn't sure if she was talking to them, or to her bones, but it was Killian who answered, his words dark as he turned to look right at him.

"We need to find our allies," Killian began, his eyes shining as he looked from Drake to Zoe. "And I only know of two people that can do that."

27

ELLIOT

I SLEPT LIKE A ZOMBIE.

And no, that does not mean I slept like the dead.

I slept like a zombie. You know, an undead monster that's limbs fall off and jaw lulls open in hopes of a bite of flesh and who knows what else. Tossing, turning, and I am sure drooling and moaning also occurred. The only thing that didn't happen was brain eating, but I had plenty of that in my dream to make up for it.

My sleep was pock-marked by something that lingered between nightmares and magical romps through a forest that I was sure could not exist in real life. No where was that green, no where was filled with so many vines and birds and perfect little red topped mushrooms.

It was a place that was made of children's laughter and glitter bombs. I could have romped through that forest all night and been perfectly fine with it. Even if I did end up farting glitter for the next month. But it was not to be. Falling asleep with such horrifying facts in my head had seriously done a number on me.

I went from dreaming about children sized people

dancing through a sparkling forest, to a long stone hall with walls that stretched a hundred feet high. Massive arches soared over me, pulling my eyes toward the end of the hall where a wall of glass glittered in a tapestry of a hundred hues.

Maybe hall was the wrong word.

This was clearly a cave, a massive tunnel that sparkled the same as the forest, glittered with what I could have sworn at first sight to be magic. Except this was a little too moist to be glitter. A little to red.

I knew it was a dream, but I swear I could feel the cool air of the cave prickle against my skin. I could feel the fear clench through each muscle, weaving through them like some kind of barbed wire. Tearing, ripping, shredding.

Pulling at a memory that I had tried far too long to push away. A dream I had nearly forgotten, but standing here...

I knew I had been here before.

And this place was very, very real.

"Well, well, well," A slither of a voice said behind me, the deep mocking of a woman shaking the barbed tension and threatening to rip it out.

I whipped around at the sound, but nothing was there, nothing but a mirror of the hall I had turned from. The same blood smeared rock extended away from me, the same swathes of color from what I was sure was a stained glass window beaming in the distance.

"What are you doing inside of my tracker," the voice snarled in my ear, tickling my skin and this time I jumped, fists up and at the ready.

I had never thrown a punch before, let alone fight anyone, chances were high that I didn't even know how. Dream or not, I wasn't going to let that stop me.

It didn't matter, however, there was no one there. Nothing but the same hallway, the same walls...

I whipped around, sure I would catch he owner of the voice, sure I would find the door.

Nothing but glass and stone. I spun again. Stone and blood. Again. Glass and stone and the deep rumble of a laugh. Forget the barbed wire, this sound was a twisting knife.

"Catch me if you can, little girl," the voice came again, the tinkling laugh mocking me as I continued to spin and turn in a quickly growing panic.

This was stupid, and I was stupid for letting my subconscious control me like that. It was a dream and I could make it go away, same as I had with so many others.

"Go," I hissed into the long hall, and with a loud roar of what I could have sworn was an avalanche, the frightening place was sucked out of my mind like water down the drain.

The hall, the window, the echo of a laugh, it all siphoned away until I was left alone, standing in the dark with only the heavy thump of my heart.

Bang. Bang. Bang.

No, my heart didn't sound like that.

The door. It was a door.

The bed shifted behind me as Jarron got up, his warm arm snaking away before he covered me in blankets, trapping in all the heat. It was so warm, so comfortable, lying here snuggling into the blankets. I very nearly fell back asleep, that was until the door to the hotel room creaked open and the dull light from the hallway flooded in, igniting the air in stars.

Sparkling glitter, all over the walls. It was like in my dream, like in the forest. The light was the same. Dull and yet somehow warm.

Like the bed.

I pressed myself into the pillow, my mind pulling me back to sleep. Back into the forest.

Trees sprouted up in my subconscious like weeds. They tangled over the hotel room until it was only that same glittering forest, the light from the door shining like the setting sun through the massive trunks.

Reality and dream blended together to the point that I couldn't tell them apart. Everything was mashed and muddled and strangely comfortable.

"She's called me twice," A voice echoed through the trees, sending multi colored birds soaring toward the bright sun. "I don't know how much longer I can hold her off."

I recognized that voice. At least I thought I did. There was something off about the way Killian spoke. Something I couldn't quite place. I turned, following the sound through the trees, darting around wide trunks and skipping over the undergrowth like I was in some kind of dance.

I forgot about the voice before it came again.

"You have been back only a few hours," Jarron said from behind me, the sound distanced and strained as it sent the broad silver leaves into a shimmer. "For this to work you need to control her. If all you can manage is a few hours then perhaps you are not the right man for the job."

Jarron chuckled, and I turned, how could he be so far away? Was I lost? I stepped toward him, darting under a branch that I was sure wasn't there before. was this forest getting thicker?

"You try to control her," Killian snarled, and I turned again, into the dark forest that was swallowing his voice, the leaves shivering along with his breathing until his snap was nothing more than an angry breeze.

No, not angry.

Frightened.

Killian was frightened.

Although why he would be scared I had no idea. Hell, I had no idea *how* he could be so scared. He was always so strong, so dark. Even when he was scowling, I didn't see him getting so scared. But something was clearly terrifying him.

The forest reacted to the thought as though it was a bomb, birds exploded from the branches as though they had been shooed away, the sound of wings and the loud tweets of despair rippling through the air, until it was all I could hear. Killian's low panic was bathed in it, Jarron's frustrated snap little more than a crack of a branch.

I needed to get out of here. Something was wrong. I batted at the birds, pushing through the trees, desperate to reach the soft cushion of my bed and fall back into it.

Fall back into reality.

Reality didn't seem to want me. No matter how hard I ran, my subconscious had trapped me in this half-awake forest, listening to a conversation that I wasn't one hundred percent sold on being real.

"That's your job, *your highness*," Jarron said with a laugh, the sound breaking through the tweets of more than a dozen birds.

"It's not my job to deflect that woman," Killian snarled, the snap cracking like a branch in my subconscious. "If it was up to me I would have her beheaded."

The harsh tone had returned, the anger so abrupt that it stabbed through me, plunging through the forest as it dissolved back into bulky shadows or a broken TV and the ribbon of light that streamed into the room, Jarron's cut-out clearly defined in the shadow of the carpet.

"That's not the song I heard her singing in your bedroom

last week." Jarron taunted, and I tensed, the implication clear even if I had no idea what they were talking about.

A woman. He hated a woman. It couldn't be me because I was nowhere near singing in his room last week.

Forget the forest, I was wide awake now, clenching the pillow that still smelled like Jarron to my chest.

Of course Killian had lovers, probably a multitude of lovers. It suddenly made sense as to why he was so distanced now. I was getting in the way of his chorus line of lovers.

Yes, my blood was boiling. At least I wasn't breaking out in flames now.

"A lot has changed in a week," Killian said, his voice lined with enough malice that it only bristled me more. "And thanks to our past, she is starting to get suspicious."

"Of course she is," Jarron said with a laugh that did nothing to calm the rage that was bubbling inside of me. "You need to control her. Keep her away from us, and away from what we are doing here. And most of all, block your mind."

My heart lifted, my phoenix bristling inside of me in hope that even through his parade of tall powerful dragon beauties he would still pick me.

"Easier said than done."

I guess not.

"Then block yourself from Ellie," Jarron provided and I flinched, a stab plunging through my heart as that hole began to rip open again. Jagged red pain ripping me in two and alarming my phoenix until she was practically screaming to get out. forcing her back, I locked her away as I had for some many years, sure that I wouldn't be able to hold her for long.

I shifted my weight, trying to dislodge the agony that

was spreading over my chest, secretly hoping that I could catch sight of him, that maybe it was someone else. Or maybe he wasn't talking about me at all.

It didn't work either way, there was only a single ribbon of light and the faded beige wallpaper.

I restrained a growl of self-loathing and curled into a ball, my groan and the rustling of blankets drowning out Killian's response. Which was probably for the best.

I may be fine, but I don't think my phoenix could handle being told she wasn't wanted right now. I had caught enough things on fire for one night. The room still smelled like smoke, and the blanket Jarron had stolen from a maid's cart was hardly cutting it, a chill was starting to creep over me, and I don't think it was entirely from Killian.

"You say that as if I want to be around her in the first place."

So much for drowning out my rejection letter.

I don't know if that counted as being dumped, but it sure felt like it. At least, what I thought being dumped would be like. Numbing agony ripped through my heart, shredding it to pieces as I pulled the pillow into me, suddenly wishing I could return to the trees and pretend that this horrible conversation was a dream.

Maybe it was. I was far too numb to be awake anymore.

"I don't like being around her."

Any warmth that I had found had turned to ice. Or rather, massive icicles straight to my heart. They stabbed and sliced me apart as I lay there, tears silently streaming down my face. That loud uncontrollable part of me wanted to jump from the bed and confront him, but I couldn't grab hold of my emotions, or my calm enough to do that and sound like a sane person.

Even if I could move. I was pretty sure all of that stabby ice had turned me to lead.

"You need to figure this out, Kills, because you are putting everyone in danger," Jarron said, his voice harsh as the light from the hallway began to dim, the door closing me in with my pain.

A lone gasp of air escaped as Jarron turned from the door to face me, his drooped expression making it clear he could see my tears. Damn reflective drama drops.

I wiped them away and tried to give him a smile, but the thing fell flat and he sighed, crawling over the bed to reach me.

"I take it you heard?" He whispered into the dark, as if he was afraid of being overheard.

I pressed my lips together in a tight little line. It was the only response I could give him that wouldn't end in explosion. He seemed to understand. Without a word, he gathered me into him, wrapping me in his arms as he pressed me against him, holding me to him from chest to toes in the tight pressure of a cocoon.

A tight, pain-erasing little cocoon.

"Don't worry, darling," he whispered in my ear as he smoothed my hair. "Killian will take care of it, I promise."

The words were far from soothing, in fact that only twisted the ice blade more, stabbing it into me with precision. I flinched, his arms tightening as he began to train his fingers up and down my spine.

It didn't take away the pain, it didn't even numb it, but it felt nice to be held, and to be wanted.

And right then, it was enough, so I leaned into him. My phoenix screaming in my head, as I cried myself to sleep in his arms.

28

ELLIOT

I woke up cranky and ready to breathe fire.

I had never breathed fire before, but after watching Zoe and the boys do it, and feeling the hot flames lick against my tongue I was pretty sure I could accomplish the feat if I focused enough.

It was good that the circus was dark tonight and we had the night off. I was so high strung that I didn't want to risk anything happening on stage. You know, like time freezing, falling, bomb spitting 'anything'. I also didn't want Stacia to take my part for the night, and stubborn as I was I would have gone on anyway.

Being dark was the best thing.

Overhearing Killian and Jarron's conversation from last night felt like a bad dream. A bad dream mixed with other weird and equally as bad dreams until my night was one long streak of bull shit.

It smelled as bad too.

I tried to push the feeling away, but it grew with each minute that the memory of last night was allowed to fester.

Didn't help that I woke up with deep bone aches that

neither Jarron or Drake could seem to soothe away. Jarron even went so far as to steal a kiss, after I exited my shower this morning. He risked painful fire for me, and while there were definitely sparks, the aches did not dissolve, and my bad mood continued to grow.

I knew I needed to see Killian. It was his touch that would calm the painful bone splintering that was cracking through my body. But I also knew that seeing him would result in angry yelling and confrontation about last night. I wanted neither, which left me with option b: stubbornly powering through it.

Which, I guess, meant also looking like I was in the middle of eating a lemon.

Yum Yum.

"Is shooting people with eye daggers part of your new act?" Drake asked as he sat beside me, dripping with sweat from practicing the current move we were working on. Jarron was still up in the air working on it, tangled in silks as he stubbornly tried to best his brother.

No competition my ass. At least this part of it was entertaining. I sipped at the coffee Drake had brought me. Normally it would take the edge off, but even the delicious brew wasn't helping.

"I didn't sleep well," I said, cringing as Jarron slipped a bit, thankfully he caught himself that time. Not that it would have ended in disaster. He may be stubborn, but I wasn't dumb enough to let him work without a spotter, and one of the Ukrainian gymnasts had been happy to help out.

"Yes, that is the lie you have been spewing all day," Drake said, giving me a sly grin. "Forgive me for not believing you."

Ugh, of course, he of all people would call me out on it.

"I would believe it if I were you," I snarled, he only smiled more, his eyes filled with that all knowing gleam.

"Did last night with Jarron go okay?" He asked, the humor slipping from his face, only to be replaced by concern.

I swallowed, choosing to occupy myself with coffee as Jarron enthusiastically waved from the other side of the gym.

Yes, last night went great. Even with the terribly painful conversation it didn't end with a disaster. I could still taste him on my lips, I could still feel his heat underneath my fingers as I kissed him. It took far too much willpower to stop myself from licking them. From tasting him. My phoenix was not helping that fight, she wanted to taste him as much as I did.

"It was fine." Lies. So many lies.

"Did you get the answers that you needed?" His voice was soft as he leaned closer, his eyes catching the sun and melting them into pools of honey.

I wanted to tell him yes, I wanted to sigh and nod and make everything all better. But I couldn't and I hated it. Drake seemed to sense that, the tiny smile he gave me sympathetic as he brushed a strand of hair from my face.

"From Jarron," It was probably the first truthful thing I had said all day.

He nodded once, the smile fading from his lips a bit.

"I understand that," he said, his focus pulling from me to the blonde model who was now talking to Stacia. I tried to ignore the twist of jealousy that was trying to overtake me, something that was easier said than done with how my phoenix was envy-raging.

Thankfully Drake helped, his hand soft against my cheek as he pulled my focus.

"Jarron is very genuine," he whispered, letting his fingers trail down to my hand as he scooted closer, his warm fingers intertwining with mine, something I may have pulled away from a few days ago. Not anymore. "I have always trusted him. It always hurt when he chose not to fight with us, but I could see his doubt even then. When he found me, I never questioned his sincerity. He was very easy to forgive."

Drake's eyes were clear and calm as he spoke to me, his fingers trailing over my skin and sending a wave of warmth through my veins. I restricted the sigh and pressed my lips together. I wanted to calm, but it wasn't Jarron that was agitating me.

Drake understood that too.

"Killian is another story," he said, a darkness taking over his features and he finally looked away, leaving me feeling cold and tense as I sat in my worry. "Killian has always been our father's son. We each had different qualities, different strengths. But he always preferred Killian, and Killian made it his life's work to become like that bastard. I could hardly believe it three years ago when Jarron told me he was fighting against the man."

"Do you believe it now?" I asked, my voice soft.

Drake sighed heavily and turned back to me, but all the warmth was gone from his eyes, he looked as cold as I felt, leaving the two of us to sit in our little ice blocks.

"I believe he doesn't want our father to claim the throne forever," he said, his voice hard as his fingers tightened around me, pinching painfully at the joints. I would have pulled away, but I was trapped under Drake's intensity. "I believe he wishes to take the role of Dragon King for himself."

There was something else there, some hidden lie interlaced with his words. Like a bruise just under the surface, I could feel it, I couldn't quite figure out where it had come from.

"So you trust him?" I asked, quirking an eyebrow as I tried to understand.

"I trust him to keep you safe."

He seemed certain of that. I didn't think I could get on that bandwagon. Sighing, I pulled my legs into my chest, letting my shoulders sag over my knees like I was made of play dough.

"You are either melting into yourself for an amazing human Popsicle act, or you don't believe me." Drake said with a low chuckle, I couldn't find it in me to join. I sunk lower, watching Jarron as he thankfully pulled away from the blonde bombshell that was still actively stalking my guys.

My guys.

Ugh. Let's pretend I did not think that.

"I don't not-not believe you," I mumbled into my knees, watching as Jarron walked toward us, waving jovially.

It took me a full second to realize that he wasn't waving to me. He had made so many friends here. His sparkling smile helped with that.

"You are going to have to talk to him, you know," Drake whispered, leaning in to me. "Just like Jarron. But don't worry, I get it. He scares me too. You are free to take all the time you need."

I jerked up, ready to finger waggle and counter with some nonsense about how nothing scares me when Killian plopped down on the mat next to me and sent me toward him with a jerk. Right into his lap.

"Why, hello there," He said with a smile so sly, so big, that I could probably have filled it with water and bathed in it.

Of course he has that brilliantly gorgeous smile, and those amazingly matching dimples when I am pissed at him. Thank goodness I didn't want to cry at him like I did last night, not that it made the volatile emotions any less dangerous. They were just more like wrestling-slash-yelling match level dangerous now.

Which wasn't going to help anyone. Not now, and certainly not here. Stacia and her cronies were already gossiping about Killian's arrival. He wasn't here often, and when he showed up it always caused a little bit of swooning.

I let out a squeak and jumped from both lap and mat before either of his large hands could pull me into him and keep me there. And he tried, well, at least I think he did. When I looked back he was still looking into his lap, hands frozen in mid smother.

Shock lined his face when he looked up to me, confusion clear in his wide green eyes. The color was more bottle green today, and I leaned into the color, leaned into him.

No, not today. Not right now. I wasn't ready.

I wasn't going to fall for it, his confusion. I had heard him last night. He couldn't stand to be around me. Had he been able to shut me out of his heart so quickly? I hadn't. I couldn't. Even with all the growls and glares and what I had heard him say yesterday, I still wanted him.

I wanted to jump back into his lap. Wrap my wings... er... arms... around him.

Ugh.

"I guess I better get working," I announced, a little bit too grumpily and strolled away before either of them could respond, making my way over the mat toward the long silk as they mumbled behind me.

"Come practice with me," I said to Jarron who was heading in the opposite direction, toward the brother convention I had left.

Jarron smiled, but I could tell it was forced, the poor guy was heaving, his usually fluffy blonde hair dripping with sweat, or water, or both.

Didn't matter either way. I had already established that Jarron could make sweat look sexy.

"Give me a minute, darling. You are working me like a battle horse today." he said between gasping breaths.

"I think you are doing that to yourself." I retorted, resisting the still pulsing urge to look behind me. "No competition, right?"

Jarron gave me a wink and a knowing smile before looking over my head toward his previous destination, "I take it you are running away from the new arrival?"

I pressed my lips together, I didn't have to answer that.

"Well don't stay away too long," Jarron said softly, running his palm over the bare skin of my arm before he leaned in, and pressed his lips to my cheek.

Dangerously close to my mouth.

Judging by the snap of profanity that filled the tent as he pulled away I would have to say it was *too* close to my lips.

The swoop of my stomach and sudden overdrive of heart were definitely in agreement with that. I forced myself to take in a shuddering breath as he pulled away, his eyes full gold with the smirk he was giving me.

"No competition," I repeated, any chance of sounding authoritative had been wiped away with the touch of his lips against my skin.

Jarron only laughed, his hands trailing down my arms as he stepped away, heading right toward whatever battle he had begun. I would have been mad, I would have stormed over and demanded them to knock it off. But I couldn't. Now was not the time.

Darn it all, I knew I was avoiding Killian, but I would

have to take it, even though every step away from him ripped my bones apart.

I needed him, I needed his touch. More than that, I wanted him. I wanted to see that wide smile spread over his face.

If only I could get his voice out of my head *'You say that as if I want to be around her.'*

Just thinking of that moment, of the words twisting over his lips, and my heart rate picked up for other reasons, my muscles tightened, and I wanted nothing other than to scale the silks and disappear into them.

For hours. For days. For as long as it would take.

So I climbed.

I climbed and I spun and wrapped and I dropped. I swung and I climbed.

I danced.

I soared.

And I let my worries float away in the folds of the silk. I let my fear travel along with it, until it was just me in the sky. Feeling the hot stale breeze of the fans, the air full of dust, chalk, and rosin. Closing my eyes, I pretended I was dipping through the clouds of a sunset, diving through the damp air before rain, the shimmering breeze of a sunrise.

The memory brought a smile to my lips, and I let the imagery fall over me as I wrapped the silk over waist and arms and tilted back, hanging upside down like a bat.

A phoenix-bat. The imagery made me smile more.

"You look so free up there."

The sunset vanished like a balloon under pressure, my phoenix bristling in a weird combination of need and loss. My eyes popped open to the bizarre face of Killian, standing only a foot away from me, his normally handsome feature twisted awkwardly as I hung upside down.

I quickly flipped myself over, not giving him an answer or a chance to touch me as I began to untangle myself from the silks. I suddenly didn't feel too much like rehearsing anymore.

Not that I was rehearsing so much as soaring. I couldn't make the smile come that time.

"What are you doing here?" I asked as I wrapped my legs around the silk and began to climb down.

The wide smile that graced his face flinched away, probably from the harshness in my voice, but I didn't care. I didn't even know why he was smiling, I was pretty sure I had heard him swear me off forever last night.

Again, stabbing pain. Even my phoenix felt it that time, but probably because I was now walking away from, and not towards, the thing she wanted most.

"Protecting you," He said, his voice cautious as he followed me.

"I'm pretty sure I don't need protecting right now," I said as I snatched my water bottle and a towel from the edge of the mat. "Too many people, not many dangers."

He made a face that was close to the dark scowl that I had gotten so used to before the corner of his mouth ticked into the tiniest of smiles, popping that dimple and sending my stomach into a glorified cha-cha. He was starting to make me feel like a freaking yo-yo.

The string that connected us had been pulled so tight by my inner shifter that I was sure one misstep would see me flinging back into his lap.

I bit my cheek and secured my feet to the ground as though they were lead.

"No people, many dangers," he said as he gestured around him to the brightly lit, and very empty, tent.

"What the..?"

"You've been up there for hours."

So I had. The practice tent was completely empty, the heavy plastic skylights in the ceiling peering into a dark, star-strewn sky.

It would have been beautiful, if I wasn't absolutely torn with frustration.

So much for my great plan to avoid Killian. Instead, I had found myself with him, alone. Unfortunately for him, I wasn't any less grumpy.

"That still doesn't answer why you are here?" I said with a snap, digging through my gym bags for my warm ups, or any other article of baggy clothing that I may have brought along.

I wasn't having much luck.

Curse my obsession with cute leotards.

"I told you, I am protecting you. "

"That answer really isn't cutting it for me," I said grumpily, still rifling through my bag.

He sighed, stepped toward me and held his hand out so politely that for a second I would have sworn he was going to ask me to marry him. You know, if he didn't hate me.

"That, and I would like to take you to one of my favorite restaurants."

Well, that was unexpected.

I stopped my search, knowing it was in vain anyway, and looked at him, trying to figure out what game he was playing at.

"Is your favorite restaurant a cave in the mountain?"

I was hesitant. Both the raw eating of the flesh of a goat and some sort of damsel in distress situation came to mind, but I wasn't going to bring any of those up.

"Dragon's don't have caves," he said, a wicked little smile pulling over his lips.

Simultaneously, I wanted to run away and dive into that grin. Best if I get out of here.

"I know," I said, grabbing the bag and throwing it over my shoulder in preparation to leave. I wasn't quite ready to be alone with him just yet. "Jarron told me."

Two words and the darkness I had seen in his eyes streaked over the bright emerald as both his eyes and his jaw hardened into that scowl I hated so much.

And there it was. The truth in his eyes, hatred and frustration glinting so powerfully he might as well have been a tornado. I had been trying to be polite, I had been trying to calmly exit and pretend that being around me wasn't causing him pain.

But that scowl. That truth.

No one could stop my anger from exploding after that.

"Why do you do that?" I asked, letting the bag fall from my shoulder. It hit the ground with a thud that might as well have been a slap with how Killian flinched.

"Do what?" He said, the scowl only growing.

"That," I yelled with a wild gesture toward the look in question, my voice strained in exasperation. "Look at me like I have ruined your life. Try to pretend that you have any interest in me when it is very clear you hate me."

Another flinch. Although with the way his eyes widened it may as well have been a stab to the heart.

"I don't hate you." It was hard to believe that with the temper that was boiling behind his steadily darkening eyes.

It was doing nothing to help me calm my own temper.

"And yet you sound like you want to rip my head off, and look at me as though you are ready to do the same." I exclaimed, my phoenix snarling like fire through my veins.

"This look is not for you."

347

I narrowed my eyes at him, "Then why is it looking at me?"

"This look is..."

"It doesn't matter," I snapped, cutting him off. "I heard you last night. Whatever lie you are about to tell me is already null and void."

"You heard me talk to Jarron, and you obviously misunderstood," he said, his voice now raising to a roar, his fists tightening against the slick fabric of his suit pants.

Killian was massive, his chest was probably double the width of mine, he stood a good head and shoulders taller, and his arms might be the size of my thighs. Provoking him was not a good idea. My gut instinct was begging me not to, my logic pulling me away. At this point even the bristling need of my soul had backed down, my phoenix whimpering in fear at my foolhardy tirade.

Yes, I was a fool, but I also didn't care. I plowed forwards, stubbornly slicing through the last of my logic in my tirade.

"I understood enough. You said you didn't want to be around me. I think it was pretty black and white," I ranted, hating when my voice caught, the damn pain of rejection attempting to boil past my rage.

Chill out tears, you can have your moment soon enough.

"I wasn't talking about you."

His eyes, his voice, everything about him screamed warning. And me? I laughed. A low twitch of a madman that echoed over the empty tent, every emotion finally bubbling over.

I don't think I had ever felt so out of control before. That was my cue to leave.

"You keep telling yourself that, honey," I said with as much mocking as I could force into my voice, well aware the hot, angry, bastard tears were flowing freely now. "You know as well as I do what you really meant."

I grabbed my bag, ready to sprint out of the tent and into the night when his hand wrapped around my forearm and our connection reacted.

Heat raced through me as though I had been thrown in fire, it spread from his fingers and through every bone, flooding me until it was everywhere. My phoenix perked up at the heat, my own fire joining to the flame that Killian had sent through me as though it had been called. As though it wanted nothing more than to join with his flame, with him. Like the warmest blanket, like the most perfect fire, it was everywhere, and I sighed, cursing the sound as it escaped my lips.

"I do, but it seems you don't," Killian said from behind me, his voice softer than I had expected as he turned me around to face him, my feet stumbling as I fought the action, my heart and soul pulling me in two different directions.

I wanted nothing to do with this lying bastard, and yet I couldn't seem to force myself away.

Fight it, Ellie.

"I was speaking of one of my father's servants," Killian said, his eyes soft little pools of bottle glass as he stepped toward me, pushing me back until I was flat against the stretching ladder, the hard wooden rungs digging into my back. "The woman fancies herself my mate, and forces herself into my bed."

"And... and you let her in," I hissed, trying to force a snap into my voice and failing. Killian only smiled now, the dark grin pulling both dimple and shadows into sharper focus. He looked as he had in the alley; dark, mysterious, and panty-dropping sexy.

The heat that his touch was still sending through me was making it hard to focus, let alone hold onto my anger.

"Not any more. Dabria is a viper I have never wanted to deal with. My heart only wants one," he whispered, his hand moving over the skin of my arm, while the other began to trace my neck, my jaw. I shivered, the chill of his breath against my neck reacting to the heat that was surging between us.. "I only want to share my bed with one person now. And I am waiting patiently for her."

The bright moss of his eyes were making it very clear who he was talking about, the twist of both soul and stomach were making it clear I wanted it too. Not that it was even close to being a possibility. Even without Zoe the chastity belt I could still smell the fire from last night.

"I only want you."

I think the last of my frustration and anger melted away.

"Then... then why do you look at me like you hate me?" I said, wrapping one of my hands around the wooden dowel of the stretching ladder, as if the sturdy piece of wood could keep my knees from buckling.

Killian had his own ideas to keep me standing. His hands wrapped firmly around my arm and neck as he stepped closer, his hips pressing into mine as he locked me between him and the ladder.

"Because I am not very patient," he said, his voice a whisper as he leaned over me, his eyes drifting to mine. His cool breath whispering over my lips. "And I really don't like to share."

And I thought I was having trouble thinking before.

It was impossible now, as he began to lean closer, as his breath whispered over my lips, so close I could feel the heat of his skin.

I could nearly feel his kiss...

"I will get what I want, Ellie," He said, the ice of his breath extinguishing the heat of the fire. "I don't care who stands in my way. I will end them."

The fire was gone in a puff of smoke, the need, the want. It was all gone, vanished as though it never existed.

There was only rage.

My eyes smacked open to his calm serene face, his lips puckered in expectation of a kiss that would never come.

"Oh, hell no."

I pushed him away, a loud crack of wood echoing around the tent as I ripped the dowel from the ladder, my hand compressing the wood as I held it, all the rage pulsing through me.

I didn't even know I could that, but my anger wouldn't even let me process the fact that I had snapped a three inch cylinder of wood like a twig.

"You are mine, Ellie," He said, that same low rumble of pride echoing in his voice.

It was possibly the worst thing he could say.

Without even thinking, my hand swung forward, the dowel whacking him hard between the legs. He shrieked and doubled over before I could aim again, sending my second smack right into the top of his head.

The massive man shrieked and wailed as he danced around, fixing me with tear filled eyes that only screamed rage.

I had no sympathy. I didn't care. He deserved it.

"I am not something you can claim," I barked, grabbing my bag as I watched him howl and hold his head and groin in the middle of the floor. " And I won't let anyone own me."

I don't think I could have gotten out of the tent fast enough.

29

ELLIOT

FOR ONCE, THE HEAT OF THE DESERT FELT NICE. WELL compared to the heat of the furious control freak I had just left, and even then, that was a low boil compared to the rage that was rippling over my skin, sending waves of smoke over my arms.

It had to be near a hundred outside, but the breeze was ice water in comparison.

I needed it. Although it did little to help me calm down. I needed to get as far away from Killian as possible and settle my nerves before I turned into something violent and scary.

Like a bomb. And judging by both heat and smoke I was on my way to becoming one.

Normally I would run right to Zoe, my best friend could always solve my problems. This time, however, I knew exactly who I needed.

If only I knew where the heck he was.

"Drake," I breathed into the night, the rage boiling down and making room for the hot, disgusting tears that were making a grand return. Because of course they would. "I need you."

I had barely said the words before those strings that I had been feeling inside of me since I had bonded to the boys tightened like a whip. It snapped against my heart like a fishing line that was pulling me toward the hotel.

Right to him.

"Drake," I said again, the tears falling harder now as I followed the pressure of my dragon sonar, my phoenix pushing me forward so fast I was sure she thought I could fly without her. Tumbling over my feet, I moved into a sprint, suddenly worried that the man whose balls I had busted was going to follow me.

Judging by the wailing behind me, I would say he was trying. I needed to disappear into the hotel and then it would be fine.

Well, it would be fine as long as the heart string trick didn't go both ways, which I could no longer guarantee.

So, I ran faster, my bag jumping over my spine as the door grew closer.

I was only about half way there when light flooded over the dark parking lot, the thick metal slab I had been heading to swinging open as a man whose lean muscle I recognized at once came tumbling out, running to me as fast as I was running to him.

"Elliot!" He yelled as soon as he caught sight of me, his arms wide as he gathered me in. "What's wrong? Oh, honey, please tell me you are okay."

I didn't have a chance to explain, hell, I couldn't even catch my breath over the fact he had called me honey, before Killian's howls turned into something much more feral, and the calm night was torn to shreds by a sound I don't think I could ever forget.

A scream, no a roar that rumbled through the earth, the

ground shaking as my bones began to ache. I wanted to say it was an earthquake, the rumble of the earth, the crash of thunder.

The lie didn't hold. It couldn't after the sky drowned in fire.

The dark, inky night was smothered but massive tongues of yellow and black that cut through the stars like knives. Rippling. Waving.

Massive drops of liquid heat began to fall around us as the flames retreated, a fiery boulder the size of a sedan smashing into the parking lot not far from us. The black ember broke apart at the impact, melting the asphalt as rivers of the brightest red began to ooze from the center. Like a yolk from an egg it spread toward us. Except it wasn't an egg.

I wasn't sure how much heat my phoenix-shifter body could take, but I wasn't about to test it on this thing. It was melting away the parking lot like it was butter, I was sure it could melt away us.

"Drake!" I called in alarm, trying to move away from the flame, but his wide eyes were locked behind me, right toward the sound, toward the flames that were turning the night to day.

"Oh crap," Drake moaned, he didn't have to tell me what was there. I knew.

I knew because I could see the shadow of the massive dragon against the hotel. I knew because I could see the faces of fear peek out of the windows, and feel it mirrored in me. Mind numbing panic. I couldn't look away from the shadow, even the powerful phoenix inside of me was shivering, pushing me back towards safety.

"Call Jarron," Drake gasped, his voice hard as he looked to me from the creature Killian had become, his eyes flaring red. I could tell the color wasn't from the flames behind me. They were from the flames inside of him.

"Jarron? How?" I questioned, moving to turn, but Drake pulled me right back to him.

"However you called me."

"I...I... I don't know what I did." I stuttered, my fear growing as the shadow on the side of the hotel began expand, the ground shivering below us. He was coming closer. "I said I needed you."

"Well, I need him, now. I can't hold Killian off... he's too strong... he won't listen... and if I shift..." He stopped, his eyes pinching shut as his hands gripped my arms harder. I could taste the agony that was running off of him. I waited, needing answers, but he only sighed and fixed me with a look that was only fire.

"I will do anything to protect you, Ellie," He bellowed over the dragon's roars. "But if I shift, Ellie, I need you to run. Run as hard and as fast as you can. Don't shift. Just get away from here."

That was no where close to the answer I wanted, "Why?"

My question was drowned by a scream, drowned by a heavy thud that shook the earth and nearly sent me to the ground. Everything shook in a pulse like a drum, the loud scrape of nails on a chalkboard twisting through my spine.

"Promise!" Drake didn't wait for a response before he pressed his lips against my cheek in the tiniest of brushes, and then he was gone, a shadow walking into the fire that was erupting through the sky like a geyser.

It was then that I turned, the earth shaking as an absolute explosion of fire ripped from the mouth of the beast that I saw for the first time.

The white canvas of the practice tent lay around him in shreds, the main performance tent in threat of collapse from the massive beast that had emerged in the middle. He was as large as the tent, as large as the hotel that was the only chance of safety I had.

Yet, I couldn't move.

Covered in scales of the darkest green, the thing looked to be a giant gemstone, except for a shimmer of black that covered the massive beast. Both in wings, scales, and in the massive spikes that covered its head and back. The black reflected the night as though it was the sun, the flames that ripped from its throat doing the same. Black and red that somehow ate the light, and glistened with it.

Like poisonous oil.

The creature screamed and spread its wings, the massive leathery span wider than the tent as it's snake like neck raised up. With a scream-like roar it sent another line of liquid black into the burning sky before it collapsed back down, its taloned hands gripping the last of the tent and sending it tumbling down with a thunderous creak of metal.

He looked nothing like Falcor.

This was dark, twisted, medieval. This was terrifying.

I jumped as the dragon roared again, it's long neck twisting around as it's bright emerald eyes fixated on me, gleaming with a scowl that was hauntingly familiar. I cringed at the look, stepping back as the eyes left, twisting to face the minuscule shape of Drake.

Compared to the beast before him, Drake looked like nothing more than a doll that could be thrown around. As the dragon lowered his head to face him, I had the distinct impression that that was exactly what was going to happen.

"No," I gasped, my heart dropping as I watched spirals of smoke twist from the dragon's scarred nostrils, the ribbons drowning Drake's tiny frame.

Eaten. Thrown. Either way, I wasn't about to let that happen.

Fool that I was, I didn't think, I ran.

The hot air began to boil the closer I got, the smell of smoke and what I was sure was ash filling my head until it was all there was, a world on fire. It wasn't just the air.

The asphalt burned from more of those fire strewn boulders, little rivers of molten dragon fire running over the black until I was running and leaping through a landscape straight out of hell.

The very mortal part of my brain begged me to turn around but my phoenix, no my heart, pushed me forward. I needed to help them, both of them. I couldn't let Drake face him alone. I may not have exactly caused this, but that didn't change what Killian did. I had every right to stop his little power play, that didn't mean he could go off and throw a hissy fit about it.

"You must calm, brother," Drake said as I got closer, his voice low and distorted through the crackling flames.

I half expected some deep grumbling voice to come from the dragon, but there was only a growl, only a snarl and a puff of smoke that pushed away the deep grey wall of the still burning fires. I stepped past a wall of flame as the smoke cleared, leaving me only steps from where Drake stood facing the dragon. Drake's normally towering frame stood strong, but it wasn't even half as tall as the head of the beast that glowered at him, hovering before him as fire and smoke licked behind his razor sharp teeth in warning.

Killian's snake-like eyes stared into his brother, the bright green startling against the oil slick color of his scales. From back there the creature had been terrifying. But here, feet from him, I couldn't deny the beauty or the ancient perfection on Killian's dragon. There was still danger there, still fear, but my heart beat faster, my Phoenix screaming in both need and want.

I stepped forward, unable to look away as I navigated through the burning rivers of Killian's temper tantrum.

"You will only call him and put us all in danger, especially Ellie," Drake's voice was calm, barely even a shake present as he bargained with his brother, but he had obviously said the wrong thing. Mentioning my name brought back all the rage into Killian's eyes, the large spines on the back of his neck perking to attention as he lifted his head and spewed another line of jet black flames to the stars. The fire ripped through the night before they began to fall back down to earth in the same balls of death.

I shrieked and darted behind some wreckage from the tent, as if the flimsy ruins would protect me from a ball of concentrated dragon fire.

I needed to get it together, but now that I was here, I wasn't sure what I needed to do, or even how to do it.

"You must calm, Killian," Drake said, his voice in that same weird deadpan I had heard when I first arrived. I peeked over the crumpled remains of the tent, watching as Drake put his hands forward like some kind of wizard casting a spell. maybe he was, with that voice... "You must reverse your shift."

A weird white sheen began to creep over the dragon's eyes before Killian shook his head, knocking both the color and whatever Drake was trying to do from existence. A snarl rippled from Killian's throat, his frustration evident as his hands began to grind against the ground. Long talons dug into the asphalt, that same ear piercing screech ripping through the air as Drake stepped back, stumbling over feet and fire in an effort to escape the claws, escape the black flames that were rumbling in Killian's throat.

"I can't shift," Drake mumbled as he fell back, a pain in his voice as his skin began to quiver.

I didn't know what he meant. I had heard them say stuff like that before, but hearing the pain in his voice, hearing the fear from before. It was like a trigger against my soul, and with my phoenix heating and trembling inside of me I vaulted over the remains of the tent and sprinted right toward them.

Jumping over a wide river of lava I threw myself between the massive head of Killian's dragon, and the heaving, crumpled form of Drake. He wasn't crying, he wasn't panicked, but I could tell he was in pain, I could tell he was scared, but not of the creature before him. And strangely, as I faced the beast that was three times bigger than I was in my animal form, I wasn't scared either.

"Stop, Killian," I heaved, watching the black flames in his throat grow. "You need to stop this."

The dragon's eyes narrowed at me, the flames in his throat burning brighter as the emerald of the dragon's eyes dug into mine much the same way that Killian's had minutes before.

"You need to stop," I said again, as if that would somehow stop the burning that was pouring from his throat, little drops of fire seeping between his teeth to drop to the ground like acid. "Come out of there so we can talk about this."

"Elliot," Drake choked out, rushing to his feet and pulling me away from the teeth of the beast that were now only about a foot away. "You need to get out of here!"

"I'm not letting you face this alone!" I screamed in return, stubbornly staring Drake down as he reached for me, his hand soft against my arm.

Well, it was for a moment, before those same sharp

claws of Killian's monster swiped through the air and sent that man tumbling away from me, into canvas and metal and who knows what else.

"Drake!" I screamed, ready to run after him, to pull him from the remains and fly him out of here if I had to. It would be easy, I could already feel the warm heat of my shifter press against my skin, eager to escape. I would pluck Killian's eyes out on the way if it came to that.

I didn't get more than a few steps before those same claws pulled through the air, this time closing around me. The dragon reared back, lifting me higher and higher, until the burning heat of the parking lot left, and it was only smoke and the strangely chilly air of summer.

"Stop this, Killian!" I screamed, fighting against the hard green scales of his knobby fingers, pressing against the black claws that were so perfectly intertwined I might as well have been in a cage. "You can't do this. I don't belong to you! I don't belong to anyone!"

The dragon screamed at that, the sound of his roar filled with the crack of heartbreak as his head whipped around, eyes boring into me so close that I could feel the wet of his arm-long teeth against my skin, taste the ash of his breath on my own tongue.

Of course, that might have been my own fire, my own ash. As my rage continued to fuel my phoenix, ripples of smoke and flame began to dance over my skin. The flames were different than when Jarron had kissed me, that had been scary yes, but there was something beautiful about it. This was terrifying. This looked dangerous.

"You are not fucking Godzilla," I snarled, stopping my fight against scales and claws to look him right in the eye. "I don't want you like this."

I said the words, I saw the snap of pain and anger in his

eyes but I only let it fuel my own. With my own scream, I let a line of fire explode from me, smacking against the side of his head with a bang and a pop of an explosion.

His roar ripped through the air, the sound so loud it shook the smoke. He growled as his claws loosened, and with one well-placed wiggle I slid free from his grasp, tumbling through the air to the burning ground below. It was too close to shift, but it didn't matter, I had done this enough. I twisted through the air, landing hard on my feet as Drake sprinted right up to me, Jarron right on his heels.

"You aren't going to give me a chance to catch you, are you?" Drake said, all humor lost from his voice as the dragon spun around to face us, the ground shaking as his massive feet slammed into the ground, the grind of his claws grating against my spine.

"Fucking idiot. He's going to destroy everything," Jarron grumbled as he pushed past me, stepping right up to the beast who was now ripping apart the last of the performance tent. "What happened?"

"I... I kinda punched him in the balls." It was the most I could say. I wasn't about to go into the whole territorial, possessiveness Killian had displayed. Besides, who knew what these two would do when it came to that.

Given the threat to Killian's manhood, the two men just laughed.

"Nice," Drake said giving me an appraising nod. "One hit to the nads and he is breathing fire."

I was pretty sure it was more than that, but I wasn't about to question him now.

"I wish he had more control over his dragon," Jarron said with a sigh as the dragon in question let out another ear-splitting roar. "He always was a drama-queen."

This time I joined Drake's chuckle.

"Hey dip-shit!" Jarron called when he got close enough to the beast to pull his focus. "Would you mind ending your fit long enough that we can maybe not put the girl of our dreams in danger?"

Jarron was calm, if not a little pissed, but his choice of words had only enraged Killian more. The dragon reared up on his hind legs, towering over the three of us as his fire burned bright as his roar rattled the ground.

Cringing at the sound, I stepped toward Jarron, pulled forward by my phoenix, by the sound that ripped from Killian's throat. This one was different.

Something was wrong.

"Fu---" Drake began, his face falling as the roar of Killian's dragon turned into something darker, the fire that I had seen burning behind his throat following suit.

Killian's flames had been black, black with streaks of red. It had been beautiful in this deep terrifying way. But the fire that burned behind the oil-green of his scales had begun to change, all color draining from them as a sneer ripped over his eyes, a deep hatred that was meant only for Jarron.

The flames grew darker, until all the air was being sucked from my lungs, all warmth drained from my bones. It was like being plunged into ice water, surrounded by a weight and a cold that would surely kill you.

I only felt fear, there was only sadness. Even Jarron stepped back, he stepped back from Killian and looked at me with eyes so bright, so sad, that I knew at once what they meant.

Goodbye.

"No," I gasped, reaching toward him as sparks of the purest white flew from my fingertips, and time stopped.

30

ELLIOT

It was different this time.

Even with the ice that was pressing against me, the air didn't feel quite so heavy. It didn't hold me in place, just everyone else.

The rumble of black fire sat in the neck of Killian's dragon, frozen as it churned and boiled in its need to escape. To impale Jarron with whatever weapon he held. I couldn't let it.

I began to sprint forward. Giving Drake one last look, not knowing how this was going to pan out. He stood with both fear and panic on his face, Zoe and Suvi were a few steps behind, the eldest of the dragons carrying the old woman in their attempt to reach us.

To stop whatever was about to happen.

I was going to stop it first.

And if the look on Drake's and Jarron's faces were any indication, it was going to kill me.

I didn't stop to think, I pulled myself forward, my phoenix screaming as I pressed myself between Jarron and the tumbling fire, right as time picked back up again, and the black abyss that Killian held inside of him began to break free.

I held my arms out, desperate to protect Jarron, to stop whatever was about to happen. Face scrunched together, I turned away, bracing for the burning heat. Instead, I got a punch to the gut.

A dragon snarled somewhere around me as a boulder intersected with my side, throwing me through the air in a tangle of arms and legs before I landed in a pile of smoldering canvas, the heavy material grinding against my skin as I slid down it only to collapse in a heap.

"What the hell?" I snarled as I tried to untangle myself, everything hurting as a deep roar trembled in the air around me. I half expected the world to be alight with the flames of whatever explosion Killian had been about to unleash. But it was calm. Well, calm except for the low roar that rumbled in the ground beneath me.

"Get up," a harsh female voice said as a hot hand wrapped around my forearm, pulling me to my feet and to a very cross looking Zoe. "You need to get out of here."

The level of fear in her voice was like a battering ram, it sucked all the emotion from my chest until I was left standing, numb and terrified, before my best friend who was staring behind me like she was seeing a monster.

But it wasn't a monster, it was a dragon. She was one, and I knew she had seen Killian in his dragon form before.

"Zoe?" I asked, but anything else I had been planning to say was sucked from the air as a roar filled every free space in my mind.

The sound rattled my bones, it ripped through my heart as the pain, the agony, behind it screamed to life, and I was sure my soul ripped in two. The scream of my phoenix blared right alongside as I turned, expecting the worst, and instead facing what I was sure was death.

A dragon lay on the ground, covered in blood and lines of glimmering gold that on first glance looked beautiful. Until the writhing beast screamed again, and it's agony ripped me in two. The lines of gold were cut into the massive beast like an infection, blood pouring from each deep cut. They zigzagged over its left wing, with several more massive gashes having torn open that side of the body. My heart sunk, my soul aching as it screamed again, and what I was seeing hit home.

This wasn't Killian.

This dragon was larger, it's scales a light red-brown that at any other time I was sure would glitter, melt like the color of brown sugar. Covered in blood, writhing in pain, it was horrifying.

"Drake," I heaved, my heart ripping from my chest as I tried to understand what I was seeing.

They said he couldn't shift, they said his dragon was broken... but this. I swallowed, ready to rip Killian's head from his shoulders. I would have if he didn't stand right before the howling maw of the writhing dragon, both he and Jarron in human form, hands out as they tried to comfort the beast that was clearly dying.

"No."

"You need to go," Zoe practically screamed in my ears, pulling me around until all I could see was her. "You have to leave before he gets here."

"Who gets here?" I stuttered like an idiot, not understanding what was happening. I didn't need to go. I needed to be right there, with Drake. I tried to pull away, to run toward him, but Zoe held on harder.

"The King."

Her answer only added to the ice that drenched my soul. Pain. Fear. I felt them both, but I couldn't move. I couldn't run.

My heart only wanted to be in one place.

"But he..." I turned toward Drake, toward the pained sounds that were slowly slashing at my heart. "He's dying."

She didn't even try to tell me I was wrong, she sighed, pulling my focus away from the three men that, even though one of them was kind of a stubborn asshole, my heart and soul had connected to.

"He's been banished. the king will know he has shifted." Zoe said, her voice choked, "he will be here soon to finish him off."

"No!" the word exploded from me, and I ripped from the tight grip of her hands running through flames, rubble, and ruin to reach the writhing dragon.

"Ellie, stop!" Zoe screamed behind me, but I ignored her, tearing away as I sprinted toward him.

Drake's dragon was huge, even laid on the ground his heaving chest towered over me. His roar shook the earth as I ran, his claws digging into the asphalt as I sprinted toward where Killian and Jarron were. Jarron was now smoothing the bleeding scales on his face, while Killian ran about like a wild man using his suit jacket to try to slow the flow of blood, but there was too much.

Too many cuts. Too much blood.

It was Killian I reached first, my rage propelling me forward.

"What did you do?" I screamed as I shoved into him, the now human form of him feeling like nothing against the beast he was hiding inside.

Killian stumbled back, blood soaked jacked and shirt spraying over both of us with the motion. His eyes were hard, dark, and filled with so much pain that his hurt echoed the snarl of the dying creature.

"I didn't do anything." Killian said, the low grind of his voice breaking with pain. "You stopped me before I did anything. You stopped me," he paused, wringing blood from the jacket as his shoulders sagged. "He shifted to protect you. These are old wounds."

He finished with a sigh, rushing back to the massive dragon with the blood soaked jacket, as if it would do any good. The gash was as deep as I was tall, the blood that poured from it, like a river against my shoes. The smell of iron filled my head, the warm wet against my ankles felt like shackles, the hard pressure cutting into my soul.

"What happened?" I asked desperate for someone to answer. Desperate to know. To fix it.

Tears boiled over as I stepped toward Jarron, reaching the massive head of Drake's dragon, the melted honey in his eyes staring at me as he whimpered in pain, tears the color of warm butter trailing down his glistening scales.

"He was branded as a traitor," Jarron said, his voice cracking as he placed his head against his brothers snout, the two of their eyes closing together. "I'm so sorry, brother. I would give my life to change this."

"He was cut, and the fae forced him back into his human form, leaving his dragon to die a slow death," Zoe provided as she came up behind me, standing guard as I stepped forward, wanting to touch him, to comfort him, but unsure of how. "His wounds have festered, and with the Fae's magic unbound, our father knows where he is. He has broken banishment. The punishment for that is death."

My eyes snapped to hers, my fingers hovering centimeters from the warm scales of the man who had so quickly stolen my heart. Who my soul was screaming for.

"We can't let that happen," I pleaded over the low growl of Drake's dragon, turning to everyone, desperate for an answer, for some magic button I could press and make it all better. "There has to be something we can do."

"There is nothing, child," Suvi said, her eyes warm as she walked up behind Zoe. "We cannot reverse the shift and he cannot do it himself as broken as he is."

"No." I am not sure the word made it out, it may as well have just been a gasp in my head.

"You need to get out of here before the king comes, Ellie," Zoe said, trying to wrap her hand around my arm again, but I jerked away, taking a step closer to Drake, his long scaly hand stretching forward, curling over the ground in front of me as though he was protecting me.

He was, and even through his pain I could see the warm passion in his eyes. I could feel my own pulling me toward him, needing him, one last time.

"I'm not going anywhere."

"You know Drake would want you to," Zoe said, but even I could hear the uncertainty there.

I could see the same questioning in Killian as he stood, covered in blood, his ruined jacket still hung at his side. He wasn't going anywhere, and neither would I.

"Come, Ellie," Jarron said, pressing his forehead to his brother's one last time, before he turned to me, his hand outstretched, "I'll go with you."

He stood there, hand reaching toward me like it was some kind of death sentence, for me. For Drake.

"No," I whispered, stronger this time, as I closed the gap between Drake and myself. "I won't leave him. I won't leave any of you."

The words burned in my soul, pulsing at an emotion that had been hovering under the surface for days. I was too stubborn to hear. I was too stubborn to see. *My guys.* I had said it. I knew it. But I don't think I realized how deep that went.

My head turned to Killian, to the man who stood in his own misery, covered in the ash of his dragon and the blood of his brother, and I think I might have understood him, understood what he was trying to say. Just a bit.

Yes, he didn't want to share. Yes, he was a little bit of a stubborn jack-ass. But he didn't want to own me.

I was his as much as he was mine. As they all were.

"You're mine," I whispered to the three of them as I stepped closer, peering to the honey of Drake's eyes, and pressed my palm to the hard scales right below his eye.

The touch was a tidal wave, a rush of fire that sparked so violently that my back arched, my teeth grinding together as it pressed against my skin. The pressure was so strong I expected my phoenix to escape, but she stayed inside, content against my heart as the fire of my connection with Drake ravaged my body, as my skin began to glow.

It was just my hand at first, the skin glowing in a brilliant white that radiated from every pore like a spotlight, but the more the pressure grew, and the more the heat pressed against my skin, the more I began to glow. The same light seeped from between Drake's scales in ribbons of white, cascading into the night and creating a million new, beautiful, stars.

Light twinkled over me as I gasped, the heat rising until it felt as through my veins were on fire.

I had always been able to take heat. I had so much fire inside of me that it never bothered me. But this was different, this was a flame that wanted to devour me. This pulled my soul inside out.

A scream ripped from my throat as the boil in my veins

reached a temperature I could no longer withstand, and my knees buckled, back arching as I fell to the ground in an agony that I was sure would end me. I couldn't survive this.

Screams ripped from my throat as I writhed on the ground, until hands wrapped around me and pulled me into chests and arms until I was surrounded. Pressed in on each side. Warm hands touching, pressing, calming. With each touch, a soothing calm moved into me, the heat of our connection calming my bones, my muscles, and finally the still boiling torrent of my blood until I was floating in a cloud. There was no more pain. Only a calm perfection, like a spring rain, or the smoke of a candle.

I could smell both.

With a sigh that would stretch over the Grand Canyon, my eyes fluttered open to Jarron's awe-stricken face, his hands soft against my arm, against my neck as he held me in his lap, Killian right beside, his large palms hot against my back, and my leg.

And then there was Drake, his beautiful face smeared with blood and ash as he sat calmly on my left, his arms enveloping me. Pain echoed in his eyes as he tried to smile, the look strained as he held my hand, leaning against Killian, who sat beside him.

"Drake," I sighed, and he smiled, although it was barely able to break the corner of his mouth. "You're..."

Alive? A man? I wasn't sure which word fit, but it didn't seem to matter. The glittering honey of his eyes said enough.

It was all it took to pull me in.

It didn't take much. He was right there, so close he was a part of me. My hand tightened around his, around whoever else held my hand as I leaned in, and pressed my lips to his. He didn't jerk away, he didn't freeze. Instead, he melted into my touch as a soothing fire rippling through my blood as we connected.

I didn't kiss him long, but as I pulled away, I didn't feel a bit ashamed either. Even with my other two dragons surrounding us.

"You saved me," he gasped, his voice strained through the pain as he answered the unasked question. "And don't ask me how, because I don't think any of us know."

"I do," Suvi said with a smile so broad that it stretched her face in a way I had never seen before.

All of us turned toward her, even Zoe, who was looking like she had been hit by a train.

"And, I think I know why you need these three boys beside you, child," Suvi said from somewhere behind me, I didn't even turn to look, I couldn't tear my focus from Drake even if I wanted to. Which I didn't.

"Don't leave us hanging," Jarron prompted, his voice lacking it's trademark chuckle.

"Your mate is one of the Fae."